The River Folk

Born in Gainsborough, Lincolnshire, Margaret Dickinson moved to the coast at the age of seven and so began her love for the sea and the Lincolnshire landscape.

Her ambition to be a writer began early and she had her first novel published at the age of twenty-five. This was followed by thirteen further titles, including *Plough the Furrow*, *Sow the Seed* and *Reap the Harvest*, which make up her Lincolnshire Fleethaven trilogy, and her most recent novels, *The Fisher Lass* and *The Tulip Girl*. Married with two grown-up daughters, Margaret Dickinson combines a busy working life with her writing career.

www.margaret-dickinson.co.uk

Margaret Dickinson

The River Folk

PAN BOOKS

First published 2001 by Pan Books
an imprint of Pan Macmillan, a division of Macmillan Publishers Limited
Pan Macmillan, 20 New Wharf Road, London N1 9RR
Basingstoke and Oxford
Associated companies throughout the world
www.panmacmillan.com

ISBN 978-1-4472-1059-7

1 3 5 7 9 8 6 4 2

A CIP catalogue record for this book is available from
the British Library.

Typeset by SetSystems Ltd, Saffron Walden, Essex
Printed and bound by CPI Group (UK) Ltd, Croydon, CR0 4YY

Visit www.panmacmillan.com to read more about all our books and to buy
them. You will also find features, author interviews and news of any author
events, and you can sign up for e-newsletters so that you're always first to hear
about our new releases.

For Dennis, Mandy and Zoë

Acknowledgements

My birthplace, Gainsborough, is the inspiration for the setting of this novel although the story is entirely fictitious. I am very grateful to the members of The Delvers Local History Group (Gainsborough) and also to the Gainsborough and District Heritage Centre, for information and help received from their publications and exhibitions.

The *Maid Mary Ann* is modelled on the keel *Comrade*, now owned by the Humber Keel and Sloop Preservation Society. My sincere thanks to the members of the society and, in particular, to the crew of *Comrade* for a wonderful day's sailing on the Humber and for answering all my questions. (Any errors are mine, not theirs!)

My love and thanks to friends, Barry and Margaret Watson. Thank you for coming sailing on the Humber with me, Barry, and for not jumping ship when I was allowed to take the tiller!

I would also like to pay tribute to the book, *Humber Keels and Keelmen*, by the late Fred Schofield, formerly owner of *Comrade*. This book was a wonderful source of inspiration and information.

As always, my love and thanks to my family and friends for their loyal encouragement and support and special thanks to Zoë and Scott for setting up my web site. www.margaret-dickinson.co.uk

Prologue

'Daddy, I'm sorry. Please, let me come up.'

The young girl stood at the bottom of the ladder leading up from the cabin on to the deck of the ship that was her home. The sliding hatch above her was open and through it she could see the stars. But tonight, they held no fascination for her.

'Daddy,' Lizzie cried again, her voice rising with fear. It was not being left in the dark confines of the cabin that frightened her, nor the sound of the water lapping against the side of the vessel, nor even the gentle rocking of the ship as it was lifted on the river's evening tide. The girl scarcely noticed any of these things, so much a normal part of her life were they. The terror that was gripping her heart, squeezing the breath from her body and making her legs tremble was the sound of her parents on the deck above her. They were quarrelling, shouting at one another and it was she, Lizzie, who had made her father so angry.

'Mam,' she tried again, but the cry froze on her lips as she heard her mother scream. And then, though she could hardly believe it, she heard the sound of a slap. In the lonely darkness, her chin trembled and tears filled her eyes. Surely her daddy wouldn't hit her mother. Not her daddy. He had never raised a hand to anyone in his life as far as she knew. He had never smacked her, Lizzie

1

thought, not once. Not even when she was her naughtiest and stayed on the riverbank playing with her friend, Tolly, instead of coming on board ship when her father was ready to sail. More than once, he had missed the tide because of her. But even then, he would just look so disappointed, so hurt by her naughtiness, that she wanted to fling herself against him, bury her face in his neck and say, 'I'm sorry, Daddy. I will be a good girl. Truly, I will.'

It was what she wanted to do now, but, when they had come back to the ship from visiting her grandmother, her father had said sternly, 'Lizzie, go below.'

For once, she had not dared to disobey him but now, as she heard her mother cry out again, this time followed swiftly by a splash, she climbed the ladder calling out shrilly, 'Mam. Mam!'

Her father was leaning over the side, searching the inky water. He called her mother's name, a wailing sound that echoed across the river through the darkness and made the child shiver. She had never, in all her life, heard her father sound like that. So desperate, so stricken, so hopeless.

The long, drawn-out sound was borne on the wind and lost in the deep, shadowy waters of the river.

'Mary Ann. *Maaary Aaan!*'

Part One

Bessie

One

1919

Bessie Ruddick slammed down her rolling pin and wiped her floury hands on her pinafore.

'I aren't having that racket coming through me kitchen wall,' she muttered. She stood listening for a moment to the sounds of a man and woman quarrelling in the house next door that had been empty for several weeks.

It must be let again, Bessie thought. The noise grew louder and now she could plainly hear the man's vulgar language. There was a thud and then a woman cried out, 'No, no, don't. Please, don't . . .'

'That does it,' Bessie said aloud. She marched out of her own house and, turning to her left, covered the few strides that brought her to her neighbours' door. Balling her fist, she thumped on it. She waited a few moments, but when no one answered, she bellowed, 'I know you're in there, 'cos I've heard you.'

Across the yard, Minnie Eccleshall appeared in her doorway. 'What's up, Bessie? Trouble?'

'You mind your business, Minnie Eccleshall, and let me mind mine.'

Minnie only grinned, folded her arms and leant against the doorjamb. Sparks were about to fly and there was, like as not, going to be a bit of fun.

A sash window grated upwards and Gladys Merry-weather poked her head out. 'Am I missing owt, Min?'

'Nowt to speak of, Glad. Just our Bessie on the warpath.'

'Right. I'll be down.' Gladys's head disappeared and seconds later she emerged from her own house to join her next-door neighbour. 'You told Phyllis? She wouldn't want to miss this.'

'She's out. Gone up town.'

'What's it about?'

Minnie shrugged. 'Dunno. But whatever it is, it sounds serious.'

Both women jumped as Bessie thumped the door again and shouted, 'Come on out here, mester, where I can see you, instead of skulking in there.' She raised her hand to batter the door once more, but as she did so it was pulled open and her fist almost met the nose of the man standing there.

'Oh. There you are,' Bessie said unnecessarily, for a moment caught off guard.

'Whaddo you want?' The man's voice was gruff and uncouth.

Bessie folded her arms across her ample bosom, behind her, she knew that Minnie and Gladys would be nudging each other. Of course, they knew the signs. Oh, this newcomer to Waterman's Yard was in for a battle royal.

'I want,' Bessie said slowly and clearly, 'a bit o' peace in me own house. I don't want to hear you shouting and bawling through me wall.'

She heard Minnie laugh and say in a voice deliberately loud enough for Bessie and the man to hear, 'That's nowt to what he'll hear when our Bessie gets going at her lot. She's a nerve.'

'Shush,' Gladys tried to warn Minnie. 'Don't let her hear you, else . . .'

Bessie ignored what was going on behind her and wagged her forefinger close to the man's face. 'This is a respectable neighbourhood, I'll have you know.'

His thin lips curled. 'Respectable? You don't know the meaning of the word, missis. You river folk, washed up with the tide, you were. All along the river.'

Bessie's glance raked him from head to foot. The man was unshaven with more than one day's growth of stubble on his gaunt face. He wore a grubby, collarless striped shirt, a black waistcoat with only one button and stained trousers. His thinning hair was black and, to Bessie's disgust, so were his fingernails.

'I want to meet your wife, mester.' A note of sarcasm crept into Bessie's tone that only her listening neighbours recognized as she tried a different tack. 'Just to make her feel welcome, like. See if there's owt we can do to help.'

'There ain't.' The man began to close the door but it was to find that Bessie's bulk had stepped firmly across the threshold.

Bessie Ruddick was a big woman in every way. She stood as tall as any man – taller than a good many. Her shoulders were broad, looking as if she could swing a sack of coal on to her back without a second's thought. Her face was round and jolly and, usually, her eyes shone with merriment. But at this moment her cheeks were blotched red with fury and her eyes sparked fire. Her voice was deep and resonant and when Bessie Ruddick got angry, her bellow could be heard by the ships passing by on the River Trent that flowed just beyond the road leading to the yards and alleyways.

''Ere,' he began, but, caught off guard, he was no match for the big woman.

'You there, love?' Bessie bellowed, calling into the dark interior of the house.

Unwisely, the man caught hold of Bessie's arm. 'Now look 'ere, you keep your nose out of our business and get your fat arse back to your own house.'

Slowly Bessie looked down at the dirty hand on her arm. Then, only inches away, her gaze met his. Suddenly, the man found his waistcoat and shirt grasped by two strong hands that almost lifted him off his feet.

''Ere . . .' he tried again, but found his breath somewhat restricted as the neckband of his shirt cut into his throat.

'No, mester. You look 'ere.' Bessie, though his nearness repelled her, thrust her face even closer to his. 'I heard you shouting at your missis and then I heard her cry out. Now unless I'm putting two an' two together and makin' five, you hit her, didn't you?'

The man's arms were flailing helplessly and his face was beginning to turn purple.

'Leggo, you owd beezum.'

'Now, now,' Bessie warned, tightening her hold. 'No rude names. Else you'll have my Bert to deal with when he comes home. When you hear his boots tramping down that there alley, you'd better hide, mester. My Bert doesn't like anyone being rude to his missis.'

Minnie and Gladys clutched each other, convulsed with laughter. Even from the other side of the yard they could sense the man's fear.

'He – he hasn't met Bert Ruddick yet, then?' Minnie gasped.

'Can't have, Min.'

The man, still in Bessie's grip, had found a little strength. 'Elsie,' he called weakly. 'Elsie. Come here, woman. Quick.'

As a thin, timorous woman appeared out of the

8

shadows, Bessie loosened her grasp and the man fell against the door. He backed away from her, his hand to his throat.

'You're mad, you are. We're not stopping here, Elsie. Pack yer things, we're going.'

The woman drooped. 'Oh Sid, I can't move again, I . . .'

'You'll do as I say . . .' he began, his voice rising, but when Bessie took a step towards him, he backed away and turned towards the inner room, almost falling over his feet in his haste to escape. 'She's mad, I tell you. Just get rid of her.'

Elsie tried to smile weakly at Bessie, but tears welled in her eyes and she touched her bottom lip where blood oozed from a gash.

Softly, Bessie said, 'Did he do that to you, love?'

'No, no. I – er – fell. Tripped over a packing case. You know . . .'

Bessie shook her head. 'No, love, I don't know. My feller'd not lay a finger on me.'

Despite everything, the little woman smiled as she murmured, 'No, I don't suppose your feller would, missis.' The smile faded as swiftly as it had come and she sighed heavily. 'I'm sorry if we disturbed you.' She glanced back over her shoulder and then moved closer as her voice dropped to a whisper. 'You haven't seen a little lass about the yard, have you?'

Bessie shook her head. 'No, love. Your lass, is it?'

The woman nodded. 'She's run off somewhere . . .' She jerked her head backwards. 'When he started. I'm worried she might get lost. And with the river so close . . .'

'Not from round here, then?' Bessie said. She was only trying to make friendly conversation, but Elsie's eyes widened in panic.

'No, no. Never even been to Elsborough before, till Sid . . .' She broke off and dropped her gaze. Then she mumbled, 'He's looking for work.'

'Aye well, it's not easy. Just back from the war, is he?'

She heard the woman pull in a sharp breath before she said, hurriedly, as if latching on to Bessie's question like a drowning person grasping for a lifeline, 'Yes, yes, that's it. Just home from the war.'

'Elsie . . .' Her husband's voice came warningly out of the shadows behind her.

The woman jumped and then stepped back nervously and made to close the door. 'I must go. If you see our Mary Ann, send her home, will you?'

'Aye,' came the man's rough voice again. 'You do that, missis, 'cos I'm going to tan her backside for her when I get hold of her, so you might hear a bit more yelling and screaming.'

Bessie raised her voice and shouted, 'I'd better not, mester, 'cos next time, I'll bring my Bert with me.'

Across the yard Minnie and Gladys leant against each other, tears of helpless laughter running down their cheeks.

'Bye for now, love,' Bessie was saying to the woman. 'I hope you're going to be happy here in Waterman's Yard.'

The woman closed her eyes and seemed, for a moment, to sway. 'Happy?' she murmured, for all the world as if she meant to add, 'What's that?'

Two

Bessie heard her husband's cheerful whistle echoing down the hollow-sounding arched passageway that led into Waterman's Yard.

Half the townsfolk of Elsborough lived in the yards – a conglomeration of houses that had been hastily built in the spaces behind the larger, grander buildings fronting River Road to accommodate a rapidly expanding population. Regarded by many as insanitary places and a breeding ground for disease, nevertheless the residents of the yards were a fiercely independent and proud community and none more so than the families who earned their living from the river.

The Waterman's Arms, for years a hostelry for sailors, keelmen and watermen of all description, stood proudly on River Road. Nestling behind it was Waterman's Yard.

As she heard his boots ringing on the cobbles of the yard where the sun rarely reached, Bessie bent to take the shepherd's pie out of the oven. Its potato topping crisp and brown, she placed it, piping hot, on the table as Bert stepped into the house and called, as always, 'Bessie, my angel, light of my life. I'm home.'

Bert Ruddick was a little ferret of a man, small and thin with sharp features and mischievous, beady eyes that missed nothing. His brown hair, turning grey now, was soft and silky. He had worked on, or beside, the river all his life, finding any kind of job he could. He was unskilled

11

but his experience of the river and all her moods was second to none and it was a mark of his worth that whilst he had never had a regular job, he had never once been out of work. He was known as a purchase-man, whose casual labour was 'purchased' by the masters of the keels and sloops that plied the River Trent near Elsborough.

'Summat'll come in with the tide, Bess,' had always been his motto and it always had for even if there was no work available aboard ship, there was often plenty to be had on the wharves.

Bert loved his wife with a fierce pride and the marvel of it to him was that she loved him in return. What was it he'd heard someone say once? Something about love being blind and seeing with the heart and not the mind? Well, that must be the case with him and his Bessie. What she saw in him, a scrawny, pint-sized river dweller, he couldn't imagine. But as to what he saw in her, now that was a different matter. A fine figure of a woman she'd always been. Still was, in his love-blurred eyes. To him she wasn't the overweight, loud-mouthed woman that others saw. To Bert Ruddick, Bessie was a Boadicea and together they'd raised three strapping lads. Thank goodness they'd all taken after their mother for size, Bert would thank his lucky stars as he downed pint after pint in The Waterman's Arms and good-naturedly took the teasing of the men around him. Whatever they said about him, no one could deny that he had sired three handsome devils, who would break a few hearts around here before they were much older.

Smiling, Bessie went to meet him. Bert put his arms around her waist as far as he could reach and laid his head against the soft, well-known pillow of her bosom, whilst she clutched his head to her breast and planted a noisy kiss on the thinning hair.

'Tea's ready,' she said.

He lifted his head and sniffed the air appreciatively. 'Smells good, Bess.'

'Shepherd's pie. Just the way you like it.'

'You always do everything just the way I like it.'

Bessie chuckled, but only said, 'Wash your hands. The lads'll be home soon.'

As he soaped and scrubbed his hands vigorously in the deep white sink in the scullery, he asked, 'Any news?'

It was a question that had become a routine throughout the terrible war that had just ended, a question that had to be asked and yet the answer had always been feared. Now, perhaps, any news might be happier.

'We've got some new neighbours at last.'

'Really?' Bert straightened up and reached for the towel. 'You met 'em yet?'

Bessie pulled a face. 'Yes, but I aren't struck with 'em. I've had a run in with the feller already.'

'Oh dear,' Bert tried to look serious, but failed.

'You can smile, Bert Ruddick. I reckon he's a wife-beater.'

Now Bert's face was sober as he sat down at the table. 'I don't like the sound of that, Bess.'

'You should have heard the racket coming through this wall this afternoon. Swearing and carrying on. Then I heard a woman cry out and when I went round, she'd a gash on her lip. She said she'd fallen, but I didn't believe it. She's terrified of him, you can see it in her eyes.'

Shaking his head, Bert picked up his knife and fork. 'Well,' he said, knowing his beloved wife almost better than she knew herself, 'while they live next door, she might get a bit of peace from him.' He glanced up at her as he added shrewdly, 'Because you're not going to stand by and see someone knocked into the middle of next week, are you?'

Despite the gravity of their conversation, Bessie laughed. 'You're right there, Bert, and—'

Whatever Bessie had been going to add was lost as the back door opened and they heard Dan calling, 'Mam, where are you?'

Tall and broad-shouldered, his dark brown hair curling on to his forehead, their eldest son appeared in the doorway of the kitchen. Dan's jaw was firm and square, his nose straight and his mouth wide and generous and, more often than not, smiling. But at the moment his face was serious, his hazel eyes worried. 'Mam, there's a little lass standing in the middle of the yard by the pump. She looks as if she's been crying. I tried to talk to her, but she shied away from me.'

Bessie followed him into the scullery and together they peered through the window at the young girl. Dressed in a dirty cotton dress, the hem ragged and uneven, her tangled black curls looked as if they hadn't seen a comb in days, let alone soap and water. Her face was thin and tears had washed pale streaks through the grime.

'I bet she's the little lass from next door,' Bessie murmured and went on to tell her son about the new arrivals. 'The woman asked me if I'd seen her.'

'How old do you reckon she is?' Dan asked.

'Anywhere between ten and thirteen. Difficult to tell.'

'But she's sucking her thumb. She's a bit old to be doing that, isn't she?'

Bessie gave a wry laugh. 'Aye, lad, and you'd be still sucking your thumb, I reckon, old as you are, if you had that feller next door for a dad. Come on, let's go and see what we can do.'

'Give us a minute, Mam,' Dan said, sitting down on a stool, 'while I get me boots off and I'll be right with you.'

Dan removed his flat cap and then eased off his heavy leather seaboots and thick socks, pushing his feet into a pair of slippers. Then he took off his gingham neckerchief and the thick woollen gansey that nearly all keelmen wore aboard ship and slipped on a checked shirt that Bessie kept hanging behind her scullery door for him to change into. His brown corduroy trousers he kept on. 'Right, Mam, ready when you are.'

Whilst Dan hovered near the back door, Bessie crossed the yard towards the girl. Closer now, she could see a faint bruise on the girl's jaw, purple turning yellow. And she was barefooted too. Bessie clicked her tongue against her teeth. Such neglect.

Bessie frowned. The girl was just standing there, motionless, with her thumb in her mouth. She was not even looking about her with a child's natural curiosity. She was silent and so still. That was what worried Bessie. At that age, Bessie's own lads would have been running riot about the yard, yelling and shrieking, with the neighbours appearing at their doors calling, 'Shut up, ya noisy little beggars. Bessie, can't you keep them lads of yours quiet?' But Bessie would only smile and lean against her doorjamb, arms folded, to watch her healthy, growing boys.

This child was quiet. Unnaturally so, to Bessie's mind.

'Take your thumb out your mouth, lass. You don't know where it's been.' Bessie was teasing gently, but the girl, apart from a darting glance upwards at the woman towering over her, made no sign that she had even heard.

The sight of this pathetic child touched Bessie Ruddick's big heart and her voice was soft as she asked, 'Are you the little girl who's come to live next door to us? Are you Mary Ann?'

Again, a swift glance from eyes that Bessie could now see were dark brown and fringed with long, black lashes. There was suffering in those soulful eyes, Bessie thought. She could see it, even in one so young.

'Poor little bairn,' the big woman murmured, resisting the urge to gather the child into her arms and carry her into her own home.

The girl had looked away again, but now there was a tiny nod of the head. Bessie thought quickly. She was obviously terrified to go home, and with good reason, if her father carried out his threat.

'I 'spect your mam's busy getting things straight. Tell you what, would you like to come into my house, seeing as we're going to be neighbours? You can have a bit of tea with us, if you like. My Bert's already tucking into his shepherd's pie. How about it, eh?'

The girl stared up at her for so long now that even Bessie felt disconcerted by the look. Still, she did not speak.

Bessie held out her hand and, after staring at it for a moment, slowly the girl put her own grubby hand into it and allowed herself to be led towards Bessie's door. Then, suddenly seeing Dan standing there, she hung back.

'It's all right,' Bessie soothed. 'It's only Dan. He's big, but he's as gentle as a lamb.'

He must have sensed the young girl's reluctance, for Dan moved away from the door and disappeared into the house.

'Now then,' Bessie said, leading her into the scullery. 'Sit up on that stool there and let's wipe them mucky paws.' She reached for a damp cloth from the draining board. Gently, she took hold of the thin wrist. Feeling the bones, the big woman tutted to herself.

'You want feeding up a bit, lass, don't you? Come on, let's have that out of your mouth. A big girl like you didn't ought to be sucking her thumb, you know. It'll go all white and wrinkly and you'll end up with crooked teeth, an' all. Our Duggie – he's me youngest – used to suck his thumb when he was a bairn. The times I 'ad to creep into his room in the night and take it out of his mouth. But he's got the loveliest white teeth now you ever did see,' Bessie added proudly. 'And it's all thanks to me. There you are, all clean. Now, let's go and get you a bit of tea.'

Leading her into the kitchen, Bessie said, 'We've got a visitor, Bert. Make room at the table.'

Dan grinned at them. 'Already have, Mam. Come and sit next to me, little 'un.'

Slowly the child moved to stand next to Dan, but she didn't sit down. She glanced at the chair and then up at Bessie.

'You can sit down, love, it's all right,' Bessie said, aware that in many households, children stood to have their meals. Only the grown-ups had chairs. In the Ruddick household, Bessie's boys had all been provided with chairs from the day they left school and started work.

'You're a man now and earning, so you've a right to sit down to eat,' she'd said to each one in turn as they reached school-leaving age.

'You're a guest,' Dan smiled down at her.

The girl sat down gingerly on the chair. Bert laid down his knife and fork and picked up an empty plate. 'Like some pie, lass? And some peas?'

'My mam's shepherd's pie could win prizes,' Dan said and winked at her.

At that moment, Ernie, Bessie's second son, slipped quietly into the room and sat down at the table.

'This is Ernie,' Dan said. Ernie nodded shyly towards her, but then his gaze was firmly fixed upon his plate. 'He's quiet, too,' Dan went on. 'Never says much. But you wait till Duggie comes home. We'll none of us get a word in edgeways then.'

'I'll put Duggie's in the oven,' Bessie said, piling food on to a plate. 'And keep it warm. He'll be late, as usual.'

But only ten minutes later, the back door was flung open and the youngest Ruddick boy entered the house in a flurry of noisy greetings.

'Mam. Dad. I'm home.'

'Think we can't hear you, lad?' Bessie said, but she was smiling as she said it and already getting up again to take his meal from the oven. 'You're early, for you?' She glanced at Mary Ann and explained. 'Duggie's always late. I tell him, he'll be late for his own funeral.'

'Hello, who's this?' Duggie, his brown hair flopping on to his forehead, bright eyes twinkling and a grin that seemed to stretch from ear to ear, sat down opposite their visitor.

'The little lass from next door. They've moved in today,' Dan told him.

'Hello, little-girl-from-next-door,' Duggie said cheekily. At once the girl scrambled up from her chair and stood behind Dan, peering over his shoulder at the newcomer.

Bessie almost laughed at the comical expression on Duggie's face. Already, she understood the child's fear of men, but her youngest son, the noisiest, funniest scallywag of the three brothers, was staring open-mouthed at the girl's reaction to him. It was certainly not how girls, whatever their age, normally treated him.

'It's all right, love, he's a noisy devil, but he won't hurt you,' Dan patted the chair beside him. 'Come on, sit down.'

The girl slid back into her chair, her gaze still on Duggie.

'What's your name, then?' Duggie tried again and Bessie was touched to hear the gentleness in his tone. Even Duggie, bless him, had been quick on the uptake, she thought. 'That ugly brute you're sitting next to,' Duggie was saying, pointing his knife across the table, 'is Dan and this,' he added, nodding towards the taciturn figure beside him, 'is Ernie. And I'm Duggie, the good-looking one.'

There were derisory guffaws around the table from the rest of the family, apart from Ernie, but Duggie only laughed, the loudest of them all. Ernie, with neat dark hair and wearing a white shirt and tie, chuckled softly, but did not speak.

Duggie leant forward as if sharing a confidence. 'Ernie's got a posh job in an office in one of the warehouses on River Road. He keeps ledgers and things. He has to write down all what the ships bring in and take out. That's why he wears a smart white shirt to go to work, but he has a skin the same colour, 'cos he's always indoors, see? Me,' he added proudly, 'I work on Miller's Wharf at the moment but, one day, I'm going to be an engineer. I'm going to get an apprenticeship at Phillips' Engineering Works. Do you know it? They made tanks in the war and—'

'That's enough chatter from you, our Duggie,' Bessie said. 'Get on with your tea.'

As they ate, Bessie kept a surreptitious eye on the child. At last, the young girl took her thumb out of her mouth and picked up her knife and fork. Bessie noticed that she watched every movement Dan made and attempted to copy him.

Dear me, Bessie thought to herself, has the child reached twelve or so without having learnt basic table manners? Pity for the girl almost robbed Bessie of her own appetite as she watched the child eating very little of the food placed before her. She picked at the shepherd's pie and vegetables and played with the apple charlotte that followed, patting it with her spoon and then mixing it with the custard before spooning only a little into her mouth. Then she pulled a wry face.

'Give the little lass a spoonful of sugar, Bessie love,' Bert said kindly, noticing the girl's grimace. 'Mebbe the apple's a bit tart for her.'

Bessie rose from the table at once and went in search of the sugar, returning to heap generous spoonfuls over the girl's pudding. But still, Mary Ann pushed the food around her bowl and made little effort to eat it.

'So, are you going to tell us your name?' Dan asked when the meal was finished.

Again there was silence. Then, as they watched her, she raised her hand slowly and put her thumb into her mouth once more. Her huge eyes continued to stare at each one of them in turn, but returned each time, Bessie noticed, to Dan.

Dan leant forward, resting his elbow on the table, watching her with concern in his eyes. At eighteen, he was now a man, whereas the younger ones – even Ernie at only a year younger – still had boyish features.

Bessie Ruddick counted herself a lucky woman. None of her family had been involved in the dreadful war that had just ended the previous year. Her boys had been too young and her beloved Bert had been too old – just. They had felt the effects of the war, of course, as had the whole country, but she gave thanks every day of her life that her sons' names would not appear on the war memorial that the town was planning to erect in memory of its war dead.

The war had touched Waterman's Yard, though, for Amy Hamilton had lost her husband in 1916 and then her only son too. He had gone through four years of war to be killed with cruel irony only days before the armistice had been signed. Now Amy had locked herself in her house in the corner of the yard and rarely ventured forth. Not even Bessie had been able to prise her out. At least not yet, for Bessie was not one to give up a battle. She'd have Amy Hamilton out of that house and back in the land of the living one of these fine days or her name wasn't Bessie Ruddick.

For the moment, however, Bessie's attention was taken up with the little girl who sat at her table.

'Has she said anything, Mam?' Dan murmured.

Bessie, her gaze still on the girl, shook her head.

'Maybe she can't talk,' Duggie said.

With surprising speed, the thumb was pulled out of her mouth. 'Of course I can talk.' Then she popped her thumb straight back into her mouth and glanced around at them triumphantly.

Bessie laughed. 'There you are, our Duggie, that's telled you.' But Duggie only grinned, pleased that his remark had at least sparked a response.

'Come to live next door to us, have you?' Dan prompted. 'That's nice.'

'Well,' Bert stood up. 'I'm off for me pint, Bessie love. All right?'

''Course it is, Bert.' She heaved herself up from her chair and began to stack the dirty plates. 'I think it's time you went home now, love. Must be nearly your bedtime.' She paused before asking sensitively, 'Will ya dad have gone out, do you think? Does he go to the pub for a pint in the evening?'

There was fleeting fear in the child's eyes and all the Ruddick family saw it. Dan, for the first time, noticed the faint bluish mark on the child's jaw and glanced at his mother. A swift look of understanding passed between mother and son as Bessie gave a little nod. She saw her son's mouth tighten in a gesture so like her own.

'I'll take you home, little 'un, but first, are you going to tell me your name?'

She removed her thumb briefly and wriggled down from her chair. She moved to stand beside Dan and looked into his face on a level with her own. 'Mary Ann Clark and I'm twelve, nearly thirteen.'

Dan stood up. 'Well, Mary Ann Clark, twelve-nearly-thirteen, then you're quite old enough to allow me to walk you home in the moonlight.' He tapped the side of his nose and winked at her as he added, 'But don't you be telling my girlfriend, Susan.'

Bessie watched as Dan held out his hand to Mary Ann. The girl looked up at him, standing so tall above her now. Suddenly, a beaming smile illuminated the girl's face. Her brown eyes sparkled with mischief and two dimples appeared in her cheeks as she put her hand trustingly into his.

Three

'Mam, what's going on in that house next door?'

When he returned from taking Mary Ann back home, Dan's face was grim.

'You might well ask, lad.' Bessie's mouth was tight.

'This poor woman came to the door. She's got a cut lip that's swelling out here.' He held his hand about three inches from his own mouth, exaggerating the woman's discomfort but Bessie got the message. 'And wasn't that a bruise on the kiddie's jaw?'

Bessie nodded. 'I reckon so.'

'So? What are you going to do?'

Dan knew his mother well enough to know that she would not be able to ignore what they both guessed was happening within that household.

'Keep me eyes and me ears open,' she told him. 'And be round there like a shot.'

'She seems a nice little thing. Held me hand and skipped along at the side of me, she did.' He paused and then met his mother's gaze. 'But she didn't say any more. Not even to her mam. Do . . . do you think she's, er, well . . .?' He tapped his forefinger to the side of his head. 'Y'know? All right?'

Bessie frowned. 'I'd need to know her a bit more before I could be sure.'

'Mm.' Dan was thoughtful for a moment, then he

seemed to shake himself. 'Well, I'd best get mesen changed if I'm to see Susan tonight.'

'Mind how you go and don't be late in.'

The young man grinned at her, put his arm about her ample waist and kissed her cheek. 'Yes, Ma. No, Ma. Three bags full, Ma.' Then he stepped smartly back out of the way as Bessie's hand came up to smack his face. But the gesture was playful and affectionate with no strength or malice behind it.

'Go on with you,' she smiled at him. 'And give me love to Susan. Time you named the day with that lass, y'know, else you'll be losing her. She's a nice girl.'

'Oho, I'm not ready to tie the knot yet awhile. I want me own ship first.'

Bessie shook her head, but there was fond pride in her tone as she murmured, 'You remind me so much of me own father, Dan. He didn't marry me mother until he skippered his own ship. Mind you, he never owned it. But I reckon he thought of it as *his* boat. I was born on the river, y'know.' She grinned. 'Somewhere between here and Newark.'

Dan knew it only too well, as did all their family, but he listened patiently to his mother's reminiscing. 'Aye, it was me dad's life's ambition to own his own ship.' Her tone became wistful. 'But he never managed it.' Then she smiled at her eldest son as she added softly, 'Maybe you'll achieve it for him, lad.'

Dan grinned. 'I mean to have a damn good try, Mam.'

Bessie was dozing, her feet on the warm brass fender, when Bert came home from The Waterman's Arms.

'He was in the pub,' Bert said without preamble as he lowered himself into the chair opposite his wife.

Bessie opened one eye. 'Who was?'

Bert jerked his thumb towards the wall. ''Im from next door. Sid, er, Clark, was it the little lass said?'

Bessie nodded.

'He bought me a pint.'

Bessie closed her eye and said drowsily, 'I hope you didn't buy 'im one back.'

Bert spread his hands. 'Bessie, my angel, a chap's got to play the game, y'know.'

Now both Bessie's eyes flew wide open. 'You mean you did?'

Bert shifted uncomfortably. 'You've got to be sociable with the chap.'

'You may have to be, Bert Ruddick, but I certainly don't. Not if he knocks his missis about and clouts that bairn of his.'

'Are you sure about that, Bess? I admit I was a bit wary of 'im at first – after what you'd said. But I have to say, he seemed a nice sort of a chap.'

Bessie snorted. 'Well, he would be, wouldn't he, Bert Ruddick, if he bought you a pint?' Then she smiled as her husband had the grace to look sheepish. She cocked her head on one side, listening. 'Mind you, I don't hear any thumps and bumps from next door now, so mebbe I've got it all wrong. Mebbe that little woman really did fall over a tea chest like she said.' She shrugged her well-rounded shoulders. 'And as for the bairn, well, kids is always getting bumps and bruises, ain't they?'

Bert nodded, watching Bessie as she levered herself out of the chair. 'Come on, Bert. Time for bed.' She held out her hand and hoisted him to his feet. Then she smiled coyly down at him. 'Feel like a bit of a cuddle, Bertie?'

Bert shook his head. 'Oooh, Bess, light of my life. Now be gentle with me. I've got a headache . . .'

Bess gave a deep-throated chuckle and pulled him towards her, clasping his face to her bosom. 'It's not ya head I'm after, Bert Ruddick.'

It was a ritual they often played when alone and, giggling like two young lovers, they climbed the stairs to their bedroom.

It was two thirty in the morning when they heard the sounds coming into their bedroom through the thin wall. First a thud and then a woman's cries. A man shouting and then the chilling sound of a child's high-pitched screaming.

'I'm not having this,' Bessie muttered, throwing back the bedclothes and heaving herself out of bed. 'Bert – get the boys up. All of 'em.'

'Aw, Bess, do you think you should interfere? The feller'll be drunk. Why not wait till morning?'

Bessie rounded on him. 'Listen to that bairn. By morning, she could have been knocked into the next world. And if she hasn't, then that poor little woman probably will have been.' She wagged her forefinger at him. 'I'm not having it, Bert. Not in our yard.'

Bessie was pulling a shawl around her shoulders over her long nightdress and thrusting her feet into well-worn slippers. In the moonlight, shining fitfully into the room, she fumbled to light a candle.

'Are you shifting, Bert Ruddick, or do I have to face him on me own?'

Bert sighed and rolled out of bed. There was no denying his Bess. Every time she got into her battling mood, part of him shrank away, but the other half of him admired her spirit and wished he was more like her.

'Shouldn't we get the police?'

'Huh!' Bessie was scathing. 'What can they do? You know they don't like interfering. A man's home is his castle and all that rubbish. No, Bert, it's up to us to sort it out.'

Bert shrugged and gave in. Not for the first time, he smiled ruefully to himself as he opened the bedroom door to carry out his general's orders and marshal the troops.

The yard was alive with activity as if it were the middle of a busy day rather than halfway through the night. Candles flickered, sash windows were thrown open and heads peered out. Doors opened and men, dressed in vests and long johns, shouted, 'What's all the racket?' 'What's going on?'

Only Amy Hamilton's house remained in darkness.

From her bedroom window, Minnie Eccleshall shouted gleefully. 'It's our Bessie. Battling Bessie's on the warpath again. Eeh, but yon man doesn't know what's going to hit him.'

Gladys Merryweather was already at her door. 'She's got all her lads with her an' all. And Bert.' She raised her voice. 'You there, Phyllis? This'll be good.'

The Ruddick boys and their father formed a semicircle around Bessie as she thumped on the door of the neighbouring house. 'Come on out here, Sid Clark.' She waited and, for a moment, there was silence in the yard, as everyone seemed to be holding their breath. Then into the quietness came the rasping sound of a window being pushed upwards and, above their heads, Sid's slurred voice asked, 'Wha'd'you want?'

'You. That's who!' Bessie folded her arms as she looked up at him. 'Get yourself down here and open this door. I want to know if that kiddie's all right.' Her voice dropped a little as she added, 'And ya missis, too, if it comes to that.'

' 'Tain't none o' your business.' He shook his fist, not only at Bessie but at all the watchers around the yard. 'Get back to your beds all of you and mind your own business.'

Then he slammed the window closed and wrenched the thin, tattered curtains together but at that moment Bessie, close to the door, heard the child whimpering on the other side.

She knocked on it again, but this time quietly so that the man in the bedroom above would not hear. 'Mary Ann? Open the door, love.' Bessie tried the doorknob, but the door was locked. 'Unlock it, lass. Can you?'

There was a moment's pause whilst they all heard her fingers struggling with the lock. Then there was the sound of a key turning. Bessie tried the door again and it opened. Dressed only in a vest and knickers, her thumb in her mouth, the girl was shivering and sobbing quietly, trying, Bessie guessed, to keep the sound low so as not to anger her father more.

'Aw, me little love . . .' Bessie gathered her into her arms and, though Mary Ann was no longer a small child, Bessie picked her up. The girl wound her arms around the woman's neck and buried her face in her shoulder. For a moment, Bessie patted her back soothingly, rocked her and murmured, 'There, there. It's all right. It's all right.'

There was nothing else she could say, though even to Bessie the words had a hollow ring. Now, inside the darkened house, Bessie could hear the man lumbering down the stairs and through the rooms towards the back door, knocking furniture over in his path. Bessie prised Mary Ann's clinging arms from around her neck and handed her to Dan.

'Tek her into our house, Dan. Out of his way.'

Dan reached out, gathered the girl into his arms and

carried her away. As he went, Bessie heard him murmuring to her, 'You come with me, little 'un. I'll soon razzle up the fire in the range and you can have a nice drink of hot milk . . .'

Bessie turned to face Sid Clark, who was now standing in the open doorway, swaying from side to side, his hands against the doorjambs on either side for support.

'You interfering owd beezum. I'll have the law on you for this. Ab . . . abduct . . . abduction, that's what it is.'

Bessie spoke loudly and clearly. 'And I'll have the law on you. Knocking your missis about and frightening your lass half to death. Have you touched her, 'cos if you've laid a finger on that bairn, I'll . . .?'

'Oh aye.' The man was smirking now, confident of his ground. 'And what do you think the law'd do, eh? They can't touch a man in his own home. Not for chastising his own, they can't.'

'Oho,' Bessie said sarcastically. 'You know all about it, don't you? Had the coppers round to your house more than once, I bet.'

The man glowered. 'I told you – mind your own business.'

'If a child's getting hurt, then it is my business. I'll make it my business.'

'Well, she ain't. I never laid a finger on her.'

'What about your wife?'

'That's nowt to do wi' you. A man's got a right—'

'No man's got a right to belt anybody,' Bessie thundered, her voice carrying through the black night and echoing round the yard to the listeners. 'Least of all, a little thing like her, who can't stand up to you.'

'Like to take me on yourself, would you?' the man sneered. 'Reckon you could, do you, missis?'

Bessie pushed up the sleeves of her nightdress. 'Oho,

wouldn't I just, mester . . .' she began, and took a step towards him.

'Bess . . .' came Bert's warning voice, but either side of her, her two remaining sons moved closer.

The man blinked, and glanced around at the menacing faces. Swiftly, he stepped back and slammed the door. From behind its comparative safety he shouted, 'I'll have me day with you, missis, you see if I don't.'

'Not if I see you first, mester, you won't,' Bess shouted back and gave the door one last thump, whilst Bert shook his head worriedly and muttered, 'Leave it now, Bess.'

'But I want to see his wife's all right, I—'

'You've done enough, lass,' Bert said firmly. Then beneath his breath, he added, 'More than enough.'

Four

'You go back to bed, all of you. You too, Bert. You've all got work in the morning. I'll stay down here with Mary Ann. I'll make her a bed up on the couch in the front room and sit with her.'

Bert knew there was no sense in arguing, so he reached up to kiss his wife's cheek and then pattered back up the stairs to his cold bed. He hated sleeping without his Bess beside him. Her presence was warm and comforting. His sons, too, yawning now that the excitement of the night was over, went back to their beds.

The child was soon drifting off and Bessie watched over her, tenderly stroking her hair and carefully removing her thumb from her mouth. When Mary Ann was asleep, Bessie tiptoed back into the warm kitchen to sit in her armchair by the glowing coals. She left the door between the two rooms open so that she could hear the child if she stirred. Bessie leant her head back and closed her eyes. She sighed heavily. She knew Bert didn't agree with her interfering, but she could not stand by and see a child at risk. Nor that poor woman if it came to that, although where she was concerned Bessie felt a trace of irritation. Why did Elsie put up with such treatment? Why didn't she up and leave him and take her child with her?

Bessie's innate honesty answered her. You've never been in that situation, Bessie Ruddick, nor are you ever likely to be, so don't judge others till you know how

31

you'd be yourself. 'I know one thing, though,' she murmured aloud. 'I wouldn't put up with it.'

The following morning, when the menfolk had gone to work, including Sid Clark, Bessie wrapped the child in a shawl and took her next door.

'You there, Mrs Clark?' When no answer came, Bessie opened the door and walked into the house.

Smashed crockery littered the floor of the scullery. As Mary Ann still had no footwear, Bessie lifted her over the sharp slivers of pottery and moved towards the living room. There she glanced around her and then shook her head in disbelief. The contrast between this house and her own home was stark.

Bessie kept her house lovingly polished and although it lacked natural lighting, like all the houses in the yards, which were hemmed in by other buildings, Bessie's home was never gloomy. In some houses, the front door led straight into the main room of the house. In the early days of their marriage, however, Bert had built Bessie a scullery, so that entry into the Ruddicks' house was through this and then into the kitchen. Here, her family had their meals at the table in the centre of the room and sat around the warm fire in comfortable easy chairs in the evening. Beyond the kitchen was Bessie's front parlour, used only at Christmas and on special occasions. In this room were Bessie's family heirlooms. A glass-fronted china cabinet holding her treasures. A grandfather clock in a mahogany case with a brass face and a pendulum that swung with a comfortingly dependable rhythm. On the sideboard was Bessie's most prized possession; a model of a keel with its one large, square sail and smaller topsail, patiently made by Bessie's own father.

But in this house, where Bessie was standing, looking about her with growing unease, there were no such comforts, no family possessions of any kind. The grate in the range was cold and the few bits of furniture scattered about the room looked as if they had come straight from the scrap heap.

'Mebbe they have,' Bessie murmured, shrewdly.

She set the child gently on the one sagging armchair and straightened up. Then she glanced at the door she guessed led to the stairs. Was the woman still in bed? Bessie bit her lip, wondering if she should venture upstairs. She glanced down at the child, but Mary Ann had curled up and fallen asleep again.

Bessie opened the inner door and peered up the stairwell. 'You there, missis?' Silence. Bessie frowned. 'Mrs Clark?' Still no answer, but as she put her foot on the first step and took hold of the banister, she heard a movement above and glanced up to see Elsie Clark approaching the top of the stairs. Relief at seeing the woman alive and on her feet flooded through Bessie. 'I've brought your little lass home.'

The woman was hiding her face with her hand and her voice croaked as she said, 'Thank you.'

Bessie sighed. 'Come on down here, love, and I'll make you a cup of tea.'

'There's no need. I'm fine.'

'You don't look it,' Bessie said with blunt kindness. ''Ow about I put the kettle on while you get dressed.'

Even from the bottom of the stairs, Bessie heard the woman's heavy sigh. Flatly, Elsie said, 'No point. I've no tea or milk or sugar. I – I'll be going shopping later. Just moving in, an' that. Y'know . . .'

Her voice trailed away and now, as if she could not be bothered to hide the truth any longer, her hand fell away from covering her face. Bessie, in the light from the window near which the woman was standing, could see her bruised and swollen cheek, one eye almost closed.

'You get dressed, love, and let me have Mary Ann's clothes. Then you're both coming round to my house.'

'Oh, but I—'

'No "buts",' Bessie said firmly. 'You're coming.'

Half an hour later, Mary Ann was tucking into a bowl of porridge whilst her mother sat beside Bessie's range, holding her hands out to the warmth and gratefully sipping a cup of tea.

Forthright as always, Bessie asked, 'Why do you put up with it, love?'

Elsie's shoulders sagged. 'What else can I do?'

'Leave him.'

'Where would I go?'

'Haven't you any family?'

Elsie's head drooped so low, her chin was almost resting on her chest. Her voice muffled, she said, 'They don't want to know me. You see . . .' She bit her lip and then glanced anxiously towards Mary Ann. Her voice little more than a whisper, she went on, 'They all tried to warn me against him. My mam and dad, even my two brothers and my sister. But I wouldn't listen. You might not believe it . . . Bessie, is it?'

Bessie nodded.

'Well, you might not believe it, Bessie . . .' Elsie Clark shook her own head as if she did not quite believe it herself. 'But fifteen years ago, Sid was a good-looking feller. A real charmer, smart and, I thought, quite ambitious. He was a drayman for a brewery.' Her eyes misted over as she remembered her youth and falling in love for the first time. 'But he didn't intend to stay a drayman forever, he said. Oh, he was handsome then,

34

Bessie, sat up on the front of his dray, driving them two great horses that were dressed out with horse-brasses and bedecked with ribbons.' Now she sighed heavily as she dragged herself back to her unhappy present.

'What went wrong, Elsie?' Bessie prompted.

'The war. That's what went wrong.'

'Ah.' Bessie's tone was suddenly more understanding. 'Well now, I can sympathize, but only a bit mind you, 'cos even if he has been to Hell and back – and by all accounts that's what it was for a lot of 'em – it doesn't give him the right to batter you about.'

'He . . . he had a bad time.'

'So did a lot of 'em. Them that's lived to tell the tale.' Briefly Bessie's thoughts went to Amy Hamilton shut away in her house of sorrow. 'And a lot never even had the chance to live to remember it. It's still no reason why you should put up with the treatment he's handing out to you now.' She jerked her thumb towards Mary Ann, still sitting at the table. 'And what about yon little lass? Does he hit her, an' all?'

Swiftly Elsie said, 'No, no. At least . . .' Her gaze met Bessie's momentarily and then fell away again in embarrassment. 'Not like he goes for me.'

'But he does hit her?' Bessie persisted, determined to get at the truth.

Elsie nodded. 'When she's naughty.'

'Naughty? Her?' Bessie was scandalized. 'I wouldn't think the bairn's got it in her to be naughty. Not what *I'd* call naughty, anyway.'

'Oh, she can be quite a cheeky little madam at times. And disobedient.'

Bessie sniffed, disbelievingly. 'Well, personally, I like to see a child with a bit of spirit.'

There was silence in the kitchen for a moment until

Mary Ann pushed back her chair and came to stand beside Bessie. Her thumb in her mouth, she leant against her and rested her head on the comforting shoulder. Bessie put her arm about the child. 'Now then. Feel better?'

Mary Ann nodded.

'And now we'd better get you to school, hadn't we? You'll just make it in time, if we hurry.'

Mary Ann's brown eyes regarded Bessie solemnly. She removed her thumb from her mouth and declared, 'I don't go to school.'

''Course you do. Everybody's got to go to school.' Bessie turned towards Elsie. 'Does she think she's old enough to leave? She isn't, you know, because they've just put the leaving age up to fourteen, haven't they? Won't she have to stay on?'

'I – she can't go to school. I haven't had the chance to get her into one. What with the move and everything . . .' Elsie's voice trailed away yet again.

Mary Ann's voice piped up. 'I haven't been to school for a year.'

'Mary Ann – please . . .' her mother began and then, defeated, glanced at Bessie. 'We – we've been moving about a lot. I had to go where I could find work and since he's been home . . .'

She said no more but the unspoken words hung in the air. 'Since he's been home, it's been worse still.'

'Right then,' Bessie said decidedly. 'If you like, Elsie, I'll take her to see a friend of mine who runs a little private school.'

Elsie's eyes widened in fear. 'We can't afford . . .' she began, but Bessie held up her hand.

'Don't worry about that. Miss Marsh is a lovely lady and she'll tell us what we ought to do. You won't have to pay a penny, love, so don't worry. Now, come along,'

Bessie said, at her happiest when she was taking charge of a situation. 'Let's get that grubby little face washed and that hair combed and I'll take you along to see my friend, Miss Edwina Marsh.'

Five

'Bessie. What a lovely surprise. What brings you here?'

Edwina Marsh herself opened the heavy oak door set between white pillars. The large, three-storey house was situated near the town's bridge over the River Trent.

'This little lass, Miss Edwina.'

Edwina looked down at the girl clutching Bessie's hand and smiled at her. She pulled the door wider open and said, 'Come in, please. Come into my study and I'll get some tea sent up.'

'Well, if it's no trouble, Miss Edwina, I'm fair parched. We've had quite a long walk, 'aven't we, Mary Ann, all along River Road? And, of course, we had to stop and look at the ships, didn't we?'

Edwina smiled. She knew how Bessie loved the river and how she would use any excuse to walk along its banks, smell the dampness and relive her memories of her young life aboard her father's vessel.

'Did you see Dan aboard Mr Price's ship?'

Bessie shook her head. 'No, they should be away downriver by now. They've gone to Hull.'

'Sit down, Bessie.' Edwina indicated a chair whilst she pulled on a tasselled rope to summon her maid.

'What would you like to drink, my dear?' she asked Mary Ann, but the girl only sucked hard on her thumb and regarded the stranger with large, solemn eyes.

'A glass o' milk, Miss Edwina, if you please.' Bessie

nodded wisely. 'She could do with a bit of building up, if you ask me.'

'So?' Edwina sat down behind her leather-topped desk. 'How can I help you?'

Bessie hesitated and glanced at the girl beside her, unwilling to speak in front of her. At that moment a knock sounded on the door and a maid, dressed in a lacy cap and a white apron over a black dress, entered. Bessie looked at her and then towards Edwina. 'Could Mary Ann go with your lass to the kitchen? I – er – I'd like to talk to you in private, if you know what I mean.'

Edwina glanced at the young girl and then met Bessie's gaze. 'Ah, yes, I understand. Of course. Mary Ann, would you like to go with Sarah? She'll take care of you and give you—'

The thumb was dragged out of her mouth as Mary Ann said, 'No, I'm staying here. With her.' And she pushed her arm through Bessie's and hugged it to her.

'Now, now,' Bessie said gently, but there was a hint of firmness in her tone. 'Be a good girl for me, eh? It's only down to the kitchen.'

Sarah stepped forward and bent to speak to the girl, who was acting like a truculent child. 'Cook's just taken a batch of scones out of the oven. Maybe she'll let you have one, thick with lovely butter and strawberry jam.' She held out her hand. 'You come with me, pet.'

Mary Ann stared up at the maid for a moment and then very slowly put out her hand to take Sarah's. Then she looked back at Bessie. 'You won't leave me here? You won't go home without me?'

'Well, I've come to see about you going to school somewhere, love, but I promise not to leave you here without telling you first.'

Mary Ann pouted. 'I don't want to stay here. I want to

go home to my mam. I've got to see if my mam's all right. You know I have.'

For the first time, Bessie saw a side to the girl that she had not seen before. Suddenly, Mary Ann seemed much older than her years. With a shock, Bessie realized now that that was what she had seen in the depths of those brown eyes, experience and knowledge beyond her years. This child had seen things that no twelve-year-old ought to have witnessed.

Bessie patted Mary Ann's hand. 'You go with Sarah, love. Everything will be all right.'

'Promise?'

'I promise.'

For a long moment she stared into Bessie's eyes, gauging if this woman was to be trusted. Satisfied, Mary Ann turned and allowed herself to be led from the room.

As the door closed behind them, Bessie let out a huge sigh. 'If ever I needed help, Miss Edwina, I need it now.'

The two women regarded each other solemnly across the desk and then the younger one reached out with both her hands and Bessie put her own into them. 'Oh Bessie, you know I will do anything – anything I can – to help you. I owe you such a debt of gratitude I'll never be able to repay if I live to be a hundred and fifty.'

They smiled at each other, but the anxiety that was in Bessie's eyes was still there, just like the sorrow that never quite left the blue eyes of the young woman sitting opposite her.

'I'll never forget what you did for our family, Bessie. And for me, especially.'

Bessie's thoughts went back to the dreadful time when Edwina's brother, Arthur, had been killed on the Somme.

Only a week later, Edwina had learnt that her fiancé, Christopher, had been killed too.

'I thought my world had ended,' Edwina murmured softly. 'And I couldn't be any help to poor Mother, grieving over her firstborn.'

'She was always very kind to me.' Bessie smiled fondly, remembering the time Edwina's mother had come to live at The Hall as a young bride. For a time, Bessie had been her personal maid, until she had left service to marry Bert. 'She even seemed to understand why I was so homesick for the river.'

At fourteen Bessie had been forced to find employment ashore. 'I could've been mate for me father aboard his ship, but I had a younger brother and me dad wanted him.' Bessie looked mournful for a moment, recalling the time when she had hated the fact that she had been born a woman. But her life in service had been made all the easier by the young Mrs Marsh.

'So,' Bessie went on, 'when I heard about Arthur being killed – such a lovely little chap, he was, as a bairn – and then you losing your young man too, well, I had to come to The Hall. Just to see if there was owt I could do. Though,' Bessie sighed heavily, 'what can anyone do in such circumstances?'

Edwina closed her eyes for a moment as if feeling again the searing grief. 'You did more for us than you can possibly know, Bessie. I was so glad to see you that day.'

They glanced at each other and Bessie knew their memories were the same. Edwina's mother had been hysterical with grief. Her father had locked himself in his study to deal with his sorrow in his own way and her brother, Randolph, had disappeared for several days. Even now, no one knew exactly where he had gone.

'There we were,' Edwina said, with a trace of bitterness in her tone. 'Supposed to be pillars of Elsborough society. Father, a leading businessman in the town. Mother, with her charitable works. And what happened? We all went to pieces. Countless other families were losing fathers, husbands, sons and . . . and fiancés and managing to get on with their lives, yet we couldn't cope. Do you know, Bessie, I truly believe that without your strength, I wouldn't have come through it.'

'Oh Miss Edwina, 'course you would. You're strong. You'd have come through right enough.' Bessie was flattered by the compliment and knew her cheeks were glowing pink, but she felt she didn't deserve it. She squeezed Edwina's hands, then released them and sat back in her chair. 'How is your mother now?'

'Bearing up, as they say. But I don't think she'll ever get over it, Bessie. I don't think any of us will.'

'No, lass,' Bessie said softly, 'you don't get over a thing like that, you just learn to live with it and carry on as best you can.' Briefly her thoughts flitted to Amy Hamilton, locked away in her house in Waterman's Yard. She hadn't seen her for two days, Bessie realized with a jolt. She really must . . . But Edwina's next words were dragging her back to her present problem.

'Now, tell me about Mary Ann.'

By the time Bessie arrived back home, she felt a lot happier. Edwina had offered to take the girl, at least for a few weeks, without payment and Mary Ann, won over by cook's buttered scones, had agreed to stay for the rest of the day, provided that Bessie promised to fetch her home in the late afternoon.

'I'll be able to assess her, Bessie, and even if she has to

go to another school, it'll make the transition easier for everyone,' Edwina had said. 'There won't be so many awkward questions asked about where she's been before. The less anyone knows about the poor child's home circumstances, the better.'

Bessie had looked at the sweet face in front of her. Edwina's golden hair was piled high on her head and soft curls fell on to her forehead. She was a pretty girl, with delicate features that belied an underlying strength of character. But in the blue eyes, there was always a sadness now that Bessie knew only time could heal. Was this lovely young woman destined to fill her lonely life educating other people's children?

'You'll meet someone else, one day,' Bessie had said aloud, gently.

Edwina had shaken her head. 'Even if I wanted to, Bessie, a whole generation of fine young men – *my* generation – has been wiped out. There are going to be a lot of war widows and spinsters, who'll never find a husband. They simply won't be there.'

With that Bessie had not been able to argue.

Bessie's contentment with her morning's work was short-lived. No sooner had she sat down in the armchair near the range, and eased her feet out of her shoes to rub her bunion, than there was a knock at the door.

'Come in, whoever you are,' she called out. 'Can't a body have five minutes' peace around here?'

Minnie Eccleshall popped her head around the door leading into Bessie's kitchen. 'There you are, Bessie. Where've you been?'

'That's for me to know and you to find out, Minnie Eccleshall. What do you want?'

Minnie, small and thin with sharp features, came and sat down opposite her. 'Any tea on the go, Bessie?'

'If you make it, Minnie. I'm fair whacked out. I've walked nearly to the bridge and back . . .' And I've got to do it again this afternoon, she thought to herself.

'Whatever for?'

'I've just told you, that's—'

'All right, all right.' Minnie jumped up again, reached for the kettle and went out into the scullery to fill it. She set it on the fire and then busied herself setting cups on the table and fetching tea, milk and sugar. Then she set the teapot to warm on the hearth.

Again she sat down. 'Have you seen Amy, 'cos neither me nor Gladys have seen her for two days?'

'No, Minnie, I ain't, so let's have this tea you're making and then we'll go across. That's if I can get me feet back into me shoes,' she added wryly.

Half an hour later the two women were banging on the door of Amy Hamilton's house.

'I didn't see a light on last night, either, now I come to think of it,' Minnie whispered, though exactly why she was whispering she could not have explained. It was as if she had a sudden foreboding. She clutched hold of Bessie's arm. 'Oh Bess, you don't think we're going to find her hanging from the ceiling, d'you?'

'Don't talk daft, Minnie,' Bessie snapped, but for a brief moment even Bessie's usual confidence deserted her.

Amy had been so depressed, and although all the neighbours had rallied round when the dreadful news had first come through that poor Amy had lost not only her husband but, later, her son too, there was a limit to their goodness. Time had passed and their patience with the grieving woman was exhausted. Only Bessie still waddled across the yard most mornings, to knock on Amy's door to make sure she was up and about and facing the day.

Bessie sighed. Even she was beginning to think that it was high time Amy pulled herself together. Nevertheless, as she felt under the loose brick near the door to retrieve the key, Bessie couldn't help thinking for the second time that day, 'It's not happened to you, Bessie Ruddick, so don't judge others till you know how it feels.'

As she turned the key in the lock and pushed open the door, she found she was holding her breath and praying silently, 'Please let her be all right. Don't let her have done anything daft.'

Six

'You there, Amy?' Bessie called.

They were creeping through the gloomy house like a couple of criminals.

'What if she's taken a bottle of pills or summat and she's lying in bed,' Minnie, close on Bessie's heels, whispered. 'Dead for two days and not one of us knew.'

Or cared enough to know, Bessie's conscience smote her, so that once more she snapped back, 'Give it a rest, Minnie. You should have been a writer with that imagination of yours.'

Huffily, Minnie said, 'I'm only trying to warn you, Bessie. That's all. I don't want you to walk into her bedroom and get a nasty shock.'

'All right, all right,' Bessie said testily. In truth, she was beginning to get even more anxious. The grate was cold, the ashes not even cleared out, and on the table stood a jug of milk, turning sour, and a loaf of bread with green mould on it.

'Come on, we'd better look upstairs, Min.'

'You can go first, seeing as you think me so fanciful.'

Outside the door of the front bedroom, Bessie, her hand on the knob, paused and exchanged a glance with Minnie. 'Here goes,' she murmured and pushed open the door. The room was in darkness but, nevertheless, they could see a mound beneath the bedclothes.

Behind her, Minnie let out a piercing shriek, startling Bessie so that every nerve in her body jumped.

The mound of bedclothes too seemed to leap in the air, bounce and then sit up with a cry of its own.

Bessie recovered the quickest and lumbered across the room to drag open the curtains. Then she turned to look at the woman in the bed. 'Oh, so you are still in the land of the living, Amy Hamilton.' She eyed her sceptically and then sniffed. 'But by the look of you, only just! You ill?'

Amy clutched at her chest and flopped back against the pillows and pulled the covers up to her chin. 'What have I got to get up for?' she said piteously and allowed the tears that filled her eyes to trickle down her temples and into her matted, unkempt hair. 'Go away and leave me alone. I just want to die.'

'Really?' Bessie said dryly. 'Not if I have anything to do with it. We can't afford flowers.' She pushed her sleeves up her arms and then turned to heave the sash window upwards. The morning air blew freshly into the stale room. Shivering, Amy burrowed beneath the covers.

'Come on out of it.' Bessie grasped the bedclothes and flung them back, revealing the thin woman curled up into a ball. 'Just look at the state of you! What would your George say if he could see you now?'

'Oh Bess, that's cruel.' Minnie's eyes were round, whilst Amy started to wail.

'Sometimes, Minnie Eccleshall, you've got to be cruel to be kind. Now, are you going to help me get her out of this bed or do I have to do it on me own? Because, mark my words, Minnie . . .' Bessie wagged her finger across the bed at her friend and neighbour. 'Out she's coming, whether she likes it or not.'

Minnie sighed and shook her head. 'You're a hard woman, Bessie. A hard woman.'

'Aye, but I'm right, aren't I? If we let her lie here . . .' Bessie said no more as with one accord they grasped hold of Amy and dragged her bodily out of the bed.

''Ere, wrap this blanket round her and tek her down-stairs. In fact, tek her across to my house. It's warm there. Make her a cup of tea and there's some porridge on the stove. Get some of that into her. I'm going to strip this bed . . .'

Ten minutes later, Bessie waddled into her own back scullery, scarcely able to see where she was going above the mound of washing she was carrying. 'Good job I was planning on lighting the copper in the wash-house today.'

There was a communal wash-house in Waterman's Yard and every week, usually on a Monday, the women gathered together to boil, wash, rinse and mangle their washing and exchange gossip. All except, in recent weeks, Amy Hamilton.

'Mind you,' Bessie was grumbling, 'with all that's been going on this morning, it's a bit late on in the day for starting a washday now.'

Minnie sniffed unsympathetically. 'Well, if you will go off on secret missions – so secret you can't tell your best friend – then . . .'

Bessie's eyes twinkled. Poor Minnie didn't like being left in the dark about what was going on in the yard. 'I'll tell you, Min. All in good time, but . . .' She lowered her voice. 'Let's see to poor Amy first, eh?'

Minnie grinned at her friend. 'Right you are, Bess. Whatever you say.' She paused and then asked, 'Er . . . what, exactly, are we going to do?'

'There's plenty of hot water in me back boiler, so you fetch me tin bath out the wash-house and . . .'

'You're not going to give her a bath in the middle of the day, Bess. And it's not even Friday.'

'And how many Fridays in recent weeks do you reckon she's given 'ersen a bath? Did you see 'er feet? Black, they are.'

'Oh but, Bess . . .'

'Don't "Oh but, Bess" me. And another thing. Have you got any clothes she could borrow while I get all hers washed? Dear oh dear, I've never seen a body in such a state in all me born days.'

'Well, I don't know about that . . .' Minnie said doubtfully.

Now Bessie laughed out loud. 'I could lend her some of mine, but she'd be able to wrap 'em twice round 'ersen, wouldn't she?'

As Minnie turned to go, Bessie called after her, 'And don't go telling Phyllis. It'll be all round this yard and the ones on either side of us, if you do. You might as well splash it across the weekly *Elsborough News* as tell Phyllis Horberry.'

Minnie grinned over her shoulder. 'All right, Bess, I won't. But you have to admit, Phyllis does bring home some choice bits of gossip now and then.'

Bessie chuckled, then her face sobered. 'Aye, but I don't want poor Amy being one of them.'

'All right, Bess,' Minnie said again and trotted off to do as her friend bade her.

The sight of their neighbour stripped naked tore at the hearts of the two women and pricked their consciences.

'Ya nowt but skin and bone, Amy lass,' Bessie whispered as she gently soaped the woman's hair and Minnie tipped a jug of water over it to rinse the suds away. 'Whatever have you been doing to let yasen get in such a state?'

Amy said nothing but submitted meekly to their minis-
trations, her arms wrapped around her knees drawn up to
her chin. Her crying had stopped and, just once, Bessie
thought she saw the ghost of a smile on Amy's mouth as
Bessie's motherly hands washed her. She sat staring into
the glowing coals in the fire, a faraway look in her eyes.
Then the smile faded and tears welled once more.

'They had to sleep in the trenches, you know. Just
where they were. In the cold and the wet and the mud.
And rats, as big as cats, would snuggle up under their
armpits at night.'

Bessie shuddered inwardly and glanced at Minnie. She
had turned white. Stoically, Minnie said nothing but bent
her head, continuing to soap Amy's feet.

They let Amy talk, hoping that unburdening her terrible memories might help her. 'And sometimes, they
hadn't proper food. Just bully beef and biscuits were all
they had. Just think, Bessie . . .' Amy gave a sob. 'My boy
– my baby – dying out there in all that. He was crying for
me – I know he was crying for me. And I wasn't there to
look after him, to keep him warm and safe. I wasn't there,
Bessie. I wasn't there.'

'Stand up, love,' Bessie ordered gently, but found that
together they had to lift Amy bodily to stand up and step
out of the tin bath. Then Bessie wrapped a thick, warm
towel around her. For a moment she put her arms about
Amy and held her close, trying to transmit some of her
own strength into the frail, grieving woman. 'There, there.
You sit by the fire here. That's it. Now, did you eat some
porridge?' When Amy did not answer, Bessie turned to
Minnie. 'Did she?'

'Only a couple of spoonfuls.'

Bessie nodded and bent towards Amy. 'Now come on,
lass. Let's get you into these clothes Min's brought across

for you. Then you can sit here for the day and have a bit of dinner with us. It'll only be cold meat and pickle, 'cos me and Min's going to give your place a good going over.'

'Oh Bess, I don't know about that,' Minnie began. 'My ol' man'll be home for his dinner and—'

'Your Stan won't mind. He's got the kindest heart I know in a man.' She grinned broadly, ''Cepting for my Bert, of course.'

Minnie smiled back. 'Oh, of course, Bess.'

The smiles faded on the faces of both women when they looked back again to their friend.

'We've got to help her, Min,' Bessie said quietly. 'We'd never forgive ourselves if . . .' She left the words unspoken but Minnie, her friend of many years, understood perfectly.

The two women had a busy day, but by the time Bessie had to go to meet Mary Ann from school as she had promised, Amy's house was positively gleaming. A fire burned brightly in her range. There was hot water in the boiler behind it and food on her table.

'Sorry, it's not more, Amy lass, but I've a regular army to feed at my house.' As she said the words, Bessie heard Minnie's sharp intake of breath and knew the woman thought her tactless. As she had worked through the day, Bessie's thoughts had not been idle ones. At first, she had dwelt on the woman Amy had once been.

She remembered the Hamilton family coming to Waterman's Yard. It was in the spring of 1900. Bessie remembered the date clearly because she had been expecting Dan when Amy and George had arrived to live in the corner house with their little boy, Ronald, who was just learning to walk. She had thought at the time, a playmate for my boy, so certain had Bessie been that her firstborn would be a boy.

The Hamiltons had been a quiet family. George did not work on the river but had a job in the local engineering works. He was a reserved man and didn't mix much with the other men in The Waterman's Arms. He was friendly enough and always so polite, touching his cap when he met any of the women who lived in the yard and smiling his slow, gentle smile. Ronald, as he had grown, had resembled his father. He had been timid and studious and had rarely joined in the rough and tumble games of the other children. Who would have thought, Bessie shook her head sadly, that he would have been one of the first in the town to volunteer in 1914 and him only sixteen?

His mother, too, at first had seemed shy but Bessie had drawn her into the small community of Waterman's Yard. Soon Amy had revealed a lively sense of humour and a sharp wit that, on a Monday morning when they all worked together in the wash-house, had had all the women reeling with laughter. Before long she was exchanging banter with Bessie and the others and was well able to defend herself when the occasional quarrel broke out.

Bessie longed to see the poor woman Amy had now become restored to the person she had first known, and by the time she and Minnie closed the door on Amy's now spotless house, Bessie had a plan of action. In fact, she had two, one concerning Amy Hamilton and the other Mary Ann Clark.

As regards Amy, Bessie had no intention of pussyfooting around her, minding every word she said for fear of upsetting her. Amy, she had decided, would have to come back into the real world and she, Bessie Ruddick – with the help of Minnie and everyone who lived in their yard – was the woman to do it. She remembered Edwina's mother clinging to her and wailing aloud, 'Oh Bessie, what shall I do? What shall I do without him? My boy. My baby.'

'You've Master Randolph and Miss Edwina to think of, madam,' Bessie had said. 'Miss Edwina's hurting too. She needs you.'

But Mrs Isabella Marsh had been so lost in her own anguish that she had been unable to give comfort to her daughter, who was grieving for two men in her life she had loved. For a while, Bessie had mothered both the sorrowing women.

And now it seemed she had to start again with Amy.

Bessie's plans for Mary Ann were less straightforward. This would be interfering in the lives of people she hardly knew and she doubted she would have the backing of her own family or neighbours.

Then she smiled to herself. She wasn't nicknamed Battling Bessie Ruddick for nothing.

'So, how did you enjoy your first day back at school, Mary Ann?'

The girl, though still sucking her left thumb and clinging on to Bessie's hand with her right, nevertheless was hopping and skipping alongside her.

'Tek that thumb out of your mouth and talk to me properly 'cos I know you can. And walk nicely, Mary Ann. You're too big now to be acting like a two-year-old.'

Mary Ann promptly removed her thumb and glanced up coyly at Bessie. A smile touched her mouth and the two dimples deepened. 'It was nice. That lady you know, she was ever so kind.'

'And did you make some friends?'

Mary Ann pulled a face. 'Not really. They all seem a bit posh and stuck up.'

Well, they would, Bessie thought to herself, seeing as the children who went to Miss Marsh's school came from the moneyed folk in the town.

She felt a tug on her hand as the girl said, 'Let's see the boats. We might see Dan.'

'Not this afternoon, Mary Ann. He's gone to Hull.'

'I want to see them anyway.'

Bessie didn't need asking twice. Any excuse, her Bert always said, and she was down to the river like a water rat making for its home.

They went down the slippery steps of one of the staithes, almost to the water.

'Be careful,' Bessie said, gripping the young girl's hand. 'I don't want you falling in the river. You'd get carried away by the current and caught amongst the weeds, else be swept under the wharf there. Then we'd never get you out.'

'Has there ever been anyone drownded?' Mary Ann asked.

'Oh aye, one or two,' Bessie said, 'so you just hang on tight to me.'

They stood on the step above the water line and looked up and down the river.

'What a lot of boats.'

Bessie beamed, her gaze taking in the riverside scene. 'Aye, there is, an' all. See that down there? That's the packet boat just coming back from Hull. It goes every day and calls at several places down the river as well as teking folks all the way to Hull and back again at night.'

'Where's Hull?'

'It's a big port on the Humber. This river . . .' Bessie pointed to the water flowing past just below their feet, 'is the River Trent. It flows into the Humber and then that river flows into the North Sea.'

'Oh.' Mary Ann did not seem to understand.

'You ask Miss Edwina tomorrow at school. She'll show you on a map and then you'll be able to see just where Dan has gone.'

Mary Ann smiled up at Bessie and the older woman was amazed, yet again, to see how the smile altered the child's face. It was suddenly alive with fun and mischief. Bessie's kind heart longed to see that look on the young girl's face all the time, in place of the haunted, frightened look that fear of her own father caused.

Further down the river, men off-loaded sacks from a ship on to the wharf, running with a wheelbarrow up and down a long gangway from ship to shore. Beyond that, a crane lifted heavy cargo on to the land.

'When I was your age, I lived on a ship. The one me dad skippered. In fact,' Bessie added, with pride, 'I was born on board.' She laughed. 'Somewhere between here and Newark.'

'I'd like to live on a boat.'

'A ship, Mary Ann. A vessel that size is called a ship. Their proper name is a keel. My dad was a keelman and so's Dan. And then there are sloops. But they're all ships. Don't you let our Dan hear you calling them boats. Boats are the little ones you row . . .'

Bored now with Bessie's explanations, Mary Ann tugged at her hand. 'If Dan's not here, then let's go home, Auntie Bessie.'

With a stab of guilt, Bessie realized that the child no doubt wanted to see her mother, wanted to know that she was all right.

'Come on, then.' They turned and began to climb the steps, Bessie taking one last, lingering look at the water and the ships and busy wharves.

'Will Dan be home tonight? Which way will he come?'

'Upriver. Up on the tide. There'll be a fair one tonight. I'll be down later to see the Aegir.'

'What's that?'

'The tidal wave that comes up the river all the way from the sea. It comes twice a day, just like the sea goes in and out, but you can't always see it clearly. Sometimes the waves are only like ripples. But when it's what they call a spring tide, then we get lovely big waves.'

The girl frowned uncomprehendingly. 'I've never seen the sea. At least, only in pictures.'

'You ask Miss Marsh tomorrow,' Bessie said again. 'She's got some nice pictures of the Aegir. She'll show you. She'll explain it all to you.'

'Can I come with you tonight to see it?'

'Oh well, now, I don't know about that. It might be past your bedtime.'

The girl pouted and then put her thumb in her mouth.

As they reached the top of the steps, Mary Ann said solemnly, 'I'd like to see the ogre tonight, Auntie Bessie. I might not be here after tomorrow. Maybe we'll have moved again.'

Bessie stared down at her. 'Moved again? But you've only just got here.'

The girl shrugged, accepting the inevitable. 'We don't stay nowhere long.'

'Oh, I see,' Bessie said. But she didn't. She didn't see at all. And to her amazement the little girl's words had brought the older woman a strange sense of loss.

She might not have known Mary Ann for many days, but already the child had wound her way around Bessie Ruddick's heart.

Seven

At about half past eight the following morning, when the communal wash-house was full of steam from the bubbling brick-built copper in the corner and Bessie's raucous singing could be heard echoing round the yard, Mary Ann, thumb in her mouth, appeared at the door. She said nothing but waited until Bessie spotted her.

'Hello, love. You just off to school, then?'

The large brown eyes regarded Bessie soulfully. Then she removed her thumb briefly to ask, 'Are you going to take me?'

'I'm a bit busy this morning, love, as you can see. Can't your mam take you?'

The girl shook her head. 'She's in bed.'

Bessie tutted to herself. 'All this staying in bed,' she muttered. 'Must be catching.' She sighed. 'All right. We'll just run across and ask Mrs Eccleshall to keep an eye on the copper. I'll take you this morning, but after that, you'll have to go on your own. You're a big girl now. By rights, you ought to be working. It's only 'cos they've upped the age you leave school that you're stopping on.'

'My dad says I can't. He says I've got to earn some money.'

'Oh aye,' Bessie said wryly, 'for him to spend in the pub, I suppose. Well, he'd better think again because it's against the law and they'd have him in prison if they found out he was sending you out to work instead of to school.'

'Would they? Would they really send him to prison?'

Bessie turned and stared at the girl in surprise. There was no fear in Mary Ann's tone, no dread that her father might be sent to jail. Bessie blinked and stared harder. If she hadn't been so young, Bessie would have said that on Mary Ann Clark's face was a devious, scheming expression.

The older woman shook her head, castigating herself for such thoughts. 'She's only a bairn,' she murmured. Yet Bessie was beginning to see that Mary Ann was a mixture of childishness and worldliness. So used to her own sons, who had always shown surprising maturity for their ages, Bessie found it unusual. But when she thought about it, Duggie could leap in seconds from being the hardworking lad on the wharves, with dreams of becoming an engineer, to a mischievous prankster, playing tricks on the unsuspecting Bessie and even, though not very often, putting one over on his older brothers. The thought crept into her mind now that perhaps, young though she was, this perceptive child realized that if Sid Clark were sent away, life for her mother and for her would be a whole lot easier.

When she returned from the long walk along River Road almost to the toll bridge, Bessie's first thought was to check on Amy Hamilton. Finding that she was up, dressed and had eaten some breakfast, Bessie crossed the yard again to knock on the door of the house next to her own. When she got no response, as was her usual habit with her near neighbours, she opened the door and went inside.

'And if she dun't like it,' Bessie murmured to herself as she did so, 'she can lump it.'

Remembering how she and Minnie had startled Amy – and themselves – Bessie mounted the stairs calling out, 'Elsie? Are you there?'

She glanced in the first open door and saw that there was no proper furniture at all in the room, just what looked like a straw mattress on the floor, the only covering a dirty grey blanket. In the far corner sat a doll and one jigsaw puzzle. Bessie shook her head in disbelief. Is this how that poor child was obliged to live? Angry and disgusted, she turned away and lumbered towards the closed door across the landing. Flinging it open, she called again, 'Elsie, where are you?'

This time the shape beneath the bedclothes did not leap up in fright – it did not even move. Bessie stood a moment, her hand to her mouth. 'Oh dear Lord,' she whispered, 'don't say he's done for her.'

She was lying with her face to the wall and, from where Bessie was standing near the door, Elsie Clark did not appear to be breathing, although in the light from the dirty window Bessie could not see clearly. She tiptoed across the room, went around the end of the bed to bend over the woman, whose head was buried beneath the thin blanket. Gently, she touched her shoulder. 'Elsie?'

To Bessie's great relief the form stirred and a muffled voice said, 'Go away. I've got flu or summat. You don't want to catch it.'

Bessie laughed aloud in relief. 'A bit of the sniffles doesn't bother me. I haven't had a day's illness in me life. Not that I can remember, anyway. Great strapping lass like me,' she joked. 'Come on now, sit up and I'll make you a cuppa.'

'Please . . .' The woman's tone was pleading, fearful almost, Bessie thought. 'Leave me alone. If Sid finds you here . . .'

'And I aren't frit of him, neither,' Bessie snorted, 'so come on, let's be having ya.'

She tugged at the blanket until, with a sigh of resignation, the woman gave in and sat up with a wince of pain.

'Oh, my good night!' Bessie exclaimed. She didn't need to ask what had happened. She could see.

Elsie's face was a mass of bruises, some older than others. The most recent injury appeared to be to her left eye, which was so swollen it was closed. She sat up in the bed holding her left arm and, through a lip that was still swollen from two days previously, murmured, 'I reckon me arm's broken.'

Bessie, staring at her, sat down heavily on the end of the bed as she asked, yet again, 'Aw lass, why do you put up with it?'

The woman shook her head. 'You don't understand. And I can't explain it all. He doesn't mean it. I know he doesn't and he's so sorry afterwards.'

'Huh, I'd make the bugger sorry,' Bessie muttered and added to herself, and I probably will. Aloud, she said, 'I'll make you that tea I promised and a slice of toast and then I'm calling the doctor to you, me girl.'

'Oh Bessie, no. I can't afford . . .'

'Ne'er mind about that. I'll pay, if necessary. If that arm is broken, it's got to be seen to.'

That evening, Bessie was waiting for Sid Clark to arrive home. When she saw him with a pathetic bunch of flowers in his hand, she stepped out of her door and barred his way.

'Oh aye, and where did you pinch them from, eh? Off some poor beggar's grave in the churchyard?'

'Get out of me way. The missis'll have me tea ready.'

'She will, will she? She'll have a job. She's in hospital.'

'Eh?' To Bessie's satisfaction, the man had the grace to look startled and even a little afraid. 'What's up with her?'

Bessie let out a wry, humourless laugh as she felt, rather than saw, Bert and two of her sons appear and come to stand behind her. Out of the corner of her eye, she saw Minnie and Stan Eccleshall emerge from their house across the yard, to be joined by their neighbours, Gladys Merryweather and her husband, Walter. And Phyllis Horberry, never one to miss a bit of drama, peered out from her half-open door.

'What's up?' Bessie raised her voice so that it was loud enough for the whole yard to hear. 'You have the gall to ask, "what's up?"'

Sid Clark shifted uncomfortably from one foot to the other, glancing around him at the watching faces, but Bessie continued without pity. 'She's black and blue from head to foot, Sid Clark, and her arm's broken. That's what's up.'

There was a murmuring around the yard like a cool breeze of disapproval and the Eccleshalls and the Merryweathers moved closer.

Sid dropped the flowers to the ground and stepped back, glancing fearfully about him. Bessie stepped towards him and wagged her forefinger in his face. 'Now listen here, you. It's got to stop. While you live in this yard, you don't lay another finger on her, you hear? Else you'll get a taste of your own medicine.'

Sid glared at her and then, with a sudden movement, dodged around Bessie and made for his own door.

'Oh,' Bessie shouted after him, almost as an afterthought but in fact it was calculated as a barbed parting shot. 'If you're interested where your daughter is, she's in our house. And that's where she's staying till her mam gets home. And even then, well, we'll see, won't we?'

From the doorway of his own home, the man turned and, feeling safer now, sneered. 'Yer welcome to the little bitch. Yer can keep her as far as I'm concerned.'

He slammed the door and Bessie heard the key turn in the lock.

'Aye, you lock yasen in, Sid Clark,' she bellowed. 'That's the only place you're going to be safe from now on, and even then, I wouldn't be too sure, if I was you.'

Eight

Dan returned home late that same night.

'I hope you don't mind, lad,' Bessie said, almost as soon as he stepped through the door, 'but I've put that little lass in your bed.' Then she explained to him what had been happening during his absence.

''Course I don't, Mam. I'll sleep on the couch tonight. It's only for one night anyway. We'll be off again on tomorrow afternoon's tide.'

'It might be a bit longer than that,' Bessie pulled a wry face. 'I daren't let her go home until her mam's out of the hospital.'

Dan shrugged his broad shoulders and smiled at his mother's anxious face. 'I don't mind. When I'm home for a longer stretch while she's here, me and the lads can play musical beds and all take turns on the couch.'

Bessie nodded, relieved. 'You're a good 'un, Dan. You all are. I just can't let mesen send her back to be on her own with 'im.'

Dan patted her round cheek with a display of affection. 'And you're the best of us, Mam. You and that big heart of yours.'

'Go on with you.' Bessie smacked his hand away playfully, but the flush on her face showed her pleasure at his compliment.

The following morning, Mary Ann was up early and much to Bessie's surprise and delight was soon trotting back and forth between the back scullery and the kitchen carrying the plates from Bessie to the table for the men's breakfast. Then, when all were tucking in to bacon, egg and fried bread, Mary Ann stood beside Dan's chair watching him eat.

'Aren't you going to sit down and have some breakfast, love?' he asked.

Mary Ann nodded and pulled her chair close to his. She looked at him coyly out of the corners of her eyes and then reached out to take a piece of bacon from his plate.

'Oi, I didn't mean take mine,' he laughed, amused by her audacity.

Bessie appeared from the scullery, carrying two more plates. 'What's going on?'

'She's nicking our Dan's breakfast,' Duggie spluttered.

Bessie placed a plate of food in front of Mary Ann. 'There's no need for that, lass. Here's yours.' Then she sat down herself and picked up her knife and fork.

But Dan only grinned and winked at the young girl, to be rewarded with the most dazzling smile that Bessie had seen from her yet, the dimples in her cheeks deepening prettily.

By heck, Bessie thought, she's going to be a stunner, this one, when she's older. She'll break a few hearts before she's done. Just as long as it isn't one of my lads. Aloud, she said, 'Eat up, love, time you were setting off for school. Give my love to Miss Edwina if you see her.'

The brown eyes widened. 'Aren't you going to take me?'

'You know the way. You're big enough to go on your own.'

Mary Ann's lower lip trembled. 'I'll get lost.'

'No, you won't,' Bessie said, gently but firmly. 'You turn left at the end of our alley on to River Road and keep going until you get nearly to the bridge and it's the big red house with the white pillars on the right hand side of the road.'

'It's all right, Mam, I'll walk along with her. I'm going to see Susan.'

Bessie sniffed. 'Think I was found under a Christmas tree, lad? That's in the opposite direction.'

'Who's Susan?' Mary Ann asked at once.

'She's his young lady,' Duggie volunteered. 'They're walking out together.'

'Are you going to marry her?' The question was a natural one, yet to Bessie's knowing ears, there was a sharp edge to the girl's tone. Poor bairn, the older woman thought, her view of marriage can't be a happy one. Maybe, she thought, while she stays in this house, we can show her a different kind of family life.

'He'll be daft if he doesn't,' Duggie said, tapping the side of his nose and winking. 'Her father owns the ship he works on.'

'Now, Duggie, you young scallywag, don't go putting ideas into the bairn's mind that aren't true,' Bessie scolded. 'Susan's a lovely girl and our Dan wouldn't go marrying someone he wasn't in love with. 'Sides, there's some might think it was a disadvantage marrying your boss's daughter.'

Dan grinned good-naturedly at his brother and punched him lightly on the shoulder.

Bert rose from the table. 'Well, Bessie, light of my life, much as I'd like to stay home with you all day, I'd better get myself off to work.'

Heaving herself up from her chair, she fetched her husband's jacket and scarf and held it for him to slip his arms into the sleeves. Tenderly, she wrapped the muffler around his neck. Then she planted a loud kiss full on his mouth. At once Bert responded: his hands resting on her well-rounded hips, he kissed her in return. 'Bye bye, my angel. Be a good girl . . .' he chuckled. 'At least till I get home.'

'Oho,' Bessie patted him playfully on the cheek. 'Chance'd be a fine thing, with all the work I've got to do looking after you lot.'

The young men were used to this kind of affection between their parents, but Mary Ann was staring openmouthed at the older couple, and her astonishment grew as all three sons also kissed their mother before leaving the house themselves to go to their various occupations. Even at her tender age and despite her unfortunate home circumstances, Mary Ann could see that it was not an action made out of duty, but given with true affection. Close on Dan's heels as he made to leave the house, she too stopped in front of Bessie, threw her arms around her and pressed her face into Bessie's bosom.

Bessie stroked the girl's hair, but instead of silkiness, Bessie felt it thick with dirt and grease. She cupped Mary Ann's face in her hands and kissed her forehead. 'We'll wash your hair tonight, love. I've some lovely shampoo you can have a bit of. It'll make it ever so pretty. Off you go now with Dan. You'll be all right walking home on your own tonight, won't you?'

For a moment, Mary Ann's eyes clouded but then she nodded. As Bessie watched them go and heard their footsteps echoing down the alley, she heard Mary Ann's high-pitched voice chattering to Dan.

Suddenly and with pleasant surprise, Bessie realized that not once that morning had she noticed the child with her thumb in her mouth.

'You didn't get lost then?' Bessie greeted Mary Ann when she appeared in the yard late in the afternoon. 'Here, you can make yasen useful. Put these pegs in the peg bag for me while I get this washing in. We're going to give you a nice bath and wash your hair before the menfolk come home. And then,' she added hastily as she saw the doubt in the girl's eyes, 'I've got a present for you.'

'A present for me? What is it?'

'Ah, now you'll have to wait and see.'

Bessie bundled more of Amy Hamilton's sheets and pillowcases into her basket and picked it up. Earlier in the day Bessie had had to coax Amy out of her bed once more. Helping her to wash and dress, Bessie had discovered a bundle of dirty bed linen stuffed into the bottom of a wardrobe.

'I don't know,' she grumbled to Mary Ann now, but without any real grudge, 'I seem to be doing nowt but wash this week. Come on, lass. I can iron these later.'

A little later, as she knelt beside the tin bath in front of the fire, it also crossed Bessie's mind that she had not bathed so many people in one week since her boys had been little.

'What did you do at school today?' Bessie asked as she lathered Mary Ann's hair, massaging the child's scalp with her strong fingers.

'Miss Edwina's learning me 'broidery.'

'Is she now? That's nice. Miss Edwina does lovely embroidery. I'll tek you to the church some time and show you the altar cloth she's done. It's beautiful. There now, bend your head while I pour this jug of clean water over you to rinse off the soap.'

As she stood before the fire, submitting herself to Bessie's vigorous towelling until her skin glowed, Mary Ann asked, 'Where's me present then?'

'There on the fireguard. I thought you'd have noticed by now. Not very observant, are you?'

The girl twisted round to look at the clothes warming on the fireguard. Undergarments and a blue cotton dress with smocking at the neck.

'I did see them,' Mary Ann said, 'but I didn't think they were for me.'

Bessie laughed. 'Well, I don't think I could squeeze into them, do you?'

Mary Ann put her arms round the woman's neck as Bessie knelt on the peg rug and kissed her cheek. The towel slipped from her naked body and Bessie was pleased to see that, whilst she was thin, the girl's skin was a healthy colour and her body firm and supple.

'Come on,' Bessie said, 'let's try them on. Minnie – Mrs Eccleshall – brought them across. She has a daughter. She's away working in service now. But Min's a terrible hoarder and she hasn't thrown her daughter's old clothes out. They're not new, of course, but there's plenty of wear left in them. Put your arms up. That's it.'

Bessie sat back on her heels to look at the girl. 'Fits you a treat. I thought it might be a bit big, but Min's girl was tiny so it's not bad. Not bad at all. Now let's rub your hair dry.'

Towelled dry, Mary Ann's hair fell in curls and waves to her shoulders.

'Black as a raven's feathers and just as shiny now. You've got lovely hair, lass. You ought to learn how to take care of it yourself. Still, enough for now . . .' Bessie pulled herself up. 'I must get the tea. My Bert and the boys'll soon be home.'

'And Dan? When will Dan be home?'

'He's gone back on his ship. Up to Newark this time, I reckon he said. He'll not be back for a day or two.'

'Oh,' Mary Ann said and put her thumb into her mouth.

Nine

After tea, when Bert had gone for his nightly pint and Ernie and Duggie had disappeared, Bessie glanced at the clock on her mantelpiece and said, 'Come on, Mary Ann, I'll take you to see the Aegir. Tonight's a big one. So come on. I don't want to miss it.'

When they arrived at the Miller's Staith, there were already several people lining the steps that led right down to the water's edge.

'There you are, Bessie, I thought you wouldn't miss tonight's tide,' a voice called.

'Saved me a place, have you, Min?' Bessie lumbered down the slippery steps to stand beside her neighbour. 'I thought you'd have called for me.'

'I would've,' Minnie said, 'but I've only just got here mesen on me way back from town. If I'd come home first, I'd have missed it.'

'Oh well, in that case,' Bessie's eyes twinkled with mischief, 'I forgive you.'

'Ta very much, I'm sure.'

The two women smiled at each other and then, as someone shouted, 'It's coming,' they turned, like everyone else, to look downriver, leaning dangerously forward to get a better view.

Bessie grabbed hold of Mary Ann. 'Don't you go falling in the water and get swept away. We'd never find you.'

''Course the best place to see it,' Minnie said, 'is Bourton corner.'

Bessie nodded excitedly. 'Yes, yes, it is. It swirls round that corner and you think it's going to come up and over the bank.'

'Wouldn't be the first time,' Minnie muttered and then, her excitement rising too, she clutched Bessie's hand and said, 'Here it comes, Bessie. Here it comes.'

The tidal wave, foaming at the crest, swept majestically up the river, rippling up the banks on either side and rocking the boats moored at the wharves. Behind the first wave front, which raised the level of the whole river until the tide ebbed, came smaller ripples, the whelps, like young following their mother.

'I don't like it,' Mary Ann cried, clinging to Bessie.

'Don't be silly, it won't hurt you.' For once Bessie was irritated by the girl's childishness. Nevertheless, she held on tightly to the girl's hand, afraid that Mary Ann might try to get away and, in so doing, topple into the water. 'Don't you think it's lovely? Just look at that big wave. Come all the way from the North Sea, that has, Mary Ann. Right up our river for miles and miles.'

The water surged just below where they were standing and splashed up the steps, sending spray on to their feet.

'I don't like it,' the girl wailed. She pulled herself out of Bessie's grasp, turned to scramble back up the steps and pushed her way through the watchers.

'Mary Ann, wait. Wait for me,' Bessie cried and turned to follow her, but felt Minnie's hand restrain her.

'Let her go, Bess. She'll find her way home. It's only across River Road. Don't let her spoil your fun. We shan't see another one like this for a while. Just you enjoy it.'

Bessie turned back towards the river, but Mary Ann being so silly had spoiled her excitement and her pleasure, and the wave was gone now, leaving only ripples in its wake. The onlookers began to disperse.

'I suppose,' Bessie said to Minnie, thinking aloud, her generous nature forgiving the girl's foolishness already, 'I shouldn't have expected her to love the river like we do, Min. The Aegir can be a bit frightening if you've never seen anything like it before.'

'I 'spect she's not used to the water,' Minnie suggested.

Bessie shook her head. 'Probably not. She told me she'd never even seen the sea.'

'There you are then,' Minnie said, as if that explained everything.

The two friends reached the top of the steps and turned to smile at each other.

'I'd better go and find her and see if she's all right,' Bessie said as they approached Waterman's Yard.

Minnie sniffed. 'She'll be all right, Bess. Do you know, I've never seen you fuss after anyone so much in all me life? An' that's saying summat.'

'Mebbe it's because I've never had a little girl of me own,' Bessie said wistfully.

'That little madam's got you wrapped around her little finger, Bess. You want to watch it.'

But Bessie only smiled.

A week later, Elsie Clark was still not home from the hospital and Mary Ann continued to stay with the Ruddick family.

'What gets me, Bert,' Bessie murmured sadly as they lay side by side in bed, 'is that Mary Ann doesn't seem bothered about either of them. Her dad or her mam. Now 'im, I can understand, but you'd've thought she'd have wanted to go to see her mother in the hospital.'

'I thought you took her on Sunday afternoon?' Bert murmured sleepily.

'I did, but I nearly had to drag her there.'

'Wasn't she pleased to see her mam when you got there then?'

There was a moment's silence whilst Bessie lay staring into the blackness, thinking. 'I suppose so,' she said at last. 'But it was odd. Not like I'd have expected a young girl to act when she hadn't seen her mam for several days. I mean, I wouldn't have liked my lads to act like that if I was in hospital, Bert.'

Bert's soft chuckle came through the darkness. 'Bess, my angel, if you were ever in hospital – God forbid,' he added with fervent reverence, 'me and the lads would be camping outside that hospital door, I can tell you.' Then he went on, 'And was her *mam* pleased to see *her*?'

'Well, yes,' Bessie said slowly. 'Sort of, but even then it wasn't how I would have been if I hadn't seen one of me own for a few days. Elsie thanked me for looking after Mary Ann and told her to be a good girl and that, but there wasn't the affection there, the love. You know?'

'Mm, I can guess what you mean.' He turned on his side, preparing for sleep. 'Ne'er mind, Bess, we've enough love in this house to spare a bit for that little lass, haven't we?'

Not for the first time in her life, Bessie thanked the good Lord who had brought Bert Ruddick to her. As a young girl Bessie had been obliged to leave the river to go into service, yet she had always hankered to return to life afloat. Her marriage to Bert had put an end to those dreams, but her happy years with him had been worth the sacrifice. Although, Bessie chuckled to herself softly in the darkness, it wouldn't do to tell him that too often.

*

One afternoon, Edwina accompanied Mary Ann home from school, stepping into Bessie's kitchen and sitting down, completely at ease in surroundings that were very different to her own home.

She drew off her gloves and said, 'I'm lending Mary Ann an embroidery frame. May we fix it to the edge of your table, Bessie?'

'Of course you can.'

From her bag, Edwina took out a small circular frame with two rings of wood, which fitted over each other, the outer one with a tightening screw. She fitted the frame to the table by means of a clamp and then she stretched a piece of canvas over the smaller of the two rings and placed the larger one over it so that the material was trapped between the two and stretched tightly.

'That leaves you free to work with both hands,' she explained. Taking a blunt-ended embroidery needle, she threaded it with coloured silk and took a couple of running stitches through the fabric to secure it.

'Now, Mary Ann, watch carefully. We call this cross-stitch or gros-point. You make a diagonal stitch like this and then you bring your needle back up through there and then down again through that tiny square, crossing over the first stitch you've just made,' Edwina explained. 'But all the top stitches must lie the same way, usually from the bottom left to the top right corner. See? Now you try.'

The young girl's black hair, which Bessie had washed again earlier that day, was shining, tied back now from falling in unruly curls around her face. Her expression was one of rapt concentration as she followed the gentle guidance of the young woman sitting beside her. Edwina's fair head bent close to the young girl's and Bessie was pleased to see that the sombre black which Edwina had worn for more than a year following the deaths of her brother and her fiancé had now been replaced by a smart, close-fitting costume of deep purple. It was still too dark a colour for Bessie's liking, but it was a start, she told herself. She liked to see Miss Edwina in royal blue, a vibrant colour that complemented her hair colouring and accentuated the colour of her eyes. But those eyes had not sparkled with joyous laughter for a long time now. Edwina was still the gentle, kind young woman she had always been, but the light had gone out of her eyes and out of her life.

Bessie sighed. So many lives lost in that dreadful war with scarcely a family untouched by its tragedy.

She fervently hoped that what they said was true, that it was the war to end all wars.

'That's very good, Mary Ann,' Edwina was saying. 'Come and see, Bessie, how neat Mary Ann's stitches are.'

Bessie stood behind them, peering over to see the girl's work. 'They are,' she said, unable to keep the surprise from her tone. 'Have you done sewing before? Has your mam taught you?'

Mary Ann shook her head.

'I reckon you've got a natural talent then, lass. What do you say, Miss Edwina?'

'It's a little early to say that, I think, but she's certainly a fast learner.' Edwina smiled. 'At least, at sewing and embroidery.'

The girl looked up and her own smile transformed her face. Her brown eyes sparkled with mischief and the dimples in her cheeks deepened. 'I like doing this much better than horrid sums and reading stuffy books. And who'd I want to be writing to anyway? Only Dan.' She giggled. 'And the postman doesn't deliver to his ship.'

Edwina laughed and, as she rose from her chair, she touched the girl's hair in an affectionate gesture. 'Well, as long as you promise me you will still try hard with your sums and your reading and writing, I'll promise to teach you all I can about embroidery. How's that, eh?'

The girl pulled a wry face, but then smiled. 'All right, as long as you promise that I'll be able to sew as good as you. I'll be able to make an altar cloth like the one Auntie Bessie showed me in the church that you'd done, won't I? I'll be able to dedicate to all sailors like Dan?'

For a moment Edwina's eyes were bright with tears. Bessie held her breath. The child had unwittingly touched a raw nerve.

During the time Mary Ann had been staying with them, Bessie had taken her into the parish church to see the beautiful altar frontal that Edwina had worked.

'She did it after she lost her brother and the young man, Christopher, she was going to marry,' Bessie had told Mary Ann as they stood admiring the beautiful purple brocade material with intricate embroidery worked in gold thread. 'They were killed in the war and she presented it to the church in their memory.'

The girl had been silent as they walked down the long path from the church. As they crossed the road, Bessie had pointed and said, 'And that's where Miss Edwina's family lives.'

The Hall was a large, timber-framed medieval manor house, the centre of which was the great hall, with wings of smaller chambers to the east and west. At one corner stood a brick tower with turrets and ramparts and arched leaded glass windows.

'They reckon Henry the eighth once slept there.'

'Who's Henry the eighth?'

'Ah well, now, you'd better ask Miss Edwina that, lass. All I know about him is that he had six wives.'

'Six? All at once?'

'Oh, I don't think so.' Bessie had scrabbled back in her

mind, trying to recall her scant lessons in history. Failing to remember more, she took refuge in Edwina's name again. 'You ask Miss Edwina. She'll know.'

Mary Ann had glanced back before the church disappeared from their view as they turned a corner. 'I'd sooner she learnt me how to 'broider,' Bessie had heard her murmur.

'I'm sure she will if you ask her nicely.'

That was how it had started. Since that day Mary Ann's only interest in her education had been centred solely on learning how to embroider. Bessie and Edwina contrived together to encourage the girl as much as they could and yet at the same time coax her to try harder at her other lessons.

Now, they moved away from Mary Ann, whose head bent over the frame and whose nimble fingers threaded the needle in and out of the canvas with amazing sureness.

'I think you're right, Bessie,' Edwina said in a low voice as the two women moved into Bessie's back scullery so that the girl should not overhear their conversation. 'I think she could well have a natural talent. I noticed it the very first time I gave her some sewing to do at school.' Edwina smiled. 'It's just a shame that her interest in writing and sums isn't as great.'

'Oh well, we can't be good at everything. I'm not much good with sums mesen.' Bessie smiled broadly. 'I leave all that to Bert. He's the clever one.'

'Now come, Bessie, don't belittle yourself. You're a wonderful wife and mother. A marvellous homemaker and . . .'

'Go on with you, Miss Edwina,' Bessie laughed.

'It's not flattery, I assure you. Mary Ann could do a lot worse than follow your example.'

Bessie sighed. 'Well, I'll try to help the little lass as

much as I can as long as they're here, 'cos I've really taken
to her. And so have Bert and the lads.'

'She certainly seems to have taken to your Dan.'

Bessie laughed. 'She idolizes him. Trots after him everywhere he goes when he's home, given half a chance. And
when he's away, she brings his name into every conversation nearly.'

'She talks about him a lot at school, too, and when I
give her an essay to do, it's always about Dan or this
family.' Edwina paused and then asked, 'What did you
mean just now when you said, "as long as they're here"?'

Bessie shrugged. 'It seems the Clark family move about
a lot. They've been here a month now and according to
what Mary Ann says that's about the longest they've
stayed anywhere recently. I had a run in with her dad
when they first came and one or two since then, too.'
Bessie's mouth tightened. 'You know she's in hospital,
don't you? Her mam?'

Edwina nodded. 'How is she?'

Wryly, Bessie said, 'Doesn't seem too anxious to come
home. And who can blame her? But when she does, he'd
better watch out 'cos I'm not putting up with 'im
knocking her about any longer. These walls . . .' she
jerked her thumb towards the wall between her own
home and the Clarks' house, 'are pretty thin. I can hear
everything that goes on, so I'll be keeping me ear out for
any more bumps and thumps.'

'Do you get a chance to talk to Mrs Clark?'

Bessie shook her head. 'I've talked to her more in the
hospital than I do when she's here. Keeps hersen shut
away in the house. Only comes out now and again to go
to the shops and then she scuttles in and out of the yard
as fast as she can. Bert has a pint now and again in The
Waterman's . . . with him.' Bessie's voice was scathing as

if she could not bring herself to give her neighbour even the common courtesy of using his name. 'Mind you, I don't hold with him being pals with the feller.' Her shoulders lifted again as she added reflectively, 'But maybe my Bert's right in what he says.'

Edwina hid her smile and asked, 'And what does your Bert say?'

'That if we're friendly with them, then maybe we can help all the more.'

'I think he has a point,' Edwina said softly. 'It certainly means we – and I do mean "we", Bessie – can help Mary Ann more.'

'I'd like to try and help her mam, but I can't get close to her. I have tried. I've been to visit her a couple of times in the hospital without Mary Ann and tried to talk to her, but she just clams up.'

'I'm sure you've done your best,' Edwina soothed.

'I can't be doing with these folks who shut themselves away. There's another one across there.' Bessie nodded towards the house in the corner of the yard. 'Amy Hamilton. I know she's suffered a terrible loss. But she's not the only one.' Bessie's eyes softened and briefly she reached out and touched Edwina's hand. 'I wish she had more of your spirit, lass.'

The sadness in Edwina's eyes deepened and there was a catch in her voice as she said softly, 'To lose a husband and a son must be even harder than the loss I've had to bear. I know my own mother and Christopher's mother too are devastated. It – it just seems such a tragic waste of young lives.'

Bessie was frowning. 'From the bit I did glean from Elsie Clark, it's something to do with the war that's made her husband act the way he does.'

'The men suffered some horrific experiences. Perhaps Mr Clark is to be pitied rather than blamed, Bessie.'

Bessie was not prepared to be quite so understanding. 'Mebbe you're right, Miss Edwina. Even so, I don't reckon it gives him the right to knock his wife and bairn about, do you?'

In that Edwina had to agree. 'No, Bessie, I don't.'

Mary Ann was still sitting at the table late in the afternoon when Dan flung open the back door with a flourish and called, 'Mam, Mam, you there? I'm home and I've brought Susan to see you.'

Bessie straightened up from the range oven where she had just placed a steak and kidney pie to cook for her family's tea, but she had no time to move to meet her son and his young lady or even to call out a greeting, before Mary Ann gave a delighted shriek, dropped her needle and jumped up from her chair, knocking it backwards on to the floor in her haste. As Dan appeared in the doorway, Mary Ann flung herself at him so that the big man lifted her up into his arms and swung her round.

'Hello, little 'un. My, you're looking bonnie. That's a pretty dress. It suits you.'

He set the girl on the floor and stood back to admire her. Mary Ann preened and twirled around in front of him, holding out the skirt of her yellow cotton dress like a dancer pirouetting before an appreciative audience.

'Your mam got it for me from the market and Miss Edwina shortened it for me because it was too long.'

'It looks very nice.' He smiled down at her. 'Very grown up.'

Nothing he could have said could have pleased her

more, but as he stepped aside and drew the girl standing behind him forward, the smile on Mary Ann's face faded.

'This is Susan. We're . . .' The tall, good-looking young man seemed suddenly embarrassed. 'We're walking out together.' He glanced towards his mother. 'I talked to Susan's father yesterday and he's agreed we can see each other.' He put his arm around Susan. 'So now we've come to tell you.'

Bessie lumbered towards them, throwing her arms wide, trying to embrace them both at once. She let out such a bellow of laughter, it seemed to shake the walls. 'That's wonderful. You're very welcome, love. Make yourself at home. You'll stay and have tea with us, won't you, 'cos my Bert'll want to see you?'

As Bessie chattered on excitedly, she was uncomfortably aware that Mary Ann was standing very still and silent now, staring resentfully at the newcomer.

Ten

'When's the wedding, then?' Duggie teased, as the Ruddick family sat around the table. The stranger in their midst blushed. She was not really a stranger, for she was the daughter of the owner of the ship on which Dan served as mate, but it was the first time she had visited their home as the girl Dan was courting.

'Take no notice of him, love,' Bessie said and lightly pinched her youngest son's ear lobe. 'You just behave yourself, our Duggie.'

But Dan only grinned. 'Not for a while yet. Not until I've got me own ship.'

Duggie let out a guffaw. 'Reckon you'll be waiting a long time then, Susan.'

Ignoring him, Dan turned to her. 'We could live aboard then. You wouldn't mind that, would you?'

Susan's blush deepened and she glanced up shyly. In a soft voice, she said, 'Of course not. I was born aboard the *Nerissa*. It was only when my elder brother reached school age that we got a house on shore.'

Bessie beamed, but before she could open her mouth there came a chorus from all her family, who knew her so well that they could predict her words. 'Eh, that'd be grand, our Dan. It'd be just like the old days.'

Bessie let out such a loud laugh that soon the whole family was convulsed. Even Susan, her shyness forgotten amidst such warmth, leant against Dan's shoulder, laughing until the tears ran down her face.

The only person at the table not joining in the merriment was Mary Ann.

'I hear your Dan's courting, then?'

'Aye, I thought you'd be first to know, Phyllis, but keep it to yasen for a day or two, will you? I haven't even had chance to tell Min and Gladys, let alone Amy.'

Phyllis smiled. 'My lips are sealed.'

Bessie cast her a wry glance and gave a grunt of disbelief as she thrust a peg firmly over Bert's long johns on the washing line. Phyllis Horberry couldn't keep a secret no matter what dire threats were made. A grapevine was nowhere in it, Bessie thought. Phyllis was more like a town crier when there was a choice bit of gossip going the rounds. Bessie sometimes wondered whether Phyllis herself didn't sometimes start the rumours.

'I reckon she sits up at night making it all up,' Bessie had said to Bert on more than one occasion when Phyllis's latest bit of tittle-tattle seemed particularly incredible.

On this occasion, however, Bessie could not, nor indeed had she any wish to, refute Phyllis's statement.

Phyllis Horberry seemed to consider herself a little above the other inhabitants of Waterman's Yard. She always dressed smartly and, as much as her purse would allow, tried to follow the fashion of the day. Her husband, Tom, was the local lamplighter and Phyllis worked in a draper's shop in Pottergate. Neither of them had any connection with the river whereas both Minnie's husband, Stan, and Gladys Merryweather's Walter worked, like Bert Ruddick, as casual purchase-men.

'So when's the wedding?'

'Give 'em half a chance, Phyllis. They've only been walking out officially for a couple of days. You'll have me with grandbairns before I can turn round.'

'You'd like that, though, wouldn't you, Bessie?'

Bessie's expression softened. 'Aye, I would.'

Phyllis nodded beyond Bessie's shoulder. 'Looks like you've got a ready made one already, the time she spends at your house.'

Bessie smiled. She had no need to turn round to see Mary Ann coming towards them.

'Hello, love,' Phyllis smiled. 'How are you? How's your mam? I haven't seen her about lately. Is she poorly?'

Bessie hid her smile. It was by no means the first time she had witnessed Phyllis swinging into action. This was how she found out all her news. A barrage of questions so that her 'victim' felt obliged to answer.

Not so Mary Ann. The girl merely stared up at the woman, her thumb in her mouth, and said nothing.

'Cat got ya tongue?' Phyllis said, though not unkindly. 'Well, I'll have to be off. Can't stand here chatting all day. See ya, Bessie.'

'Bye, Phyllis. Now, love . . .' she turned to Mary Ann. 'You off to school then?'

Mary Ann said nothing but continued to stare, now at Bessie.

'Off you go, then. Your mam's coming home today but you can still come and see me when you get home tonight. I'll be doing me ironing if this lot manages to get dry today.' She pulled a comical face. 'And I'll be very pleased to be interrupted.' Still there was no response from the girl. 'You can stay to your tea with us if your mam doesn't mind, although I 'spect she'd like to see you herself, wouldn't she?'

Her brown gaze still steadily upon Bessie, Mary Ann asked, 'Will *she* be there again? With Dan?'

'Amy.' Bessie banged on her neighbour's door. 'Amy, love, are you there?'

The door flew open. 'There's no rest for the wicked when you're around, is there, Bessie?'

Bessie grinned and stepped across Amy's threshold. 'I've brought you a steak and kidney pie, love. It's nice and hot so pop it in your oven to keep warm while you do yourself a few taties.' Bessie looked at her neighbour. Amy was looking much better, so she risked a gentle jibe. 'You ain't forgotten how to peel a few taties and boil 'em, 'ave ya?'

The smile, so long unused, began tentatively at the corner of Amy's mouth and then, quivering, spread across her face. Then she reached up and put her arms about Bessie and laid her head against her shoulder. 'Oh Bessie, what would I do without you? What would any of us do without you?'

Embarrassed by the unaccustomed display of affection, Bessie patted Amy's back. 'There, there, you'll be all right, Amy love. You'll be all right.'

Her voice muffled against Bessie's shoulder, Amy said, 'It'll only be thanks to you if I am.'

'Come on, now, before I drop this pie.'

Amy stood back and wiped the tears from her eyes. 'You're right, Bessie. I know you are. My George wouldn't have wanted me to carry on this way. I will try, really I will.'

Bessie beamed with delight and relief. 'I'm pleased to hear it,' she said, as she bent to put the pie in the oven of Amy's range. She closed the door and straightened up again. 'And your Ron wouldn't want to see his mam grieving like this either, Amy. He were a lovely lad – bright as a button and never without a smile for you, even if he was a bit on the shy side. He'd not have liked to see you this unhappy for the rest of your days, now would he?'

Amy's lower lip trembled and she caught it between her teeth. Tears welled in her eyes again and Bessie thought for a moment that she had pushed things too far too soon. But then, Amy nodded and said, 'You're right, Bessie. I know you are. But it's just . . . so hard.'

Bessie patted her friend's arm but for once could find no words. She couldn't say, 'I know,' because she didn't. She didn't know what it would be like to lose her Bert and one of her lads. At the mere thought of it happening, Bessie could feel her throat constrict and tears prickle at the back of her eyelids, but she could only guess at the devastation this poor woman must be feeling at the loss of both her husband and her only child. That was the reason that Bessie's patience for Amy's grief was unlimited.

'You know, Min,' Bessie said a short while later to her friend, 'I reckon Amy's really on the mend. Oh, she'll never get over it. I 'spect you never do get over something like that, do you? But I reckon she's starting to pull herself together a bit.'

'Not before time,' Minnie replied tartly.

'Don't be too hard on her, Min.'

Minnie smiled across the kitchen table as the two women, their week's washing hanging together on the lines outside in the yard, took a well-earned break over a cup of tea and a biscuit. 'You're a funny woman, Bessie

Ruddick, and no mistake. Ranting and raving one minute and soft as a brush the next.'

Bessie shook with laughter. 'That's me, Min. That's me to a tee.'

Min laughed with her. 'But I wouldn't change you, Bessie. Not one hair of your head. Life's certainly never dull when you're around.' She took a sip of her tea and then asked, 'So, what's your next project? The woman next door, I take it, 'cos you seem to have taken charge of the little lass already.'

Bessie sighed heavily. 'D'you know, Min, for once in me life I don't know what to do. I have to admit I've never come across a feller before who knocks his missis about. I know we've got a few ruffians living in the yards, I can't deny that. One or two drunks, the odd gambler here and there and one or two not quite as honest as they might be, but in the main, the river folk are a hard-working lot and I've always been proud to be one of 'em, but him, well . . .'

'He's not one of us, though, is he? I mean, he's nowt to do with the river, is he?'

'No. He's a drayman. So she says. But where he works now, I don't know. He goes off every morning as if he's going to some sort of work somewhere, but that's all I know.'

Minnie laughed. 'It's a mystery, all right. But I know the very woman to solve it.'

Both women laughed as together they said, 'Phyllis!'

Eleven

'Hello, Elsie. How are you?' No one was more surprised than Bessie to see their new neighbour struggling up the alleyway between the houses and across the yard laden with shopping bags. 'Been doing your Christmas shopping? It'll soon be on us now, won't it? Only three weeks to go.'

Elsie Clark lowered her bags and put her hand on her thin chest. But there was a smile on her face as she said, 'This is going to be our best Christmas ever. Sid's got a good job and he likes it here.' She nodded towards Bessie. 'Your husband's made him feel welcome, having a pint with him in the pub, an' that. I'm very grateful. He's settled down a lot now.' She gave a nervous laugh and added, 'If you know what I mean. And as for our Mary Ann, I never have seen her so happy.'

In the weeks since Elsie had been home from the hospital, Bessie had not once heard the Clarks quarrelling. Elsie's arm was better and there were no bruises on her face.

'I'm glad, love. Here, let me help you with those.'

'Oh no, no, it's all right,' Elsie said quickly. She bent and picked up the bags again. 'I didn't get cleared up before I went out. Me kitchen's a tip.'

Bessie laughed. 'You've no need to feel embarrassed on my account. You should see mine sometimes. Looks like it's been hit by a tidal wave. I remember sometimes on board ship when I was a bairn, 'cos the weather can be rough, 'specially in the mouth of the Humber near Hull, y'know. Well . . .'

'I'm sorry, Mrs Ruddick . . .'

'Call me "Bessie". Everyone else does.' Bessie gave a raucous laugh. 'I hardly know who you're talking about when you say "Mrs Ruddick".'

'All right, Bessie, then. But I must go. Sid'll be back soon and I haven't got his tea ready. Is Mary Ann home? Have you seen her?'

Bessie shook her head. 'Now you mention it, I haven't. I hadn't realized it'd got so late.'

'I wonder where she's got to?' Worriedly, the woman murmured almost beneath her breath so that Bessie had to strain to catch the words, 'I hope she's home before Sid, else there'll be trouble.'

'I bet I know where she is,' Bessie said suddenly as she remembered. 'Dan's ship's unloading at Miller's Wharf. Look, you go and see to your shopping and start your old man's tea and I'll go and look for her. I bet the little minx is there.'

'But what about your own tea?'

'In the oven keeping hot. They all come in at different times, my menfolk, so I have it ready early, all plated up for when they decide to appear.'

'Well,' Elsie said, doubtfully, 'if you're sure, I would be grateful.'

'Off you go, love. I'll go and find her.'

Mary Ann was not at the wharf.

'Hello, Mam. What are you doing here?' Dan greeted his mother. 'Come to hold me hand on the way 'ome, have ya? We're just about done, so if you hang on a minute . . .'

Bessie's laugh echoed across the dark waters of the

river. 'I don't reckon it's your old mam's hand you want to be holding, is it, lad? Not now. No, I'm looking for Mary Ann. She's not come home from school. I thought she'd be here waiting for you. Have you seen her?'

Dan shook his head and a worried frown creased his forehead. 'It's a bit late for her to be out, isn't it, now it's dark so early? School finished ages ago, didn't it?'

Bessie nodded. 'Yes. I thought she'd be here. I told her mam not to worry, that I'd come and find her. I was so sure she'd be here.'

'We'd best get looking for her then, hadn't we?'

'Well, yes, but you must be tired and hungry.'

'No "buts", Mam, I'll help you find her.'

They had walked away from the wharf and were now standing in River Road.

'Do you think she could still be at school?' Dan asked.

'She could, I suppose. But it wouldn't be like Miss Edwina to keep her there this late. Not without letting her mam or me know.'

'Could she have got lost?'

'She shouldn't have. She knows the way home well enough by now, unless . . .' Bessie pondered and bit her lower lip.

'What, Mam?'

'It is nearly Christmas and all the shops in the town are so pretty. I shouldn't think the poor little mite's expecting to get much for Christmas. Maybe she just went to have a look, you know.'

'And she might have got lost, you mean?'

'I don't think she knows the town very well. She's been into Pottergate and the Market Place with me a couple of times, but if she took a wrong turning . . .'

'Come on, we'll go and see if we can find her.'

Together Bessie and Dan wound their way through the

narrow streets where the houses were so tall on either side that the alleyways were dark even on the brightest day. Now, they would have been pitch black if Phyllis's husband, Tom Horberry, hadn't been round already to light the lamps on the brackets set high on the wall. Twisting and turning, they came to one of the town's main streets. Pottergate ran down to the river ending in the Packet Landing, where boats and the steam packet to Hull moored. Rounding the corner by the Woolpack Hotel, which stood close to the Packet Landing, its clientele travellers on the early boats to Hull, Bessie suggested, 'We'll walk up towards the Market Place. That's where she might be.'

Now they were passing shops which, tonight, were all keeping late hours to catch the Christmas shoppers. A baker's where mince pies, Christmas cakes and chocolate Yule logs filled the window. Then a flower shop where Christmas trees stood on the pavement outside, leaning drunkenly against the windows, whilst holly wreathes and bunches of mistletoe adorned the inside.

Past the shoemaker's, the grocer's and a china shop they walked without even glancing in the windows. Usually, Bessie loved ambling down Pottergate and would dawdle to look in every shop, but tonight she was anxious and hurried on, panting a little, as fast as she could. Dan, with long, easy strides, kept his pace to match his mother's. He too ignored the shops, his worried glance scanning the milling crowd.

'Happy Christmas to you, Bessie.' A voice came out of the shadows and she turned to see Tom Horberry wobbling down the middle of the street on his bicycle.

'And to you, Tom,' Bessie replied automatically and then added swiftly, 'have you seen Mary Ann?'

Tom dismounted and wheeled his bicycle towards

them, and in the glow from the lighted shop windows, Bessie could see the puzzlement on his face.

'You know,' she said, unable to keep the impatience from her tone, 'the lass who's come to live in the yard. Next door to us.'

Tom's expression cleared. 'Oh aye, I know who you mean now.' Then he shook his head. 'No, sorry, I haven't. Lost, is she?'

'I hope not,' Bessie muttered. Already she was moving on.

'I'll keep a look out on me way home, Bessie,' Tom called after them. 'If I see her, I'll take her home with me.'

Bessie waved her hand in acknowledgement and called back over her shoulder. 'Right you are.' Then in a lower voice she murmured to Dan, 'But I doubt she'll go with him. I don't think she even knows him. And she's funny with men, isn't she?'

'I think she's getting better. She was laughing with our Duggie the other day.'

Despite her anxiety, Bessie grinned. 'Well, who wouldn't?'

On they went again until they reached the jewellers' on the corner where the street opened out in the Market Place.

'There she is,' Dan said suddenly.

'Where? Where?'

He pointed. 'Over there. Just coming out of that draper's shop.'

'That's where Phyllis works. Mebbe she's been talking to her. And just look at her,' Bessie said, 'skipping along as if she hasn't a care in the world and us worried half to death.'

She felt Dan's hand on her arm. 'Now, Mam, don't have a go at her. That little lass doesn't get a lot of fun in her life and you're only mad at her 'cos you've been worried. After all, she's old enough to go into the town by herself now, isn't she?'

Bessie's anger subsided in a second. 'Yes, you're right, lad. But even so, she ought to know just to tell one of us where she's going. Even if her mam wasn't at home, I was. Or one of the other neighbours.'

She saw Dan's white teeth as he grinned at her in the dim light. 'Let me tell her, she'll take it better from me.'

'You're right there, lad. All right, you just give her a gentle ticking off and I'll say no more about it.'

As they neared Mary Ann, Bessie raised her voice. 'There you are, love. We thought you'd got lost.'

At the sound of her voice, Mary Ann stopped, and when she saw Dan, she gave a little hop of delight and ran towards them. 'Dan, Auntie Bessie. Were you looking for me?'

She pressed herself between them and linked her arms through theirs.

'We just wondered where you'd got to, love,' Dan said gently, looking down at her. Bessie noticed that there was a note of firmness in his tone as he added, 'You ought to let one of us know where you're going, though, if you're not coming straight home from school. 'Specially now it's getting dark earlier. All right?'

Bessie saw the girl glance up at him, adoration in her eyes. 'All right, Dan. I'm sorry if you were worried . . .' She turned her head briefly to include Bessie. 'I won't do it again.'

'Good girl, but just say you're sorry to your mam as well, won't you?'

Mary Ann laughed. 'She'll not care. She'll not notice I'm not there.'

'That's where you're wrong,' Bessie couldn't stop herself from saying now, 'because it was the first thing she asked me when she got back from shopping. Were you home?'

Mary Ann stopped suddenly and, with her arms through theirs, both Bessie and Dan were brought to a halt too. 'Shopping? Me mam? Me mam's been out shopping?'

Puzzled, Bessie looked down at her. 'Well, yes. It's nearly Christmas.'

'But me mam never goes out shopping. She . . .' For a moment Mary Ann hesitated and then blurted out, 'She hasn't any money.'

'She must have. How does she buy food and that?'

In a small voice, Mary Ann said, 'Me dad gets the food.'

Bessie was quick to notice that the girl said 'gets' and not 'buys' and for a brief second she wondered if Mary Ann was implying that her father stole what they ate.

Her next words refuted this. 'Me dad goes to the market last thing, when the stall-holders are closing up, you know. He gets bargains and he haggles with the stall-holders till he gets things for . . . for next to nothing. He says me mam's too weak to argue. She'd give in and pay them what they asked.'

Above her head Bessie exchanged a glance with Dan as they moved on again.

'She's been out shopping this afternoon 'cos I saw her come back mesen loaded with heavy bags.'

'Maybe she's been out buying your Christmas present, eh?' Dan grinned down at her.

Mary Ann grimaced as if she did not believe it, but then she smiled coyly up at him as she said, 'That's what

I've been doing. I've been getting you a Christmas present.'

'Me? Now why should you go spending your money on me, love?'

''Cos I wanted to.'

The uneasy feeling crept over Bessie again. 'Getting' not 'buying' the girl had said.

Keeping her tone deliberately light, she asked, 'Been saving your pocket money, have you?'

'Oh no, I don't get any pocket money.'

There was silence before Bessie was obliged to ask, 'So where did you get the money to buy Dan a present?'

Mary Ann replied promptly without a hint of hesitation. 'Miss Edwina gave me some.'

'Oh,' Bessie said, unsure now what to say. Had the girl asked Miss Edwina or had that kindly soul realized that poor Mary Ann would have no money of her own with which to buy presents? She resolved to have a quiet word with Edwina, but now all she said was, 'That was very kind of her.'

Bessie felt Mary Ann squeeze her arm. 'I'll show you later, Auntie Bessie, but you've to promise faithfully not to tell Dan.'

Beside them, Bessie heard Dan's deep chuckle.

'I reckon we'll have a party on Boxing Day evening. What d'you say, Bert?'

'Whatever you like, my angel.' Bert knew better than to point out that it would be a lot of expense and hard work for his Bessie. He didn't mind the cost so much; the lads were all very good and chipped in with extra house-keeping money for their mother at such times. But he did worry about all the extra work it would mean for his wife. He knew she worked from dawn to dusk – and beyond – to look after him and their three sons, besides involving herself with the neighbours and their problems. To his Bessie, the inhabitants of Waterman's Yard were one big family, even, he smiled to himself, Sid Clark.

It was as if she could read his mind, for her next words were, 'I suppose we'll have to ask *him* from next door?'

'You can't very well leave him out, can you, love? After all, Mary Ann's bound to be here and I expect you'll want to ask Elsie. So . . .' He spread his hands.

'Yeah,' Bessie sighed, but planted a kiss on the top of his thinning hair as she passed his chair. 'You're right, Bert. I couldn't bring mesen to miss him out, 'specially not at Christmas.'

Bert chuckled and asked impishly, 'So, have you bought him a present?'

'No, I have not,' was the swift retort. Then, realizing he was teasing her, she grinned and added, 'I'll leave that to you. An extra pint in the pub, eh?'

Bert pretended to groan. 'Why do I dig a hole for myself every time?'

''Cos you're an old softie and I always have to have the last word.'

Bert looked up at her coyly, 'Well, most of the time, my angel. Only most of the time.'

'Talking of presents, Mary Ann's embroidering a hand-kerchief for Dan with a big curly "D" in one corner. She says that she's doing something for me at school. Miss Edwina's helping her, but she won't tell me what it is. Says it's to be a surprise. And that reminds me,' Bessie murmured more to herself now than to Bert, 'I still haven't had a word with Miss Edwina about the money. Reckon I'll have a walk up to the school tomorrow morning.'

Twelve

'So did the little minx ask you for money to buy a present for Dan?'

Edwina bit her lip. 'Er, well, not exactly.'

Bessie nodded and smiled, 'Ah, I thought so. You gave her some. Oh Miss Edwina, you are good, you—'

Edwina was shaking her head. Softly she said, 'No, Bessie, I didn't give her any money.' She met Bessie's gaze steadily and the sadness that was always in her eyes deepened, but now for a very different reason. 'Two shillings went missing out of my purse last Thursday.'

Bessie closed her eyes and groaned. 'Oh no.'

'I thought, at first, it was the kitchen maid. But she's been here six months and nothing has ever gone missing before. Then I remembered I sent Mary Ann from the classroom to fetch a book from my office.' Edwina waved her hand to indicate the bookcase standing against one wall of the room where they were sitting. 'My purse was lying here on my desk.' She spread her hands. 'I know, I know, it was careless of me. I shouldn't have left it lying about, but I didn't think that anyone here would . . .' Her voice trailed away sadly.

'What are you going to do? Bring the police in?'

'Oh no, Bessie. Heavens! Not for two shillings.'

Bessie shook her head. 'It's not the amount that matters, Miss Edwina, if you don't mind me saying so. It's the principle.'

'Well, yes, but . . .' Edwina put her hand to her forehead. 'Oh dear, how silly of me to have put temptation in that poor child's way. She has so little in her life. I should have realized.'

Bessie gave a wry sniff of disapproval. 'Don't blame yourself, Miss Edwina. You're not used to having children in your school whose parents haven't a ha'penny to scratch their backsides with. If anyone's to blame, then it's me for bringing her to you. Besides, she should know better than to go stealing. Her circumstances aren't *that* bad. Mind you,' Bessie's kind heart forced her to reconsider, 'with Sid Clark for her dad, it isn't any wonder really.'

'What do you know about her background?'

'Very little. I haven't learnt any more about the family since the day I brought her here. They're a close lot. He doesn't even loosen his tongue when he's having a pint with my Bert.' Grimly, she added, 'Mebbe they have got summat to hide.'

Edwina sighed heavily. 'Do you want to be here when I speak to her?'

Bessie considered for a moment. 'No. 'Tain't my place, really. If anyone ought to be here it's her mother. Or her father, God forbid! But not me.' She heaved herself to her feet. 'What are you going to do, Miss Edwina? Expel her?'

'Goodness, no!' Edwina was shocked. 'I'm going to try to help her.'

'It's very good of you. Maybe too good. I hope she won't throw your kindness back in your face.'

Edwina, too, rose and walked with Bessie to the door. 'Leave it with me. I'll give the matter some thought before I do anything.' She sighed as she added, 'It's at this sort of time that I miss Christopher the most. He was so calm and level-headed in a situation like this. He would have known exactly the best way to handle it. And he was kind as well, he wouldn't have wanted to be too harsh on the child, I know.'

Bessie patted Miss Edwina's hand. 'You'll do the right thing, I know you will.'

When Mary Ann arrived home that afternoon, Bessie saw her crossing the yard and going straight to her own home instead of skipping into the Ruddick house as she always did.

Oh dear, Bessie thought, it looks like Miss Edwina's said something already and the girl daren't face me. But half an hour later Mary Ann appeared at Bessie's back door, holding two badly wrapped small parcels in her hand.

Bessie noticed at once that although there was a smile plastered on the girl's face, her eyes were red, but all Mary Ann said was, 'I've brought your presents round. One for you and Uncle Bert and one for Dan.'

Bessie smiled. 'I thought you'd have kept them until the party.'

'Oh no, I want you to have them on Christmas morning.'

'You won't see us open them, though, will you?'

The disappointment showed plainly on the girl's face. A smile tugged at the corner of Bessie's mouth. The little minx, she thought, she's angling to be asked here for Christmas Day. Then she relented. Bending down she said, 'Tell you what. As long as ya mam doesn't mind, you can come round after dinner on Christmas Day. About three o'clock and we'll all save our presents and open them then, eh? How would that be?'

The girl's eyes shone and she flung her arms around Bessie and pressed her face against her. 'Oh Auntie Bessie. Thank you. That would be wonderful.'

'But you must remember to ask your mam,' Bessie said firmly and then added, 'and then you're all coming to our little party on Boxing Day, aren't you?'

'Now, Amy, I won't take no for an answer. You're coming to our party.'

'I will if I'm back, Bessie.'

'Back? Back where from?' Bessie asked, surprised.

'I'm going to me sister's in Lincoln on Christmas Eve and staying over. I was planning to come back on Boxing Day, that's if I can get here. I don't know if there'll be any trains running.'

Bessie nodded. 'In that case, I'll let you off, 'cos I'm glad to hear you're going to your sister's. It'll do you good to get away for a bit.'

A ghost of a smile lit Amy's tired face. 'I don't know about that, Bessie. I daren't stay away too long. What'd I do without you to bully me?'

Bessie chuckled and the two women smiled at one another.

'So? What happened? Did you speak to her, 'cos she's said not a word to me.'

Once more Bessie was sitting in Edwina's study, a cup of tea in her hand and, under cover of the desk, easing her feet out of her shoes.

'Yes, I did. She was heartbroken, Bessie, that I'd found her out and begged me not to tell you or Dan. I didn't tell her that it had been you who had alerted me. She doesn't think you know anything about it.'

'But she admitted taking it?'

'Oh yes. She wanted to buy Dan a Christmas present.

You see . . .' Edwina sighed again. 'I suppose I must have put the idea into her head in a way.'

'I wish you'd stop trying to take the blame, Miss Edwina. There's no excuse for her being light-fingered.'

Edwina smiled. 'No, no, you're right, Bessie. Of course you are. But as I was saying, I suggested that she make something for you – I can't tell you what, I don't want to spoil her surprise – but of course I provided her with the materials. I actually gave her some money to go into town one lunchtime and buy what she needed. So,' Edwina spread her hands, 'I suppose when she wanted to get Dan something, she thought I wouldn't mind.'

'I know you wouldn't, but did you tell her that she should have asked you?'

'Oh yes, I was very firm about it. I said what she had done was stealing and that if she ever did such a thing again I would have to get the police in and tell her father and . . . and you and Dan.' Edwina shook her head. 'Do you know, she didn't bat an eyelid when I mentioned the police or her father. But when I threatened to tell you and Dan she became almost hysterical.'

'I could see that she'd been crying when she got home, but she never said a word to me about it.'

'Of course she wouldn't. Nor will she. The last thing she wants is for you or Dan to find out.'

There was silence between them for a moment before Edwina added, 'The thing that shocked me the most was when she said, quite offhandedly, that if her father found out he'd take his belt to her.'

Bessie placed her empty cup and saucer down on the desk. 'He would,' she said shortly. 'There's no doubt about that.'

'Then we'll have to make sure he doesn't find out, won't we? I think she's learnt her lesson.'

'I hope so,' Bessie said, with feeling. 'I really hope so.'

Thirteen

'Bert, this has been one of the best Christmas Days we've ever had. An' that's saying summat, 'cos we've had some good 'uns.'

'It's all thanks to you, my angel.' Bert kissed his wife soundly. 'I don't think I've ever eaten so much in my life.' He patted his stomach, though there was not an ounce of spare fat on his thin frame. 'I'll be as round as you are soon, if you keep feeding me like that.'

'Eh, watch your cheek, m'lad, else you'll not get your last present of the day when we get to our bed.'

Bert chuckled happily, safe in the knowledge that his wife would not carry out her dire threat. They were sitting contentedly by the fire's last glow at the end of a hectic and happy day. Early in the evening, Dan had left to go to Susan's house and the other two boys were out, continuing the day's merrymaking in their own way.

'Aye, it's been a grand day, love. We've not been able to make merry properly for a few years now, have we?'

'Not while the war was on, no. And even last year, with it only having just finished a month or so before and all those poor lads trickling home, well, it was difficult, wasn't it?'

Bert nodded.

'But this year,' Bessie smiled. 'It's different. Even Amy's bucking up now. And when we get into the New Year. Fancy, 1920 already. Makes me feel old, Bert.'

'Old?' Bert grinned. 'You'll never be old to me, light of my life.' Then his smile faded a little as he added, 'There was only one sad moment.' He sighed and shook his head. 'When that poor little lass came in from next door and sniffed the air and said how good your dinner smelt.'

'Oh dear, yes. I never thought for a moment that her mam wouldn't have cooked a proper Christmas dinner.'

'Ne'er mind, love.' Bert was smiling broadly again now. 'She got one, didn't she?'

Bessie laughed, remembering the plate she had set before Mary Ann, piled high with turkey, stuffing, sausage and bacon rolls, potatoes and Brussels sprouts. 'Where she put it all, I don't know. She must be like you, Bert, got hollow legs.'

'I don't know about that, love. But one thing I do know, she's got clever fingers.'

Bessie's eyes followed his gaze to the framed sampler now hanging in pride of place above their mantelpiece. It had been Mary Ann's gift to Bessie. Worked in cross-stitch on canvas were Bessie and Bert's names with the date of their marriage and beneath it were listed the names of their three sons with their dates of birth. Round the edge were tiny images of things that were important in their lives: wedding bells, a house, a ship and a cradle.

'And them hankies she gave our Dan. I suppose she embroidered them an' all,' Bert said.

'Er, yes.' Bessie's pleasure at the sight of the gift that the girl had given Dan had been marred by the memory of how she had acquired the money to buy it.

'What is it, Bess?'

'Bert Ruddick,' Bessie smiled at him, 'you know me a mite too well, don't you?'

'Well now, I could see a little cloud come into those sparkling eyes of yours when I mentioned the lass's gift to our Dan. What is it that bothers you, eh? Think she's getting a bit too attached to him, d'you?'

Bessie's eyes widened in astonishment. That thought had never entered her mind.

Bert nodded, understanding at once. 'You hadn't realized, had you? She's growing up, love, and young girls of her age start to look at young fellers, now don't they? She's fallen for our Dan and no mistake.'

'Oh Bert,' Bessie said. 'I never gave it a thought. I just thought, well, that she'd taken to him. You know, her being an only child an' that . . .' Her voice trailed away. 'Oh dear,' she murmured.

'You still haven't told me what's bothering you. If it's not that, then what is it? And don't try telling me "nothing".' He wagged his finger at her in playful admonishment.

So Bessie told him the full story, but at the end all Bert said was, 'Poor bairn.'

Bessie opened her mouth to remonstrate with him, but before she could utter a word, he said, 'I know, I know what you're going to say, my angel, and of course you're quite right. Nothing gives anyone the right to take another's belongings, but even so . . .' He gave a huge sigh. 'Even so, I still say, "poor bairn."'

Bert heaved himself up and held out his hand to his wife. 'Come on, light of my life. If you're to give the lass and her mother and father, to say nothing of half the neighbourhood an' all, a good party tomorrow night, you'd best be up the wooden hill, down sheet lane and into blanket fair. Come on.'

It all began so well. Mary Ann was the first to arrive for the party, dressed in a red dress that Bessie hadn't seen before.

'Miss Edwina gave it to me. It's brand new. I've never – ever – had a new dress before. Isn't it lovely?'

'It most certainly is,' Bessie agreed, marvelling yet again at Edwina's generosity of spirit.

Everyone in the Ruddick family complimented Mary Ann on her appearance and Duggie chased her round the front parlour, in use in honour of Christmas, with a sprig of mistletoe. Next came Minnie and Stan Eccleshall closely followed by the Merryweathers and the Horberrys.

Last of all Elsie and Sid Clark appeared at the back door and were ushered in to join the throng. Bert put a glass of beer into Sid's hand and Bessie steered Elsie in the direction of Minnie. 'You know everyone, don't you?' Bessie said and then carried on without waiting for an answer. 'Here, Min, you look after Elsie for me while I see to things. Mary Ann, you come and help me carry the sandwiches through. Dan, get Stan a drink, will you? Duggie, put that mistletoe down and make yasen useful.'

At first the atmosphere was a little strained but as the beer flowed, everyone began to relax. All, that is, except Phyllis Horberry and her husband, Tom. Bessie could not help noticing, despite being so busy looking after everyone, that whenever Sid Clark turned to speak to one of them, they coldly ignored him and turned away.

'Phyllis,' Bessie said in a loud voice above the chatter. 'Give us a hand in the kitchen, will you? I'll get to the bottom of this,' she muttered as she headed back towards the kitchen hoping Phyllis would follow her. At that moment a knock sounded at the back door.

'That'll be Amy, I 'spect. I'll just let her in.'

'I'll go,' Phyllis said swiftly.

From her scullery as she cut more bread and butter, Bessie could hear the low murmur of their voices and then, as she emerged carrying two plates, the two women glanced at her and their conversation ceased abruptly.

'Hello, Amy,' Bessie said cheerily and, careful how she phrased her words, asked tactfully, 'Have a nice time with your sister, did you?'

'Nice time? Nice time, you say?' Amy's voice was shrill and with more fire in it than Bessie had heard in a long time.

Bessie smiled. 'Oh dear, got sore knees, have you, love?' The extent of Bessie's tactfulness was limited. Amy's sister, Clara, was a devout Catholic who would no doubt have spent much of the Christmas period attending services and dragging a reluctant Amy with her. Amy, once a regular churchgoer herself, had had her own Christian beliefs badly shaken by the loss of her husband and son. Since that time she had never, to Bessie's knowledge, set foot in the parish church, a defect which was high on Bessie's list of priorities to remedy.

Amy was stepping towards her, her thin neck stretching forward, like a chicken about to peck a rival. 'Is it true?'

Bessie blinked. 'Is what true?'

'What Phyllis says?'

Bessie glanced at Phyllis, who was wearing a strange expression. It was a cross between her usual, self-satisfied smile when she had just imparted a particular juicy piece of gossip and a sudden look of panic.

'Amy, no, don't say anything.' Phyllis put out her hand to restrain Amy. 'I only told you in case you'd rather not come in. But don't spoil Bessie's party. Me and Tom were just going. He doesn't want to stay. Not now he knows.'

'Knows?' Bessie said sharply. 'Knows what?'

'About that Sid Clark,' Amy spat. 'Where is he? I'll tell him a thing or two . . .'

Before either of the women could stop her, Bessie hampered as she was by carrying two plates of bread and butter, Amy whirled about, rushed through Bessie's kitchen and into the front room.

'Oh law. I'm sorry, Bessie, I didn't mean . . .' Phyllis began, but Bessie was too busy hurrying after Amy to stay and listen to her.

Amy flung open the door with such violence that it crashed against Bessie's prized china cabinet and the glass in the doors shattered. Amy, however, was unaware of what she had done.

'Where is he? Where is that bloody coward?'

Everyone in the room seemed turned to stone as Amy launched herself forward towards Sid Clark, her fists flailing. Dan was the first to recover his senses and leap into action. He caught hold of Amy around her waist, but not before she had landed one punch at Sid's shoulder.

There was little weight behind it for Amy, though like a wild thing at this moment, had little real strength. Sid staggered backwards more from shock than from the blow, the pint of beer he held in his hand slopping over on to Bessie's best square of carpet, which had taken her and Bert ten years to save up for.

'Here, here, what's got into you, Amy?' Bessie crashed the plates she was carrying down on to the table and rushed to help Dan.

'He's a bloody conchy, that's what he is. Phyllis has just told me.'

All eyes turned to look at Sid Clark and then suddenly the room seemed to erupt. He swung his beer mug round, smashing it into his wife's face, sending further splashes of liquid up Bessie's wallpaper. 'You bloody bitch. You and your big mouth.'

Before anyone could reach her, Elsie had crumpled into

a heap. Then Sid lunged, hand outstretched, towards Mary Ann. Catching her by the hair, he yanked it viciously. 'Or was it you, telling these fancy friends of yours?'

Now Bessie swung into action, her family behind her. Only Dan, still struggling to hold Amy, did not move forward.

'Leave her alone,' Bessie bellowed, and whilst Bert and her three younger sons grasped Sid Clark, Bessie reached out for the girl and pulled her into the safety of her arms. 'What's all this about? Phyllis . . .' Bessie looked around the room, but the person who had thrown this particular stone into the pond and caused more than a ripple was nowhere to be seen. 'Tom, get that wife of yours in here this minute. I want to know what has caused all this.'

A moment later, Tom brought a reluctant Phyllis in.

'Now, everyone calm down and let's sort this out. Bert, help Elsie up, will ya, and sit her in that chair. Are you all right?'

The woman, still dazed, nodded. Her face was not cut, miraculously after such a blow, but a red and ugly swelling was beginning to show.

'And you,' Bessie ordered Sid. 'You sit down, an' all.'

Against her Bessie could hear Mary Ann's soft whimpering and the sounds of her thumb being sucked vigorously. She bent over her and whispered, 'There, there, love, it's all right. It's all right.' They were only words of reassurance, for Bessie was well aware that things were far from all right. 'Now, Phyllis, just tell us what this is all about.'

Phyllis glanced at Amy, who, though quiet now, was still staring at Sid, hatred in her eyes, before saying, 'He was a conchy in the war. He spent most of the war in a prison cell in Lincoln jail. Someone at work told me. A friend of hers told her because her husband is a warder at the jail. Somehow, he even got out of being sent to the Front as a stretcher-bearer.' Phyllis, warming to her story now, nodded knowingly. 'That's where most of the conchies ended up, but not him.'

'That was a job and a half,' Bessie muttered. 'It'd take some guts to go out picking up the wounded and—'

'How would you know anything about it, Bessie Ruddick?' Amy screeched suddenly. 'When your husband and all yer sons stayed safe at home here?' The pitch of Amy's voice rose. 'Were they conchies an' all?'

Bessie's face flamed. 'You know very well they weren't, Amy, and if you say any such thing about my Bert or my lads, you an' me are going to fall out.'

'Your Dan could have gone,' Amy persisted.

'No, he couldn't. He weren't old enough. He's only just eighteen now.'

Amy's mouth was tight with resentment. 'My lad volunteered and he was only sixteen. *Sixteen*, Bessie. All the way through he went. Four years of hell and then he gets killed only days before the peace is signed. And then I have to live alongside folks like *'im*.' She flung her arm out towards Sid. 'If I had my way, he'd have been shot.'

'Aw, come now, Amy . . .'

'Don't you "come now, Amy" me, Bessie Ruddick. I've seen it all. Palling on with 'em. Having them here, in your own home and taking their kiddie to Miss Edwina's school. Oho, I bet your fancy friend won't be so ready to help when she finds out just what the kid's father is. Not when she lost her brother and her fiancé. Oh no, Miss Edwina will understand, even if you don't.'

With that parting shot, Amy pulled herself free of Dan's hold and marched out of the room, slamming the door so that the already battered china cabinet yielded up yet more broken glass.

For a moment there was silence in the room, then Bessie turned her look upon Sid. 'Is it true? What she says?'

'A man's got a right to follow his own conscience,' he growled. 'I don't hold with war and killing other folks. I'm a peaceful man – if I'm left alone.'

Bessie's eyes narrowed and her lips tightened as she struggled with her own feelings. She'd no time for the men who hid away at home whilst others gave their lives for their country, but a tiny part of her could sympathize with someone who genuinely believed that war was wrong and that they should take a stand against it. She had heard that some very eminent people had suffered abuse because of their beliefs. It took a courageous man to stand alone against family, friends and neighbours and even the world at large. For that very action meant ridicule, hatred and imprisonment. In some cases, they had given their own lives in the cause of peace, for she had heard that many had been shot for cowardice.

Bessie frowned. She had never met a conscientious objector before and, of course, she didn't know Sid Clark well enough, didn't know him at all, but he didn't strike her as a man of unshakeable principles. She regarded him thoughtfully. There was a veiled threat in his final words and his sentiments didn't quite ring true. Not to her ears. Here he was, she thought, bold as brass in her front room claiming to be a peaceful man when he was a wife beater and not above ill-treating his daughter. Oh no, Bessie couldn't see it and she prided herself on being a good judge of character.

'Get him out of here, Bert,' she said quietly now. 'Tek him to the pub while I see to Elsie and this little lass.' She glanced around the room. 'The party's over, folks.'

Fourteen

'Well, did you ever?' Minnie had managed at last to close her gaping mouth. 'What do you make of all that, then, Bess?'

The rest of Bessie's guests had gone, but Minnie had stayed to help clear up the remnants of the shattered party.

At Bessie's bidding, Bert and his sons had taken Sid to the pub.

'Try to find out more of his side of the story, Bert. I don't like to condemn a feller afore he's had chance to defend himself. But we've got to get at the truth if we're to help 'em.'

Bert had nodded. He didn't hold with conchies. Hadn't a scrap of sympathy for them, but he knew his Bessie was thinking more about the man's wife and daughter than about Sid. If it meant living next door to the feller for the sake of that little lass and her mother, then Bert – and his sons – would do it.

Phyllis had scuttled away as if she couldn't get leave quickly enough, her husband close behind her, and they were soon followed by the Merryweathers and Stan Eccleshall. Bessie herself had taken Elsie and Mary Ann back to their own house. The girl had begged to stay, tears running down her cheeks, but Bessie had been firm. She needed time to herself for once, although she was glad to have Minnie's company and help now.

In answer to Minnie's question, Bessie said slowly, 'I

suppose it could account for his behaviour. He must have had a tough time.' She was trying to be fair to the man, but it was hard to be rational and, for once, even Bessie's tender heart failed. 'But it don't give him the right to knock his wife and bairn about.'

'I've never seen Amy so riled,' Minnie said, as she swept up the broken glass whilst Bessie scrubbed at the stain on her carpet.

'As far as Amy's concerned, you know what they say, Min?'

Minnie looked up. 'No. What?'

'It's an ill wind that blows nobody any good.'

'How d'you mean?'

'It could stop Amy wallowing in self-pity. Now she's got someone to direct her anger at, it might drag her out of that terrible depression.'

Minnie shook her head. 'Oh, you're getting too deep for me, Bess. All I know is, I don't reckon this is over. Not by a long chalk, I don't.'

Two hours later when the men were still not home, Bessie went next door to check on Elsie and Mary Ann.

'Can I come in, love?' she called, but pushed open the door and stepped inside without waiting for an invitation.

Elsie was sitting huddled near the range, even though there was no fire in the grate. There was no sign of Mary Ann.

'Little lass in bed, is she?' Bessie asked, moving to sit down in the chair opposite the woman.

Elsie nodded.

'Eh, but it's cold in here,' Bessie shivered. 'I'd light you a fire, but it's a bit late now. The room'll hardly get warm afore you go to bed, will it?'

'There's no wood or coal,' Elsie murmured.

'I'll bring you a bucketful round in the morning, then,' Bessie said, trying to be cheerful. 'Always difficult to gauge what you're going to be needing over the holidays, ain't it?'

She knew she was making excuses to save the woman's pride. There was no coal in the house, Christmas or not, and, she suspected, very little food. Before the fracas, Bessie had noticed Sid Clark tucking into her sandwiches as if he hadn't eaten for a week. And she hadn't forgotten Mary Ann's round eyes at the plateful of Christmas dinner Bessie had placed before her. She had thought the Clark family was going to have a good Christmas when she had seen Elsie loaded with shopping. She must have been wrong, Bessie thought.

'Now, love, do you want to tell me about it? Maybe, if I know the full story, I can help.'

Elsie shrugged her thin shoulders. 'I doubt it, Bessie. We'll just have to move on again. Everywhere we go, somehow, someone seems to find out about us and we have to go.'

Bessie gave a wry snort of laughter. 'I could have warned you about Phyllis Horberry. A ferret's got nothing on her when it comes to a bit of gossip.' She put her head on one side and regarded the pathetic little woman. She felt sorry for her and for the young girl upstairs, who was probably lying on that old mattress, sobbing herself to sleep and sucking her thumb until it was white and wrinkly.

'Maybe if the folks round here knew the truth, they could sympathize a bit. Worth a try, ain't it?'

Again, the disconsolate shrug. 'You can't expect someone like poor Amy Hamilton to understand,' Elsie said reasonably. 'Can you?'

112

Bessie sighed. 'Not really, if I'm honest with you.'

'Sid never used to be like he is now, Bessie. I want you to believe that. He was quite a good husband and father. Oh, he always drank a bit and it always made him nasty tempered, but he never knocked me and Mary Ann about. Not . . . not until he came out of prison.' Elsie sighed. 'After the war finished and he came home, it still wasn't over.' Flatly, she added hopelessly, 'It never will be over. Everybody thinks that in Sid's case he was hiding behind the name of being a conscientious objector just to get out of going to the Front.'

'I suppose,' Bessie said thoughtfully, 'folks think that, if he'd been genuine, he'd have gone as a stretcher-bearer, like Phyllis said.' She paused and asked softly, not wanting to bring this poor woman any further pain, but needing to get at the truth. 'Wouldn't he?'

Elsie gave a deep sigh. 'It grieves me to say it, Bessie, but I have to agree with you. That's what he should have done.'

'Then I'm sorry for you, Elsie,' was all Bessie could say. 'Very sorry.'

As she went home, Bessie had the uncomfortable feeling that Minnie's words were prophetic.

This wasn't over by a long chalk.

Fifteen

Minnie's prediction came true a week later.

Bessie and Bert woke with a jump at two o'clock in the morning on New Year's Day to hear the screams coming through their bedroom wall from the house next door.

The Ruddicks' New Year celebrations had been quiet and just within their own household. Their sons had stayed at home to see the New Year in with their parents and Susan had been invited to spend the evening with them. Dan had set off to walk her home just after midnight. The rest had gone to their beds soon after one o'clock, although Bessie had slept fitfully, listening with half an ear for Dan to arrive home.

'Daft, you are,' she had muttered to herself. 'He's a grown man now.'

'What, love?' Bert had murmured sleepily. 'What d'you say?'

Bessie had chuckled. 'Nothing, sweetheart, just me worrying about our Dan.'

'He'll be all right, he's . . .' Bert had begun, but the sentence ended in a gentle snore.

Bessie had lain awake for a while, staring into the darkness imagining, quite irrationally, all the different sorts of trouble Dan could get involved in if he encountered revellers roaming the streets. But gradually her heavy eyelids had closed and she had fallen into a half sleep.

Then the commotion had begun and, at once, she was fully awake.

'Oh no,' she groaned as she levered herself out of bed and lumbered across the room to light the candle on the mantelpiece. 'I've been afraid of this. Come on, Bert.'

Although he sat up and lowered his legs to the floor, Bert said, 'Do you really think we should interfere, my angel?'

'I aren't lying here listening to that racket and doing nothing about it.'

There was another cry of pain followed by a thump and, plainly through the wall, they could hear Sid shouting obscenities.

'Just listen to the man. Have you ever heard owt like it?'

Bert gave a wry smile. 'Well, yes, I have, love, amongst sailors and workmen.' He shook his head. 'But it's not the sort of language you like to hear a man using to his wife.'

There was a thud against the wall and the sound of splintering wood. Then, suddenly, there was silence. An eerie, uncanny silence that sent a chill through Bessie.

'Oh Bert, what's he done?'

But Bert was swinging his legs back into bed and lying back against the pillow.

Shocked, Bessie said, 'You're not just going to lie there and do nothing, Bert Ruddick, are you?'

'What can we do, Bess? If we go round and bang on his door, he'll not answer it. So, short of breaking it down, how are we to get in?' He paused and then asked quietly, 'Do you want me to call out the police?'

Bessie shivered and got back into bed, though she did not, for the moment, blow out the candle. 'I don't know. I really don't know what to do, Bert. I just hate to think of that poor woman – and Mary Ann – having to put up with that lot.' She nodded her head towards the wall.

Bert snuggled down further beneath the covers. 'It seems to have settled down now. I expect he got blind drunk. She told you he was worse then, didn't she?'

'Mm,' Bessie murmured, her hearing still tuned to any sound coming from next door. 'What worries me now is, why has it gone quiet so suddenly?'

Despite the gravity of their conversation, Bert chuckled. 'That's the trouble with you, my angel. Never satisfied, are you?'

For once, worried as she was, Bessie did not pick up on his teasing innuendo. Bert turned on his side, his back to her, but Bessie still sat up in bed, a shawl around her shoulders, listening intently.

'I can't hear anything,' she muttered. 'It's *too* quiet now.'

She waited a few moments more and then, exasperated, swung her legs out of the bed again, saying, 'I'm wide awake now. I'm going down to make some cocoa. D'you want some?'

There was no answer from her husband, so, pushing her feet into her slippers and taking the candle, Bessie plodded down the stairs and into the kitchen. Minutes later she had just settled herself into Bert's armchair near the dying embers in the range when she heard the back door open and close very quietly. The inner door opened and a shadowy figure stepped silently into the room. Bessie saw him start as he saw the lighted candle on the table and her sitting in the chair.

'You waiting up for me, Mam? Am I going to get a clip round the ear for being late home?'

He stood over her, towering above her, this big, handsome son of hers, her firstborn.

Bessie chuckled. 'I don't think I'll bother. You're a bit big for that now.' Then she added, wagging her finger at him playfully, 'But don't think I wouldn't if I thought you deserved it.'

Dan, too, laughed softly and sat down opposite her. 'Any cocoa going? It's cold out and I've had a long walk home.'

As Bessie got up to get him a mug of cocoa, she asked, 'Did you get your ear clipped yon end for Susan being late home?'

'No, the Prices were still merrymaking. The house was ablaze with light and they'd got friends and neighbours round. I reckon it'll go on till dawn.' He grinned at her in the flickering candlelight. 'But I thought seeing that her dad is me boss and I'm due to sail one of his ships downriver tomorrow on the afternoon tide, I'd better look willing and get to me bed.'

'You mean today, lad,' Bessie said. 'It's New Year's Day now. The first of January 1920. Can you believe it?'

'So, what are you doing still up?'

'Oh, I've been to bed once, but then there was this unearthly racket from next door. He's been at it again.'

Dan cocked his head on one side and listened. 'Seems all right now, though. Drunk, was he?'

Bessie handed him his cocoa and sat down heavily with a sigh. 'I 'spect so. He was shouting and swearing and carrying on. There was thuds and bangs and then she was screaming.'

Dan looked suddenly worried. 'Who? Mary Ann?'

'No, I don't think so. I think it was his missis. Elsie.'

Dan relaxed slightly, but angry disapproval was still in his eyes. 'He's still got no right . . .' He broke off and sighed. 'Still, it seems to have stopped. Let's hope he's fallen into a drunken stupor.'

'It went quiet all of a sudden, though. That's what's worrying me.'

'But you've not heard the little lass? You've not heard Mary Ann?'

Bessie shook her head. 'No.'

'I reckon if it had been anything really bad, she'd have come round here. Don't you? She knows by now, surely, that she can come to us for anything, doesn't she?'

'I think so,' Bessie agreed. 'I hope so.'

'Come on then, Mam,' Dan said, draining his mug and standing up. 'Let's both get to our beds, eh?'

'Aye, you're right, lad,' Bessie said as she got up, and then she added, with feeling, 'At least I hope to God you are.'

Sixteen

'I ain't seen hide nor hair of any of 'em this morning, Min, and I'm worried sick now.'

'Mebbe he's sleeping the booze off and she and the little lass are having a lie-in while he's quiet.'

Bessie sighed. 'Sounds reasonable, I suppose, after all the shenanigans last night, but . . .' she bit her lip. 'I'd feel better if I just saw one of 'em.'

They were standing outside Minnie's door, arms folded and looking across the yard towards the Clarks' house.

There was not a movement to be seen. No curtain moved, no window or door opened.

'I can't stand it any longer,' Bessie said. 'I'm going across there and I don't care if I do wake 'em up.'

'If you rouse the sleeping tiger,' Minnie warned, 'you'll get more than you bargained for. And she'll not thank you neither if she's gettin' a bit o' peace.'

Bessie had taken a step forward but now she stopped again and groaned. 'Oh Min, I don't know what to do.'

'Leave it till dinner time and then if we've seen nowt by then, well, I'll come with you.'

Bessie considered. 'All right. Good idea. Yes, that's what we'll do.'

Midday came and still there was no sign of life from her neighbours, so Bessie crossed the yard once more and rapped sharply on Minnie's door. 'Come on, Min, if you're coming, 'cos I'm going to see what's what.'

Minnie opened her door, untying her apron. 'I'm right with you, Bess.'

Together, they approached the house and Bessie raised her hand to knock, but before she could do so, Minnie clutched her arm and said, 'Listen, can you hear summat?'

Bessie was motionless with her arm still raised in the air. From behind the door came a whimpering like an animal in pain.

'Oh my God,' Bessie breathed. She grasped the door-knob, turned it and pushed, but the door did not yield.

'It's locked.' Instead of raising her arm again, she put her face close to the door and called softly, 'Is that you, Mary Ann?'

The whimpering beyond the door grew louder until it became a wail.

'It is her,' Bessie said. 'I'm sure it is.' Raising her voice again, she said, 'Mary Ann, love, open the door.'

The two women standing outside saw and heard the doorknob move, but still the door did not open. The girl's crying increased. 'I can't. There's no key.'

'What? But there must be,' Bessie said, getting more and more agitated by the minute. Something was dread-fully wrong behind that door and now she was castigating herself inwardly for having waited so long before trying to find out just what had happened.

'Look on the floor, love. Has it dropped out?'

There was a scrabbling sound and then, 'I can't find it.'

Then Bessie jumped as Mary Ann thumped on her side of the door. 'Get me out, Auntie Bessie, get me out.'

'I wish Bert or one of the lads was here.' Bessie bit her lip and then said suddenly, 'I know. Min, what time is it?'

'Dunno. About twelve, I think.'

'Right. You stay here. I'm going for Dan. With a bit of luck, he won't have sailed yet.'

She was halfway across the yard before Minnie called after her, 'He'll not come, Bessie, if he's ready to sail.'

'He'll come,' Bessie muttered, pulling her shawl closely around her as she hurried through the alleyway between the houses. 'When he knows it's for that little lass, he'll come.'

Only minutes later, she was hurrying back again to Waterman's Yard, Dan loping along beside her.

'You're sure it's Mary Ann behind the door, Mam?'

'Certain,' Bessie puffed. 'Called me Auntie Bessie, didn't she? "Get me out, Auntie Bessie," she said. "Get me out." Like a trapped animal. Poor little mite.'

'But where's her mam?'

'I daren't think, lad,' Bessie said grimly.

'Right then,' Dan said, equally adamant. 'Break down the door, it is.'

When they arrived back, other neighbours had gathered.

Gladys had joined Minnie outside the Clarks' house and, from her doorway, Amy Hamilton was shouting unwanted advice. 'Leave 'em to it. I don't know what you're bothering with them for. If I'd my way I'd . . . I'd lock the house up and set fire to the lot of 'em.'

Minnie, imbued with some of Bessie's spirit, rounded on her. 'Shut up, Amy. It's the little lass and her mother we're bothered about. Not him. I'm with you there. He can go hang, for all I care.'

'Tarred with the same brush, the lot of 'em,' Amy ranted.

'You can't blame the bairn. Be fair, Amy.'

'Be fair, you say. Is it fair that my Ron threw his life away to save the likes of his miserable hide?' She jabbed her finger towards the house. 'Who thought about my Ron, eh?'

'We all thought about your Ron and your George, Amy,' Bessie said, coming across the yard and catching the gist of the conversation. 'You know we did. We still do, but it doesn't mean we have to turn our backs on Mary Ann just because of what her father is.'

'And what would you know about it, Bessie Ruddick?' was Amy's parting shot as she slammed her door with such force, it seemed to rattle on its hinges.

Dan went straight to the door and called out, 'Mary Ann? Are you there, love?'

At once they heard her cries. 'Dan, oh Dan. Help me, please help me.'

'Listen, love. Calm down. We'll get you out. But first of all, try to stop crying and tell me, can you really not find the key?'

'No, no, it's gone. Dad's locked the door and gone. And me mam. I can't find me mam.'

Dan turned and his eyes met his mother's terrified gaze as she murmured, 'Oh my dear Lord, what has he done?' Then with renewed vigour, she said, 'Get that door down, son.'

Again Dan put his mouth close to the door and shouted, 'Mary Ann, listen to me, love. Get right away from the door, 'cos I'm going to break it down and I don't want to hurt you. Do you hear me?'

'Yes, Dan.'

'Do you understand, love? Stand right back out of the way.'

Her voice sounded fainter now, further away, as she said again, 'Yes, Dan.'

Dan gave a small nod of satisfaction and stood back. First he kicked at the door near the lock, trying to break it and then he put his broad shoulders against it and heaved until the wood splintered and gave way. Pushing it aside, he stepped inside and held out his arms.

The girl rushed to him and he picked her up and held her close. She wound her arms about him and buried her face against his neck, sobbing wildly.

For a few moments he just held her, patting her back and soothing, 'There, there. You're safe now. It's all right.' Then gently he prised himself free of her clinging arms and set her on the ground. 'Now you go with Mrs Eccleshall to our house.'

'No, no . . .' Mary Ann began, but when Dan said, firmly, but kindly, 'Please do as I ask, Mary Ann, because I want me mam to come upstairs to see to your mother. Understand?'

Biting her lip, the tears still running down her face, the girl nodded, 'But you'll come in a minute.'

'As soon as we can,' was all he would promise.

As Minnie led her away, Mary Ann looked back at Dan, stumbling as she did so instead of looking where she was going. Only Minnie, holding her hand, prevented her from falling.

'Right, Mam,' Dan said soberly and with no relish for what they had to do. 'We'd better have a look-see.'

'Oh lad, what are we going to find?'

'I daren't think, Mam,' Dan said, but nevertheless he led the way into the house and, following Bessie's direction, went upstairs and into the main bedroom.

As he pushed open the door, Bessie knew, like her, Dan was holding his breath.

The bowl and jug on the washstand had been smashed on the floor and the stand overturned. Two spindly-legged chairs had been broken as if they were matchwood and the bed had been overturned and rested at an angle against the wall.

'I bet that was the loud thud we heard,' Bessie muttered, her wide eyes taking in the scene of devastation before them.

'But where is she?' Dan said, looking round. 'Where's Mrs Clark?'

'Mebbe she's gone with him.' Her voice hardened. 'Mebbe they've both scarpered and left the little lass . . .'

'No,' Dan shook his head. 'Surely no mother would leave her child.'

Bessie cast him a wry glance but said nothing. Dan might be a man now, but in some ways he still had a lot to learn about the world and its cruel ways.

'You don't think . . .' he was saying and pointing with a finger that shook slightly, 'that she's under there?'

They exchanged a glance that said, 'Well, if she is . . .'

Dan heaved the bed away from the wall and it fell with a crash on to the floor. Elsie was lying face downwards, squashed against the skirting board, and before Dan even turned her over very gently, they both knew that there was little or no chance of her being alive.

Seventeen

Now, of course, they had no choice. The police had to be called.

'I'll have to go, Mam. If I miss the tide, Mr Price might sack me.'

'What? When you're walking out with his daughter?'

Dan sighed. 'That wouldn't make a scrap of difference to Mr Price. In fact, it would make it worse, because he'd think I was deliberately taking advantage.'

Bessie sighed. 'You're right, Dan. Jack Price is a hard man. I know him of old.'

'Mam, tell the police when they come that I'll be home tomorrow and I'll go straight to the station and give them a full statement. It'll only be the same as yours anyway.'

Bessie nodded. 'You go then, lad. I'll give you a few minutes to get aboard, else if your ship's not halfway down the river, they'll likely fetch you back.'

Despite the gravity of the moment, Dan smiled. 'Thanks, Mam. Good luck.'

Wryly, Bessie said, 'I reckon I'm going to need it, lad.'

As Dan's heavy boots clattered across the yard and away down the alley, Bessie went towards her own house, biting her lip. 'I wish my Bert was here,' she muttered to herself. 'I could do with him here right this minute.'

How on earth was she going to break the dreadful news to Mary Ann?

The girl's first question, however, was not about her

mother, nor her father. 'Where's Dan?' she demanded the moment Bessie set foot in the kitchen.

'He's had to go back to his ship, love. Come and sit down with me a minute. Min, have you got that kettle boiling? I could do with a strong cuppa.'

'Yes, Bess.' Minnie scuttled between kitchen and scullery and only when they were all sitting around the roaring fire in the kitchen range did Bessie say gently, 'Mary Ann, we've found your mam, love.' She glanced at Minnie, but her neighbour was looking even more round-eyed and fearful than the young girl was. 'I'm afraid . . .'

'She's dead, isn't she?' Mary Ann took the words from her and Bessie held her breath, unable to guess exactly how the girl was about to react.

Bessie nodded. 'I'm so sorry, love, but yes, she is. And . . . and I must call the police. You understand that, don't you?'

Mary Ann was staring at her. Her calmness was unnerving. Bessie had steeled herself to cope with hysterics, but Mary Ann sat quietly and it was obvious by her next words that she was thinking rationally and, for her age, with adult logic.

'My father killed her, didn't he?'

Bessie gulped. 'I'm afraid it does look that way, yes.'

'And now he's gone?'

Bessie nodded.

'He locked me in, didn't he? Locked me in that house with my mother lying dead somewhere . . . Where was she?'

'Did you look in their bedroom?'

Mary Ann nodded.

'So, you saw the bed against the wall?'

Again the girl nodded.

'She . . . she was under that.'

Beside her Bessie heard Minnie gasp and, turning to glance at her, saw that she had turned white.

'Here, give me that cup before you drop it,' she said, getting up at once. 'Now, head down between your knees. I can't do with you fainting on me just now, Minnie Eccleshall.'

A little roughly, though not unkindly, Bessie took the cup and saucer out of Minnie's shaking hands and thrust her head into her own lap. 'Now, just stay like that till you feel better.' She glanced at Mary Ann. 'You all right, love?'

Although the girl nodded, Bessie was still worried. Her reaction was unnatural. Although it would be hard to deal with, she almost wished Mary Ann would cry, rage even. At least that would be more normal. But she just sat there, staring ahead of her, her face expressionless, her hands lying idly in her lap, as if her mind was completely blank.

Perhaps it was, Bessie thought. Perhaps that was going to be the girl's way of dealing with it. Just not to think about it.

Slowly Minnie sat up. 'I'm all right, Bessie, honest. Sorry. Now, what do you want me to do?'

'Finish your tea first,' Bessie said, sitting down again herself and picking up her own cup. She glanced at the clock. Dan had had a good half an hour's start now. Time enough, she thought. She mustn't be much longer fetching the police or they would want to know why she had delayed calling them. 'Then,' she went on, 'if you'd look after Mary Ann, I'll see to everything else.'

Minnie nodded gratefully and gave another little shudder, pleased not to have to go into the house next door. 'You can come home with me, Mary Ann.'

Bessie nodded her approval. Although it was only just across the yard, at least in Minnie's home, Mary Ann would hear less of the comings and goings next door.

As she saw them out, Bessie whispered to Minnie, 'Keep her the far side of your house, if you can. The less she sees the better, poor bairn.'

Minnie nodded. 'There's only me scullery window looks over this way. I'll do me best, Bessie.'

Bessie patted her friend's shoulder. 'I know you will, Min. Thanks.'

As Bessie stood in the middle of the yard awaiting the arrival of the police, Amy opened her door. 'What's going on, Bessie? What are you standing there for?'

Bessie glanced over her shoulder towards the alleyway, but there was no one emerging from its shadows into the yard yet.

She moved towards Amy and said in a low voice. 'There's trouble at the Clarks' house. The police are on their way. I've just been to the station to fetch them.'

Amy smiled maliciously. 'Good for you, Bess. Get the bugger arrested, that's what I say. Sling him back in jail where he belongs. Let him rot . . .'

'He's not there, Amy. He's gone.'

Amy's mouth dropped open. 'Gone? Gone where?'

Bessie shrugged. 'Dunno.'

'So why . . .?' Amy began and then her eyes widened. 'You don't mean he's done for her?'

'Well, she's dead. That's all I know for certain. But it looks like it.'

Even Amy, for a moment, was shocked. Then her mouth was a grim, tight line. 'I can't say I'm surprised. That's all his sort are good for, battering defenceless women. I told you he was no good. That's what comes of having a conchy in our yard. I hope they find him and hang him.'

Grimly, Bessie said, 'If they do find him, that's exactly what they will do. Hang him.'

'Hanging's too good for him,' Amy said now, perversely. 'They should throw him to the women. All us women, who've lost someone in the war. We'd soon show him what we thought of a conchy.'

'Oh Amy,' Bessie sighed sadly. 'Don't be so bitter, love.'

'Bitter? Bitter, you say? Don't you think I've got good reason to be bitter?'

With that Amy slammed the door just as Bessie heard what sounded like an army of heavy boots thundering down the alleyway and into the yard.

'So, Mrs Ruddick. You and your son found the body, did you?'

Bessie faced the burly, solemn-faced policeman. He was not in uniform but had introduced himself as Inspector Chapman. He seemed to be in charge of a sergeant and several younger constables, who were dashing about doing his bidding.

Bessie licked her dry lips. 'Yes. My son Dan has had to go back to work. He said to tell you that when he gets back tomorrow, he'll come straight to the station to see you.' She tried to smile winningly at the man. 'I'll tell him to ask for you, shall I?'

The man was unmoved and said sternly, 'He should not have done that, Mrs Ruddick. He should have waited here.'

Bessie bristled. 'He's on one of Mr Price's ships and

he'd have missed the tide, else. Expect him to lose his job, do you?'

'This is a very serious matter, Mrs Ruddick.'

'I know that,' Bessie snapped. 'I've got eyes in me head, ain't I? But, like I said, he'll come and see you just as soon as he gets back tomorrow. Besides, I was with him. He can't tell you any more than I can.' Craftily, she added, 'Not as much, really.'

'Oh? Why is that?'

'Because me and Bert heard all the rumpus going on in the night.'

'And who might Bert be?'

'Me husband, of course.' Bessie was fast losing her patience. She had got off on the wrong foot with this man, she knew, so she took a deep breath and tried to hold on to her composure. 'Dan wasn't even here.'

'Really?'

'No. His young lady had been here with us to see the New Year in and he'd taken her home.'

'I see. We shall need her name and address to verify that.'

'Whatever for?'

'To confirm your son's alibi.'

'Alibi? What on earth should my Dan need an alibi for?'

'No need to get alarmed, madam. It's just routine.'

'Is it, indeed. Well, it sounds a very silly routine to me, if you start accusing innocent folk, who just try to help. It's obvious who's done it, ain't it?'

'Maybe. Maybe not,' the man said carefully. 'We have to make our inquiries and you'd do better to assist us, Mrs Ruddick.'

'I'm trying to,' Bessie snapped again, 'if you'll let me get a word in edgeways to tell you.'

Now the man listened whilst Bessie explained in detail all that had happened the previous night. When she fell silent he asked, 'Had you heard such noises before last night?'

Bessie's mouth tightened. 'Oh yes. From the day they moved in, we knew what he was, but I had a go at him . . .' She was about to recount how she had threatened Sid Clark on his own doorstep, but she was fast becoming very wary of this policeman. She doubted that he would see her side of such a situation. He might even run her in for menacing the man, or something as daft.

For once, Bessie held her tongue, but it was, even she realized, with great difficulty.

'Do you know anything else about the family? You mentioned a girl?'

'Yes, Mary Ann. She's across at my neighbour's house.'

'Does she know what's happened?'

'I told her.'

'And?'

Bessie shrugged. 'I don't think it's sunk in yet. She's only thirteen.'

'I shall have to have a chat with her, since she was in the house all night.'

Bessie shuddered inwardly. What this dour man's questioning would do to poor Mary Ann she dare not think.

131

Eighteen

'Now then, me little lass, you come and sit down in Mrs Ruddick's kitchen with me and we'll have a little chat, shall we? Perhaps this nice lady would make us a cup of tea. Should you like that, eh?'

Bessie's mouth dropped open. Inspector Chapman was like a different man. Mesmerized by the sudden change in him, she watched as he took hold of Mary Ann's hand and led her across the yard, walking on her right hand side so that his tall, broad frame shielded her from even having to see her home.

'Now,' he said kindly, as they entered Bessie's house. 'You sit there. My word,' he spread his large hands out towards the warmth as they sat down either side of the range. 'This is a nice fire, isn't it? Get yourself warm, love. Cold old day, isn't it? And this little bit of trouble doesn't help, does it?'

Little bit of trouble, he called it. Well, that was one way of looking at it, Bessie supposed. Just about the worst that could happen to anyone had happened to Mary Ann and he was calling it 'a little bit of trouble'.

Bessie went into her scullery and set about making a cup of tea, but she kept her ears attuned to what was going on in her kitchen.

'I'm sorry to have to ask a lot of questions, love, but you're old enough to understand that we have to find out what's happened, don't we?'

Bessie could not hear if Mary Ann answered, but she heard the man continue. 'So, were you there last night? All night?'

Again there was a pause and Bessie presumed Mary Ann was merely nodding or shaking her head in response.

The big man's voice was very gentle now as he asked, 'And can you tell me what happened?'

There was a long silence before Bessie, carrying a tray of cups through, heard Mary Ann say haltingly, 'Me dad came home drunk. It was very late. Later than usual. Gone midnight.'

'Does he get drunk very often?'

Now Bessie was in the room setting the tray on the table and saw Mary Ann nod.

'And then what happened?'

'We'd gone to bed, me mam and me.'

'And where did you sleep? In that little room at the top of the stairs?'

Again, she nodded.

'And your mam?'

'In the big bedroom. With . . . with me dad.'

'Yes?' Gently Chapman encouraged her.

'Well, he was banging about. Falling up the stairs, you know.'

Now the man nodded, but Bessie noticed that he never took his gaze away from Mary Ann's face. He was watching her intently.

'Then I heard him get into bed. It creaks, their bed. And I heard her crying out, "No, no, please don't." Then I heard him making funny noises, sort of grunting and the bed was creaking and me mam was still crying.'

Chapman and Bessie exchanged a look but neither said a word as the girl continued, recounting now things she didn't perhaps fully understand, but the older man and woman understood only too well.

'After a bit it went quiet and I thought he must have fallen asleep but then I heard him shouting at her. "Shut up, you silly bitch, I've every right."' Mary Ann paused and wrinkled her forehead. 'At least, I think that's what he said. Then he said, "What sort of wife are you, eh?" And then he was swearing and . . . and hitting her. I heard the slaps and her crying out. Then . . . then it got worse. There was thumps and bangs and . . . and then I didn't hear me mam no more.'

She was sitting rigidly upright, twisting her hands together in her lap, her eyes wide in her pale face, as she was obliged to relive the nightmare.

'And your father?'

Bessie was very tempted to intervene to save Mary Ann any further anguish, but she knew the policeman was only doing his job and she had to admit that he was handling a very sensitive situation in the best way possible.

'After it all went quiet, he went out.'

'Did he come into your room? Did he say anything to you?'

Mary Ann shook her head. 'No, I had a chair lodged under the doorknob. I . . . I thought he might. Sometimes . . . sometimes he's hit me an' all. But I don't think he even tried my door. I think he just rushed out. I heard him going down the stairs and then the back door slammed. A bit later, I went into me mam's room but the bed was tipped up and she wasn't there. I didn't go downstairs because I was frightened he'd come back and catch me. I'd have been in for a belting if he had.'

Bessie and Chapman exchanged another grim look.

Now Mary Ann looked from one to the other. 'Me mam was under the bed, wasn't she?'

Chapman nodded.

'If . . . if I'd found her, could I . . . I mean . . .?' Mary Ann's voice broke and faltered.

Catching her meaning, Chapman reached forward and patted her hand. 'No, no, love. I'm sure you couldn't have done anything by then to help her. You mustn't think that.'

Bessie was feeling her own stab of guilt. If she had gone round there when the noise had first started, maybe she could have prevented the catastrophe. Then she sighed. Unlike Mary Ann, Bessie was old enough and wise enough to know that whatever she had done, it had been a tragedy waiting to happen.

All she could do now was to help Mary Ann.

When Dan didn't arrive home the next day, Bessie began to worry.

The previous twenty-four hours had been, Bessie thought, probably the worst she had experienced in her whole life.

The whole afternoon had been taken up with Inspector Chapman and his questions. Then he had asked a young constable to come into Bessie's kitchen and write everything down, so that both Bessie and Mary Ann had to go through it all again.

Poor Elsie's body had been taken away and there would be a post mortem, Chapman told them, and an inquest. The house had been sealed up and no one – not even Mary Ann – would be allowed to enter it.

'If the child needs anything,' Chapman said to Bessie as he left, 'get one of my men to get it for her. There'll be someone here, certainly for the rest of today.'

Bessie nodded. 'Just her clothes. If they could just bring her clothes out. She's only in her nightie.'

'Right, I'll see to that for you. Thank you, Mrs Ruddick, you've been most helpful.' His voice became stern again. 'But please make sure your son comes straight to the station and asks for me personally, will you?'

'I will,' Bessie replied shortly, beginning to bristle indignantly again.

When Bert and her other sons had arrived home that night, they had been shocked to hear the dreadful news, but Bessie was comforted by their presence. She no longer felt as if she were carrying the burden alone.

'You couldn't have done anything, my angel,' Bert reassured her in the privacy of their bedroom in the early hours of the morning, when neither of them could sleep. 'I doubt we could have got into the house anyway.'

'We should have broken the door down and got in,' Bessie said.

'We know that now, Bessie love. But law-abiding citizens can't go breaking folks' doors down.'

'We had good reason, Bert. We could hear what was going on.'

Bert sighed. 'I know how you feel, love. I feel the same, but I still don't think there's anything more we could have done.'

Bessie could not answer him, for she knew that as long as she lived she would never entirely rid herself of the prickle of guilt she felt. If only . . .

'They want to see Dan. He's to go straight to the station when he gets home. I hope he won't get into trouble with the police. That feller, Chapman, was mad he'd gone.'

'Well, he would be,' said Bert reasonably. 'He's only doing his job.' He chuckled then. 'Poor Dan. It was a rotten choice to have to make. Risk the wrath of your employer and maybe the sack or get on the wrong side of the law. Not an enviable choice.'

Bessie snorted. 'You'd think Jack Price would be a bit more understanding.'

'He isn't and he never will be. He's a hard case, Bessie. And I should know 'cos I've worked for him on and off for twenty years.'

'I like his lass, though. Susan. She seems a nice girl for our Dan.'

'Mm,' Bert said thoughtfully. 'She is. I'll grant you that. But I'm not so sure Dan isn't stacking up a load of trouble for himself by getting involved with his employer's daughter. That's not going to be an easy situation.'

'That's the least of my worries at the moment, Bert,' Bessie said wryly.

'I know, love, I know.' Bert had kissed her then and had added, 'Now, let's try and get some sleep because tomorrow's not going to be a lot easier than today's been. Let's just hope that the police aren't too hard on our Dan, eh?'

But now, by late the following afternoon, Dan had still not appeared.

'Shall we take a walk down to the river and see if we can see Dan's ship?' Bessie suggested.

Mary Ann jumped up, a spark of interest brightening her eyes for the first time. 'Ooh yes, let's.'

'Right, get ya coat, then.'

They crossed the yard without even glancing at the house next door, walked down the alley and out on to River Road.

'Now then, let me think,' Bessie paused a moment. 'Where's he likely to be? Dixon's Wharf today, I reckon. Let's try there anyway, shall we? Come on, it's this way.'

The wharf was busy and Bessie and Mary Ann had to be careful not to get in the way of the men unloading the cargo from the ship moored there.

'Is that Dan's ship?'

'Yes, that's the *Nerissa*.' Bessie squinted against the bright winter sun glinting on the ripples on the river. 'But I don't see Dan.'

'He'll have gone to the police station, won't he?'

'He might have, but I'd have thought he'd have come home first.'

'Mrs Ruddick. Mrs Ruddick.'

They both heard the voice calling Bessie's name and turned to see Susan hurrying towards them.

The young woman held a handkerchief to her face and was obviously very distressed. It was clear that she had been crying. Automatically, Bessie put out her arms to catch hold of her. 'Why, lass, whatever's the matter?'

'Oh, Mrs Ruddick. It's Dan. He's been arrested.'

Nineteen

'I want to see that feller, Chapman.' Bessie faced the desk sergeant in what her neighbours would have called her 'Battling Bessie' mood. 'And I want to see him now.'

'I'm sorry, madam. Inspector Chapman is not available. Can I help you in any way?'

'Then I want to see my son.'

'Your son, madam?'

'Dan Ruddick. You've got him here, haven't you?'

The man leafed through a large book in front of him. 'I don't believe so, madam. What makes you think he's here?'

'Susan,' Bessie jerked her thumb over her shoulder towards Susan and Mary Ann standing behind her, 'says he's been arrested.' She turned towards Susan now. 'That's what you said, didn't you?'

'I . . . it's what my father said.'

'And when was this, miss?'

'Well, I – er – don't know when, exactly. I just presumed it was when they docked back here this morning.'

'Docked, you say? Ah now, wait a moment. If you'll just sit down over there . . .' He turned away towards an open door leading into a room behind the reception area.

'Oi, wait a minute . . .' Bessie began, but Susan pulled at her arm and whispered, 'I think he's gone to ask someone. Let's sit down and wait.'

With ill grace, Bessie sat down on a wooden bench seat

set against the wall. 'I don't know. What a carry on. As if our Dan has done anything wrong.'

They waited for what seemed like an age, but, in fact, it was only a few minutes, before the sergeant returned.

'Yes, I thought so,' he began as if answering his own unvoiced question. 'It seems our colleagues in Hull arrested two men yesterday in connection with an incident which has taken place in – er . . .' He consulted a piece of paper he held in his hand. 'Waterman's Yard.' He looked up. 'Would that mean anything to you?'

Bessie heaved herself up and lumbered towards the desk. 'Yes,' she replied shortly, only just managing to hold on to her temper. 'It would.'

'The inspector is at this moment travelling to Hull to bring back both prisoners.'

'Prisoners? What on earth do you think you're doing arresting my lad? You've no right. No right at all. All he did was to go to his work. All right, all right, I know mebbe he should have stayed and seen the policeman before he went, but he'd have missed the tide and prob- ably got the sack.' She glowered at the man behind the desk. 'Not that that would have bothered any of you, I suppose. You probably don't have any idea how import- ant it is.'

'I can't tell you any more than that, Mrs – er . . .?'

'Ruddick. Mrs Ruddick. I'm his mother.'

'Well, Mrs Ruddick, I am sorry but I'm not at liberty to tell you any more than that.'

Bessie's frown deepened. 'Oh, so you could then. I see. Like that, is it?'

The sergeant said nothing. 'If you call back later today, maybe I'll have more information for you then.'

Muttering, Bessie turned to go. 'Come on,' she said to

Mary Ann and Susan. 'We're wasting our time here. We're not going to get anything else out of him.'

She had begun to move towards the door when she stopped suddenly and turned to face the man again. 'Wait a minute. You said they'd arrested two?'

'That's right.'

'Who's the other one?'

The sergeant pursed his lips and began, 'I'm not at liberty . . .' but Bessie finished his sentence for him.

'. . . To tell you. Thanks, mester, for nothing.'

Bessie's anger carried her along the street and back towards the river.

'Does your father know anything?' she asked Susan.

Susan walked quickly beside her whilst Mary Ann had to take little running steps to keep up with them. Despite her size, Bessie was remarkably nimble on her feet when she was seething with indignation.

'I don't know,' Susan said worriedly. 'He was awfully angry. I . . . I didn't stay to ask him much.'

'Right then,' Bessie said. 'I'll see him.'

'Do be careful, Mrs Ruddick,' Susan said worriedly. 'Please don't make it any worse for Dan. Father's very cross about it all.'

But Bessie was too furious herself to listen to Susan's warning. 'Well, he's no right to be. I'll give him a piece of my mind.'

As they approached the wharf they saw Susan's father coming down the gangway from his ship.

'Jack Price,' Bessie bellowed, her voice echoing along the riverbank. 'I want a word with you.'

'Oh you do, do you?' The man was glowering as they neared each other. 'I could have lost a valuable contract through your son and his shenanigans. I've a good mind to sack him.'

'It's putting you and his job first that's caused the trouble,' Bessie snapped.

Jack Price gave a wry laugh. 'Oh no, it isn't. That's not even the half of it.'

Bessie stared at him blankly.

'He's been arrested, Bessie, for aiding and abetting a wanted man to evade arrest.'

'Eh?' Bessie said and now her voice was a high-pitched squeak of disbelief.

'Clark had stowed away on my ship.' Jack's tone was indignant. 'And the police think that your Dan had something to do with it, being as how you're neighbours and Clark is a drinking pal of your Bert's.'

Bessie spluttered with rage, hardly able to get the words out. 'How can they . . . how dare they . . . you don't think that?'

When Jack did not answer, Bessie gasped, 'Jack Price, you can't think that of Dan. Not of my boy. We've known each other years, Jack. Why, we went to school together.'

'When you were there, Bessie.' Even amid his anger, Jack could smile at the memory of the time when school and Bessie had not seen much of one another. Living on her father's ship had not been conducive to regular education. But Bessie was at this moment in no mood to be humoured, not even by being reminded of her own fond memories.

Jack's mouth hardened again. 'I'm sorry, Bessie, but I've to think of my own business. You must see that.' He turned towards his daughter, standing a little way behind Bessie. He pointed at her and said, 'And you, my girl, are not to see Dan Ruddick until all this business is cleared up. I don't want you involved. You hear me?'

Though tears ran down Susan's face, she did not argue.

'Get yourself home, now, and help your mother,' Jack ordered. With one look of desperation at Bessie, Susan, without a word, did as she was bid.

Bessie's anger flared again. 'So you think he's guilty, do you?'

'Bessie, go home, will you? If the lad really had nowt to do with it, then his job's here for him. But if he did . . .' Jack Price did not finish his sentence, but the unspoken words were clear enough as if he had shouted them from the rooftops.

'If he did, Jack Price, then you'd better keep your head down, because you'll see pigs flying past.' Bessie turned and grabbed hold of Mary Ann's hand. 'Come on, lass. We're going home.'

Later that afternoon, Bessie returned to the police station but once more all they would tell her was that Sid Clark and Dan had been brought back to Elsborough police station and were now in the cells.

'You'd better get your lad a solicitor,' was the only advice they would give her.

'A solicitor!' Bessie wailed later to Bert. 'How on earth can we afford to pay for a solicitor?'

'Have you spoken to Miss Edwina?' Bert asked. He was as worried as Bessie, but had taken the news much more calmly. 'Her father's a magistrate. Perhaps he can help?'

'Oh Bert . . .' Dramatically, Bessie flung her arms around him. 'I never thought of that. Mind you, I ain't been thinking straight all day. What would I do without you, Bert? I'll go first thing in the morning. I know she'll do what she can. She'll believe in my lad, even if that rat,

Price, doesn't. Do you know?' she went on indignantly. 'He's told Susan that she's not to see Dan any more. Now that tells you a lot, doesn't it?'

Behind her, Mary Ann smiled.

Twenty

'Of course, I'll do whatever I can.'

In her own way, Edwina was as indignant as Bessie. 'It's unthinkable that Dan would be involved in any way. I'll speak to my father as soon as I get home.' She reached out and took Bessie's hand. 'Try not to worry, Bessie. The police had to do their job and just remember, they don't know Dan like we do. But it'll be all right. I promise you. Sid Clark must have known that Dan's ship was leaving the following morning.'

Bessie nodded, hope lighting her eyes now as she listened to Edwina's calm and rational explanation of what might have happened. 'Mebbe he heard someone talking about it in The Waterman's,' she suggested.

'There you are, then. Maybe he even thought, in his twisted mind, that Dan *might* help him. Not that he would, of course,' Edwina added hurriedly. 'What happened in Hull? Do you know?'

Bessie shook her head. 'They won't tell us anything.'

'I'll try to find out for you. In the meantime, have you brought Mary Ann to school?'

Bessie nodded. 'Yes, I thought it best for her.'

'I'm sure you're right. I'll make sure all the staff know what's happened and we'll look after her. I'll walk home with her tonight. You know what other children can be like and the news will be spreading like the proverbial wildfire by now.'

Bessie nodded sadly. 'Poor little lass. I wonder what's going to happen to her?' She felt Edwina's thoughtful gaze on her and looked up. 'What?'

'Can you look after her for a few days at least?' Edwina asked. 'Just until we can find out if she's any relative, who would take her in?'

Bessie's answer was swift. 'Of course we can. As long as it takes.'

It was already dark in the enclosed confines of Waterman's Yard when Edwina and Mary Ann arrived at Bessie's home late that afternoon.

'Come in, come in. The kettle's boiling. Mary Ann, you nip across to Minnie's. She's been baking and promised me one of her apple pies.' Bessie winked at Edwina. 'Minnie Eccleshall's pastry is legend around here. Not even I can get it as light as she does. Come in, Miss Edwina. Here, let me take your hat and coat. Go on, Mary Ann, there's a love.'

When the girl was safely across the yard, Bessie said, 'I arranged all that with Minnie earlier, just in case you had owt to tell me.'

Edwina nodded. 'I have. I managed to see my father at lunchtime. It appears that Dan has been arrested because they believe he helped Sid Clark to escape by allowing him to stow away on the *Nerissa*.'

Bessie nodded, but held back her impatience. That much she knew already.

'Naturally, Dan is protesting his innocence and pointing out – and there are witnesses to this, Bessie – that it was he who raised the alarm when he saw the man trying to sneak off the ship at Hull.'

'But they don't believe him?'

'Not yet, but they will,' Edwina said confidently. 'I've got in touch with our solicitors and Mr Riggall promised to go to the station and see Dan this very afternoon.'

Bessie let out a sigh of relief. 'Thank you, Miss Edwina.' She wrinkled her forehead. 'I expect we can scrape up for his fees.'

Edwina waved her hand as she removed her gloves and sat down in Bert's sagging armchair. 'Don't worry about that, Bessie, please. My family retains Riggall and Bates on a permanent basis.' She smiled impishly. 'I'm sure that little bit won't be noticed on the account.'

'Oh Miss Edwina, but we couldn't . . .'

'Yes, you can and you will, Bessie Ruddick. You're looking after the girl, aren't you? If we all do our bit, then . . .'

She said no more as the door opened and Mary Ann appeared, carefully carrying an apple pie, hot from Minnie's oven.

'Now, doesn't that look a treat?' Bessie said. 'What say we all have a piece, eh? With a nice helping of cream?'

Dan arrived home about eight o'clock that evening to a rapturous welcome from his family and a tearful, clinging one from Mary Ann.

'There, there, love. It'll be all right,' Dan patted her awkwardly and looked over the girl's head for help from his mother.

Briskly, but not unkindly, Bessie said, 'Now, now, Mary Ann. Let our Dan get inside the door. I bet you're hungry, lad, aren't you?'

'What happened?' Duggie demanded. 'Is everything all right?'

Dan pulled a face. 'Sort of. I'm released on bail pending

further inquiries. They haven't dropped the charges yet, but Mr Riggall seems sure they will. It's thanks to Miss Edwina that I'm here at all. If it wasn't for her, I'd still be locked up in that awful cell.' He gave a dramatic shudder and glanced sympathetically towards Mary Ann. He wondered if she was thinking about her own father, locked up in a similar cold, dank place. 'Worst of it is,' Dan went on, 'I'm not allowed to leave the town, so I can't sail.'

Bessie exchanged a glance with Bert, who said, 'That's a blow, lad, because the way Price is feeling at the moment, I doubt he'll find you work elsewhere.'

'No,' Dan said gloomily, 'and I don't expect he'll let me see Susan either.'

Bessie put her hand on his shoulder. 'There are other ships and other employers. Once all this business is over, it'll be all right.'

'Maybe,' Dan murmured. 'But don't say it, Mam. Don't say there's other girls, 'cos I don't want to hear it.'

Quietly, Bessie said, 'I wasn't going to, lad. I wasn't going to.'

Mary Ann, sitting next to Dan, slipped her arm through his and leant her head against his shoulder, smiling gently.

The tiny community of Waterman's Yard rallied around Mary Ann. Even Amy grudgingly acknowledged that whatever had happened was not the girl's fault. But she could not and would not have a scrap of sympathy for the man.

'If I had my way,' she said loudly for all to hear, 'they'd not only hang the devil but draw and quarter him an' all and stick his head on a pike near the bridge for all to see his shame.'

Bessie smiled wryly at the change in her neighbour. At least, Bessie thought, she's showing a bit of spirit at last. Anything's better than that dreadful wallowing in self-pity.

'Aye,' Bessie murmured to herself more than once. 'It's an ill wind that blows nobody any good.'

The police were now satisfied that they had the right person in jail awaiting trial for murder and, to everyone's relief, all charges against Dan were dropped. With the examination of the crime scene complete, the authorities gave permission for the house the Clarks had occupied to be cleared, cleaned and re-let.

'I can't see anyone wanting to come and live there,' Minnie Eccleshall shuddered. 'I don't even want to set foot in the place.' She eyed Bessie fearfully. 'You weren't going to ask me to come with you, Bessie, were you?'

Bessie weighed the key she held in her hand thoughtfully. 'The owners have asked me to see to the clearing out. Everything belongs to Mary Ann by rights, though there's nothing in there that's worth a brass farthing, if you ask me. Still, there might be some bits and pieces she'll want.'

Appalled, Minnie said, 'You're not expecting that poor little lass to go in there, are you?'

'Heavens, no. What do you think I am, Minnie Eccleshall? No,' she added grimly. 'I'll see to it. And when you've got a rotten job to do, then I always say it's best got over and done with. So, if you're not going to be a help, Min, at least don't be a hindrance.'

'Sorry, I'm sure.' Min said huffily as she stepped back smartly out of the way. But still, she did not offer to help Bessie.

Even Bessie's stout heart quailed a little as she opened the door that had been repaired and stepped inside. Hands on hips, she stood in the centre of the kitchen and surveyed the broken chair, the rickety table, the dirty curtainless windows. There was nothing here that made a home, nothing worth keeping for Mary Ann. And despite Miss Edwina's endeavours to find someone, it seemed that Mary Ann had no relatives who were willing to take her.

'I made contact with her mother's family,' Edwina had told Bessie only the previous day and shook her head sadly. 'They won't have anything to do with her. They just don't want to know. Can you believe it?'

Bessie had shaken her head sadly. 'I can believe it, yes. Because it happens. But I don't understand it.'

Now, as Bessie stood in the silent, tragic house, she said aloud, 'Well, Bessie Ruddick, me girl, you always did hanker after a daughter. And now it looks like you've got yourself one.'

Part Two

Mary Ann

Twenty-One

1921

'Now you remember all I've told you. Miss Edwina's given you the most marvellous chance, Mary Ann. Taking you on as an upstairs maid, and as her personal maid too. You don't know how lucky you are. I started work at The Hall when I was thirteen as a scullery maid and I had to work me way up. And the cook they had there then was a right tartar, I can tell you . . .'

Beside her, Bessie prattled on, but Mary Ann was listening only with half an ear. Her mind was busy with her own plans for her future – plans that certainly included what Bessie and Miss Edwina had mapped out for her, but Mary Ann's own ambitions went much further than either of them could guess.

Bessie was right about one thing though, the girl conceded. She was lucky, very lucky, that Miss Edwina had offered her a job in her own home, for The Hall was only just a few streets away from Waterman's Yard and a mere couple of hundred yards from the river.

Mary Ann smiled. From today on, she was a working girl, a grown up and, best of all, she would be living and working only a short distance from Dan.

'Are you listening to me, lass?' Bessie prodded her arm.

'Of course I am, Auntie Bessie,' Mary Ann answered

with pretended obedience. 'I'm to be a good girl and work hard and be a credit to you and to Miss Edwina.'

'Aye well, that an' all, lass.' Now Mary Ann felt Bessie's comforting hand take hold of her arm. Her voice was gentle as she added, 'But most of all, lass, I want you to be a credit to your poor mam. Don't ever forget her, will ya?'

They stopped on the path outside the entrance to The Hall and turned to face each other. Although she had grown rapidly in the past year, Mary Ann still had to stand on tiptoe to reach up and kiss Bessie's cheek. The girl had, as Bessie put it, 'filled out in all the right places'. Now she was no longer the skinny little waif, but a pretty young girl with an impish smile and a sparkle in her eyes, on the brink of womanhood. Mary Ann said nothing in response to Bessie's plea, but merely smiled, stepped back and with a little wave moved towards the back door of The Hall.

'See you on Sunday afternoon, Auntie Bessie. Give my love to Dan when he comes home tonight.'

Then she was gone, running lightly across the grass towards the stately building that was now to be her home.

Mrs Nellie Goodrick was nothing like Mary Ann had expected the cook at The Hall would be. She had pictured someone like Bessie on baking day. Tall, maybe, but round and jolly and red-faced from the constant heat of the oven. So the appearance of the woman standing before her, hands on hips, her steely, unfriendly gaze raking Mary Ann's appearance from head to toe, was a surprise – and not a pleasant one.

Nellie Goodrick was certainly tall, but with little shape to the bony body covered by her copious white apron.

The apron and the white cap were the only things, Mary Ann thought, that made her look like a cook. She had cold grey eyes and a nose like a bird's beak above a thin-lipped mouth that seemed constantly pursed in disapproval.

'So you're the new girl, are you?'

Mary Ann decided meekness would be her greatest ally, at least on her first day.

'Yes, ma'am,' she answered, keeping her voice low and deferential.

'I hope you know how lucky you are? This position should have been young Clara's by rights. She's been here long enough to be promoted from just a general maid.' The woman gave a quick shake of her head. 'But there you are, life isn't always fair, is it?'

Life had been decidedly unfair to Nellie Goodrick. Not only had she not even been in the queue when the looks were given out, but she had also allowed bitterness to warp her personality. Her forty-six years of life had been spent solely trying to please others. Firstly her parents, from whom she had never managed, not once, to illicit an endearment or a gesture of pride towards her. Secondly, her husband, whom, in a short-lived marriage, she had also, it seemed, failed to please. And so, it had been her lot to be in service from the age of thirteen, the last twenty years in the employ of Bertram Marsh and his wife, Isabella, here at The Hall.

Mr and Mrs Marsh kept themselves aloof from their servants. They were kindly, always fair, but distant. Their eldest son, Arthur, who had been killed on the Somme, had been quiet and shy and had scarcely spoken more than a few dozen words with the woman who prepared all the food he ate. As for Randolph, the second son, who was now, because of the death of his brother, the heir to the Marsh estate, well, what Nellie Goodrick thought about him was best left unsaid. Her opinions, if ever voiced, would earn her instant dismissal from this household.

There was really only one person within the household for whom Nellie had any affection, such as her unloved and unloving heart was able to feel – Miss Edwina. And it was for this reason alone that Nellie Goodrick strove to keep her resentment at the arrival of this girl in check. And this girl especially, for they all knew of Mary Ann's tragic circumstances. Unlike the inhabitants of Waterman's Yard, the servants at The Hall believed in the saying 'bad blood will out'. There was certainly bad blood flowing through Mary Ann Clark's veins in Nellie's opinion and, as she had remarked at the supper table in the kitchen only the previous evening, 'Miss Edwina will regret bringing her here. You mark my words.' Everyone around the table from Peter Deakin, The Hall's one and only manservant, to Clara Dobson, the general maid, and the kitchen maid, Jessie Banks, had indeed 'marked her words'.

Now she saw the subject of her words standing before her in person, Nellie felt no compunction to change her mind. The girl had a bold look, she thought, and she was pretty, far too pretty to work here. Nellie sighed. No doubt within a very few months she would be the third girl to depart hastily in tears and without a reference, having believed Randolph Marsh's seductive protestations of love. It was on the tip of her tongue to warn the girl, but the bitter resentment against anyone who was even remotely attractive rose in her throat and choked her warning.

Mary Ann stared back at the woman unflinchingly. Far from being daunted by the cook's animosity, she saw it as a challenge.

In the last year or so since the tragedy of Waterman's Yard, as it had been headlined in the local newspaper, Mary Ann had changed. Welcomed into the Ruddick family household, she had been spoiled and petted by them all. Bessie and Bert had immediately treated her as their daughter, as if she had been born to them late in life, the gift of their dreams.

For the boys, she had been a younger sister to be teased and spoiled and protected and each, in their own way, had done so. The extended family, the other inhabitants of the Yard, had shown her nothing but sympathy, and Mary Ann had blossomed in the warmth of their affection like a flower under the sun's warm rays. Her life would have been perfect if it had not been for the dreadful shadow of her father's crime. There was not a person in the town who did not know all about it and who she was. Whilst the residents of the Yard might be kindly, other people were less understanding. There was no escape unless she went right away, but that would mean leaving Dan and the rest of his family.

'The best way,' Miss Edwina had counselled, 'is to hold your head high and live through it. I know it's difficult, especially when you're so young, but it's the only way. You can't run all your life, Mary Ann. Wherever you go, however far away from here, people have a habit of finding out about you, and you would have to run again and go on running.'

Mary Ann had agreed. 'I don't want to leave here, Miss Edwina. You and Auntie Bessie and everyone in Waterman's Yard have been so kind to me,' she said winningly. But the real reason why she wanted to stay in Elsborough Mary Ann had kept to herself.

During the time that the trial of Sid Clark and the impending death sentence upon him were constantly in the news, there had been no respite from people's interest in her. Not until the sentence had been carried out could Mary Ann begin to build her new life.

'I want to go, Auntie Bessie,' she had declared the day before her father was due to be hanged at nine o'clock in the morning at Lincoln prison.

Bessie had looked at her aghast. 'Oh love, whatever for?'

The girl had shrugged. 'I just need to go. I need to be there.'

'You mean . . .' Bessie had faltered, for once completely lost for words. 'You want to see him once more before . . .?'

At this, Mary Ann had shaken her head vehemently. 'Oh no, I never want to see him again.' Her dark eyes had held Bessie's and her mouth had hardened as she said, 'I just want to be there to know he's really dead and never coming back.'

Bessie had put her arms around her and tried to draw the girl's rigid body close. 'Aw love, he's been found guilty. Even if he was to get a last-minute reprieve and they didn't hang him, he's never going to get out of jail again. I promise you, he's never coming back.'

It had been Dan who had taken her, very early the following day, to Lincoln. They had stood in the grey, dank morning outside the grim walls of the prison on top of the hill. There was a small gathering and Mary Ann caught brief snatches of the murmured conversations around her.

'They reckon he's not shown a scrap of remorse at what he's done.'

'The bastard!'

'Aye, well, he were a conchy, weren't he? What can you expect?'

'Too cowardly to fight the enemy, eh, but he could batter his poor wife to death . . .'

'There's a kiddie, isn't there? A girl?'

'Aye, poor wench. She'll be an orphan after this morning's work.'

''Spect it'll haunt her for the rest of her life.'

Mary Ann stood stolidly silent. Not so much as the twitch of a muscle or the flicker of an eyelid betrayed the fact that she had overheard. Only Dan, squeezing her hand in comfort, knew.

The words went on, floating around her head.

'He's not long now. It's gone eight. The chaplain will be with him now.'

'Then he'll be taken from the condemned cell to a room right next to the scaffold,' one man said, and added, almost with a note of pride, 'I've seen the place.' Then he gave a dramatic shudder. 'By heck! I wouldn't want to be in his shoes at this moment.'

Now Mary Ann's fingers tightened on Dan's hand, although neither of them spoke or even glanced at each other.

At a quarter to nine, they heard the distant tolling of the prison bell and then, just as the hour of nine o'clock struck, they saw a black flag being hoisted on the prison tower.

'That's it, then,' a voice behind them said. 'That's him done for. And good riddance, I say.'

The murmuring amongst the crowd seemed to grow louder and when, a few minutes later, a warder appeared at the door and attached two notices to a board on the wall outside, the onlookers surged forward. The declaration, signed by the Under Sheriff of Lincolnshire, the Governor and the Chaplain of the prison, stated that 'the judgement of death was this day executed on Sidney

Clark'. Beside it, another notice announced that a surgeon had examined the body and pronounced the said Sidney Clark dead.

'Come on, love,' Dan said softly. 'Time we went home.'

Mary Ann slipped her arm through Dan's and turned her back on the place where her father had died. She would never, she vowed silently, think of him again.

'Well,' Nellie Goodrick said, 'I suppose Clara had better take you up to Miss Edwina's room.'

Mary Ann smiled her best smile and even dropped a tiny curtsy. 'Thank you, Mrs Goodrick,' she said prettily.

Clara Dobson was as sour-faced as the cook and took no pains to conceal her resentment of the newcomer. 'Miss Edwina's never had a maid before. What she wants to bring you here for, I don't know. I've always done everything for her.'

For the moment, Mary Ann kept her mouth tightly shut, even pressing her lips together to stop them mouthing the retort that sprang to her lips.

The other girl grumbled on. 'You needn't think yourself above the rest of us. You'll have to muck in and help with the housework, like everyone else has to.' Mary Ann felt her belligerent glance. 'We're not exactly overloaded with servants here. It's a big old house and takes a lot of looking after.'

She's right there, Mary Ann thought, as she followed the girl. It is a very old house.

They passed through the great hall, which was the very centre of the medieval house. There was little furniture in the room, but the vast timber arched roof was awesome. Each roof-truss was cut from a naturally curving oak tree and carved by craftsmen long since gone.

Mary Ann gazed about her. For a brief moment, she felt strangely in awe of the room's size.

'Through here,' said her unwilling guide sharply, leading the way up a wooden spiral staircase towards the east wing, where the furnishings gave the old rooms a more modern appearance, along passages that nevertheless still creaked with age, until Clara opened a bedroom door and stood aside for Mary Ann to enter. 'Here you are, then. You'd best get busy being Miss Edwina's personal maid. And don't ask me what you're to do, 'cos I aren't helping you. Not ever. So don't ask.'

Mary Ann passed close to her, entered the room and looked about her. Whilst the walls and ceilings could not hide their age, the furnishings were pretty and feminine, indicative of the young woman who slept there.

Mary Ann turned and, with a smile that dimpled her cheeks and lit up her eyes, said in response to the sullen maid's statement, 'I won't, Clara. Believe me, I won't.'

Twenty-Two

'How've you got on, then? Everything all right?'

Bessie was waiting at the door for her on the following Sunday afternoon, just like any anxious mother awaiting the return of her daughter for the first time since starting work.

Mary Ann gave a little skip and ran the last few steps across the yard to throw her arms around the woman she thought of as her mother now. 'It was all right. I don't see much of Miss Edwina because she's at school all day. But I clean her room from top to bottom, just like you've taught me. And I sort out all her clothes and tidy all her drawers.' Mary Ann laughed and the merry sound echoed around the yard. 'For someone who's so good at needle-work, there's a lot of her things need mending. Miss Edwina might have shown me how to do pretty stitches, but you've shown me how to darn and mend, Bessie, and that's going to be a lot more use to me now.'

Bessie hugged the girl to her. She had missed her. Even though she was only a street or two away, the house where Mary Ann now lived and Bessie's home in Water-man's Yard were worlds apart. But Bessie knew every inch of the inside of The Hall and she had been imagining Mary Ann's every move during the days she had been away.

'What were the rest of the staff like with you? And the master and the mistress?'

'I only saw the master striding through the great hall,' Mary Ann began as Bessie drew her into the warm kitchen and fussed over her. 'The mistress came into Miss Edwina's room once to see what I was doing. She seems a nice lady, but she always looks so sad and . . . and vague, somehow. As if she's not quite aware of what's going on around her.'

Bessie's face was sober. 'She's lost her boy. Her eldest son. Her firstborn. Think how I'd feel if I lost Dan.'

Mary Ann's eyes were horrified. 'Don't, Auntie Bessie. Don't say such a thing.'

'It's all right, love.' Bessie patted the girl's arm, angry with herself that she had touched on even the thought of a personal tragedy. Mary Ann had already had more than her share of trouble without imagining more. Swiftly, bringing the conversation back to safer ground, Bessie said, 'What did the mistress say to you?'

'She just asked me if I was all right and that she hoped I'd be happy with them.'

'That was kind,' Bessie murmured and added, 'and the rest of the staff. What was Nellie Goodrick like with you?'

Mary Ann laughed. 'I reckon her face'd turn milk sour.'

Bessie chuckled. 'Poor Nellie. She came as a kitchen maid just before I left to marry my Bert and she was a poor scrawny thing then.'

'And,' Mary Ann went on, 'Clara Dobson reckons I've taken her job so she's very unfriendly.'

'Oh dear, that's a shame.'

Mary Ann shrugged and there was a tight determination to her mouth. 'She doesn't bother me.'

'What's your own room like?'

Mary Ann, like all the other servants at The Hall, was obliged to live in. She pulled a face. 'All right, except that

I have to share with Clara and neither of us are happy about that.'

'And, er . . .' Bessie seemed hesitant now. 'And what about Mr Randolph? Have you met him yet?'

'No. He's away.'

'Ah. Now, you just be careful of him, love. He's got a bit of a reputation where pretty young housemaids are concerned.'

'Don't worry about me, Auntie Bessie. I can take care of myself.' Mary Ann put her head on one side and listened. Hearing no other movement in the house except for the sounds in the kitchen, she said, 'Where is everyone?'

'Bert's upstairs on the bed, snoring his head off after the big Sunday dinner I've just given him. By the way, I've saved you a plateful if you want it, love.'

'And the others?'

'They're off out somewhere. Don't ask me where.'

'And Dan? Where's Dan?'

'So you're the new little maid?'

Mary Ann, sitting in a window seat, her back to the latticed, leaded window, her head bent over her needle-work, looked up to see a man standing a few feet in front of her. Without doubt, he was the most handsome man she had ever seen. Handsomer, even, than Dan, she had to admit. He was tall with smooth fair hair and a broad forehead. His nose was long and straight and his jaw strong and square. Indeed, his features were so well balanced they could have been carved by an artist's chisel. His mouth curved in a mocking smile and he held his head slightly on one side, one fair eyebrow raised in a sardonic question.

He moved closer. His voice was rich and deep as he asked her, 'And what is your name, young lady?'

She stood up, laid her work aside and bobbed a little curtsy. 'Mary Ann, sir. You must be Mr Randolph.'

He laughed softly. 'So you've heard about me?'

'Miss Edwina has spoken of you, sir.'

This was quite true, for Edwina had said only that morning before leaving to go to her school, 'My brother returns today.' She had smiled and added, 'He's a handsome devil, Mary Ann, and unfortunately he is only too well aware of it. He's also a shameless flirt with pretty young girls. You, my dear, fall into that category, so please be warned.'

Her words had been spoken with humour and yet there had been an underlying caution in them and they had echoed Bessie's earlier warning. Standing before him now, Mary Ann could see why. Young though she was, she could see the interest sparking in his eyes as his glance travelled slowly and appraisingly up and down her slim body. Mary Ann returned his stare steadily, not in the least fazed by his interest in her.

'You're a bold one,' he murmured. 'New maids usually blush and simper on meeting me.'

Mary Ann smiled, knowing that her own brown eyes were full of mischief.

He moved closer still and reached out, touching her chin with his forefinger. Nearer now, she could see that his eyes were a startlingly bright blue.

'We shall have to become better acquainted, Mary Ann.'

'Randolph.'

He let his hand fall away as they both heard Edwina speak behind them. She entered the long room and came towards them smiling. 'Now, now, you leave my little

Mary Ann alone. Besides, unless I'm much mistaken, Mary Ann has eyes for no one but Dan Ruddick. Isn't that right, Mary Ann?' Without waiting for confirmation or denial, she continued, holding her face up to Randolph for his brotherly kiss, 'And he's a big burly skipper of one of Mr Price's keel boats that goes up and down the river. So you'd better beware.'

She patted her brother's chest playfully and then moved to pick up Mary Ann's needlework.

'That's very good, my dear. Excellent, in fact.' She looked up and smiled. 'I think you'll achieve your dream one day of being able to embroider a banner for the church. What do you say, Randolph?' Edwina held out the circular embroidery frame, which held the stretched piece of peach-coloured satin upon which Mary Ann had been working in coloured silks.

Randolph cast a disinterested glance upon it. 'Yes, very nice. Well, I must be off. I'll see you at dinner, Edwina.' Then he turned and strode away down the room.

For a moment both young women stood watching him and then Edwina touched Mary Ann lightly on her arm and said, 'Come, it's time I taught you how to outline this silk work with gold thread.'

Together they sat on the window seat, their heads bent over the delicate embroidery, but before her eyes, all Mary Ann could see was the handsome face of Randolph Marsh.

Randolph filled The Hall with his presence.

'Whenever he comes into the house,' Mary Ann told the Ruddick family one Sunday afternoon when she had been working at The Hall for several weeks, 'it's like a whisper runs through the house. "Mr Randolph's home,

Mr Randolph's home." And everyone scuttles about like he's some god.'

They were all sitting around the table for Sunday afternoon tea. It was a family ritual that they all enjoyed. They exchanged their news, reported what had happened to them in their working life the previous week. Told funny stories or found sympathy and, often, advice for their problems too.

'His mother indulges him,' Bessie remarked, as she poured the tea from the huge teapot and handed the cups around the table. 'In her eyes he can do no wrong. And since he's a chip off the old block, as they say,' she smiled and explained, 'just like his father was when he was that age, well, Mr Bertram isn't going to find fault with him either, is he?'

'That's not always the case, though, is it, my angel,' Bert remarked. 'Sometimes when a son is exactly like his father and they're both strong characters, then there can be a clash of personalities.' His grin widened as he winked at Mary Ann. 'Mind you, with my lot, I know my place.'

Mary Ann smiled back. Bert Ruddick was what she would call a lovely man. Kind, generous, sensible and down to earth, but when it came to strength of character, then there was really only one member of the Ruddick parents' incredible partnership that could be called 'strong' and that was Bessie. But Mary Ann was beginning to realize that Bessie was a wise woman. Whilst she took the lead in almost everything, she always acted as if she deferred to her husband's wishes and she never allowed anyone to voice the notion that it was she, and not he, who wore the trousers in their house.

'You're quite right, Bert,' Bessie was saying now. 'But your boys respect you, don't they? I'm not sure that Mr Randolph respects anyone.'

'He seems very fond of Miss Edwina,' Mary Ann put in. 'He's always very kind to her.' She wrinkled her forehead thoughtfully. 'In fact, he treats Miss Edwina better than anyone else. Even better than his mother. He's a bit . . . a bit . . . sort of . . .' The young girl sought for the right words to express what she felt. 'Offhand with her. Do you know what I mean?'

Bessie nodded, her mouth tightening for a moment. 'I do. It's because Mrs Marsh is so soft with him – always has been – and he knows it. Miss Edwina, now, she stands up to him. She sees right through him and won't stand for his nonsense. So,' Bessie shrugged at the perverseness of human nature, 'he respects her far more than he does his indulgent mother.'

'Do you think Miss Edwina will ever get married?' Mary Ann asked.

Before Bessie could answer, Duggie said, 'Didn't you know? She's waiting for me. Tall, dark and handsome. I'm just what she's looking for.'

Bessie's laugh rang out. 'Dark, I'll grant you. But as for the rest, well . . .'

Duggie laughed the loudest of them all. He was the shortest member of the Ruddick family, but his shoulders were broad and strong from his work on the wharves along the river. He was not conventionally good looking; his nose was a little too large, his jaw slightly too square, but his dark eyes sparkled with mischief and good humour. His black curly hair, an unruly mop, coupled with his weather-beaten skin gave him a gypsyish appearance. 'I never liked school when I had to go,' he was saying now. 'But if I could go to Miss Marsh's, I'd go back tomorrow.'

'Aye, and it'd do you some good an' all,' his mother teased. 'Mebbe you'd have got that apprenticeship at the engineering works you're always going on about, if you'd worked a bit harder at school, m'lad.'

There was a moment's silence around the table and Mary Ann held her breath, but then Duggie adopted a hangdog expression and pressed the palm of his hand over his heart. 'Aw, Mam, cut me to the quick, you have.' Sitting next to Mary Ann, he pretended to dissolve into tears and hid his face against her shoulder.

'The truth sometimes hurts, lad,' Bessie said.

Duggie raised his head, gave an exaggerated sigh and then grinned amiably. 'Yeah. You're right, Mam. Of course, you are.' He glanced at Mary Ann and winked. 'It's me own fault if I'm going to have to work on the river all me life.'

'You could do a lot worse.' At once, Bessie sprang to defend not only Bert, but Dan too. 'If truth be told, lad, I'm proud that you *do* work on the river. Much better than being in a smelly old factory.'

'Ernie works indoors. You're proud of him and his posh office job, aren't you? Even if it is still only a stone's throw from the river.'

Bessie opened her mouth to reply but to everyone's surprise Ernie spoke. 'I sometimes wish I was out on the river instead of stuck indoors.'

The whole family and Mary Ann stared at him, waiting for him to go on, but a flush of embarrassment crept up the young man's neck. He looked down at his plate, crumbling a piece of bread between his fingers. Then, as if to cover his discomfort, everyone seemed to speak at once.

'You're doing well there, Ernie,' his father said. 'You stick at it, lad. Maybe one day you'll be office manager.'

'I envy you in winter,' Dan grinned. 'Nice and warm indoors. I'll swap you, if you like.'

'Can you get me a job there?' Duggie joked.

'We were talking about Miss Edwina,' Bessie said, glancing at Mary Ann. Her smile faded as she added, 'And no, I doubt she will ever get married now, if I'm honest, because I don't know whether she'll ever meet anyone who will match up to Mr Christopher in her eyes. It was a match made in heaven. They were ideally suited and were so in love. You could see it in their eyes.' She sighed heavily. 'It's a cruel world.'

Now there was silence around the table for a few moments, the only sound the clatter of knives and forks against plates.

At the end of the meal, Dan stood up. 'I'll be on me way then.'

Everyone looked up at him and then Mary Ann rose too and slipped her hand through his arm. 'Are you going to walk me home, Dan?' she said, her head coyly on one side. 'But I don't have to go yet. I don't have to be back at The Hall until nine.'

For a moment Dan looked embarrassed. 'Well, I . . . er . . . I've arranged to go out tonight, Mary Ann. Perhaps Duggie . . .?' He looked hopefully across at his younger brother.

'Yeah, I'll walk you back, Mary Ann.'

Mary Ann pouted. 'You always see me back on a Sunday night, Dan.'

'Maybe he's meeting someone. A girl,' Duggie tormented. 'Oho, I'm right. Look at his face.'

Under their scrutiny, Dan's face reddened even more.

'Who is she, Dan? Come on, you can tell us.'

Bessie stood up and began to gather the plates into a pile. 'Leave the lad alone. He's big enough and ugly enough to look after himself. He'll tell us when he wants us to know.'

Dan shot his mother a grateful look, but even so he said, 'You might as well know, I suppose. I'm seeing Susan.'

'Susan!' came a chorus of surprised voices and Bessie added, 'Not behind her father's back I hope, lad, else you're stacking up trouble for yourself.'

'No, no. He's given his permission. She was waiting for me yesterday on the wharf. I thought it was all over – for good – but it seems she asked him if she could see me again and he agreed. So . . .' He shrugged and then glanced down at Mary Ann, seeming about to speak to her. But she, after staring at him in shocked silence for a moment, snatched her hand away from his arm and sat down heavily on her chair. For the first time in ages, Mary Ann's hand crept up towards her face and, almost of its own volition, her thumb crept into her mouth.

She was aware that Dan was still hovering close by, looking as if he didn't know whether to go or to stay. Mary Ann felt his hesitant gaze upon her but, stubbornly, she refused to look at him.

'Don't stand there dithering, lad,' Bessie was saying briskly. 'Get off with you, if you're going. And you, Mary Ann, can stop that sulking this minute and come and help me with the washing up.'

But Mary Ann continued to sit quite still, sucking her thumb and staring into the fire.

Twenty-Three

Mary Ann walked quickly through the dark streets with Duggie trying to keep up with her.

'By heck, you walk quick for a girl. What's the hurry? Got a train to catch, have you?'

'It's cold and I'm getting wet,' she snapped.

Duggie laughed. 'Little bit of rain won't hurt you. You ought to work outdoors in all weathers like me.'

'Well, I don't and I don't want to.'

'Oho, getting used to the soft life, are we?' he teased, but there was no malice in his tone. Duggie hadn't a drop of spite in him, but Mary Ann was in no mood for his jocularity.

She stopped suddenly. 'You needn't come any further.'

'Our Dan'd knock me head off if I hadn't seen you to the door and summat happened.'

Through clenched teeth Mary Ann said, 'If "your Dan" had been so bothered, he'd have come with me himself.'

There was a moment's silence before Duggie said, 'By heck, you're jealous. You're jealous of him going to meet Susan, aren't you?'

Mary Ann glared at him. Through the darkness she could not see his face, but she knew he was laughing. She could hear it in his voice.

'What would you know about it, Duggie Ruddick?' With that parting shot, she whirled about and was gone, running along the wet pavement to get away from him as fast as she could.

She heard him calling behind her, 'Mary Ann, Mary Ann. Wait. I didn't mean . . .'

She rounded the corner, and before her loomed the dark shape of The Hall, lights twinkling from its leaded windows. He wouldn't follow her any further now. He would know she was home. Near the door leading into the kitchens and thence to the servants' quarters, Mary Ann leant against the wall to catch her breath. She rested her head against the rough brickwork, closed her eyes and gave a low groan.

Now the whole Ruddick family would know of her love for Dan. Duggie was the last of them to be able to keep a secret. She could imagine him telling them all, could see them sitting round the fire laughing together at her foolishness. Maybe Dan would laugh the loudest. The thought wounded her and she let out another low moan.

'What's the matter? Are you hurt?'

Mary Ann jumped as the voice came unexpectedly out of the darkness.

'Oh! Mr Randolph. No – I mean . . .'

'What are you doing out here in the dark?' He moved closer, towering over her. 'Waiting for a young man, perhaps?'

'Oh no, sir.'

'Really? You surprise me. A pretty little thing like you must have a string of admirers.'

'No, sir,' Mary Ann said again, trying valiantly to make her tone sound prim. 'Mrs Goodrick would flay me alive if I had a follower.'

'Indeed?' He paused and then asked, 'So, what are you doing out here, skulking about in the dark?'

'I'm not skulking,' Mary Ann flashed indignantly, quite

forgetting for the moment to whom she was speaking. 'I've just come back from my afternoon off and – and . . .' Ingenuity came to her rescue. 'I – I think I've twisted my ankle coming up the path. I was just resting against the wall for a moment. I . . .' She began to embroider the tale. 'I felt a bit dizzy with the sharp pain.'

'Pray allow me to assist you.' The words sounded concerned and yet his tone held a hint of derision, as if he didn't quite believe her and yet was willing to play along.

'I'll be all right, sir, thank you. If I can just get inside.'

'You didn't ought to put any weight on it, if you have sprained it, my dear.'

Before Mary Ann realized what was happening, Randolph had bent down, put one arm beneath her knees and the other about her waist and lifted her up into his arms. She gave a cry of protest, but his only answer was a soft laugh.

Moments later, they were in the room that Randolph called his den and he was setting her down gently into a leather armchair at the side of a crackling fire.

The room, at the far end of the east wing of the sprawling old house, had been the boys' playroom. As they had grown older they had called it their den, where they could be alone together or where they could invite their friends without disturbing the rest of the household. Sadly, only Randolph now enjoyed its privacy. Not a day went by when he did not miss his quieter, more sober, brother, although not for one instant would he ever have admitted what he believed to be a sign of weakness – that of pure, unadulterated affection for another human being.

'Which foot did you hurt?'

'The . . . the right one.' Mary Ann was feeling apprehensive. What if he could tell that she had not hurt her ankle at all?

Randolph sat down on a footstool and took Mary Ann's foot into his hands. He unlaced her boot and gently slipped it from her foot. Then his hands slid up her leg to find the top of her stocking. Mary Ann's eyes widened. 'Don't . . .' she began, but he only smiled in the firelight.

'If I'm to be your doctor, then you must allow me to examine you properly.' His voice was deep and somehow hypnotizing, silencing her protests almost before they had begun.

Gently, he eased her stocking down and drew it from her foot. With strong fingers he gently pressed around her anklebone. His head was bent over her foot and Mary Ann noticed that his hair was thick and springy and that, despite his efforts to smooth it, there was a tiny, wayward curl behind his ear. For some irrational reason, she had the urge to reach out to touch it.

'There doesn't seem to be anything broken, nor is it swollen.' He looked up at her then, his eyes, shadowed and unfathomable depths in the flickering light from the fire, the only illumination in the room. In little more than a whisper, he asked, 'Where does it hurt?'

Mary Ann ran her tongue around her lips, which were suddenly dry, naïvely unaware how provocative her action was to the man kneeling before her. 'It doesn't now,' she said. 'It must have felt worse when . . . when I did it than it really was.'

Randolph smiled in the dim light. 'I'm sure it did.' He spoke the words so softly that she was unable to tell whether he believed her or not. He was still kneeling in front of her, stroking her foot with his fingers in a caress that suddenly became stronger, more urgent. 'Perhaps a little massage will help,' he murmured.

He was stroking the area around her ankle and then smoothing the top of her foot and gently wriggling each of her toes. His touch, intended to heal her imaginary hurt, was, in fact, driving that other hurt from her heart and her mind. He leant towards her, looking up into her face. 'Is that better?' he asked, his voice soft and deep.

'Yes . . .' Mary Ann gulped at the strange feelings enveloping her. A tingling sensation was coursing through her, making her feel as if she was blushing all over her body. Her heart was beating faster than normal and now it had nothing to do with having run the last few yards to the back door of The Hall. 'Yes, thank you, sir.'

She tried to pull her foot out of his grasp, but his hands held it and his fingers continued to fondle her toes. 'You have a very delicate foot, Mary Ann. And such trim ankles. I wonder – I long to know – are your legs as perfect? Are you every bit as perfect all over?' His hand was creeping once more beneath her petticoat.

Mary Ann reached forward and pushed away his searching hand. 'Please, sir. I must go.' With a sudden, sharp movement, she wrenched her foot away from him and bent forward to retrieve her boot and stocking, but before she could reach them, he had taken her by the shoulders and was drawing her gently up.

'Can you stand on it without pain?'

Pretending to test her weight upon it, Mary Ann nodded. 'Yes, sir, I think so. Thank you for your kindness, but I must . . .'

The rest of her words were silenced as he bent his head and found her mouth with lips that were hungry for the taste of her. 'You sweet, pretty little thing,' he murmured against her mouth. 'What kind Fate brought you to me?'

It was the first time that anyone had kissed her with the passion a man has for a woman. It frightened her, yet at the same time exhilarated her. The blood was pounding in her ears, her heart was thudding beneath her ribs as Randolph kissed her and stroked her hair.

Then he was straightening up, drawing away from her and leaving her bereft, washed upon the shore by the tide of a shared passion and then abandoned. He took both her hands in his and gently, reverently, kissed each of her fingers in turn. The touch of his lips sent a shudder through her.

'My dear, I would not hurt you for the world. You are far too sweet and innocent. Come, sit with me.' He sat down in the huge armchair himself and drew her, unresisting now, on to his lap. 'I've seen you about the house, Mary Ann, and oh . . .' He rested his cheek against her breast and she felt sure that he must hear her heart, taking wild, leaping somersaults. 'How I've longed to hold you, to touch you. And then, tonight, there you were. A damsel in distress and me, your knight in shining armour. Sweet, sweet Mary Ann.'

Mary Ann said nothing. She did not know what to say. She had not the words to express the excitement, the heady emotion that filled her heart and tore her rational mind to shreds.

Somewhere a door banged and Mary Ann jumped, pulling away from him. He reached out and caught hold of her. 'Don't be afraid. No one will come in here, I promise you.'

'I . . . I must go, sir. I must.'

He nodded and stood up too, towering over her. Resting his hands lightly on her shoulders, he looked down into her upturned face. Then he traced the outline of her cheek with his forefinger.

'Sweet, sweet girl. This is our secret. You know that, don't you?'

Mesmerized, Mary Ann nodded. 'Yes, sir. Of course, sir.'

Tenderly and with great gentleness, he kissed her once more, then held her hand as he led her across the room. He opened the door a little to stand listening for a moment before whispering, 'The coast is clear. Off you go. And remember, this is our secret. Our very own wonderful secret.'

Blushing, Mary Ann smiled and passed through the doorway, carrying her boot and her stocking. The door closed behind her and, as she paused, she thought she heard his deep, soft laugh beyond the panels. She smiled and hugged her arms around herself. She, too, felt like laughing aloud and shouting with sheer joy. Instead, she crept away, hurrying swiftly along the passages and corridors with the silence of a wraith until she reached the safety of her own room.

Luckily for Mary Ann, Clara was asleep, lying on her back, her mouth wide open and snoring noisily.

Mary Ann wrinkled her nose in disgust. It seemed so unfeminine for a girl to snore. True, Clara had adenoidal trouble and couldn't help it, but still . . .

Mary Ann stretched her arms above her head and let out a sigh of sheer delight. Slowly, she began to undress in the moonlight shining in through the skylight that afforded the only natural lighting in their attic bedroom. Running her hands over her body, savouring the feel of Randolph's hands upon her, Mary Ann smiled to herself.

I can do better for myself than you, Daniel Ruddick.

Twenty-Four

The following morning Mary Ann was disappointed to find that Randolph was not in the dining room waiting for her to serve his breakfast.

Keeping her tone devoid of any particular interest, she asked, 'Will Mr Randolph be in to breakfast, Miss Edwina?'

'I don't think so, Mary Ann. I understand he left early this morning for Yorkshire. He'll be gone a few days.' Edwina rose from her place at the table and smiled. 'Would you like to come to the school this afternoon? I was wondering if you would like to teach the little ones a few basic embroidery stitches.'

Mary Ann swallowed her disappointment and smiled brightly. 'I'd love to, Miss Edwina.'

'Good. Then we can walk home together later and call to see Bessie.'

Mary Ann nodded, although the smile faded from her mouth. She avoided meeting Edwina's gaze and busied herself clearing away the breakfast dishes. She would love to see Bessie, but, for the first time ever, she hoped that the rest of the family would not be at home.

That afternoon, Mary Ann sat surrounded by seven eager little girls. Each held a piece of linen, some coloured wool and a needle.

'Now,' Mary Ann began, smiling around at them all. 'I don't know all your names, so each time I speak to you, you must tell me what your name is until I can remember it for myself. All right?' Seven small heads nodded. 'First of all, I must warn you about the needle. You must be very careful not to hurt yourself or anyone else. When you are not working with it, you must fasten it on to the corner of your piece of work. Like this.'

She held up a small piece of linen and threaded the needle in and out of the material until it was securely fastened. 'Never leave your needle lying about and always keep a piece of thread in it and attached to some material. Now, let's begin . . .'

For the next hour, Mary Ann worked happily with the children, showing them firstly how to make small, neat running stitches about an inch in from the edge of the material. Then she taught them how to do buttonhole stitch about the very edge of the fabric. Some of the tiny fingers found this very hard, pulling the thread too tightly so that it puckered the material. Mary Ann seemed to spend most of her time picking out the stitches and then showing them again and again.

Towards the end of the afternoon, Edwina slipped into the room and sat at the back of the class watching and listening. As the bell sounded and Mary Ann allowed her charges to put their work away, Edwina moved forwards.

When the girls had trooped from the room to retrieve their coats from the cloakroom, she smiled and asked, 'Now, did you enjoy that?'

Unable to keep the surprise from her voice, Mary Ann said, 'Yes, I did. I didn't think I'd have the patience, but they were so keen and willing to learn.' She pulled a face. 'Even though some of them don't seem to have held a needle before.' She blushed a little as she remembered.

'Still, I can't say much about that, can I? I didn't do any sewing until I met Bessie and then you.'

Edwina smiled kindly. 'You have a natural talent for it, Mary Ann. Always remember that not everyone is lucky enough to have your gift. You must be very patient with those who have not.'

Mary Ann nodded. 'Do you mean you want me to do it again?'

'Would you like to?'

Mary Ann's eyes shone. 'Yes, please, Miss Edwina.'

With school over for the day and the children gone, Edwina and Mary Ann walked along River Road towards Waterman's Yard. For a while they walked in silence for Mary Ann's thoughts were busy. At last she said, 'Do you think I could be a teacher?'

To her, a teacher was someone of standing, someone to be admired and looked up to. It would make her more equal to Miss Edwina. More equal with her brother, Mr Randolph.

Carefully, Edwina said, 'I don't see why you shouldn't. But it would mean a lot of hard work, Mary Ann.' Edwina did not like to tell the girl that because of her background, Mary Ann's early education had been badly neglected, and that to become a fully fledged teacher, one had to pass examinations. But the girl had intelligence and was quick to learn. There was no telling what Mary Ann could do if she put her mind to it.

When they arrived at Bessie's home, she and Minnie were sitting in the kitchen enjoying a cup of tea.

'I'll be going,' Minnie said, standing up at once.

'Please don't let us drive you away, Mrs Eccleshall,' Edwina said, but Minnie insisted.

'No, no, miss. It's time I was going. If my Stan's tea isn't ready when he steps through the door . . .' She pulled a comical face, but they all knew that she was only joking. 'I'll see you tomorrow, Bessie. Going into town, are we?'

'Of course. It's market day.' Bessie heaved herself up. 'I'll be ready. Now then.' She turned to Mary Ann with her usual greeting. 'How are you, love?'

'Fine, Auntie Bessie,' Mary Ann said, and plunged into recounting her afternoon at the school, ending by saying, 'Miss Edwina thinks I might be able to be a teacher, if I work hard.'

She saw the two women exchange a glance, but all Bessie said was, 'That'd be nice, love.'

They drank tea and ate a slice of Bessie's plum bread. Then Edwina rose and pulled on her gloves. Mary Ann, too, put down her cup and made to rise.

'You can stay for the evening if you wish, Mary Ann. I'll tell Mrs Goodrick I've given you permission. But please, be home by nine o'clock.'

Instead of leaping at the chance to remain in the Ruddick household, and especially taking the opportunity to see Dan, Mary Ann hesitated. If Duggie had told the rest of his family about her feelings for Dan, then she could expect to be teased unmercifully. And if Dan knew, then she would wish the floor to open up and swallow her whole. Then Mary Ann raised her head defiantly. What did it matter now, anyway? She could laugh it all off as one of Duggie's japes. For Dan was seeing Susan again, and hadn't she, Mary Ann, got someone now who was really interested in her? Someone far more handsome and dashing and eligible than a man who sailed up and down the river on a barge. You've missed your chance, Dan Ruddick, she thought. I've got better fish to fry.

She smiled. 'Thank you, Miss Edwina. I'd love to stay.'

'Right then,' Bessie said. 'You can make yourself useful and lay the table.'

They all laughed as Edwina said, 'I'll be on my way before I'm given a job. Please give Mr Ruddick and the boys my regards.'

'I will,' Bessie said going to the door with her. 'And I know they'd send you theirs.'

The Ruddick menfolk came home one by one, each greeting Mary Ann in their different ways. Bert with quiet affection and with serious enquiries as to her health, her wellbeing and her happiness in her situation, Ernie with shyness and only a few, hesitant words and Duggie with his usual ebullience. But now, there was an extra twinkle in his eyes that teased her without a word being spoken.

And then Dan, the last to come home, how would he greet her? Mary Ann held her breath.

His pleasure at seeing her unexpectedly was genuine and his manner towards her the same as ever. Affectionate and concerned for her – just like any elder brother. She knew now – now that she had experienced how a man behaved when he was attracted to her – that Dan looked upon her as he would a sister. He had never kissed her or touched her in the way that Mr Randolph had. He didn't love her in the way that Mary Ann had imagined she loved him.

Had she really loved Dan or had her adoration of him been just because he had shown her tenderness when she had been starved of love?

'Hello, fancy seeing you here!' He was smiling down at her. 'Everything all right?'

Mary Ann nodded and swallowed. He was the same as ever and it seemed that perhaps she had maligned Duggie in thinking he had told his family about her feelings for Dan.

As they all sat down to eat, Mary Ann began to tell them about her day, her visit to the school and the class of little girls to whom she had begun to teach embroidery.

But she was careful that not once did she mention Mr Randolph's name.

Twenty-Five

Randolph returned to The Hall three days later.

Mary Ann, passing through the great hall carrying a tray, heard his boots echoing on the tiled floor behind her.

She stopped, turned to face him and waited whilst he glanced around him to make sure there was no one else there. Then he came to her.

'Have you missed me?' His left eyebrow rose in question.

'Oh yes,' she breathed, her knees trembling. 'Where have you been?'

'Just away,' he said idly. 'On business.' He glanced around again and then leant closer, his lips brushing her hair. 'I've thought about you every minute I've been away. Come to my room this evening. I've brought a little present for you.'

There was the sound of voices and he turned from her abruptly and strode away.

The dishes on the tray she was carrying rattled together as her hands shook. Mary Ann bit her lip and tried to steady her leaping heart, and for the rest of the day her lack of concentration earned her a sharp reprimand from Mrs Goodrick, which brought a satisfied smirk to Clara's face.

*

It was late when Nellie Goodrick allowed her to leave the kitchen and, having gone to her room first, Mary Ann waited until she thought the way was clear for her to creep down to Randolph's den.

The master, Bertram Marsh, was in his study, locked away with his cigars and a bottle of port. Mrs Marsh had retired to her bedroom. She wasn't sure where Edwina was, but as she hadn't seen her since dinner, Mary Ann hoped she would not run into her as she tiptoed through the house towards the east wing. Nervously, she tapped on the door and heard him bid her enter.

He was sitting in the deep armchair and when he turned his head and saw her standing in the doorway, he rose at once and came towards her.

Closing the door softly, he drew her towards the fire. 'I thought you weren't coming.'

'I couldn't get away before, sir,' she said breathlessly.

'Oh Mary Ann, please don't call me "sir". Not when we're alone.' He pulled a face. 'Of course we must keep up the pretence outside this room. No one must know. You do understand that, don't you?'

'Yes,' she said, though her tone was hesitant with disappointment. She wanted to tell everyone. She wanted to wipe away Clara Dobson's smug expression and see the look of disapproval on the cook's face that she knew would be there. But most of all, she wanted to see Dan's face when she told him about Mr Randolph.

Randolph put his arms around her and drew her into his embrace, resting his cheek against her hair. 'Oh Mary Ann, you don't know how much I've missed you. Everywhere I went, I kept seeing your sweet little face, those dark, magnificent eyes and those pretty little dimples in your cheeks when you smile.'

He bent his head then and lifted her chin with his finger

so that she was looking up into his face. Then he began to kiss her and the room reeled around her and she was borne along on a tidal wave of a new and exciting emotion.

Gently, he pressed her down on to the thick rug in front of the warm fire. He turned down the gaslights so that the only illumination in the room came from the flickering firelight. Removing his jacket, he lay down beside her. Propping his head on one hand, he let his gaze roam all over her, until she felt disconcerted and embarrassed by his scrutiny. With his right hand he stroked the hair from her face and caressed her cheek, then he allowed his hand to stray to her bosom where, deftly, he unbuttoned the topmost three buttons of her blouse, with her hardly being aware of what he was doing. Then his hand travelled down to her waist and thence to her groin where it rested.

He bent over and as his lips pecked gently at her mouth, he murmured endearments, such words of love and longing that Mary Ann had never heard before.

'You adorable little creature. Don't be afraid, my sweet Mary Ann. I won't hurt you. I promise I won't hurt you . . .'

It was two o'clock in the morning before Mary Ann stumbled up the back stairs to her room. She was sore and bleeding, for despite his promise, it had hurt when he had entered her, for she was a virgin. Despite the traumas of her early life that had left her with a worldly knowledge, she was nevertheless still ignorant and naïve in the desires of men and women carried away by tumultuous passion.

She was shaking now with a mixture of fear and yet

exhilaration too. She was loved and desired and by such a man as Randolph Marsh.

'Let's keep this to ourselves, my darling, for now. I want you just for myself. But one day the whole world will know how much I love you and want you.'

At his words, her heart sang. He didn't mean to keep their love hidden like some grubby little secret. He really loved her and he wanted to parade his love for everyone to see. Sleep was impossible. In the cold, dark attic room Mary Ann lay in her narrow bed a completely different person to the girl who had lain there only the previous night. Now she was a woman. Her body had responded to his like a woman's and the next time there would be none of the pain. Randolph had told her so.

'Next time,' he had said, as they had lain together in the aftermath of his violent lovemaking, 'it will be just as wonderful for you. I promise.'

It was their secret – a wonderful, exciting, daring secret – and Mary Ann hugged the knowledge to herself. She would tell no one. Not even Bessie. For somewhere in the dark recesses of her mind, buried deliberately deep, Mary Ann knew that Bessie would be shocked and angry at what she had done this night.

'You're looking a bit peaky, love. Are you all right?'

Mary Ann was startled and her heart began to thump at Bessie's question. She knew the cause, but how was she to avoid telling the truth? Bessie was far too sharp not to know a lie when it was being told to her. So Mary Ann decided that the truth, but not the whole truth, was the best policy.

'I've not been sleeping very well. I'm tired.' She did not, however, add that the reason she was missing her sleep was because she spent the late hours of most nights in Randolph's arms.

'Are they working you too hard?' Bessie persisted. 'Is this teaching thing, as well as all the work you have to do at The Hall, too much for you? It'd be just like Nellie Goodrick to work you all the harder just because you're Miss Edwina's favourite.'

And Mr Randolph's favourite, Mary Ann was thinking, but she shook her head and said, 'No, no. I love doing that.'

She was silent now, her eyes downcast. It was not only the lack of sleep, but the fear too. Mary Ann was not so ignorant – Bessie in her matter-of-fact way had seen to that – that she did not know the risk she was taking. Any day, she might become pregnant. What would happen then? Would Randolph stand by her as he had promised?

'Don't be afraid,' he had whispered. 'I'll always take care of you.'

But would he marry her? The words had never been spoken. He had never said as much, but he had promised not to hurt her and, always, to look after her. So, didn't that amount to the same thing? Didn't that mean that one day she would be his wife?

'I adore you,' he told her constantly. 'I've never known anyone like you before. I've been waiting the whole of my life for someone like you.'

Starved of love for most of her young life, Mary Ann's hungry soul fed on his words. Even in the warmth of Bessie's kitchen, the memories made her shiver with desire for him, the feel of him, the smell of him and the sound of his whispered words.

'Are you catching a chill, love?' Bessie persisted in her concern.

Mary Ann forced a smile on to her mouth. 'Me? Ill? I've never been ill in me life, Auntie Bessie.' She put her head on one side as she deliberated. She must act as normally as possible or this wise, perceptive woman might start to probe a little too deeply.

So, as she always had done when she visited Waterman's Yard, Mary Ann asked, 'Where's Dan?'

Dan walked her back to The Hall that night and insisted on seeing her right to the door the servants used. Mary Ann's heart was skipping wildly, afraid that Randolph might be waiting for her in the shadows. But no, she reasoned inwardly. Randolph would be waiting in his room, their little love nest, for her to come to him.

'Are you really happy at The Hall, Mary Ann?' Dan asked her as they walked along. He reached out and took hold of her hand in the darkness and put it through his arm so that they walked closely together. 'We want you to be happy. You know that, don't you?'

Only a short time ago, Mary Ann would have been ecstatic at his action. She would have read far more into his affectionate gesture than perhaps he meant. Now, knowing that he was once more seeing Susan, she realized it was no more than a brotherly protectiveness.

Added to that, she now knew so much more about desire and she had the love of a man of position in the community, a man of standing. Oh, if she were to become Mrs Randolph Marsh and live at The Hall as its future mistress . . .

'Of course I'm happy there. Why wouldn't I be?'

'I just wondered, that's all. You've often said that Mrs Goodrick is very severe with you, and that you and Clara don't get on.'

'Huh,' Mary Ann expressed derision. 'Who are they, anyway? I don't care about them.'

'Perhaps not,' Dan said reasonably. 'But they could make your life very difficult.'

In the darkness, Mary Ann smiled to herself, hugging her delicious secret. She couldn't wait to see the look on the faces of the cook and that uppity housemaid when Randolph made the announcement that they were to be married.

'Are you going to marry Susan?'

'Oh, well now,' Dan sounded embarrassed. 'It's early days yet. Her father has only recently given permission for us to see each other again.'

'Permission? What on earth do you need his permission for?'

'Susan's not twenty-one yet. And besides, she wouldn't want to go against her father. Nor would I,' he added wryly. 'Don't forget, he's my employer. Not only that, if he were to sack me, he's got a lot of influence amongst the river folk. I'd be hard pressed to find another job round here.'

Her clear laugh rang out in the night air. Now that her sights were no longer set on Dan, she could joke about such things. 'Then you should marry me,' she said, with teasing flippancy. 'I don't have any parents to object.'

Dan did not answer and for a moment both of them were silenced by bitter memories flooding back. She felt him squeeze her hand closer to his side in the gesture of comfort.

As they rounded the corner and the dark shape of The Hall loomed before them, Dan asked, 'When shall we see you again? Next Sunday?'

'Unless Miss Edwina and me call on our way home from school in the week. We do that sometimes.'

'Are you enjoying that? The teaching, I mean?'

Mary Ann's reply was swift and genuine. 'Yes. I'm quite surprised how much I like the children. I never had much to do with other kids, being an only one and not going to school an awful lot.'

Again, the reference to her past life made Dan bring the conversation round to looking forwards, not backwards. 'Should you like to be a teacher?'

Her answer this time did not come so quickly. She had other plans now, plans that meant she would be a lady of leisure with no need to earn her own living or have any occupation.

'I wouldn't mind teaching embroidery, but to be a proper teacher, well, I don't think I could. I mean, I haven't been to school enough myself and there'd be a lot of examinations to take.'

'Would there be so many if you were just to teach embroidery?'

'No, I don't think so. Miss Edwina says that a lot of those would be practical exams and she thinks that maybe I could scrape through the written ones.' She was playing a part now, with no real intention of ever taking such examinations. She wouldn't need to as Mrs Randolph Marsh.

'Here we are then, safely to the door. You're not late are you? You won't get into trouble with Mrs Goodrick?'

'No, no. I'm in good time.' But it was not Mrs Goodrick she was thinking of. She was in good time to go up to her room and then to slip down the stairs again to see Randolph.

The windows of his room were just across the lawn between the two wings of the house and Mary Ann could not resist glancing across towards the soft lighting shining beyond the leaded panes. He was there. He was waiting for her. In fact, she fancied she saw the outline of his shape standing at the window.

With a spark of devilment, she stood on tiptoe and kissed Dan's cheek. 'I'll see you Sunday, if not before. Thank you for seeing me home, Dan. Goodnight.'

'Goodnight, Mary Ann. God bless.' To her surprise, he reached out and took her by the shoulders. Then he bent his head and kissed her firmly on the mouth.

He released her so quickly that she was caught off balance and put out her hand to steady herself against the wall. She gave a small gasp of surprise, but he had turned away and before she could utter a word he had disappeared into the darkness.

Half an hour later, Mary Ann was tapping softly on the door of Randolph's room. She put her hand on the knob in readiness for his soft, 'Come in.'

Suddenly the door was flung open, wrenched from her grasp and she found herself being pulled roughly into the room, the door being slammed behind her. Now he was gripping her shoulder so strongly that his fingers dug into her flesh.

'Who was that with you? I saw you. I saw you kissing him. I'll kill him. Tell me . . .' He shook her. 'Who was it?'

Mary Ann gave a nervous laugh and tried to make light of it. She was afraid and yet a feeling of exhilaration flooded through her. He must really love her to get so jealous.

'It was only Dan.'

'Dan who?' he shot back.

'Dan Ruddick. He walked me home, that's all. One of them always does.'

'What do you mean?' he asked harshly. 'One of them?'

'One of the Ruddicks. I lived with them before I came here. Didn't you know?'

His grip began to slacken a little, but a new fear was creeping through Mary Ann's veins now. Did he not know who she was? Did he not know her background or her terrible past?

He was calmer, but his tone was still sharp as he asked, 'Why did you live with them? Are they your family?'

'Sort of. They took me in after my parents . . .' She hesitated only momentarily before adding, 'Died.'

'The Ruddicks?' he said slowly and thoughtfully. 'They live in Waterman's Yard, don't they?'

Quietly, Mary Ann said, 'Yes.'

'And your surname is?'

Almost inaudibly, she said, 'Clark.'

'Mary Ann Clark.' He said the name as if realization had just come to him.

She looked up at him, desperately afraid now that she was going to see his face twisted with anger and revulsion, but it was expressionless as he stared down at her for what, to Mary Ann, holding her breath, seemed an interminable age.

Then slowly, he cupped her face in his hands and kissed her forehead. 'You poor little thing. I never realized who you were. What a dreadful thing to happen to anyone. And to someone as sweet and lovely as you.'

Joy and relief flooded through her. She put her arms about his waist and buried her face against his chest. 'Oh Randolph, Randolph. You do love me.'

He drew her to the hearth and they lay down together. That evening his lovemaking was gentle and giving and, more than ever, Mary Ann believed herself secure in his love.

Twenty-Six

'Mary Ann? Whatever are you doing creeping about the house at this time of the night?'

In her flight from Randolph's arms back to her own room, Mary Ann froze at the sound of Edwina's voice.

It had to happen. Night after night, she had been going to Randolph's room for several weeks now and it was only a matter of time before another member of the household caught her. Mary Ann didn't know whether to be pleased or sorry that that person was Miss Edwina.

'Are you ill, my dear?' Edwina came towards her and then, as she saw her more clearly, 'Why, you're still fully dressed.' Mary Ann saw Edwina's mouth tighten as she asked, 'Have you only just come in? Oh really, Mary Ann. No wonder you are so tired sometimes during the day. And there I was blaming myself for having perhaps expected too much of you, involving you in teaching too. You really must come home earlier than this. I shall have to speak to Bessie—'

'No,' Mary Ann interrupted. 'No, please don't do that. I . . . I won't let it happen again, Miss Edwina. I promise.'

'Well,' Edwina said doubtfully. 'Just mind you don't. Run along now and get to bed.'

Her heart still thumping, Mary Ann sped along the corridor and up the back stairs. She would have to tell Randolph what had happened. Maybe he would agree to tell everyone the truth now.

But in the morning, Mary Ann rose with tired eyes to hear from the servants' gossip that Mr Randolph had left The Hall early that morning and would not return for four or five days.

'Where's he gone?' Mary Ann asked, without thinking.

'That's no concern of yours,' Mrs Goodrick snapped, 'or of mine.' A slow smirk stretched her mouth, but what purported to be a smile did not reach the woman's eyes. 'Not that I don't know, of course.'

'So?' Mary Ann stood her ground. 'Where has he gone?'

Mrs Goodrick raised her forefinger to wag in Mary Ann's face, but before she could do so, Clara said smugly. 'He's gone to Yorkshire again, I bet.'

Mary Ann wheeled around upon the hapless house-maid. 'Yorkshire? Why? Why's he gone to Yorkshire?'

'Ah,' Clara said. There was a glint in her small, piggy eyes that sat in her round, podgy face. The girl suffered from facial acne and, this morning, the crop of spots around her chin was particularly fiery. 'That'd be telling.'

At that moment the bell above the door tinkled and Mrs Goodrick smoothed down her white apron. 'That's the mistress wanting me in the morning room. You two, get on with your work and be quick about it.'

Clara turned away, but as the door closed behind the cook, Mary Ann reached out and grasped the girl by her hair, almost wrenching the white lace cap from the girl's head. 'You just tell me what you mean, Clara Dobson, else I'll pull your hair out by its roots.'

Clara let out such a shriek and then began to scream so loudly that Mary Ann let go of her hair at once. 'Shut up,' she hissed. 'You'll have the whole household down here.'

Clara backed away from her, her mouth wide in a

series of shrill cries. 'Get away. Get away. Don't touch me.'

The kitchen door burst open and Mrs Goodrick hurried in again, swiftly followed by Edwina.

'Whatever's going on?' the cook began. 'Stop that silly noise, girl.'

'She was going to kill me. She's a bad 'un. She'll murder all of us in our beds. Just like her father did.'

'Clara!' Edwina's voice was shocked. 'I will not have such talk in this house. You will apologize to Mary Ann this instant.'

Clara was crying now. Great wracking sobs were shaking her whole body. 'It was 'er, Miss Edwina. She pulled me hair. Just 'cos I wouldn't tell her where Mr Randolph has gone.'

'Mr . . .?' Edwina began, astonishment in her tone. Then Mary Ann felt her questioning gaze upon her. Quietly now, Edwina said, 'I think you'd better come with me, Mary Ann. Mrs Goodrick, will you deal with Clara, please?'

With that, Edwina turned and left the kitchen. Subdued now, Mary Ann followed her. Edwina led the way up the stairs to the privacy of her own bedroom. She opened the door and stood aside for Mary Ann to enter the room. Then she closed the door.

Mary Ann stood in the centre of the pretty bedroom, a mutinous look on her face. Edwina leant against the door for a moment and Mary Ann felt her watching her. Edwina crossed the room to the window and sat down in a chair. She did not invite Mary Ann to sit down, but left the girl standing where she was.

'Now,' Edwina began. Her voice was still low. Edwina rarely raised her voice but now there was steeliness to her tone. 'Are you going to tell me what this is all about?'

Mary Ann glanced at her. Edwina's eyes were shrewd and knowing and for a moment Mary Ann held her breath. There would be no point in lying to Miss Edwina, she thought. Edwina would know and she would then be in deeper trouble.

If only, she thought, Randolph had not gone away. And without telling her too. He might have said something last night, but as she remembered the previous evening, she knew that all such thoughts must have been driven out of his mind. Just like there had been no room for anyone else in her mind but him.

'Why are you smiling, Mary Ann?' Edwina's voice cut into her erotic memories of their passionate lovemaking.

'I just . . .' Mary Ann began hesitantly. 'I just wanted to know where Ra—, where Mr Randolph had gone, miss. That's all.'

Edwina's eyes narrowed, and even Mary Ann, for all her boldness, found the young woman's gaze disconcerting.

'And why should that concern you?'

Mary Ann manufactured a disinterested shrug, but she knew that she could not deceive Edwina. Not for long. Already, Mary Ann could see the realization dawning in Edwina's face. Then Edwina closed her eyes momentarily and gave a low groan and murmured, 'Oh no. Not again.' She sighed and stood up and then she crossed the room towards Mary Ann and put her hand out to take the girl's arm gently. 'Come. Sit down with me. We must talk and I want you to be absolutely truthful with me, Mary Ann. For your own sake, my dear, as much as anyone else's. Do you understand me?'

Mutely, Mary Ann nodded and allowed herself to be led towards the window where Edwina pushed her gently into a chair. Then she sat down beside her. 'Tell me, am I right in thinking that you had been to Randolph's study last night when I bumped into you on the stairs?'

Edwina's gaze was penetrating, yet not angry or unkind, just dreadfully anxious.

Mary Ann swallowed and her eyes widened. There was nothing else she could do but whisper, 'Yes.'

'And?'

Now Mary Ann turned rebellious. 'And what?'

'What happened? Did he try to . . . try to . . .?'

The truth burst from her lips. Why should she keep it secret any longer? Why shouldn't the whole world know the truth?

'He didn't *try* anything. Randolph loves me. He said so. We're to be married. I know he wants to marry me.'

Edwina gasped and the colour drained from her face. 'Did . . . did Randolph say that to you? Did Randolph ask you to marry him, Mary Ann?'

The girl stared at her. For a brief, terrifying moment, a sliver of fear crept into her heart. 'Not yet. He hasn't actually asked me yet. But he will. I know he will. That's what people do when they're in love. They get married.'

She knew her words must be like shafts through Edwina's heart, reminding her of her own lost love, but at this moment Mary Ann didn't care about anyone else's feelings. She was safe in Randolph's love. It was an armour that shielded her, protected her and gave her strength against the likes of Mrs Goodrick and Clara. Even against Miss Edwina.

Edwina was shaking her head sadly. 'Oh my dear Mary Ann. I am so sorry my brother has deceived you in this way. I should have known. I should never have brought you here. Into this house.' Her mouth tightened and now there was a flash of anger in her fine eyes. It was not directed at Mary Ann, but at her absent, callous rake of a brother. Her next words were like a death knell to all Mary Ann's hopes and dreams.

'Randolph is engaged to a girl in Yorkshire and has been for the past twelve months. He will never marry you, my dear.'

Twenty-Seven

Mary Ann flew to her attic bedroom and slammed the door. She threw herself on to the bed and gave way to a storm of hysterical weeping.

'Mary Ann, let me in. I've got to change my clothes.' Clara's plaintive voice was at the door, but Mary Ann did not answer.

A few minutes later there was a sharp rap on the door and Nellie Goodrick shouted, 'Open this door at once or it'll be the worse for you, miss.'

Still, Mary Ann made no reply. Only when Edwina knocked and said in her gentle way, 'Please, Mary Ann, let me come in. Let me talk to you, my dear,' did she respond, her voice muffled with tears, 'Go away and leave me alone.'

She refused even to open the door so that Clara could come to her bed. She neither knew nor cared where the girl spent the night. Not until lunchtime the following day, when she heard that Randolph was back, did Mary Ann wash her face, tidy her hair, smooth down her dress and open the door to go downstairs. She marched straight through the great hall to Randolph's den. Anger now carrying her along, she was determined to face him.

She didn't even bother to knock but flung the door wide and stepped into the room.

'What the . . .?' he began, rising from his chair behind the desk. 'Oh,' he said then, sinking back. 'It's you.'

'Yes, it's me,' she said and stood before his desk. 'Is it true? Are you going to marry a girl in Yorkshire?'

Frowning, Randolph stood up again. 'That has nothing to do with you.'

'Nothing to do with me,' she screamed at him. 'When you seduced me in this very room. There . . .' She flung out her arm towards the hearthrug. 'Right there. You made love to me and whispered promises you didn't mean to keep. How dare you say it has nothing to do with me?'

He moved around the desk to stand in front of her. His eyes glittered with anger and his mouth twisted in a sneer. His handsome face, even to the besotted Mary Ann, was suddenly ugly. 'You didn't really think I would marry you, did you? Not even you could be so naïve, surely?'

Mary Ann gasped, staring up at him, shocked now at the change in the man she loved. Then she narrowed her eyes calculatingly as she said, 'What if I was to tell you I'm expecting your child?'

He returned her gaze with equal calculation. 'Are you?' he asked dispassionately.

'What if I was?'

He shrugged. 'You'd be taken care of.' Then with a cold smile, completely devoid of any feeling, he added, 'Just like several before you have been.'

'I hate you,' Mary Ann spat between clenched teeth, and she balled her fists and pummelled his chest. 'I hope I never see you again as long as you live.'

He caught hold of her wrists and held her fast. 'Mary Ann, my little Mary Ann.' Now his voice was soft and seductive and his sudden change of tone was her undoing. She was trembling at his touch. She loved him, she couldn't help it. However badly he treated her, she could not stop loving him. She gave a sob and fell against him. He put his arms around her and kissed her hair. 'My dear,

dear girl, you must understand, in my world, in my family, one cannot always marry where one's heart lies. It is my duty, but I will always . . .'

She dragged herself free of him, anger surging through her once more. She was on a seesaw of emotion – one moment she loved him – the next she hated him and the violence of her passion frightened her. She wanted to hit him, to wipe that arrogant, self-confident smile off his face. She really felt in that instant as if she could kill him. 'Duty?' she screamed at him again. 'What do you mean, duty? If you loved me, you wouldn't be planning to marry someone else.'

Randolph spread his hands, as if in helplessness. 'I have to, Mary Ann, but it doesn't mean . . .'

'Oh yes, it does. I'm leaving and I'll never see you again.'

She whirled around and made for the door, but his voice followed her mockingly, 'I don't think you mean that, my dear. If I so much as crooked my little finger, I think you'd come running.'

'Aw lass, whatever's the matter?'

Mary Ann flew into Bessie's open arms, weeping hysterically.

'There, there,' Bessie tried to soothe her.

Mary Ann clung to her, burying her face against the stout woman's shoulders. 'Oh Auntie Bessie, Auntie Bessie. He said he loved me. I know he loves me. They're wrong. They're all wrong.'

'Who? Who are you talking about? Now come, lass. Stop that crying and tell me what's happened.' Bessie was firm now.

'Perhaps I can enlighten you, Bessie.' Edwina's calm

voice spoke behind them. Her tone was flat with disappointment and concern.

'Oh Miss Edwina. I didn't know you'd come with her. Come in, come in. Sit down. I'll make some tea.'

Edwina held up her hand. 'Please don't trouble, Bessie. We need to talk to you before your menfolk come home. Mary Ann.' Her tone took on a note of firmness, too. 'Now stop that crying.'

But Mary Ann only wailed louder.

Bessie disentangled herself from the girl's clinging arms and took hold of her. Gently she shook her. 'Stop that this instant and sit down.'

Mary Ann's cries rose hysterically until, with a desperate glance at Edwina, Bessie raised her hand and slapped the girl smartly on the cheek. The noise ceased and for a moment Mary Ann seemed not to breathe. Shocked, she stared at Bessie and then collapsed weeping into Bert's big armchair.

'I think I'll make that tea, miss, if you don't mind. I could do with some, ne'er mind anyone else.'

Edwina nodded and, whilst Bessie swiftly mashed a pot of tea from the kettle that was already boiling over the fire in the range, she patted Mary Ann's shoulder and talked quietly to her. By the time Bessie had poured out three cups of tea, the young girl's sobs had subsided to inconsolable hiccups.

'Now,' said Bessie briskly. 'Will one of you please tell me what is going on?'

'I'm afraid it's my brother, Randolph, up to his old tricks, Bessie,' Edwina began as she took the cup and saucer handed to her.

Mary Ann felt them both look at her and then exchange a knowing glance between them. Then they began to talk almost as if Mary Ann were not present.

Edwina sighed heavily. 'You know what he's like. What he's always been like. Two young girls have been dismissed in the past because they were pregnant, and in each case they swore that Randolph was the father of their babies. Another left, also pregnant, but loyally refused to name the father.' Edwina sighed. 'But I always had my own suspicions. Goodness knows how much my father must be paying out even now to help those poor girls.'

Mary Ann saw Bessie's lips tighten and felt her glance upon her, but for the moment, she said nothing.

'It seems,' Edwina went on sadly, 'that he has filled Mary Ann's head with the notion that he is in love with her. The poor child believed he would marry her. Then she found out that he had gone to Yorkshire. She locked herself in her room. Not one of us could get her to come out. I was on the point of coming to you for help, Bessie, but then Randolph returned.'

'Yorkshire?' Bessie looked puzzled.

Edwina nodded. 'That's where Celia Thompson lives. Randolph's fiancée. He'd gone to see her to . . . to discuss plans for their wedding.'

'And does this Miss Thompson know about his philandering?' Bessie asked harshly.

Edwina smiled wryly. 'You don't mince your words, do you, Bessie?'

'Never have, miss, and I doubt I'll start now.' For a brief moment the two women shared an intimacy borne of their long knowledge of each other, which excluded Mary Ann. Then Edwina sighed heavily. 'I doubt it. And I expect he'll carry on just as before even once they are married.'

Bessie gave a snort of disapproval.

'You know how it is, Bessie. Randolph is now the son

and heir to our family's estates. He must make a good marriage.'

'I thought all that sort of thing had been swept away by the war. Seems I was wrong.'

'I wonder if it will ever be completely swept away, as you put it. Not in our – forgive me, dear Bessie – in our class.' She reached out and touched Bessie's hand and for a moment, despite the gravity of their conversation, she smiled impishly. 'You know I have always considered myself most fortunate to have been born the girl in the family. At least I can choose whom I marry. And I did.' Her eyes clouded. 'My only misfortune was to lose him.'

'Yes, miss. I know. Your Mr Christopher was a lovely man.' Bessie leant closer to her. 'But what would have happened if you had chosen someone of whom your family disapproved, eh? Just you tell me that.'

Edwina wrinkled her forehead and sighed. 'Yes, I suppose you are right. Things might have been very different then, if father had not approved of Christopher.'

'I'm sure they would have been,' Bessie said wryly. 'And it happens in other walks of life, an' all. Look at our Dan, for instance. It's taken Jack Price long enough to decide that Susan can start walking out with him again.'

'Is that what you're saying,' Mary Ann blurted out now. 'That Randolph won't marry me because his father won't approve?'

Mary Ann saw them turn to look at her, surprise in their eyes as if they really had forgotten, for the moment, that she was sitting there listening to every word they said.

Carefully, Edwina put her cup on its saucer and set it down on the table. 'My dear, I cannot hide the fact that Randolph is entering into something of an arranged marriage. There has been an understanding between our families for years that, eventually, Celia would make a suitable bride for . . . for . . .' she faltered and tears came to her eyes, 'for the heir to the Marsh estates. She has no brothers and her father wishes her to marry into a family of equal standing to the Thompsons, who have extensive estates in Yorkshire.'

'She was promised to Mr Arthur, wasn't she?' Bessie put in.

Edwina nodded. 'But after Arthur was killed, Randolph agreed to marry her instead.'

'And she agreed?' Even Bessie, who was versed in the ways of the gentry, sounded amazed. As for Mary Ann, she could scarcely believe what she was hearing.

Edwina shrugged. 'Evidently, yes.'

'So he doesn't love her then?' Hope sprang briefly again in Mary Ann's breast. 'He can't do, if it's all been arranged by their parents.'

'I expect they have become very fond of each other,' Edwina said carefully. 'I'm sure neither of our families would press them into a loveless marriage.' Though she said the words, even Mary Ann could detect that Edwina's tone lacked conviction. Always a truthful woman, Edwina was obliged to add with ill-concealed disapproval, 'Although I expect that Randolph, once he has produced an heir and a spare, will still feel able to find his pleasures elsewhere.'

Mary Ann shuddered. The revelations of the past hour had been a dreadful shock to her. She had understood nothing of the ways of the gentry, yet she knew that Miss Edwina would not lie to her. And Bessie, too, understood every word that was being said and, worse still, accepted it as being the truth.

Although she was calmer now, tears poured down Mary Ann's face as she said bitterly, 'With the likes of me, you mean?'

Neither of the women answered her and Mary Ann bowed her head in shame and cruel disillusionment.

'Hello, love. What are you doing here?'

Dan came into the house, the first home. As he looked more closely at her, his welcoming smile faded. 'Whatever's the matter?' he said at once, unknowingly echoing his mother's first question.

'There's been a bit of bother at The Hall,' Bessie said, bustling between her scullery and the table as she set the tea. 'Can't tell you now, Dan. Bert'll be home in a minute and his tea's not ready.'

Dan sat down opposite Mary Ann, who was sitting huddled close to the range, shivering miserably and, from time to time, still shedding tears.

'Are you poorly, love?'

Again Bessie spoke for her. 'No, she's not. At least, I hope she's not. I'll have to sort that out later. Oh lor', heaven forbid we've that to deal with an' all.'

'Ma? What are you on about?'

'Later, lad. We'll tell you later.'

Suddenly, Mary Ann jumped up. 'Stop talking about me as if I'm not here. And I'm not staying here while you tell them all. I don't want them all laughing at me. Duggie and . . . and . . .'

Bessie set a meat and potato pie on the table and turned to face her. 'Now you just look here, m'girl. There's no one in this house going to laugh at you. You're part of this family. They're like brothers to you and don't you forget it. Duggie may be a little scallywag at times, but 'is heart's in the right place and, besides, it's no more than you deserve. You've been a silly little girl and—'

Mary Ann covered her ears. 'Stop it. Stop it. I won't listen.'

With that she stumbled towards the door, knocking against furniture as she went. 'I won't stay here another minute. I won't stay where I'm not wanted. I'll chuck myself in the river. Nobody cares . . .'

She flung open the back door and flew across the yard, her running feet echoing back into the house as mother and son stared at each other, stunned into silence.

Twenty-Eight

Mary Ann hid behind a stack of barrels on Miller's Wharf. She curled herself into a ball, hugging her knees to her chest and burying her face in her skirt.

She heard Dan's urgent, frantic voice. 'Mary Ann? Mary Ann, where are you?' Then she heard Bessie, puffing and panting, arrive. They were standing just the other side of the barrels now and Mary Ann could hear every word they said quite plainly.

'I've just passed ya dad coming home. He'll leave a note for the lads to follow us and he'll be here himself in a minute.'

'She can't have got far.' Dan's tone was distracted. He was hardly listening to what his mother said. 'I was right behind her.' He was moving away from Mary Ann's hiding place, his voice fading as he neared the edge of the wharf over the water.

'She wouldn't really do what she said, Mam, would she? I'll never forgive myself if anything happens to her.'

'It's not your fault, lad. It's that devil at The Hall up to his tricks again. Ee, it's me to blame if anyone is. I should have known better than to let a pretty little thing like her go up there, but – well – I thought with Miss Edwina looking after her, he'd leave her alone.'

There was a pause and then very faintly, so that Mary Ann had to strain to hear her, Bessie said, 'Poor little lass. She only wanted to be loved. That's all it'd be.'

Mary Ann held her breath as she heard Dan say, 'That's what I mean. That's why I feel so badly. I should have . . .' His voice faded completely as they moved on, searching the riverbank.

She stayed hidden for a few moments longer, then she crept out and tiptoed towards the edge of the wharf, standing right on the tip of the planking. She looked down at the dark, swirling water, wondering just how deep it was. She couldn't swim and it would be very cold. She might get swept away by the current, but Dan was only a few yards away anxiously scanning the banks of the river. She could see them, vague shapes in the gathering dusk.

Mary Ann tensed herself, gave one last glance towards Dan and Bessie, and then drew in a deep breath. As she jumped into the water, she let out a piercing shriek that penetrated the night and brought Dan running.

The dark, cold water swirled around her, the strong current carrying her downriver, dragging at her clothes and sucking her beneath the surface. She struggled, pushing upwards, her lungs bursting. She didn't mean it. She hadn't meant to die. She didn't want to die. She just wanted . . .

And then strong arms were reaching for her. Safe hands held her and pulled her upwards and she gulped in the sweet, cold air.

There were no angry words as Dan carried her home, Bessie puffing alongside. No recriminations. Only loving, tender concern from each member of the family. Even Duggie fetched the tin bath and filled it with water from the boiler and then stood outside in the scullery whilst Bessie stripped Mary Ann's wet clothes and helped her into the bath. Then the older woman knelt on the peg rug and soaped her gently.

'There, there, lass. It's over now. You must forget all about him. He's not for you.' She gave a snort of condemnation. 'He's not for any nice girl, if you ask me. But then I suppose that poor lass they've chosen will have to take him on. Me heart bleeds for her, whoever she is.'

Mary Ann had been silent from the moment Dan had plunged into the river and pulled her out, spluttering and coughing. She had clung to him, burying her face against his neck as he had carried her home. She had not cried, had not spoken, but now she lifted her face and looked into Bessie's eyes as she said, 'Celia. Her name's Celia and she lives in Yorkshire.'

Bessie nodded. 'Aye, I know. Celia Thompson.' Her mouth was a tight, grim line.

'But why, Auntie Bessie? Why's he going to marry her if he doesn't love her?'

Again Bessie snorted in a most unladylike manner. But Bessie Ruddick would have been the first to admit that she was no lady and, by her next words, it was clear that she had no wish to be. 'Love's got nowt to do with it, lass. Not in their circles. Arranged marriages, that's what happens in their class. Well, all I can say, Mary Ann, is that I'm glad I was born on a ship on the river to plain and ordinary folk. Miss Celia Thompson's got my sympathy.'

'Do . . . do you know her? Have you ever seen her?'

'No. I haven't been up to The Hall since Mr Arthur got killed. 'Course I see Miss Edwina. I'm very fond of her, but I haven't much time for some of the others. Mrs Marsh is all right, in her way, and Mr Arthur was a nice young man, but he's gone now, poor feller.' She paused and then sniffed disparagingly. 'I never did think much to the master, to tell you the truth, and as for that other devil, Mr High and Bloody Mighty Randolph Marsh, well, I wouldn't spit on him if he was on fire.' She levered herself up from her kneeling position and added, 'Come on now, lass. Get yasen out of that water. Let's get you dry and let poor Dan get into the bath. He'll catch a chill, else, and you wouldn't want that now, would you?'

An hour later, the whole family was seated around the fire, Mary Ann holding a steaming mug of cocoa with a drop of whisky in it that Bert had fetched for her from The Waterman's Arms. Dan sat close by Mary Ann, casting anxious glances at her every few seconds.

'You can have my bed tonight. I'll sleep on the couch in the front room.'

'Up you go, then, lass,' Bessie said kindly and, as if adding the second part of the same sentence, Bert said, 'And have a good night's sleep, love. You'll feel better in the morning.'

Mary Ann put her mug down and stood up. She swayed a little and put her hand to her forehead. She gave a little gasp and, immediately, Dan was at her side.

'I'll carry you up.' Without waiting for any protest, he picked her up in his strong arms. 'Duggie, open the doors for me, will you?'

Duggie sprang up and leapt towards the door leading to the stairs. Then he bounded up the stairs ahead of them to open the door to his brother's room, Dan being the only one of the three brothers who now had a room to himself since Mary Ann had moved out to live in at The Hall. He went to the bed and pulled back the covers so that Dan could lay her down. Then gently he pulled the bedclothes over her, tucking them warmly around her.

'Thanks, Duggie,' Dan said, 'I'll be down in a moment.'

For the first time that evening, Duggie grinned, knowing himself dismissed. He nodded down at Mary Ann. 'Good night, Mary Ann. Sleep tight. Watch the bugs don't bite.'

Mary Ann smiled weakly at him, but she did not speak.

As the door closed behind Duggie, Dan sat on the edge of the bed and took her hand into his. His touch was warm and comforting and Mary Ann closed her eyes.

'Now promise me, Mary Ann,' Dan said, his voice even deeper with anxiety, 'that you won't ever do such a thing again. No man's worth that.'

Mary Ann squeezed two tears from her eyes. Her chin quivered and then she opened her eyes and looked at him, hoping she looked the picture of abject misery. 'I . . .' she began, her voice cracked and thick with hurt. Then latching on to the words she had heard Bessie utter, she said, 'I just wanted someone to love me.'

She felt him squeeze her hand even tighter. 'We love you, Mary Ann. You know we do. All of us. Even,' he smiled slightly, 'that young rascal Duggie.'

'I know. I know you do. But I meant . . . I mean I want someone to love me more than just . . . just like a brother.'

'Mary Ann,' he breathed and leant towards her.

She sat up suddenly and flung her arms around his neck, pressing her cheek to his face. 'Oh Dan, why couldn't you love me when I wanted you to? Why couldn't you fall in love with me? If only you had, then this might never have happened. I would never have fallen for Mr Randolph. I just wanted someone to love me and take care of me.'

His arms were around her slim waist and she could feel the warmth of his hands on her body. 'Mary Ann, Mary Ann,' Dan whispered, burying his face in her hair. 'I'll

take care of you. I'll never let anyone hurt you again.
I promise you.'

She felt a shudder run through him as he kissed her
neck and she felt once more the shiver of delight run
through her own body as his hands caressed her.

And then he was kissing her, cupping her face between
his hands and murmuring, 'You're so sweet. You're so
pretty. My little Mary Ann.' His lips were seeking her
forehead, her eyes and, lastly, her lips.

Exhilaration coursed through her. Dan would love her.
Dan would take care of her. Dan would never hurt her
like Randolph had done. She would forget all about
Randolph Marsh and, from this moment on, it was Dan
she would love.

'Now, lass,' Bessie began briskly the following morning
when Mary Ann at last appeared downstairs, bleary-eyed
and yawning. 'Bert and the lads have gone to their work,
but they all said I was to give you their love. Feeling a bit
better, are you?'

Mary Ann nodded and yawned again. She pulled the
shawl around her shoulders and sat in Bert's armchair,
putting her bare feet on the warm brass fender.

'Here, get this down you. A nice bowl of porridge. Put
hairs on ya chest, will that.'

Mary Ann took the proffered bowl and spooned the
porridge slowly into her mouth, hunching her shoulders
and bending towards the fire.

'Here, let me stir that fire up a bit, if you're cold.'

Having done so, Bessie sat down in the chair opposite
and Mary Ann felt the woman's thoughtful gaze upon
her. 'Now, lass. What are you going to do? Miss Edwina
called this morning. She says it'd be better if you didn't

go back to The Hall, but she can find you extra work at the school, if you'd like that.'

Mary Ann said nothing.

'What about it, eh?'

Mary Ann shrugged, but still she remained silent.

'Have you a better idea?'

Mary Ann shook her head.

'Well, then?'

Mary Ann lifted her shoulders again and then, looking straight into Bessie's eyes, she smiled as she said, 'It won't be for long anyway. Whatever I do.'

'Aw now, come, lass,' Bessie flapped her hands. 'Don't talk that way. You mustn't think of—'

'No, no, I didn't mean that Bessie. What I meant was, I won't be able to work for much longer.'

Bessie's mouth dropped open and then she groaned and closed her eyes. 'Oh no. Not that. I was afraid you might be. Aw lass, no.'

'Dan's told you? I didn't think you'd mind. I thought – I hoped you'd be pleased.'

'Pleased? How can I be pleased? You no more than a bairn yasen and now you're going to bring another into the world.' She frowned as if she had suddenly realized what Mary Ann had said. 'Dan? What's Dan got to do with it? Did you tell him last night? Does he know?'

Mary Ann shook her head. 'Auntie Bessie, I don't think we're talking about the same thing. You think I'm carrying Mr Randolph's child. Is that it?'

Bessie nodded.

'Well, I'm not.' That much she was sure of and now she hoped to bluff it out that she had ever lain with Randolph Marsh. That wasn't the sort of thing Bessie would like if Mary Ann were to become her daughter-in-law.

Bessie let out a huge sigh of relief. 'Oh, thank the good Lord for that.' Then she frowned. 'So if that's not it, just what are you on about?'

Mary Ann set her empty bowl down on the hearth and then smiled at Bessie. 'I'm not going to be able to work for Miss Edwina much longer because I'm going to be too busy looking after my husband.'

'Oh now, look, Mary Ann. You must get it into that head of yours, he's not going to marry you. His sort . . .'

Mary Ann shook her head. 'I'm not talking about Mr Randolph. I don't want to talk about him ever again. I don't even want to hear his name mentioned.'

'Then . . .?'

Bessie was clearly puzzled and Mary Ann's smile widened as she added, 'I'm going to marry Dan.'

If Mary Ann had hoped to drop a bombshell into Bessie's lap, she had certainly succeeded.

'Dan? Our Dan?' Bessie blustered, her round face reddening. 'But . . . but he's courting. He's walking out with Susan Price.' She shook her head and then leant towards Mary Ann, taking the girl's hand gently into her own. 'Look, love. You've got it all wrong. Our Dan was just being kind to you last night. He loves you, yes. Like we all do. Like a daughter or a sister. But if he's going to marry anyone, love,' her tone became even gentler, 'it's Susan.'

'No,' Mary Ann shook her head firmly. 'No. He's going to marry me. I know he is.'

That evening when Dan stepped over the threshold, his mother's tirade hit him with a force that was almost a physical blow. From the bedroom, Mary Ann heard the raised voices and crept downstairs to listen.

'Whatever are you thinking of, Dan Ruddick? I'm surprised at you. Leading the poor girl on after all she's been through. First, that rotten home life she had as a bairn and then that bastard at The Hall and his philandering ways, taking advantage of a young and vulnerable lass. But you! I'd have thought you'd have had a bit more sense.'

'Hold on, Ma, hold on.' Mary Ann heard his deep voice and could imagine him holding out his hands, palms outward, to fend off his mother's onslaught. 'What are you on about?'

'You! That's what I'm on about. Leading that little lass on to believe you're going to marry her. How could you?'

'Marry her?' Dan sounded surprised, as if the thought had not even occurred to him.

'That's what she said, but how she's got that idea into her head, I don't know, unless you've put it there.'

There was a moment's silence whilst Mary Ann held her breath before she heard Dan say again, 'Marry her.'

Now the words were spoken softly, as if he was rolling the idea around in his mind, pondering, even savouring, the notion.

'Well,' Mary Ann heard him say at last. 'Why not? Why shouldn't I marry her, Ma?'

Twenty-Nine

The wrangling within the Ruddick household went on for days. Whilst, in the main, the argument occurred when she was out of the room, Mary Ann was usually somewhere in the cramped house and could scarcely fail to overhear most of what was said.

'You're not serious, our Dan,' Bessie persisted. 'I don't want you hurting her. She's had enough broken promises to last her a lifetime. Tell her the truth now, lad, before it's gone too far. Tell her that she misunderstood you. That you were just feeling sorry for her because she was so upset. She'll understand. But tell her now, Dan.'

'I'm telling her no such thing, Mam. Besides, she needs someone like me to take care of her.'

'What about Susan, lad?' Bert asked in his quiet and thoughtful way when he was being serious.

'Oh, she'll be all right.' There was an unusual trace of bitterness in Dan's tone as he said, 'She'll always have her *father* to take care of her.' Gently, now, he asked them, 'But who's going to take care of little Mary Ann?' Then his voice hardened as he added, 'The likes of Randolph Marsh?'

To this, his family had no answer.

Bert shook his head sadly, 'You'll likely lose your job with old man Price if you jilt his one and only daughter. Besides, you've waited months, years almost, to get her back after that bit of trouble.'

'It was she who came back to me, if you remember, Dad. And to be honest, if Susan had thought that much about me, she'd have stood by me at the time it all happened, never mind what her father said.'

'Oh, now you're being unfair, Dan,' Bessie said.

At this moment Mary Ann stepped into the room and went straight to stand by Dan.

Keeping his voice low and his anger in check, although Mary Ann could see that his eyes were sparkling with defiance, Dan said levelly, 'No, I don't think I am, Mam. Susan knew very well that her dad was being unjust, that I had nowt to do with Sid Clark being aboard our ship.'

'You can't expect a lass like her to go against her father, though.'

Now Mary Ann, putting her hand on Dan's arm, spoke up. 'I would have done. I'd have run away with Dan sooner than do what me dad told me.'

Bessie and Bert glanced at her, looked at each other and then away.

'Aye well,' Bessie murmured. ''Appen you would, lass. But in your case, no one would have thought any the worse of you. But . . .' Bessie bit her lip, hesitating to hurt this young girl, whom she loved like one of her own, any more than she had been wounded already. But it had to be said and Bessie Ruddick had never been one to shirk saying what needed to be voiced. Gently, she added, 'But you do see, don't you, that Susan comes from – well – a loving, caring home. Her father was bound to be cautious for her, and though I could have hit him mesen for not believing in our Dan, even I could see how Jack Price must have felt. D'you see?'

Mary Ann shook her head. 'No. If Dan loves me and he doesn't love Susan, then what's the problem?'

'The problem,' Duggie, for once very serious, put in, 'is

that Dan will be without a job. And Price will see to it that he doesn't get another round here.' Then his impish sense of fun got the better of him, even in the midst of all the wrangling. 'I think you'd do a lot better to marry me, Mary Ann, than this old sobersides, anyway.' He leant across and tweaked her nose playfully. 'What do you say?'

Coyly, Mary Ann put her head on one side. 'Why, thank you, kind sir. But I must decline your offer. I am already spoken for.'

Dan, covering her hand where it lay upon his arm, smiled down at her. 'There, it's settled then. We'll be married as soon as you're sixteen.'

And they were. There was nothing Bessie or Bert or his two brothers could do to dissuade Dan from his decision. Even Susan, visiting Waterman's Yard, her eyes red-rimmed from weeping, could not break his resolve.

Mary Ann, listening outside the door into the kitchen, overheard her pleading with him.

'My father says he will give you your own ship. You can be a skipper, Dan.'

'That's bribery, Susan,' Dan said harshly, his tone implying how shocked he was that Susan should resort to emotional blackmail.

'It's not,' Susan cried. 'If you were his son-in-law, there's nothing my father wouldn't do for you. He just wants me to be happy.'

'It's not so long back that he wouldn't have had me as a son-in-law if I'd been the last man on earth.'

'You can't blame him for that. He was only trying to protect me.'

Mary Ann heard Dan's deep sigh. 'I know and I don't blame him. Not really. Not any more.'

'So why? Why are you marrying this girl? Everyone

knows she's been Randolph Marsh's latest . . .' She hesitated before adding scathingly, 'Piece.'

'Susan . . .'

'Well, it's true. She's no better than she should be. Why are you marrying her? Because I know you don't love her. Is she expecting his child? Is that it?'

'No, she isn't,' Dan said sharply.

'Are you sure?' Susan asked quietly, almost pityingly as if she believed Dan was being duped by Mary Ann's wiles.

Grudgingly, as if feeling disloyal in having to offer proof, Dan said, 'I am sure because me mother told me she wasn't. I don't think she's even – well, you know – been with him.'

Susan gave a humourless laugh. 'If you believe that, Dan Ruddick, you're even more gullible than I thought you were.'

'Susan, please, try to understand. I have to take care of her. She needs someone to love her and look after her.'

'And you're the only poor fool around to do it, are you, Dan?' Susan's tone was filled with sadness now as she said, 'If there's nothing more I can say to you, I'll go.' Her voice softened as she added, 'I wish you well, Dan. I hope you will be happy. I mean that, because I love you and I always will. You might not believe that it grieves me to say it, but I think she will only bring you unhappiness, my dear.'

Susan must have turned away from him, for the kitchen door opened so suddenly that Mary Ann was caught eavesdropping. Susan's eyes narrowed as she looked into Mary Ann's startled eyes. Then she leant closer and whispered so that Dan, still in the other room, would not hear. 'Just you look after him, Mary Ann Clark, else you'll have me to reckon with. You hear me?'

Then before Mary Ann could think of a sharp retort, Susan was gone, running across the yard, her hand to her face as if she could no longer hold back the tears.

Mary Ann watched her go.

Who would have thought that quiet little Susan Price would have had quite so much spirit? For a brief moment, even Mary Ann admired her.

Once the news got out, of course, the other residents of Waterman's Yard had their say too. Battle lines were drawn with Bessie, now defending her son to outsiders, and Minnie Eccleshall on one side. Opposing them were Gladys and Phyllis. But most vociferous of all was Amy Hamilton.

Monday morning brought them all into the yard's communal wash-house, face to face. And from Dan's bedroom window where she was sleeping now, Mary Ann heard it all.

'What's it got to do with you anyway, I'd like to know?' Bessie said, declaring war.

'Can't abide to see a good man go to waste on a little trollop like that,' Amy said primly. 'We all know what she's been up to with *him*.' She jerked her thumb in the direction of The Hall.

'She's not in the family way, if that's what you're thinking. She's not having to get married.' Bessie picked up her washing basket and turned to go indoors before her sharp tongue could say more.

'You bitch, Bessie Ruddick,' Amy muttered, her face fiery red.

'Here, here, there's no need for that sort of talk,' Minnie sprang at once to Bessie's defence. 'She only said—'

223

'I know what she said,' Amy spat. 'She's got a long memory and an even longer knife. And she knows how to wound with it, an' all.' Amy turned and stormed towards her own back door.

Inside the Ruddicks' house, Mary Ann ran down the stairs as Bessie came in.

'What was all that about?' she asked.

'Something and nothing,' Bessie said. 'Get the kettle on. I could do with a cuppa after that.'

Mary Ann busied herself and they were sitting at the table pouring out the tea when Minnie poked her head round the door. 'Any left in the pot?'

'Come on in, then.' Bessie sighed and rested her arms on the table.

Minnie sat down. 'You going to tell us then?'

'I don't know if I should,' Bessie murmured. 'Doesn't seem fair. 'Specially now.'

'Oh, go on, Bess. You know I can keep a secret. I'm not like Phyllis. And Mary Ann here, well, she'll not say owt, will you, lass?'

Mary Ann, having witnessed Minnie defending her alongside Bessie, smiled. ''Course not, Mrs Eccleshall.'

Bessie sighed. 'It's a long time ago. Me and Bert had been married nearly two years and I was expecting our Dan when the Hamiltons came to live in the yard. George had got a job at Phillips' Engineering and they'd moved here from Lincoln. Their little boy, Ron, was about eighteen months old, I think.' Bessie paused a moment and smiled sadly, remembering the golden-haired little boy learning to walk on the uneven cobbles of Waterman's Yard. 'But living in the yard then was old Mrs Jaggers and she was *the* biggest gossip I have ever met in me life.'

'What? Worse than Phyllis?' Minnie asked incredulously.

'Oh, ten times worse than her. Anyway, only a few weeks after the Hamiltons moved in, Mrs Jaggers was spreading it around that they'd had to get married. That Amy was six months gone when she walked down the aisle.'

'How had she found that out?'

Bessie shrugged. 'How does Phyllis find things out? They know someone, who knows someone, who knows.'

Minnie was thoughtful for a moment before she said, 'I'd never have thought it of Amy, though, of all people. She's always seemed so prim and proper.'

'It can happen to the best of us,' Bessie said, and then she winked at the other two like a guilty conspirator. 'I have to admit, even I was lucky not to get caught 'afore Bert put the ring on me finger.'

The two women laughed together and Mary Ann joined in, though her laughter was with relief, realizing now, even more than before, just how lucky she had been that she was not at this moment carrying Randolph Marsh's bastard.

Thirty

'So what are you going to do now that you're married?'

Once all the legalities, because of Mary Ann's age, had been satisfied, they were married quietly in the parish church. The only witnesses present were the Ruddick family members and Minnie and Stan Eccleshall.

Once back in Waterman's Yard for the 'reception', for which Bessie had spent the whole of the previous day baking, she asked the question and went on, 'It's high time you were making some decisions. All I've heard so far is a lot of talk. But you know you can both stay here, Dan, in your room, if that's what you want?'

Dan smiled at his mother. 'I know, I know. You'd like to keep all your chicks under your roof, wouldn't you, Ma?'

'She can't wait to be a grandma,' Duggie teased. 'That's what it is. So you'd best get up them stairs, our Dan, and get cracking.'

Everyone laughed, though Mary Ann lowered her head, pretending to be shy at the mention of their wedding night. In truth, she was rather nervous at the thought of what would happen when she and Dan climbed into bed together. Not because she was ignorant, for she knew all too well what to expect. But Mary Ann was desperate to deceive Dan into thinking that for her it was the first time. She thought back to the night Randolph had first made love to her. To her chagrin, she felt the familiar thrill run through her when she remembered his touch and his seductive words.

No, no, she must not think of him. She must think only of Dan now.

Thoughtful as ever, Dan was drawing the conversation away from such delicate matters, though Mary Ann hoped fervently that he did not even begin to guess at the real cause of her blushes. That night, she knew, she would have to be a very good actress.

'I shall have to start looking for a job tomorrow.' He glanced apologetically at his new wife. 'I'm afraid a honeymoon is out for us at the moment, love.'

Mary Ann slipped her hand into his and squeezed it. 'I don't mind. As long as we're together.'

Duggie made a sound as if he was going to be sick, which earned him a gentle clout from his mother. 'Don't you mock it, son,' she laughed. 'You'd do better to find yasen a nice girl.'

Duggie put his hands over his heart and threw back his head dramatically. 'But my heart is broken, Mam. Dan has stolen the only girl I've ever loved.'

The whole family laughed and Duggie's grin was the widest of all. 'There's one good thing about it, though,' he said. 'She's really our sister now, isn't she?'

Mary Ann felt a warm glow run through her, and inside her head she repeated the vows she had so recently spoken in the church. She would be a good wife to Dan. Lovingly, she smiled up at him and he reached out and touched her face gently with the tips of his fingers.

'Aye,' Bessie was saying. 'And we've got a daughter, 'aven't we, Bert?'

'Yes, light of my life, we have.' He beamed across at the couple, but then his smile faded a little as he added, 'But you're right, Dan. You should start looking straight away for a job. I've asked around for you already, but everyone is so frightened of Price's hold on this stretch of the river, you might have to go further afield.'

The interview with Mr Price a week earlier, Dan had told them all, had been short but nasty. 'He's a vindictive old devil, but I have to hand it to Susan that she hadn't told him before now.'

That had surprised Bessie. 'That day she came here, I thought she'd run straight home and tell him. I thought you were for the sack then, lad.' Bessie had glanced at her son and then away again. She had said no more, but her look had said, 'Susan must still care for you if she has kept it hidden from her father all this time.'

Understanding, Dan had nodded. 'I feel guilty enough about it, without her old man having a go at me.'

'You've no reason to feel guilty,' Mary Ann had said. 'It's no good marrying her if you don't love her. You love me now, don't you?'

'Yes, yes. Of course I do.'

'And it's not as if you were engaged to her or anything, is it?'

That had prompted a wry grimace from Dan. 'Good job I wasn't. Do you know what he said to me? If we'd been officially engaged, he'd have had me up in court for breach of promise. Can you imagine that?'

Bessie had nodded. 'Aye, with Jack Price I can believe anything.' She had looked, then, at her husband. 'What about you, Bert? Is your job safe?'

Bert had wrinkled his brow. 'I reckon. We go back a long way, Jack and me.' Bert tapped the side of his nose and winked at his wife. 'There's things I know about Jack Price that perhaps he wouldn't like aired in public. I reckon he'll let me alone.'

'Couldn't you make him give Dan his job back, then?' Mary Ann asked. 'Couldn't you sort of threaten him?'

Bessie had answered swiftly for her husband. 'It's not in Bert's nature to do things like that.'

'I think it'd be best,' Bert said quietly, 'for you to make a clean break, Dan. It'd only make things very awkward for you if you were to stay on with him, now wouldn't it?'

'Yes,' Dan was forced to agree. 'Yes, you're right, Dad.'

Mary Ann continued to help Miss Edwina at the school, both in teaching embroidery and helping out generally. They had been married for two months and Dan had still not been able to find work.

'I know how difficult things must be for you, Mary Ann,' Edwina said, 'so there'll be a little extra in your pay packet each week until Dan has found another job.'

'Oh thank you, miss. You are kind.' Mary Ann paused and then added, 'You heard then?'

Edwina smiled. 'Not much remains a secret in this town, not even from the so-called gentry.' She pulled a wry face against herself. 'But seriously, how is Dan's search for work progressing?'

Now it was Mary Ann's turn to pull a face and say, 'Not very well. So many people have business with Mr Price and they're not prepared to upset him by giving Dan a job. Mr Price has let everyone know that he believes Dan jilted his daughter and broke her heart.'

Edwina sighed. 'Oh dear.' She was thoughtful a moment and then said, 'There's someone my father knows. A boat owner near Newark. I'll see what I can do. Leave it with me, Mary Ann.'

A week later, Mary Ann ran nearly all the way home, arriving breathless and holding the stitch in her side. 'Dan. Where's Dan?'

'He's out. Why, whatever's the matter?'

Mary Ann's face was overjoyed. 'Miss Edwina's found him a job. At least, she's arranged for him to go and see a boat owner near Newark and she's put in a good word for him, so he can't fail to get it.'

'Here, here, slow down. I can't keep up with you, lass. Sit down and tell me slowly.'

Mary Ann sat down, taking huge gulps of air to steady herself. 'Miss Edwina's father knows a man who owns several boats . . .'

'Ships, love, ships,' Bessie, out of habit, corrected her.

'Ships, then.' Mary Ann was impatient to impart her news. 'And Dan's to go and see him. It's a Mr Sudbury. One of his skippers has just been taken very ill and he's desperate to find someone.'

'That's a bit of luck,' Bessie began and then she clapped her hand to her mouth. 'Oh, that sounds awful towards the poor feller who's ill, but you know what I mean.' Her face clouded. 'Dan's not a skipper though. He hasn't the experience.'

'Mr Price was going to make him a skipper if he'd married Susan, so he must have thought he was capable of being one.'

Bessie was frowning. 'How d'you know that? I didn't know that.'

'Oh, er . . .' Mary Ann realized suddenly that in her excitement she had let her tongue run away with her. 'Dan told me.' Mentally, she crossed her fingers, hoping the lie would not catch her out. She was sure Bessie would not have approved of her eavesdropping.

'Well . . .' Still, Bessie did not sound too sure, but she

smiled and nodded and said, 'At least he can go and see this Mr Sudbury. That's something, ain't it? But I shouldn't get your hopes up.'

Dan travelled to Newark the following day, leaving Mary Ann in a turmoil of excitement until she heard his footsteps in the alleyway that evening. She flew out of the house and across the yard to meet him, Bessie waddling after her as fast as she could. Dan caught Mary Ann in his arms and swung her round.

'I've got a job. I've got a job and what's more, we've got a home, an' all. Mr Sudbury says we can live aboard the ship I'm to skipper. There now, what do you think of that?'

Mary Ann gave a squeal of delight and Bessie clapped her hands. 'I'm that glad for you, I don't know where to put mesen. Wait till Bert hears. And to live aboard, an' all. Oh, I'm that envious. It's a wonderful life, Mary Ann. You'll love it.'

Mary Ann was still hugging him. 'I don't care where we live, as long as I'm with Dan.'

That evening the house was alive with chatter as Dan related all that had happened and everyone plied him with questions.

'Whatever did you tell him?'

'Does he know you've not skippered before?'

'Did he ask for references, 'cos I doubt old Price'd give you the time of day.'

'It's all thanks to Miss Edwina. Oh, but she is good.' This was from Bessie.

'One at a time, one at a time,' Dan grinned happily. 'I

told him the truth. Everything. There was no other way, really, was there? But he's a really nice chap. I took to him and I think he took to me. He's a real, larger-than-life character. He wears a check jacket and trousers and a top hat all the time and always has a cigar in his mouth. And you should hear him laugh. It's so loud it's a wonder we can't hear it from here.' If it was possible, Dan's smile broadened even further. 'It seems that John Sudbury had a run in with Jack Price some years back. He can't stand the man and they're bitter rivals now for trade on this part of the Trent. So, he's very happy to put one over on him. He said he'd heard of me. You know how river folk talk? And he'd heard nowt but good, how I was a good worker and that I was more than ready to take on my own ship. He wants me to take on all the work I can get downriver, to Hull, even into Yorkshire, if I can.'

'How's he paying you, lad?'

'Thirds, Dad.'

Everyone nodded approval, except Mary Ann who looked puzzled. 'What's that mean?'

'It's the way the earnings are shared between the owner and the captain. The owner pays certain expenses out first, then the money that's left is split one-third to the owner, that's Mr Sudbury and then two-thirds to the captain.' Dan grinned, as if he could not, even yet, believe his good fortune.

'And that's all yours?'

'Well, yes, but I'll have a lot of expenses to pay out of my portion. Casual labour, towing, horse-hauling, even lock pennies when we have to go through locks or bridges that have to be operated to let us through and then of course there's our living expenses . . .'

'Oh stop, stop. I don't want to know,' Mary Ann laughed.

Now Dan glanced apologetically at Mary Ann. 'There's just one thing. I had to tell him about the bit of trouble a while back. I thought it best to be completely honest with him. And it was a good job I was, because he'd heard all about it. He put his hand on my shoulder and said that clinched the deal as far as he was concerned. If I could be that honest about that, then he had no more worries.'

'There you are. Haven't I always told you, honesty is the best policy?' Bessie reminded him.

'You have, Ma. You have.'

'It's all down to you and your upbringing that's got Dan that job today, our mam,' Duggie teased, but Bessie only pretended to preen herself and agreed, 'Of course it is.'

The whole house shook with their laughter.

Thirty-One

'Mary Ann? Mary Ann, where are you?' Dan's voice echoed through the house on his return from another trip to Newark a week later.

'Here, Dan, upstairs. I'm just packing,' she called, then scrambled to her feet and hurried down the stairs carrying the pillowcase containing their clothes. 'What is it? Is something wrong?' But when she saw his face, she knew that there was nothing wrong at all. In fact, everything was very right.

His face was a picture of happiness and pride as he held out his hand to her. 'Come with me. I've something to show you. And Mam too. Where is she?'

'Across at Mrs Eccleshall's, I think.'

'Come on . . .' Dan was like an excited schoolboy. He grasped Mary Ann's hand and pulled her outside and across the yard. 'Let's get her. I want her to see it too.'

'What, Dan? What are you on about?'

He turned a beaming smile upon her. 'My ship, of course. Our new home, Mary Ann.'

Mary Ann gasped. 'You've brought her home already?'

Dan nodded as he rapped on Minnie's door, calling impatiently, 'Mam, Mam, are you there?' Unable to wait even the moment it took for the door to be answered, he opened it and called again. 'Mam?'

Bessie appeared. 'Whats the matter?' For a moment her eyes were worried, but she too, on seeing his face, saw she had no cause for alarm. She, quicker to guess than Mary Ann had been, said, 'You've got her? You've brought her home?' She stepped out into the yard and began at once to move towards the alley. 'Let's be 'aving a look-see, then.'

Minutes later, the three of them were standing on Miller's Wharf staring in awe at the sleek lines of the keel.

'She's not new, of course, but she's just been repaired, overhauled and repainted.'

'She looks as good as new.' Bessie's round face was aglow with delight. 'Just look at that paintwork. I like the colours. Blue, white and orange. Very smart. You'll be able to embroider him a pennant in those colours for the mast, Mary Ann.'

'So, how about it, Mam?' Dan asked. 'Are you coming aboard?'

Bessie shook her grey head. 'Oho, I don't know about that, lad. I'm a bit too broad in the beam now to be clambering up and down ladders.'

'Come on,' he coaxed. 'I want you to explain things to Mary Ann.'

'Well . . .' Bessie said, still doubtful, but she allowed Dan to help her aboard his first ship as master.

'I can't get down there,' she said looking askance at the companion down into the stern cabin. 'I'd forgotten how narrow they are.'

'Aw, come on, Mam. Your dad was a big feller, wasn't he? And he managed it.'

'Oh, go on, then,' Bessie said, 'I'll have a go, but don't blame me if I get stuck and have to stay there for your first voyage.'

Dan laughed. 'That's all right. You'd be good ballast if the weather gets rough, Mam.'

'Oh you!' Bessie said and took a swipe at him, but Dan ducked out of the way.

Dan went down the vertical ladder first and helped his mother climb down, followed by Mary Ann.

'Oh Mary Ann, she's beautiful. Just look at this lovely wood.' Reverently, Bessie ran her hands over the varnished mahogany of the cabin's interior. Every panel was a cupboard door, which Bessie was now opening and closing with excitement. 'So compact,' she enthused.

Next to the ladder down which they had climbed was a tiny stove complete with a hob on the top bar of the fireplace for the kettle or pans. It even had a minute brass fender and fire irons. On the opposite side of the ladder, on the port side and round the after end of the cabin, was a locker with cushions on it for seating.

'And that's where you put your coal,' Bessie said, pointing to a part of the locker on the port side. 'And then your pans go under there.' Now she was pointing at the lockers across the end of the cabin. Above this was a drop-leaf table and above that, the polished, built-in cupboards. On the starboard side of the cabin was a double bed.

'And look here.' Bessie was pointing to the opposite side again. 'This is what they call the spareside. It's a spare bed.' Her smile widened. 'This is where your bairn'll sleep. See?'

'Oh, so you think there's going to be one then, Mam?'

'There'd better be, our Dan,' Bessie said, closing the drawer. 'Else I'll want to know the reason why.'

Dan put his arm around Mary Ann's shoulders and gave her a squeeze.

'Oh Mary Ann,' Bessie was saying ecstatically. 'You're going to be so happy here.'

Mary Ann was not so sure. It all looked so small and

cramped and she still had to experience her first trip on the water.

They climbed back up the ladder, Bessie heaving and grunting as she did so, until they all three stood on deck again.

'You'll have to learn how to scull the cog boat,' Bessie said, leaning over to look at the tiny boat moored aft of the ship.

'The what?' Mary Ann gaped at her.

'This little boat.' Bessie beckoned her. 'It's called a cog boat and it's only got one oar and you scull it. Like this.' Bessie demonstrated as if gripping the oar in both her hands and sculling the little boat through the water.

'You'll soon learn how to do it. I used to be a dab hand at it. I could scull faster than me dad by the time I left the river.' She sighed and gave one last look at the small vessel bobbing gently on the rippling river. 'But I reckon my sculling days are well and truly over.' She laughed, but there was a tinge of nostalgia in the sound. 'Reckon I'd capsize it now. It's handy for you to get to shore to do your washing and fetch supplies, an' that. You'll soon get the hang of it all, love.'

Mary Ann thought about the cramped conditions of the cabin, the enclosed bed she would share with Dan, no doubt squashed by his broad shoulders against the side of the bunk, the tiny stove where she would be expected to do all the cooking. Then she looked down at the boat, which was her only means of transport to the shore and, she could not help the thought from entering her mind, her only escape from the ship.

'Mm,' was all Mary Ann said in reply to Bessie, but in that one sound were all the doubts and fears she was feeling inside.

Of course she had realized how different her future life

with Dan aboard this ship would be from the one she had planned as the wife of Randolph Marsh and lady of the manor. But now she was facing the reality of it.

Bessie was dragging her back from her daydreams. 'What you want to do is this. On wash days, you take all your washing in the cog boat and you scull up to the next lock or wherever there's a wash-house. If you time it right, by the time Dan gets there, you're done. And then, when he's travelling without a load you can string a line up in the hold, peg all your washing on it, open the fore and aft hatches and, as you sail, your washing dries lovely.' Bessie beamed with pride. 'And not so much as a smut or speck of dirt to be seen.' She sniffed derisively. 'Not like I have to put up with in the Waterman's Yard. I reckon half the time, me washing comes back in dirtier than what it went out.'

Bessie moved towards the gangway from the ship on to the jetty. 'See you Sunday and don't be late for yar dinner. Twelve o'clock sharp. By the way, Dan.' Bessie paused at the head of the gangway and turned briefly to ask, 'What's this little beauty called?'

Dan's laugh echoed across the river. 'I reckon it's a good omen, Mam. I thought so the minute I saw her. At the moment, she's called the *Maid Marian*. Mr Sudbury calls all his vessels after something to do with Robin Hood, but he's given me permission to alter the spelling a bit.' Dan put his arms around Mary Ann's shoulders and hugged her to him. 'From now on she'll be the *Maid Mary Ann*.'

Mary Ann fell in the river three times before she could scull the cog boat properly.

'I reckon I ought to have learnt you how to swim first,'

Dan laughed as he fished her out of the river for the third time.

'I'll soon have no dry clothes left at this rate,' Mary Ann wailed, standing, dripping, on the deck of the ship and looking the picture of misery. 'I'll never get the hang of the wretched thing,' she muttered, casting a malevolent glance at the little boat bobbing innocently a few feet away.

'You will. You're doing fine. Really you are. It's all a matter of keeping your balance. One day you'll be sculling up and down this river faster than I can sail.'

Mary Ann glanced at him disbelievingly and squelched away to find some dry clothes yet again. Laughing, Dan followed her.

'I've brought you a little present, Dan,' Bert held out a brown paper parcel. 'It's from me and yar mam.'

'Just to let you know how proud we are of you, son,' Bessie beamed.

'Oh Dan, open it, open it,' Mary Ann said, excitedly. She was still a child when it came to presents. Maybe it was because she had had so few in her young life.

Dan unwrapped the gift, a seaman's peaked cap.

'I reckoned now you're going to be a captain, you'd better look the part,' Bert said.

'Thanks, Dad.' Dan grinned and put on the cap. 'It fits perfectly.'

''Course it does,' Bessie said with pretended indignation. 'I took one of your old caps to be sure the size was right.'

'So how's married life then?' Duggie asked as they all sat down to Sunday dinner. 'Recommend it, do you? Reckon I ought to try it?'

'It'd be a brave girl to take you on,' Bessie remarked, setting the joint of beef in front of Bert whilst he sharpened the carving knife on a steel.

Mary Ann joined in the good-humoured teasing, saying, 'Who do you think would have him, Auntie Bessie?'

Before Bessie could answer, there was a knock at the back door and a voice called, 'Coo-ee. Anybody in?'

'It's Phyllis. Now what does she want? Just as we're sitting down to dinner, an' all.' Things had never been quite the same between Phyllis and Bessie since Phyllis had caused the trouble at the Boxing Day party. Ever since then, Phyllis had always seemed to take sides against Bessie in any argument.

'Minnie's my only real friend,' Bessie had said to her family after Phyllis had once again sided with Amy concerning Mary Ann's marriage to Dan. 'The rest of 'em, I can take 'em or leave 'em.'

Bert had smiled and put his arms around her waist. 'But, my angel, if one of them were in trouble, you'd be there, now wouldn't you?'

Bessie had chuckled. 'You know me too well, Bert Ruddick. That's your trouble.'

Now, as they heard Phyllis calling again, 'Anybody home?' Bessie said, ''Spect it's a bit of choice gossip she can't wait to pass on.' She raised her voice and called, 'Come in, Phyllis, if you must.'

Phyllis appeared in the kitchen doorway. 'Oh, I'm sorry. You're having your dinner. I'll come back later.'

'No, no. You might as well say what you've come to say. Bert's not carved yet and I'm still dishing up.' She turned to face her neighbour, hands on hips, and asked, 'What's the Horberry Gazette got for us this week, eh?'

'If you're going to be like that, Bessie Ruddick, I'll keep what I know to myself.'

'Pigs might fly,' Bessie murmured.

'Hush, my angel,' Bert warned softly.

Phyllis appeared to be struggling with her desire to impart her titbit of news and her need to withhold it to spite Bessie. Her desire won. She pulled out a chair and sat down at the table. 'Have you heard the news?'

'Shouldn't think so,' Bessie said and paused as she bent to lift out two tureens of vegetables, keeping warm in the oven. Placing them on the table, she added, 'Not afore you, Phyllis.'

Phyllis beamed. 'There's to be a big wedding at the parish church in June. Mr Randolph and Miss Celia Thompson have announced the date of their marriage. By, it'll be a posh affair, won't it? Nellie Goodrick says she doesn't know how she's going to cope with all the catering. Mind you, she's already made the wedding cake.'

Her news was greeted with silence. Phyllis's glance darted from one to another, coming to rest at last upon the newly married couple. 'And that's not all,' she added, and now there was a sly note in her voice. 'I've heard that Ted Oliver . . . You know him, don't you, Dan? He's the ferryman at Eastlands?'

Dan said nothing, but gave a curt nod.

'They say he's got his feet well and truly under the table with Jack Price. He's courting Price's daughter, Susan. 'Course he's quite a bit older than her, but they say Jack Price is singing his praises to the rooftops.' Again, she glanced around but, when no one spoke, she got up. 'I'll leave you to it, then. Enjoy your dinner.'

Suddenly, Mary Ann's appetite seemed to have deserted her. She glanced at Dan, fearful that he would notice, but he, too, seemed lost in his own thoughts.

Thirty-Two

'I've got my first cargo. Cement from Hull to be 'livered to Lincoln.' Dan seized Mary Ann's hand as if he couldn't wait to set off. 'Are you ready, my pretty little mate?'

'Yes, yes,' she said, trying to look as if her excitement matched his, but, inwardly, her heart was plummeting. This was it, then. Today – right this moment, it seemed – she would have to go aboard the ship, which was to be her home. They'd come back to Bessie's at weekends whenever they could, she knew, but for most of the week they would be travelling up and down the river carrying cargoes this way and that.

'Come on,' Dan was urging. 'We must catch the tide.'

From now on, Mary Ann thought, her life was going to be ruled by the tides, the currents and the wind.

The ebb tide was running strongly and as soon as they were aboard and had cast off, the current began to take them steadily downriver. From the cabin where she was stowing away their belongings, Mary Ann heard Dan calling her. She climbed the ladder and made her way carefully to him.

'When we get into the Humber, Mary Ann, you'll have to help me.' He put his arm around her. 'You're my "mate" now.'

'Oh Dan, I can't. I don't know what to do.'

Dan's arm slipped from her shoulders. 'You'll have to, love,' he said and whilst his tone was still gentle, there was a firmness in it too now. 'I can't manage everything on my own. You'll have to do exactly as I tell you. Look, we'll take our time going downriver, go with the tide and I'll show you what you have to do . . .'

The next few hours were a mesmerism of sails and sheets, rollers, lee boards and bowlines.

'I'll never learn all that, Dan,' she said at last, appalled at what he expected of her. Now Dan's reply was terse. 'You'll have to, Mary Ann. Like I said, you'll have to act as "mate".'

She stared at him. 'I thought when you talked about me being your mate, I thought you meant I was your wife. I didn't think you meant I had to help sail the boat . . .'

'Ship, Mary Ann. It's a ship,' Dan frowned, but she ignored him and gestured vaguely in the direction of the cabin below.

'I knew I'd have to cook and wash, but I didn't expect . . .' Her voice trailed away as she glanced helplessly around her. 'I can't do all this.'

She heard Dan sigh heavily and then, though he seemed to have to make a deliberate effort, he put his arms around her. 'We can't afford to employ anyone else. At least, not yet. Besides, wives often act as mates.'

There were only the two of them aboard ship and whilst keels the size of the *Maid Mary Ann* could normally be handled by a captain and mate, it was not going to be so easy when one of them was a complete novice. The son of a woman who had been born on the river and brought up almost from the time she could walk to help out aboard her father's vessel, Dan, in his excitement at having his first command, had failed to remember that his new wife was totally ignorant of life on the water.

When they got into the Humber, somehow Dan

managed to heave the sails up with Mary Ann doing exactly what he told her.

'There,' he said at last, a little breathless but smiling. 'That wasn't so bad, was it?'

Mary Ann looked down at her hands, roughened and sore with rope burns, and said nothing.

The wind filled the sails and the ship sped forward.

'Now, you ought to learn how to steer. Come here, Mary Ann.'

Gingerly, Mary Ann took hold of the carved wooden tiller.

'There,' Dan said, 'just get the feel of it.' He put his hand over hers and guided her to move the tiller to the right, then to the left, so that she could see in which direction the ship responded. 'See,' he said, 'nothing to it.' But Mary Ann could detect that the confidence he was trying to exude was forced.

'See that tall building on the far bank?' he said. 'Now, try to keep that in line with the bow of the ship.'

Mary Ann, biting her lip with concentration and with the wind from behind them blowing her hair across her face, only nodded.

That first trip to Hull was a near-disaster.

The first time Dan decided to change tack, Mary Ann went for'ard and waited for his commands.

'Stand by,' she heard him shout above the noise of the wind in the sails and the lapping water. Tensing herself against the motion of the ship, she saw him making ready, saw him push the tiller hard over to port and then release one of the ropes on the same side. She heard the rattle as he released the starboard lee board, but when she heard his command, 'Rise ya tack,' instead of operating the tack roller as he had shown her, she released the bowline.

Too late, she heard his bellow, 'No, no, Mary Ann . . .'

The sail flapped and for a moment the ship rocked and Mary Ann knew she had done something wrong, but could not, for the life of her, remember what.

'I'm sorry, I'm sorry,' she screamed, tears blinding her as she fought to keep her balance.

He came to her and, for a moment, held her close. 'It's all right, it's all right. We'll just let the ship come around and we'll try again.' Patiently, he explained again that she should not release the bowline until he commanded 'Let go'.

'I feel sick,' Mary Ann wailed. 'Take me home, Dan. Please, take me home. Take me back to Auntie Bessie.'

Dan took her by the shoulders and held her firmly. 'Now look, Mary Ann, we've got to do this together. You have to try again . . .'

By the time they reached the safety of the port of Hull, Dan was trembling with exhaustion and Mary Ann was crying hysterically. 'I hate it. I'm never coming with you again.'

'That was nothing,' he shouted back, fear at what might have happened snapping his patience. 'What do you think it would have been like if there'd been a real gale blowing?'

'Oh,' she wailed. 'I hate you, Dan Ruddick.' She flung herself away from him and almost fell down the ladder into the cabin, where she scrambled into the bed and buried her face in the pillow.

She heard him follow her down and then felt his touch on her shoulder.

'Don't cry, love,' he said wearily, the anger gone from

his tone now. 'It's not your fault. I should have realized. Mary Ann, I'm sorry. Please don't cry.'

She sniffed, but turned over and sat up, facing him with red and swollen eyes. 'What are we going to do? How are we going to get home again?'

Dan sat down and rested his arm on the table. 'I'm going to send a telegram home and ask Dad, or Duggie, to come to Hull on the train.'

'What are you going to put? "Mary Ann useless. Send help"?'

Dan actually laughed as he said, 'Something like that,' and then added swiftly as he saw her tears begin again, 'No, no, I'm only joking. I'll think of something.'

What he did put Mary Ann never knew, but the following day, whilst the cargo of cement was being loaded at a wharf not far from Hull, Duggie arrived at the station and took a hansom cab to find them.

'I've only come to help out, y'know. Just temporary. Just until you get the hang of it, Mary Ann,' he said. She had expected Duggie to tease her, to make fun of her ignorance of life aboard ship, but to her surprise, he did not. 'Because I'll soon be getting me apprenticeship at Phillips, y'know.'

'Of course you will, Duggie,' Dan said, 'but in the meantime, you can fill in the time helping me.'

'Well, that's all right then. Just so long as everybody knows.'

'You'll be all right sleeping in the fo'c'sle cabin, won't you?' Dan asked.

''Course, I will.' Duggie grinned. 'Won't be the first time, will it?'

'Nor the last,' Dan murmured, but only Mary Ann heard him. Duggie had served with Dan before as mate and there would be no need for words of command to pass between them. Each knew exactly what to do and the ship would be safe in their expert hands.

Louder, Dan said, 'Now, Mary Ann's been busy all morning down in the cabin. We'll go down and see what she's been cooking up, eh? We'll have a bit of dinner and then we can be away on the afternoon tide.'

'We'll need a tow up to Torksey,' Duggie said. 'But if the wind's fair we should be all right once we get into the Fossdyke.'

'How are we going to get towed?' Mary Ann asked, her curiosity overcoming her wish not to be involved with the sailing of the ship at all.

'Sam Bryce runs a daily service with his tugs from Hull all the way to Newark and all points in between,' Duggie explained to her.

'Right,' Dan said, climbing down the ladder into the stern cabin, with Duggie following. 'I'll see to it. But first things first. Me stomach feels as if me throat's been cut.'

Mary Ann went down after them. As she stepped off the last rung and turned to face them, it was to find them both looking at the cold grate in the stove and then at the table on which were three empty plates and, in the centre, a plate of sandwiches.

Dan lifted the edge of one and then turned to Mary Ann in horror. 'Cold fat bacon sandwiches?' he said, unable to keep the disgust from his tone. 'And not even the kettle on for a mug of tea. What on earth have you been doing all the morning, Mary Ann? I thought at least you'd have made us a nice hot stew in the beef kettle.' Before she could answer, Dan caught sight of the piece of embroidery Mary Ann had been working on. He picked it up and thrust it towards her. 'Is this what you call work? Sitting sewing all the morning?'

Easy tears filled Mary Ann's eyes. 'I . . . I didn't know how to light the fire. I couldn't find . . .'

'There's sticks and paper and coal in the locker there.' Dan pointed to the coal locker on the portside of the cabin. 'You could have asked. Duggie hasn't had a bite to eat since leaving home this morning.'

Mary Ann stared at Dan as he ranted on. She had never seen him so angry. Where was her kind, understanding husband? Her own temper flared. 'I can't cook on that silly little stove.'

'Plenty of women do,' Dan thundered, his rage filling the cabin. 'My mam's taught you to cook, hasn't she?'

'Yes, but in her kitchen range. Not on that – that *thing*.'

'It's perfectly adequate. My grandmother cooked for her whole family on just such a stove.'

'Look, it's all right,' Duggie interrupted. 'Mam packed me some grub up and I ate it on the train. And you'll soon get the hang of it, Mary Ann. Look, Dan, let's eat these sandwiches then you go and arrange about a tow and I'll show Mary Ann how to light the fire and she can cook us a meal for tonight.' He looked from one to the other, his good humour and sensible suggestions lightening the atmosphere.

Dan, still glowering, sat down. He picked up a sandwich and ate it in two mouthfuls as if to say, 'Hardly a man's meal, is it?'

Duggie sat on the other side of the table, munching happily and looking around the cabin.

'Snug as a bug in a rug, down here, aren't you? They've fitted it out nice, haven't they . . .?' Duggie prattled on saying nothing in particular and yet keeping up a constant chatter to which neither Dan nor Mary Ann replied.

When he had finished eating, Dan rose and climbed the ladder on to the deck.

'Right, then,' Duggie winked at her. 'Let's get this fire lit.' He leant towards her and, in a conspiratorial whisper, added, 'It'll be all right, love. It must all be very strange for you. And old Dan, well, he's got a lot on his mind. It's a big responsibility, being a captain, you know. Just take no notice of him. I'll help you get a meal started, an' all, and you'll soon get the hang of it.' He winked at her again, patted the bed and said saucily, 'You just give him a cuddle when you get him into this bunk tonight and he'll be all right.'

For the first time since they had left Elsborough, Mary Ann smiled. Suddenly, she threw her arms around Duggie's neck and kissed his cheek. 'Oh Duggie,' she said. 'You are good to me.'

Embarrassed, Duggie released her arms and gently pushed her from him. He laughed, trying to make a joke of her action. 'Give over, Mary Ann, you're a married woman now.'

Mary Ann put her head on one side, her cheeks dimpling prettily. Coyly, she said, 'And you're my brother now, so I'm allowed to kiss you.'

'Come on,' he said again, deliberately changing the subject. 'Let's get this fire lit.'

'Are we going home now?' Mary Ann asked when the cement in bags had been put ashore by the *Maid Mary Ann*'s derrick, straight on to the drays belonging to the builder who had bought the whole shipment. They had passed Elsborough on their way upriver to Lincoln and Mary Ann had sulked because Dan had refused to let her off the ship to go home to Bessie.

'Not yet,' Dan said. 'We're going further upriver, almost to Newark, for a load of Trent gravel.'

'Oh.' Mary Ann turned away before he could see the disappointment on her face.

'But we'll be home on Saturday,' he promised. 'And then you can have a nice hot bath in Mam's kitchen and see all your friends.'

Mary Ann held her breath, afraid that somehow he had guessed her thoughts. Oh, it wasn't the bath she was hankering for, although it would be nice to sink into the tin bath full of deliciously hot water and to smell the scented soap that Bessie shared with her. There was someone Mary Ann wanted to see, even more than she longed to see Bessie again, but her husband was the last person she could tell who that someone was.

'Is it true? Is he really going to marry this . . . this Celia?'

Mary Ann was standing before Edwina's desk in her study at the school.

'Oh, my dear.' Edwina stood up and came around the desk. She put her arms about Mary Ann. 'You must forget all about him and get on with your own life with Dan.' She stood back a little, but still clasped Mary Ann by the shoulders. Her steady gaze held Mary Ann's. 'Dan's a fine man.' Edwina sighed as she added, 'A far better man than Randolph, I have to admit it, even though he's my brother. You should be very happy with Dan. He'll not hurt you.'

'No, I know,' Mary Ann whispered, sorry that she had come here now on an impulse that had made her take a detour from shopping for supplies in the town before returning to the ship. She had thought that she could perhaps talk to Miss Edwina. Although she could talk to

Bessie about anything else, it was impossible to confide in her mother-in-law about her memories of Randolph Marsh.

'I was so happy for you when I heard you were to marry Dan Ruddick. I thought – well – that whatever had happened between you and Randolph had been just an infatuation. You're not the first young girl to fall for his flattery.' Her mouth was tight as she muttered, 'I wish I could say that you would be the last, since he is to be married at the end of this month, but if I'm honest, I can't even say that.' Edwina sighed and let her hands fall from Mary Ann's shoulders. 'Forget about him, my dear. Get on with your life with Dan and be happy. That's all we want for you. That you should be happy.'

Mary Ann lifted her chin and smiled, knowing now that she must never again speak of Randolph in this way to Edwina. Oh, she would continue to see Miss Edwina, for she loved her dearly, and she could perhaps ask after him in a casual manner, just like anyone would ask after her brother. But never again must she speak aloud her secret thoughts of Randolph.

'I will,' she said bravely, hiding the despair she was feeling inside. 'And can you keep a secret?'

She saw the wariness in Edwina's eyes as the young woman nodded.

Mary Ann's smile broadened as she said, 'I think I'm going to have a baby.'

For a moment, fear and disbelief clouded Edwina's eyes. She swayed a little and caught hold of the edge of the desk for support as she gasped, 'Oh no.'

'It's all right, miss,' Mary Ann took hold of her arm gently and led her to a chair. 'It's all right. Really, it is.' She leant over her and, looking straight into Edwina's eyes, she said softly, 'It is Dan's baby, I promise you.'

For a moment, Edwina gazed into her eyes, desperately trying to see if she was telling the truth. Mary Ann couldn't blame Miss Edwina for doubting her. In the past she had told lies when it suited her, had even stolen from Miss Edwina. And only Mary Ann knew how many times she had pinched fruit and cakes from the market stalls in the town when she had been hungry as a child. No, Mary Ann could not blame her. But for once, she was telling the truth. The child she was carrying was indeed Dan Ruddick's.

Though in her heart of hearts, how Mary Ann wished it was not.

Thirty-Three

'I'm going to be a grandma. Oh Bert, do you hear that?'

A month later, Mary Ann's suspicions were confirmed by the doctor.

Bert smiled and winked at Mary Ann. 'I hear, my angel. I hear.' He put his arms about his wife. 'But you don't look old enough, light of my life. No one will ever believe you.'

'Oh, go on with you,' Bessie said, smacking him playfully, her smile so wide, Mary Ann thought, you could tie it at the back of her head. 'And you're going to be a grandpa, Bert. How shall you like that, eh?'

'I shall like it very well. Very well, indeed. When is it due, Mary Ann?'

'In the spring. About the end of February or the beginning of March, I think.'

Bessie clapped her hands. 'It might be born aboard the *Maid Mary Ann*. Somewhere on the river, just like I was. Maybe Dan'll deliver his own bairn, just like my dad helped deliver me. Or, if you're near here, he can fetch me. I hope it's a girl. Oh, you will give me a granddaughter, Mary Ann, won't you?'

Mary Ann laughed. 'I'll try, Mam.' Since her marriage to Dan, Mary Ann had begun to call Bessie 'Mam' rather than addressing her as an adoptive 'Auntie'. It made her feel even closer to the woman, who had been more of a mother to her than her own had ever been. Bessie was delighted. She had allowed the girl to come to it in her own good time, but Mary Ann knew that every time she called Bessie 'Mam' it gave the older woman a little thrill of pleasure.

'But don't you think,' Mary Ann was saying now, 'that Dan will want a boy?'

'You can give him a boy later. There's plenty of time for that. No, we want a girl first, Mary Ann. And you can tell Dan I said so.'

Mary Ann smiled. 'Yes, Mam.'

The winter months passed comparatively uneventfully. Duggie was still mate aboard the *Maid Mary Ann*, although hardly a week went past without him saying, 'Well, I might not be here much longer. I've to see Mr Phillips about an apprenticeship . . .'

Often without Dan's knowledge, he helped Mary Ann. To her surprise it had been Duggie who had patiently helped her to learn what to do aboard the ship; Duggie not Dan, who relit the stove in the cabin for her if it went out; Duggie who praised her first culinary efforts and hung over the side of the ship to help her aboard when she returned in the cog boat.

'You come up, love,' he would call out. 'I'll get the washing . . .' or the shopping or whatever she had been ashore to do.

He had even coaxed her to learn how to take the tiller.

'It'll not happen often, Mary Ann,' Duggie told her. 'But you ought to be able to, just in case we ever get a time when we really need you to help out.'

As her pregnancy advanced Duggie fetched and carried for her more and more. He even sculled the cog boat for her, taking her ashore whenever she needed to go. If Dan didn't need him on deck, Duggie helped with the cooking whilst Mary Ann sat on the seat with her embroidery or sewing tiny garments for the expected baby. Then, when they were all three eating the meal later he would say, with pretended innocence, 'This stew's lovely, Mary Ann.'

Two weeks before Mary Ann's expected confinement, Dan said to her, 'I've got to go to Hull with a cargo, I think you should stay at home with me mam.'

'Oh I can't, Dan. She wants me to have the baby aboard the ship.'

Mary Ann had come to terms with her life afloat, although she had to admit to herself that it was only because of Duggie's presence aboard. She told herself that she was happy, that she should be grateful to Dan, and to Duggie too, for taking care of her. But she could not love her husband in the same way that she had loved Randolph Marsh. When they lay together in the bunk bed and Dan made love to her, the only way she could respond to him was by closing her eyes in the darkness and remembering those times with Randolph. Only then would her body ripple with desire and move in unison with Dan's hunger. Sometimes she bit so hard on her lower lip to stop herself from calling out Randolph's name that she drew blood.

When Dan said, 'You really have taken to the life now, haven't you, Mary Ann? I was so worried at first that you would find it so cramped aboard ship. That you'd feel . . . restricted,' Mary Ann had to bite back the hasty retort that it was only thanks to Duggie if she had. Instead, she shrugged and said, 'I've got used to it.'

Tenderly Dan reached out and spread his hand over her rounded belly. 'You're getting very big, aren't you? It can't be long now.'

Mary Ann smiled up at him. 'Do you think it could be twins?'

Dan laughed. 'What, a boy *and* a girl. That'd please Ma, wouldn't it?'

Mary Ann grimaced. 'Maybe, but I don't know how I'd cope with two.' She glanced around the tiny cabin. 'It's going to be hard enough with one. Still,' she yawned, 'I'll have to manage. And I'm coming with you to Hull. Your mam would never forgive me if I gave birth to her grandchild in Waterman's Yard instead of on the River Trent.'

Still, Dan looked doubtful. 'It's a cargo of potatoes and you know what that means.'

Mary Ann nodded. Dan would be stopping at several berths at villages along Trentside to pick up their cargo. The farmers brought their potatoes in sacks, which had to be loaded by hand, and the trip to Hull would take much longer than a straight run.

'And it can get very rough on the Humber, you know.'

'Don't remind me,' Mary Ann said at once with feeling, and Dan grimaced apologetically as he added, 'Still, you're not due for another couple of weeks, are you?'

'No. I'll be fine.'

Dan cupped her face in his hands and kissed her forehead. 'Oh Mary Ann, I do love you. I'm so proud of you the way you've learnt how to do everything. Do you know that? I'm sorry if I was a bit sharp with you at first. It was a big thing, you know, getting my first command. Am I forgiven?'

Mary Ann put her arms about him and buried her face in his chest. Unseen, she screwed up her face, for a brief moment riddled with guilt that she could not love this good man as he deserved to be loved. And there was something else too. She didn't know how to tell him the piece of news that she had heard the previous day in the town.

A week earlier, whilst they had been upriver near Newark, Susan Price had married Ted Oliver.

'Dan. Dan! I'll have to go below.'

'Not now, Mary Ann,' he yelled at her above the noise of the wind. 'I need you on deck. You'll have to stay at the tiller.'

The wind was driving up the Humber from the North Sea. Squalls of rain lashed the ship, stinging Mary Ann's face until she screwed up her eyes, unable to see, but still, doggedly, she clung to the tiller. 'I have to,' she gasped, the rain cold in her mouth. 'I have to go below.'

They were on their way back from Hull with a cargo of wheat, loaded in bulk, for one of the waterside mills in Elsborough.

'I've got dreadful pains. The baby's coming.'

Dan, his face wet with the rain, stared at her, horrified. 'For God's sake, Mary Ann. Not now.'

'I can't help it,' she screamed back at him as another pain wracked her body. She bent double, still hanging on to the tiller with one hand but clutching at her stomach with the other and gasping.

'Another half an hour, Mary Ann. Hang on if you can. Another half an hour and we'll be into the Trent.'

'Oh aye,' she countered bitterly. 'Never mind me. We've got to make the Trent. It's got to be born on the Trent.'

'Don't be stupid. I didn't mean that. It'll be calmer there. More sheltered. That's what I meant.'

Mary Ann didn't answer. As the contraction eased, she stood up and resumed her task.

'All right?' Dan's face was anxious, but he dared not let her leave yet. True, like his mother, he wanted his son or daughter born on the water, but not in it.

When they reached the calmer waters of the River Trent, the ship was stable. The wind still rocked her from side to side and flapped her sails, but now the *Maid Mary Ann* was in no danger of capsizing.

'You can go below. Duggie and I can manage now.'

'Oh thanks.' Mary Ann's tone was heavy with sarcasm. As she began to move towards the companion, another spasm of pain shot through her. She doubled over and fell to her knees.

Dan was beside her in an instant. 'Oh, love, I'm sorry. I didn't realize.'

Tenderly, now, he held her until the pain subsided, then he lifted her up and together they staggered towards the ladder. Dan went down first and then Mary Ann followed, Dan guiding her feet on to each rung. Another pain creased her and she cried out, her foot slipping so that she fell heavily against him.

'There, I've got you,' he gasped. 'You're all right. Here, let me help you get these wet clothes off.'

'I can manage,' Mary Ann snapped. 'Just go back and sail your blasted boat.'

Dan looked for a moment as if she had slapped him physically in the face, but then he said quietly, 'We'll sail a little further and then we'll drop anchor.'

Without waiting for her to argue, he climbed the ladder and disappeared. Left alone, Mary Ann leant on her hands on the side of the bed and groaned. Then, feeling another twinge, she stripped off her wet clothes and prepared the bed for giving birth. As she climbed into it, she wondered just how long it would be before she would get out of it again.

*

When Dan came down to her again, she said, 'It seems to have quietened down now. The pains aren't coming so often.'

'Perhaps it was a false alarm,' Dan said hopefully. Much as he wanted the child to be born on the river, he would have liked to have been a little nearer Elsborough, a little nearer some knowledgeable help. 'Can I sail a bit further upriver, then?'

Mary Ann ran her hands over her stomach then she nodded. 'Can we get near home do you think? So you can fetch Bessie?'

Dan leant across the bed and kissed her. 'We'll try. Hang on, Mary Ann.'

But they had only gone a few miles when Mary Ann was crying out, 'Dan, Dan. My waters have broken. It's coming, oh it's coming.'

Once more Dan anchored and came down to the cabin. 'We've only got as far as Eastlands' Ferry. Can't you hang on a little longer?'

'No, no.' Now she was writhing on the bed, her whole body bathed in sweat, her dark hair plastered to her face.

'Oh, let me die. I just want to die,' she moaned. As the pain gripped her once more, she screamed, 'I don't want it. I don't want it.'

Dan was beside himself, feeling helpless and ignorant of what to do.

There were towels and hot water all ready, but he had no idea what they were for.

'I'll go for help. I'll take the cog boat and go for help.'

Mary Ann clutched at him, her grip vice-like in her agony. 'No, no, don't leave me. I'm going to die. Don't leave me.'

'Duggie will go then.'

Once Duggie had gone, Dan sat with her, holding her

hand, wiping her forehead, his agony almost as bad as hers as he watched her suffer.

'Oh, why doesn't it come?' she moaned, lying back exhausted against the pillows.

Dan stood up suddenly. 'Where the hell has Duggie got to? He can't have been daft enough to try to go all the way to Elsborough, surely?' He stared down at her, anxious and afraid. He'd sooner face a mountainous sea than this. 'Something must be wrong,' he muttered. 'You need a midwife or a doctor and you need one now.'

'Don't leave me. Please, don't leave me.'

'Mary Ann, I have to. I'll have to swim to the bank and . . .'

Desperate now, he was already climbing the ladder as she called out weakly, 'Don't leave me, Dan. Oh, don't you leave me too.'

As she heard him step on to the deck and begin to run across it, Mary Ann whimpered, 'Why does everyone leave me? What have I done so wrong?' Then, as pain seized her again, she cried out, 'Mam. Mam!' not knowing whether it was for her own mother she called, or for Bessie.

Out of a haze of pain, she heard voices and then Dan saying loudly, 'There you are. I was just about to set off myself. Thank God . . .'

Mary Ann closed her eyes and offered up a silent prayer. Duggie had come back. Duggie had brought Bessie. Everything would be all right now. Bessie was here. Bessie would take care of her . . .

She heard Dan's boots scraping on the ladder and his voice calling out to her. 'Mary Ann? Duggie's back and he's brought someone to help you.'

Bleary-eyed, Mary Ann turned her head to see Dan coming towards her. Behind him, coming carefully down the vertical ladder, was Susan.

Thirty-Four

'Get her out. I won't have her here.' Mary Ann screamed, trying to push herself into the farthest corner of the enclosed bunk bed, away from the woman coming towards her.

'Don't be silly, Mary Ann.' Dan, in his anxiety, was frowning and his voice was unusually sharp. 'Susan's come to help you.'

'I want Mam,' she cried, the sweat shining on her face. Then, lest he should think her half-demented with the pain, she added, reverting to her childhood name for the woman she now thought of as her own mother, 'I want your mam. I want Auntie Bessie.'

Susan leant over the bed. Gently and with infinite kindness, she said, 'Mary Ann, it was too far for Duggie to go for Mrs Ruddick. Let me help you, now that I'm here. I'm sure I can, but Duggie can set off to go for his mother, if you want him to.'

Mary Ann's eyes were huge in her red face. 'How can you help?' she asked harshly. 'You haven't had a baby.'

She saw Susan wince at the deliberate shaft, but calmly she replied, 'No, my dear, but when I was fifteen, my mother had my little brother. I was there at the birth. Admittedly, I don't know as much as Mrs Ruddick, but,' she smiled now, 'I think I can safely say I do know a little more than Dan or Duggie.'

At that moment, a pain gripped Mary Ann with such

ferocity that she threw herself backwards on the bed and arched her body. Her screams echoed down the river.

'Dan,' Susan said, taking charge without any further permission or otherwise from Mary Ann, 'I need hot water, a bowl, soap, plenty of clean towels ... Ah, I see you've already made a start. Good.'

Dan, thankful to have something positive to do, hurried to do as she asked, although there was barely room in the small cabin for them to move around each other. At last, Susan said, 'I think you'd better go on deck now, Dan. Out of the way.'

But Dan shook his head. 'No, I'm staying here. I want to see my son born.'

Mary Ann, through a haze of pain and near delirium, saw Susan smile and heard her say softly, 'And if it's a girl?'

Dan's voice came clearly to her. 'I'll love her just the same.'

'Sit over there, then, and keep out of the way, Dan Ruddick. This is women's work.'

At that moment, Duggie poked his head down the companion. 'How's she doing? Anything you want?'

'We're fine, Duggie ...'

Panting between contractions, Mary Ann gasped, 'You speak for yourself,' but Susan only smiled and went on, 'But you could take the expectant father out of my way.'

'I'm staying here,' Dan declared and Duggie grinned. 'He's too big for me to shift, Susan. Sorry, you'll have to put up with him. Just watch he doesn't pass out, though.' He laughed and added, 'I'll wait up here, though, if it's all the same to you.'

Then Susan was bending over Mary Ann again. 'Now, my dear, the next time you get a strong pain, I want you to push.'

Mary Ann, between spasms, blinked at her. 'Push? Push what?'

'Well, sort of . . . bear down. You've got to help the little mite. It can't come into the world without a bit of help from you. You've got to push it out.'

'Have I?'

Susan nodded and as Mary Ann's face began to twist with the pain once more, she said, 'Come on, Mary Ann, push!'

An hour later a baby girl made her way noisily into the world. Mary Ann, weak and exhausted, was scarcely aware of Dan's triumphant shout and of Susan's smiling face as she cut the cord, lifted the child and put the red and bawling infant into its father's arms.

'You have a daughter, Dan. So you'd best forget all about having a son for this time.'

Even through her fatigue, Mary Ann was aware of Dan and Susan standing close together, their heads bent over the child, marvelling at its lusty cry and its waving limbs.

'By, she's a little fighter, ain't she?' Dan was grinning broadly.

'She's a little beauty. And just look at all that black hair.'

'Oi, what's going on down there?' A shout from above made both Dan and Susan look up with startled eyes. 'Out of me way, Duggie Ruddick. It's not you I'm after.'

'Oh dear,' Susan said, suddenly agitated. 'That's Ted. He must have come looking for me. I must go.'

'Wait a minute. You can't leave her like that.' Mary Ann saw Dan nod towards her and Susan turned back with a little start, almost as if she had completely forgotten about the mother.

'Oh dear, no. You're right, I can't. The afterbirth hasn't come away yet.' For a moment, Susan seemed uncertain, and when another shout from on deck filtered down to them, she jumped visibly.

'Susan? Are you down there?'

'Look, Ted . . .' Now they could hear Duggie trying to reason with him.

Susan whispered to Dan. 'Give the child to me. She can lie beside Mary Ann. You go up there and tell him what's happened while I see to her.'

Mary Ann lay back against the pillows. She was beginning to shiver now. All she wanted was to be wrapped up warmly and left to sleep and sleep. And she certainly didn't want the yelling infant beside her.

'It's not coming away. Can you push again, Mary Ann?'

Weakly, Mary Ann said, 'Whatever for? She's born now.'

'Yes, but there's what they call the afterbirth. It has to come away. If it doesn't, you could be dreadfully ill.'

'I am dreadfully ill now,' Mary Ann moaned, and lay with her eyes closed. 'I just want to die.'

'Don't talk like that,' Susan said, sharply. 'You've got a baby to think about now.'

'I don't want it. You can keep it.'

' "It" is a "her",' Susan reminded her brusquely. 'Now, come along. We've got to get this afterbirth out. Just sit up a minute, Mary Ann.'

Mary Ann did not move, making no effort to assist the woman who was trying so hard to help her, limited though her own knowledge was.

'Mary Ann . . .'

'Susan,' Ted's bellow came down the companion. 'You come home now. Do you hear me? I won't have you on this ship a moment longer.'

'Oh dear,' Susan muttered, wringing her hands. 'Oh Mary Ann, please . . .'

'Look . . .' Mary Ann raised her head and then heaved herself up on to one elbow. She opened her mouth to speak again, but caught her breath and was seized by a fit of coughing.

'Oh!' she cried, as she felt something slither out of her and rest, wet and sticky, between her legs.

'Thank goodness!' Susan said with relief. 'It's come away.' Then she raised her voice. 'I'm coming, Ted. I won't be a minute.'

'You'll come now, woman.'

But Susan remained where she was, busily washing Mary Ann. 'I'll be in trouble with him,' she murmured, 'but I can't leave you like this.'

Despite her exhaustion, Mary Ann was intrigued. 'What do you mean? Why should he mind?'

Susan glanced at her and then away again. In a low voice she said, 'Ted told me I was to have nothing to do with Dan again.'

'Well, you aren't. I mean, you're only helping me, aren't you?'

'Yes. But I'm aboard Dan's ship, aren't I?'

The two young women stared at each other as Mary Ann said shrewdly, 'You mean he's jealous of Dan?'

Susan nodded. 'Oh Mary Ann,' she whispered and suddenly there were tears in her eyes. 'You don't know the half of it.'

Mary Ann saw her brush the tears away impatiently and plaster a brave smile on her face. 'There. That's all I can do. But I think Dan should get his mother to have a look at you as soon as you get to Elsborough. I must go.' But even then, she could not resist putting out a gentle finger and touching the cheek of Dan's baby girl.

As she turned away and put her foot on the first rung of the ladder, Mary Ann said, 'Susan . . .'

Susan paused and looked back at her.

'Thank you,' Mary Ann said. 'I know it must have been hard for you.'

Susan nodded, smiled and then climbed the ladder. Mary Ann lay back and closed her eyes, but a second later they flew wide open as she heard Ted Oliver's voice again. 'What the hell do you think you're doing?'

Mary Ann let out a startled gasp as she heard distinctly the sound of a slap and Susan's cry.

'Now, look here . . .' began Dan's voice.

'Don't you "look here" to me, Dan Ruddick. You just keep away from her now. You hear me. She's *my* wife now. You cast her off when you took up with that little trollop down there. So you leave Susan be. She's mine.' A pause and then, 'Come on. We're going home.'

Another startled cry from Susan and Mary Ann imagined that Ted had grasped hold of his wife and was pulling her after him. Straining her ears, she heard them climbing down the rope ladder and into a rowing boat that bumped gently against the side of the ship. Then she heard the splash of oars as Ted pulled away. The sound became fainter and, at last, Dan descended the ladder and came to the side of the bed.

His face, showing none of the earlier exultation at the birth of his child, now looked grim with shock and despair.

'He hit her, Mary Ann. Right in front of me. The bastard actually hit her. We couldn't stop him.'

Mary Ann lay back and closed her eyes, memories of her early life flooding back to her. Fleeting pictures of the beatings her mother had suffered at the hands of her father. She could almost feel the bruises once more that she had received from him.

'Maybe he'll finish up at the end of a rope,' she said, bitterly.

As she drifted into an exhausted sleep, the last words she heard Dan say were, 'I'll hang the bastard mesen if I catch him hitting her again.'

Thirty-Five

'Oh Mary Ann, she's beautiful. What a little treasure. Look, Bert. Look at those big eyes.'

The new grandmother was drooling over the baby, whilst the mother was lying listlessly on the bunk, refusing to even try to get out of it.

'What's her name?'

Mary Ann, still weak and uninterested in her daughter, shrugged. 'Haven't thought of one yet.'

'Not thought of one!' Bessie was scandalized. 'Why, I'd have thought you'd been discussing names for weeks. We did, didn't we Bert? Rosemary was a favourite. Every time we picked Rosemary, didn't we?'

Bert grinned. 'Aye. Good job we never used it though, eh?' He tickled the baby under her chin. 'She's smiling at me. Look, she's smiling at me.'

'Wind,' said Bessie knowledgeably.

'Never,' Bert insisted. 'She knows who her grandpa is. She's smiling at me.'

Bessie looked at him fondly. ''Course she is, Bert.'

Mary Ann listened to them and silently ground her teeth. Why didn't they go away and leave her alone? And they could take the squalling brat that pulled and sucked at her and made her breasts sore with them.

They were looking at her, watching her, concern on their faces. 'Do you want to call her after your mam, love?' Bessie asked gently.

Mary Ann lay against the pillows and closed her eyes, remembering the thin little woman who had been so dominated, so overpowered by Sid Clark that she had not had the strength for her own survival, yet alone that of her only child. Mary Ann could scarcely remember affection or any kind of care from her mother. She opened her eyes and turned her head to look at Bessie and Bert standing there. These two warm-hearted souls had been far more like proper parents to her than ever her own had been.

'Or you could call her after yourself, or even after our Dan. Danielle. That's a nice name.' Bessie pulled a grimace. 'Bit posh, mebbe, for the likes of us. But it'd be nice.'

Briefly, the question flitted through Mary Ann's mind. Was there a feminine form of Randolph? But, of course, she did not voice the question aloud, although the thought of even suggesting it made her smile impishly.

Misreading it, Bessie said, 'You like that? Danielle?'

Mary Ann moved her head on the pillow. 'No. I'd like to call her after you, Mam.'

A flush of pleasure crept up Bessie's neck and suffused her face. Bert put his arm around his wife and squeezed her waist. 'Aw, now that's nice. Isn't that lovely, lass?'

Mary Ann was touched to see tears in their eyes.

'Me proper name's Elizabeth,' Bessie said.

Mary Ann sighed and closed her eyes again, but, seeing how much pleasure her sudden decision had given them both, the smile stayed on her mouth. 'That's settled then. Elizabeth it is. We've already asked Duggie to be her godfather. Do you think Miss Edwina would agree to be her godmother?'

'I'm sure she'd love to be,' Bessie said, as she laid the child beside Mary Ann and added softly, her voice breaking with emotion, 'Thank you, Mary Ann, for giving us a beautiful granddaughter. You've made me and Bert very happy, to say nothing of our Dan. He's fair puffing out his chest like a pouter pigeon.'

Bert moved forward too and leant over the bed to kiss Mary Ann's forehead. 'We're very proud of you, lass.'

Mary Ann felt a peculiar lump in her throat. She looked down at her baby daughter. She had been so locked away in her own discomfort that she had turned against her child, blaming its arrival for feeling so dreadful. Now, she really looked at her for the first time, seeing her through the eyes of the besotted father and the doting grandparents.

They were right, she was a pretty little thing, Mary Ann saw now. With dark wisps of hair and dark eyes, round cheeks and a surprisingly smooth skin. Her small mouth worked in sucking movements yet she made no noise and merely gazed up, unblinkingly, at the face of her mother.

'Hello,' Mary Ann said softly, gently tracing the shape of the tiny face with her finger. 'Hello, my little Lizzie.'

Mary Ann could see the relief in Dan's face when he climbed down the ladder into the cabin later to find her out of the bunk bed and sitting on the bench seat feeding her child.

'Feeling better, love?' he asked tenderly and reached out to touch the baby's head.

'Much better. I'll soon be up and about.' There was a pause before she added, 'Did your mam and dad tell you her name?'

Dan shook his head. 'Mam said you'd decided, but she said you'd tell me yourself.'

Mary Ann smiled up at him. 'We'll christen her after your mother, Dan. Elizabeth. All right?'

She didn't need to hear Dan's answer – it was written in the broad smile that wreathed his face. 'But I thought,' she went on, 'that we'd call her Lizzie. What do you think?'

Dan nodded. 'Fine by me.' He paused a moment, watching them, then he said, 'If you're really feeling better, Mary Ann, we should take the ship back to Newark. Mr Sudbury has been very kind – very understanding – but it's time I was earning us all some money again.'

'Of course,' Mary Ann said at once. 'But I can't do much just yet.'

'Oh no, no,' Dan held up his hand in protest. 'I wouldn't expect you to, my love. Besides,' he smiled down fondly at them with love and pride in his voice, 'You've enough to do looking after our daughter. Duggie says he'll do the cooking for a few days.'

Dan was a good husband, Mary Ann thought, and he would make a wonderful, loving father. She did love him, she told herself. She really did. She glanced down at the infant in her arms. Lizzie's blue gaze was fastened upon Mary Ann's face as she sucked contentedly. The baby's tiny fingers fluttered, uncontrolled, and touched her mother's breast. Mary Ann trembled beneath the feather-light touch and in that moment she vowed, I will be a good mother to you and a better wife to Dan.

And so doing, she locked away the memories of Randolph Marsh and determined to think of him no more.

Their life together – the three of them that had now become four – evolved into a pattern. Most of the time,

Mary Ann and the growing child travelled aboard the ship. She worked hard and kept the promise she had made to herself, and only when the child was fast asleep and all her chores done did she allow herself to pick up her embroidery. Now her work had a purpose, for she learnt how to smock and to make intricate delicate lace, too, with which she decorated her daughter's little dresses.

Duggie's presence still lightened Mary Ann's days and he was a second father to Lizzie. His good humour never flagged. Rarely was Duggie Ruddick seen without a smile on his face and a quick-witted quip from his tongue. And his teasing was never cruel, never barbed. He was like the brother Mary Ann had never had and she could have wished for none better.

He seemed to have a succession of girlfriends, but no one serious. Whenever they moored to load or unload, or went home to Waterman's Yard for the weekend, there always seemed to be a girl on the wharf waiting to catch a few moments with Duggie.

'You're a right Jack the lad,' Mary Ann teased him. 'Aren't you ever going to settle down?'

Duggie pretended to frown and drew in breath in a whistle. 'Not me, Mary Ann. I'm not going to stay here all me life, you know. I'll be away to seek me fortune one of these fine days.'

'Leaving? You're going to leave us? Have you got an apprenticeship?'

He pulled a face. 'I reckon that's passed me by, Mary Ann. I'm getting a bit too old now.' Then he laughed. 'Don't worry. I'm not leaving yet. Besides, it's only a pipe dream. I'll probably end me days on this stretch of river. But sometimes . . .' His face took on a dreamy expression. 'Just sometimes, when we're at Hull, I look out down the Humber and out into the North Sea and wonder what's out there beyond the horizon. I wonder what I'm missing. I get a bit restless and long to pack a few belongings on me back and head off into the unknown.' Then he gave a mocking sigh. 'But, like I say, I'll probably never do it. I like me mam's cooking – and yours,' he added hastily, 'to go too far away.'

'You needn't spare my feelings, Duggie. My cooking isn't a patch on your mam's or on yours, if it comes to that. Even I look forward to Sunday dinner in Waterman's Yard.'

'Your cooking is a lot better than it used to be, Mary Ann, and it's amazing how you manage in that little cabin, so don't belittle yourself.'

Mary Ann coloured at his praise. For all his teasing, Duggie was always truthful.

So the routine of their lives continued. Whenever they were moored in Elsborough, they spent time with Bessie and the family, and Mary Ann always tried to see Edwina. Her visits to the school, she told herself, were to keep up her learning, and to prove this to herself as much as to Edwina – and to Bessie – every time they went there she insisted that Edwina should teach her a new embroidery stitch. But when their heads were bent together over the fine stitches, Mary Ann had to bite upon her lips to stop them from asking, 'How is Randolph? Where is he and what is he doing? Is he happy?'

Then came the day when Mary Ann stepped into Edwina's office unannounced to find that Edwina already had visitors.

A smartly dressed woman was sitting on the chaise longue set against one wall of Edwina's study. She was reclining languidly against the cushions and smoking a cigarette in a long, ebony holder. She was not particularly good looking, Mary Ann thought, her eyes drawn to the stranger as she stood in the doorway, but with the skilful use of cosmetics, her hair trimmed in the short haircut of the day, and her fashionable clothes, the woman oozed sophistication. But her mouth had a petulant twist to it and her eyes, squinting at Mary Ann through the haze of her cigarette smoke, were dull with boredom.

There was a young boy, no more than a year old, sitting on Edwina's lap. As he turned to see who had come into the room, Mary Ann was startled by the brightness of his blue eyes. For an instant, Mary Ann trembled. The child's eyes were so like Randolph's that there could be no mistaking the little boy's parentage.

Edwina raised her head and smiled. 'Mary Ann, how nice. Come in, my dear. Come and meet my nephew, Lawrence.'

Thirty-Six

Edwina made the more formal introductions as Mary Ann moved forward into the room.

'This is Celia, my sister-in-law.' Tactfully, Edwina cleverly avoided mentioning Randolph. 'And this is Lawrence. He's only a couple of months younger than your little Lizzie.'

Mary Ann drank in the sight of the child. He had Randolph's fair hair and blue eyes, and as she glanced between them she could see that, although the child had inherited the shape of his mother's mouth, whilst hers wore a sulky expression, his was upturned in a cherubic greeting.

She moved forward, squatted down in front of the little boy and held out her finger for him to grasp. 'How do you do, Master Lawrence? What a handsome little man he is.'

'He's like his father.' The woman spoke behind her, her tone bitter. 'He'll no doubt break a few hearts when he's older.'

Mary Ann drew in a breath sharply. Did Celia know who she was? Did she know all about Mary Ann's affair with Randolph? And if so, who had told her? She was sure he would not have done so, so that left only one person. She glanced resentfully at Edwina, but Edwina gave a little shake of her head. Aloud she said, 'He has some of your features, Celia, surely, and he's so placid. Such a good baby.'

'He doesn't take after either of us for that, Edwina. I'm sure Randolph was a demon as a child and my mother never tires of telling me that I dispatched twelve nannies single-handedly.' Celia stubbed out her cigarette in a glass ashtray and stood up. Smoothing down her skirt, she said, 'I'd better be going. Are you sure you don't mind looking after him, Edwina? His wretched nanny has a dreadful cold and has taken to her bed.'

'Much the best thing. You don't want the little man to catch it.'

'I suppose not.' The woman sounded as if she didn't care one way or the other, only that her own life should not be disrupted. 'It's really most inconvenient. I have a luncheon appointment with Mrs Phillips.'

Mrs Phillips was the wife of one of the town's most influential men. He owned the huge engineering works that was one of Elsborough's major employers. So, thought Mary Ann, Celia had wasted no time in ingratiating herself with the town's elite.

Edwina, with no such pretensions, smiled. 'It'll be a real pleasure. If it didn't sound so horrid, I could wish that the nanny might catch a cold more frequently if it means I get the chance to look after him.'

Celia shrugged her slim shoulders. 'If that's the case, you can have him on her afternoon off and welcome.'

'But that's the only time you get to spend with him,' Edwina protested.

'I'm not very good with young children, Edwina. I don't pretend to be. I'll get on better with my son when he can hold an intelligent conversation.'

She slipped on her coat and picked up her handbag and gloves. She stood a moment looking down at the sweet picture Edwina and the child made. 'You're very maternal, aren't you, Edwina? You really should get married and have children of your own before it's too late.' Then, losing interest, she said, 'I must go. Deakin can pick Lawrence up at four o'clock in the Bentley.'

'Very well,' Edwina murmured, her attention captivated by the child in her lap. 'I'll take good care of him.'

Since her brother's marriage, Edwina had moved out of the family home and now lived in an apartment at the top of the school building. Mr and Mrs Marsh senior, of course, still lived at The Hall.

'My dear Edwina, of that I can be sure,' Celia said, as she reached the door. 'Goodbye and thank you again. You're such a treasure. Goodbye – er . . .' She hesitated, trying to recall the name she had just been given. 'Goodbye – Mary Ann, is it?'

Mary Ann nodded as she said quietly, 'Goodbye, Mrs Marsh.'

As the door closed behind Celia, Mary Ann said, 'She didn't even say goodbye to him.'

Edwina sighed. 'No. Like she said, she isn't very good with young children. She never takes a lot of notice of him. It quite upsets me to see how offhand she is with the little chap. I'm just praying that she will change once he gets a little older and, to her mind, more interesting.'

Mary Ann allowed the boy to clasp and unclasp her finger and only resisted when he tried to draw it towards his mouth. 'No, no, you're not going to chew my finger,' she laughed.

'He's still teething. See how he dribbles,' Edwina said adoringly.

Mary Ann's face sobered. 'Does she . . . does Mrs Marsh know who I am?'

Edwina shook her head again. 'If you mean does she know about your . . .' She paused briefly struggling to find an appropriate word. 'Association with Randolph. No, she doesn't.' Then she added wryly, 'At least, not unless Randolph has told her himself and I doubt that very much.'

Mary Ann said nothing, her gaze on his child as the boy played with her fingers and smiled playfully up into her eyes.

'He is a lovely little boy,' she murmured, but now Edwina was trying to draw the conversation away.

'Tell me, how is Lizzie, and, of course, Dan and Duggie? And do you see anything of poor Susan?'

Susan Oliver had become known, all along the riverbank, as 'poor Susan'. Though Dan and Mary Ann had probably been the first to know, it was now common knowledge that her husband Ted was wildly and irrationally jealous of her. She was a virtual prisoner in the cottage near the ferry, which Ted operated between the two villages on either side of the Trent, appropriately named Eastlands and Westlands. The ferryman's cottage was at Eastlands and so it was always known as Eastlands' Ferry.

Susan had no friends and saw little of her own family. It was a disastrous marriage, but Susan was trapped. Her father would not countenance the scandal of a divorce.

'He's a hard man, that Jack Price. Thank God I don't work for him any more,' Dan said often. 'He seems to blame Susan. Says she must be giving her husband cause for jealousy. What chance has she got, locked away in the middle of nowhere?'

Mary Ann would glance at him and wonder. Whenever they passed by the tiny white cottage on the riverbank, Dan would be on deck, and she knew he stood looking across the expanse of water hoping to catch sight of Susan.

But Susan was never to be seen. Very occasionally,

as they had come upriver, they would see her in the distance, pegging out the washing on the line, but by the time the *Maid Mary Ann* drew level, Susan had scuttled indoors.

Did Ted see Dan watching out for his wife, Mary Ann thought, and did he, too, wonder?

In answer to Edwina's question, Mary Ann shook her head. 'Not much. I haven't seen her to speak to since the night Lizzie was born.'

'She's got a little boy now, hasn't she?'

Mary Ann nodded. 'Yes. Tolly. He was born about ten months after Lizzie. When was Lawrence born?'

'Two months after Lizzie.'

'And I never knew,' Mary Ann murmured.

For a moment, Edwina looked embarrassed. 'I'm sorry. I should have told you. But – it was, well, awkward.'

'Is that why no one told me? Not even Bessie.' Mary Ann looked straight into Edwina's eyes. 'She knew, I suppose?'

Edwina nodded and said again, 'I'm sorry, Mary Ann, we should have told you.'

As she walked home, back to the wharf where she knew Dan would be waiting, anxious to catch the tide, Mary Ann pondered on the strange quirk of Fate that had brought three children into the world within the space of a year. Three children, who were linked in a strange way by their parents' pasts. What did life hold for each of them? Mary Ann wondered. Would their paths cross? Would they even know one another? Perhaps Lizzie and Tolly would, she mused. As long as his father didn't guard him as jealously as he did his wife. But would Lizzie ever know Lawrence?

A smile played mischievously upon Mary Ann's mouth. If Edwina was to look after her nephew on the nanny's day off, she thought, then she must try to bring Lizzie to visit her godmother on one of those days.

Thirty-Seven

Lizzie was almost nine when Mary Ann met Randolph Marsh again.

The intervening years had been kind to Mary Ann and her little family, although there had been no more children. She had found a kind of contentment with Dan and, after the shaky beginning, had grown to love her daughter although her displays of affection towards the child were spasmodic. One moment she would lavish kisses and cuddles upon Lizzie, the next she would be offhand with her and lost in a world of her own memories. To a less confident infant, such erratic behaviour would have been disastrous, but Lizzie, sure in the love of a large, extended family, appeared to take her mother's mood swings in her stride.

Lizzie was a delight to all who knew her. In looks, she resembled her mother: dark hair, deep brown eyes and dimples in her cheeks, which seemed ever present for the child smiled constantly. She was bright and intelligent and quick to learn. In her character, she took after the Ruddick family. She was forthright, even from an early age, in her opinions like her grandmother, Bessie. Yet any bossiness was quickly dispelled by her lively, teasing manner which echoed her Uncle Duggie's nature.

Her father, her grandfather and her two uncles, especially Duggie, doted on her and spoiled her. In their eyes she could do no wrong and any necessary correction had to come from Mary Ann or Bessie.

Lizzie learnt to walk on the deck of the *Maid Mary Ann* and to swim under Duggie's tuition, not in the river for the currents were too strong and treacherous, but in the town's swimming baths when they moored for a few hours at one of the wharves.

'She's not to swim in the river. You must teach her that, Mary Ann,' Dan commanded. 'Folks throw all sorts of rubbish and muck into the river.' Before she reached school age, he had built her a miniature cog boat of her own. He taught her to scull in the shallow waters of the River Trent, paying out the rope from the ship with the little craft attached to it. Then, with a mixture of concern and pride, he and Duggie hung over the side as the tiny hands manoeuvred the oar with a deftness that was in her blood.

When she reached school age, Mary Ann was adamant that Lizzie should attend Edwina's school.

'She's going to be a lady when she grows up,' Mary Ann declared, and even Bessie, who normally despised anyone trying to 'rise above their station', backed the decision. If she had been fully aware, however, of all that lay behind Mary Ann's scheme, Bessie might not have been so ready to agree. But wanting the very best for her granddaughter, Bessie even persuaded each member of the Ruddick family to contribute to the fees.

Dan missed his little girl dreadfully from the moment she stepped off the ship in her smart new uniform. Mary Ann, holding Lizzie's hand, had known that Dan was watching them as they walked the length of River Road that first school morning.

'Turn and wave to your daddy,' she had said to Lizzie before his tall, still figure was lost from their sight.

Lizzie had turned and blown him a kiss from her tiny

hand. Then she had skipped ahead of her mother, anxious to begin her new life.

Edwina, Lizzie's godmother, had loved her from the first time she had seen her, and now having the child in her charge, she found it difficult not to favour her over her other pupils.

'She's so bright and quick,' Edwina extolled Lizzie's virtues to anyone who would listen. Then she would smile fondly and say, 'But she's a little mischief at times and is often in trouble with her teacher. It's difficult to be angry with her for long, though. She makes you laugh just when you're trying to be stern with her.'

Mary Ann's secretly cherished hope that Lizzie would meet Lawrence Marsh did not happen. Often, when they were small, Mary Ann would take her daughter to see Edwina hoping they might meet the boy by chance. But Fate never decreed their meeting. And by the time Lizzie attended the school, Lawrence already had a tutor at home and then, at the age of seven, he was sent away to boarding school. In the school holidays when perhaps he visited Edwina, there was no plausible reason for Lizzie to be there.

Lizzie did, however, know Tolly Oliver.

Almost from the time she could walk, she would stand at the ship's rail and wave to the boy who lived in the ferryman's cottage.

'That's Tolly,' Mary Ann had heard Dan tell her. She had watched Lizzie staring at the boy and then dimpling as she laughed and waved to him.

It became a ritual that every time they passed by on the river, Lizzie would run to the side and wave.

'Wave to Tolly, Mamma,' Lizzie would shout. 'We must all wave to Tolly. Daddy, wave to Tolly.'

'Poor Tolly,' Dan would murmur, but it wasn't until Lizzie grew a little older that she asked her mother, 'Why does Daddy always call him "poor Tolly"? Is it because he always looks so lonely? Or is it because they haven't much money?'

Mary Ann looked down at the young child and marvelled at her perception.

'A bit of both, I think,' had been her answer. Mary Ann could not explain to the child that because Tolly's mother was 'poor Susan', it seemed natural to call her son a similar name.

'He looks so thin, doesn't he?' Lizzie mused, with an unusual understanding from one so young.

Hearing their conversation Dan had come to stand alongside them. In his hand he held a potato from the cargo they were carrying.

Thoughtfully, he tossed it up and down in his hand like a huge cricket ball.

'Wants feeding up a bit, poor lad. Shall we throw him this?' Dan smiled down at his daughter and then, above her head, he caught Mary Ann's glance.

Quietly, Mary Ann said, 'They say, in the wash-houses, that Ted hasn't much time for his lad.'

Dan pulled a face. 'Doesn't surprise me. The man's so eaten up with jealousy, I don't think he's got a loving bone in his body. He can't stand anyone to come between himself and Susan – not even his own son.' And he said yet again, 'Poor Tolly.'

Mary Ann glanced at him and was sure that secretly her husband was also thinking, 'Poor Susan.'

'Throw it, Daddy. Throw that big potato to Tolly. His mam can cook it for his dinner.'

Dan raised his arm, drew it back and hurled the

unusual missile across the rippling water to the bank. The garden of the ferryman's cottage came down to the river with no fencing or hedge between it and the slope of the bank. They watched Tolly stare in surprise as the potato landed close by him and rolled almost to his feet.

Lizzie jumped up and down and clapped her hands. 'It's for your dinner, Tolly,' she shouted, her piping voice bouncing on the breeze to him. 'It's for your dinner.'

Slowly the boy bent and picked it up. He stood a moment with it in the palm of his hand and then, even from a distance, they could all see the broad grin on his face. He waved and then turned and dashed into the house. They heard him calling, 'Mam, Mam, look . . .' But the rest of his words were lost.

Even Mary Ann was touched by the boy's pleasure. She smiled at Dan. 'That was a nice thing to do, Dan Ruddick.' She reached up and touched his cheek. Dan caught hold of her hand and kissed her fingers tenderly.

'Look, there's Tolly's mam,' Lizzie said, and Mary Ann and Dan turned back to see Susan standing in the doorway of her home. She was holding the potato and as her hand fluttered briefly in a nervous gesture of thanks, Mary Ann felt Dan let go of her hand.

It became another ritual that, as long as Ted Oliver was not around to see, every time the *Maid Mary Ann* passed Ferry Cottage, they would throw something to Tolly if the cargo they were carrying was suitable. In winter, if they were carrying house coal to the Co-op's yard in Elsborough, both Dan and Duggie would pelt enough coal to keep the cottage fire burning for a week. They watched with amusement and delight as Tolly scurried about the grass picking up the coal and putting it into a bucket.

'The lad can hardly carry it,' Duggie would laugh, but Dan would only smile and say, 'It'll keep him warm for a day or two.'

Potatoes and other vegetables were regularly hurled across the water and sometimes they even carried canned fruit, imported into Hull and distributed via the rivers and canals. Lizzie would laugh aloud as she watched Tolly picking up the cans and staring at the labels in amazement.

'Are you sure you're not making more trouble for Susan?' Mary Ann asked. 'How is she going to explain the appearance of canned fruit on her pantry shelves to a man like Ted Oliver?'

Dan shrugged. 'She'll think of something,' he said confidently.

'Well, I'm not so sure. I don't think a tin of pineapple or peaches is worth a black eye or a broken jaw.'

She turned away to go below, but she knew Dan was looking after her thoughtfully, trying to gauge whether his wife's comment was justified or whether it was really because she didn't like him giving presents to Susan.

'He can work that out for himself,' Mary Ann muttered to herself as she sat down in the cabin and picked up her embroidery. She sighed and gave a wry smile. She wasn't even sure of her motives herself, so how was Dan to guess?

As soon as she could scull safely, Dan allowed Lizzie to take her little cog boat along the shallows of the river as long as the current wasn't running too strongly, keeping pace with the ship but always in sight of her father. It was on one such day that Mary Ann, watching her from the slowly moving ship, saw Tolly standing on the bank near his home. She watched Lizzie manoeuvre her little boat towards the muddy riverbank. Above the breeze and the flapping of the square sail above her, Mary Ann heard her daughter's clear voice. 'Hello. You're Tolly, aren't you? I'm Lizzie.'

Mary Ann could not hear the boy's reply, but she saw him nod and she could only guess at the conversation that followed as the *Maid Mary Ann* moved on upriver. 'It's a funny name, Tolly, isn't it?' Mary Ann knew her daughter well enough to be sure of that first question.

His cheeks would redden as he admitted, 'It's short for Bartholomew.' He grimaced. 'I'm called after me dad's father.'

Lizzie's laughter rang out and Mary Ann watched her daughter gesticulating with her small, capable hands towards the ship and then to her own little boat. Mary Ann smiled. Now Lizzie was proudly telling Tolly how her father had made the craft himself, especially for her. The boy moved closer, right to the water's edge, so that he could see the boat properly.

Mary Ann cupped her hands around her mouth and called, 'Lizzie. Lizzie.'

When the girl looked up, Mary Ann beckoned. But the child only waved and turned her head away to talk to Tolly again.

'The little minx,' Mary Ann murmured. 'She's deliberately ignoring me.'

The ship moved on and there was nothing Mary Ann could do as she watched the boy hold out his hand to help her daughter step ashore. Then giving a little laugh herself, Mary Ann shrugged. Oh well, she thought, if that's what she wants to do, she'd better get on with it.

Mary Ann turned away and went below and it wasn't until half an hour later that she heard Dan calling frantically. 'Mary Ann, Mary Ann. Where's Lizzie? I can't see Lizzie.'

Mary Ann climbed the ladder. 'She's with Tolly. I called to her and beckoned her but the little madam took no notice.'

'And you left her there?'

'She'll be all right. She'll—'

'Why didn't you take the cog boat and go after her? You know she's to stay in sight of the ship. I don't want her sculling on the river without one of us watching her.'

'The last I saw of her she was climbing out of the boat and on to the bank,' Mary Ann told him. 'They'll be playing together. She'll be all right.'

'How's she going to catch up with us or hadn't you thought of that?'

Mary Ann blinked. She hadn't.

'I thought not,' Dan muttered and his face was dark with anger. 'You'd better take the cog boat and go back for her.'

'I haven't time . . .' she began, but Dan said harshly, 'Now, Mary Ann.'

Irritated by both her daughter's misbehaviour and what she saw as Dan's fussing, Mary Ann sculled back downriver towards the ferryman's cottage. Lizzie's cog boat was tied to a post set in the riverbank at the bottom of the garden, but there was no sign of the children.

Mary Ann drew level with the cottage. 'Lizzie. Lizzie!' she called, balancing herself in the small boat, her hand on the oar. Susan appeared in the doorway. 'Why, Mary Ann. Is something wrong?'

Exasperated, Mary Ann answered sharply. 'Lizzie

stopped to talk to your boy and now they've disappeared. I'll tan her backside for her when I catch up with her.'

Susan stepped out into the sunshine and, shielding her eyes, glanced up and down the river. A little way downstream, the ferry, with Ted Oliver at the winding gear, was leaving the opposite bank, bringing its passengers from Nottinghamshire into Lincolnshire. Swiftly, Susan stepped back into the doorway of her home so that she could not be seen from the ferry.

'He . . . he might have taken her salmon fishing, Mary Ann.' She pointed in the direction of the approaching ferry. 'Further downstream, beyond the ferry crossing. At the bend in the river. D'you know where I mean?'

Mary Ann nodded. 'Thanks, Susan.' She looked again at the woman. It was years since she had seen Susan this close and she could see, even from this distance, that the woman, who was still only young, had changed noticeably. She was thinner. Her hair, drab and untidy, was pulled back into an unbecoming bun at the back of her head. Beneath the apron she wore, the hem of her dress was uneven, as if part of it had become unstitched and she had neither the time nor the energy to mend it.

Mary Ann's clever fingers itched to repair the garment and then she laughed at herself for wanting to help the girl who had always been a rival for Dan's affection. Well, she didn't look much of a rival now, poor thing, Mary Ann thought, with a rare moment of genuine sympathy for Susan.

'I'd better go and look for them,' she called and then, pausing only to allow the ferry to pass by and the ripples it made to subside, she began to scull further downstream.

She found the children side by side, lying flat on a ledge over a shallow part of the river, their gaze intent on the water. Mary Ann sculled closer and saw them look up in disgust as her paddle disturbed the stillness.

Lizzie leapt to her feet. 'You've frightened them away, Mam. Tolly was going to show me how to catch one with his net.'

'I'll frighten you, me girl, when I get me hands on you.'

Tolly glanced fearfully from one to the other. 'I . . . I'm s-sorry,' he stammered, but Lizzie only grinned saucily at her.

'You'll have to catch me first.'

'Why, you cheeky little . . .' It was at that moment that Mary Ann became aware of a rider on horseback in the meadow behind the children, coming slowly towards the riverbank. A tall, handsome man, dressed in a black riding habit.

Mary Ann felt the breath squeezed from her body as she gazed for the first time in almost ten years on Randolph Marsh.

Thirty-Eight

'I only wanted to catch you a fish, Daddy.' Mary Ann listened with only half an ear to her wayward daughter's excuses. 'I won't do it again. At least, not without asking you first.' The child was incredible, Mary Ann thought, though her mind was still reeling. She argues like an adult, justifying her naughtiness. 'Please don't take my boat away, Daddy.'

Every nerve in her body still jangling, Mary Ann wandered away down the deck towards the bows leaving Dan to admonish the child for once.

So often Mary Ann had thought about what she would do, what she might feel, when she saw Randolph again. Would she hate him, want to fly at him and pummel him or scratch his eyes out as she had the last time they had been together? Now she was in turmoil because it had happened and she had felt none of those things. She had been totally unprepared for the thrill that ran through her. It was still there, the power that he exuded over her. The mere sight of him had made her whole being quiver.

She leant on the rail and gazed back down the river, hungry for another glimpse of him, but though she scanned the fields on either side she could see no galloping horse.

Had he recognized her? Had he known her?

He had made no move of acknowledgement. He had

merely reined in his horse and sat there, high up in the saddle, watching them.

Maybe the children had been poaching. Mary Ann didn't know if anyone owned the rights to fishing in the river. Perhaps Randolph did, for since his father's death quite recently, he had inherited the Marsh estates and all that went with them. The fields of golden corn, the meadows, streams and woodlands that stretched along the Trent valley, even the villages and many of the homes of the people who lived there were owned by the Marsh Estate. So, maybe he even owned part of the river, certainly the right to fish there.

Dan had once hinted as much when they'd all heard of Bertram Marsh's death one Sunday lunchtime in Waterman's Yard. 'That family's got too much power, if you ask me. They nearly own the folk around here. 'Tisn't right. Not in this day and age. It's nineteen thirty-three, for heaven's sake, and we're still living in a system that's almost feudal.'

'Fancy yasen as Lord of the Manor, do you, our Dan?' Bessie had asked.

'I'd make a darn sight better job of it than *he's* going to,' he'd responded, waving his fork at his mother.

'It's a shame young Mr Arthur was killed,' Bert had put in quietly. 'He'd have made a much better squire than his brother.'

'Be better still if women had the same chance as the menfolk. Miss Edwina would be perfect.'

Duggie, as ever, had teased, 'I don't know. We gave 'em the vote and now they want to rule the world.'

The family had laughed and the conversation had turned away from the Marsh family. Mary Ann had said nothing, but she had listened and now, as she stood on the deck of the *Maid Mary Ann* shading her eyes against the glare of the sun sparkling on the water, she thought, And now he's master of it all.

She saw him again one day when she was alone at the wash-house a mile along the river south of Eastlands' Ferry. She heard the pounding of a horse's hooves and her heart missed a beat as she dropped Dan's shirt back into the tub of rinsing water and hurried outside. He was galloping across the field and, as she watched, he took a hedge in a flying leap, horse and rider suspended in mid-air for a heart-stopping moment until he landed with a thud on the opposite side. Mary Ann stood watching him until he was a speck in the distance.

The day he spoke to her, once more at the wash-house, Lizzie was with her.

'Good day, Mrs Ruddick.' Sitting high above her on his restless stallion, he looked down upon her, smiling that slow, sardonic smile that still had the power to twist her heart and make her pulse race.

'Mr Marsh,' she murmured and tried to turn away, pushing Lizzie before her towards their two cog boats moored against the small landing stage.

He leant forward, resting his arm on the front of his saddle. 'So formal, Mary Ann,' he said softly and she glanced over her shoulder, looking up once more into those blue eyes, and she knew herself lost.

She tried, oh how she tried, to turn away, to step into the boat and scull back down the river to Dan and to safety. And maybe, just maybe, she would have managed it if Lizzie had not refused to respond to her mother's little push urging her towards the river. Instead, she stared up at the stranger and then smiled prettily.

'Hello,' Lizzie said. 'Who are you?'

'Lizzie . . .' Mary Ann began, but Randolph's laugh rang out. 'Don't scold her, Mary Ann. I like a child with spirit. My own son could well take a lesson from her. In fact, I must bring him to meet her. Maybe . . .' his voice was suddenly deep and low, 'maybe they will become good friends.'

Mary Ann's head shot up as she said tartly, 'Surely you wouldn't allow your son to consort with the likes of us?' Then she added pointedly, 'Mr Marsh.'

'I wasn't suggesting they should be married, Mary Ann.' Again, his voice was soft as he added, 'Though times are changing. I doubt my son will be obliged to marry where his father chooses.'

His blue eyes were holding her gaze now and in that brief moment, there passed between them explanation, sorrow; even, Mary Ann believed, a plea for forgiveness, though not a word was spoken.

'I must go,' she said hoarsely.

'I'll see you again though?'

Now there was no mistaking the entreaty in his tone. But all Mary Ann would allow herself to say, was, 'Good day, Mr Marsh.'

As they sculled, side by side, downriver, Mary Ann was aware of him keeping the pace with them as he rode along the riverbank, matching their speed. But before they came to a bend in the river and within sight of Dan's ship, Randolph turned and galloped away towards the woodland on the other side of the meadow bordering the river.

'Who was he, Mam?' Lizzie called.

Mary Ann tried to quieten the thudding of her heart, so strong that it seemed to echo the sound of his horse's hooves. She thought quickly and said, 'Miss Edwina's brother,' and as they neared the ship, she said, 'Don't tell your father or Uncle Duggie that we met him, Lizzie.'

The child's eyes were innocent. 'Why not?'

Mary Ann swallowed and then, knowing that the child would do nothing to hurt her beloved father, she answered deviously, 'Your daddy doesn't like him and it would only upset him to think we had even been talking to him.'

Lizzie's cheeks dimpled. 'All right, then. I promise.'

Their meetings became frequent and, soon, were planned.

Whilst Lizzie was at school, there was no danger of discovery, for Mary Ann waited until the ship reached the part of the river where the wash-house was situated.

'I'll catch you up,' she would say gaily to Dan as she clambered down into the cog boat, loaded with their weekly wash.

'I don't know why you don't come ahead and then let me pick you up when I get here like most watermen's wives do?' Dan remarked more than once, but the comment was said idly with no thought in his trusting mind that Mary Ann might have her own devious reasons.

Mary Ann never answered him, just waved goodbye and sculled towards the bank, her heart thumping in anticipation, knowing that in the shadows of the trees at the edge of Raven's Wood, only a field's width away, Randolph was waiting.

Thirty-Nine

'I never wanted to hurt you, you must know that, Mary Ann.'

They were sitting together with their backs against a tree trunk, hidden deep in Raven's Wood, the scent of bluebells all around them, the sound of rustling leaves and busy, twittering birds above them.

'I wish you hadn't left The Hall,' he said. 'Why did you run away?'

'How could I stay?' she asked simply.

'I would have cared for you. Looked after you. I said I would.'

'And what would your bride have said,' she asked bitterly, 'if you had installed your mistress just down the corridor?'

Randolph sighed and swished his whip at a passing bumblebee. 'You're right, of course. You couldn't have stayed there, but if only you'd given me a little time. Time to work something out.'

'Such as?'

'I would have found you a little cottage somewhere.'

The idea appalled and yet thrilled her at the same time. 'I'd have been a kept woman, you mean? Your mistress?'

'At least we could have been together.'

'You *could* have married me,' she retaliated.

He was shaking his head sadly, 'No, I couldn't Mary Ann. Not then. If I was free now, maybe. But then . . . No.'

'Because of your father?'

'Partly.'

'What then?'

Again, he sighed. 'My family name and the Marsh Estate mean everything to me. There was a clause in Great-Great-Grandfather Marsh's will that should any heir marry against the wishes of the family, then he would be cut off with a shilling.'

'They really put that? In the will?'

Randolph nodded. 'Oh, yes. And they meant it.'

'And it still counts today?'

'Yes.'

'And Lawrence? He'll have to marry someone of whom you approve or he will be "cut off with a shilling"?'

'Yes.'

Remembering the word that Dan had used, Mary Ann said, 'It sounds positively feudal to me.'

'It is,' Randolph agreed blandly. 'But then in our world, it works. Of course I might . . .' he smiled down at her, but his tone had a tinge of sarcasm, ' . . . try to be a little more understanding where my son's concerned.'

Mary Ann looked deep into the blue eyes that were so close to hers. She had seen those eyes afire with passion and she had seen them cold with rejection. Now they were calculating.

Perceptively, she said, 'And you might not.'

'It would depend, of course,' Randolph said glancing away. 'He is my only son and heir. My only child. And now, it is highly unlikely there will be any more.'

Her eyes widened and her gaze met his again as he added in a whisper, 'If you know what I mean.'

She did. Oh, she did, and her heart began to sing.

She tore her gaze away from his, fearful of what he

would be able to read in her eyes. 'Why did you never tell me yourself that you were engaged to Celia?'

'Who was it who told you?' Even after all these years his voice was harsh with anger against whoever had enlightened her.

Mary Ann, glad that she had kept Edwina's name out of the conversation thus far, said quite truthfully, 'It was common knowledge amongst the servants.'

Randolph sighed. 'Ah yes. Servants gossip. I sometimes think they know more about our lives than we do ourselves.'

Mary Ann giggled. 'I hope they don't know about us now.'

They sat together, their fingers entwined, until she said slowly, 'So, you're telling me that your marriage to Celia was a marriage of convenience? The union of two land-owning families.'

'It's the done thing, my dear, in my world.'

'Do you love her? Your wife?' She thought about Celia, the bored, discontented woman, whom she had met just that once in Edwina's apartment at the school. She certainly had not looked happy then, Mary Ann remembered. So were things any better now? 'Are you happy together?'

Randolph gave a wry laugh. 'Hardly. Haven't I just told you as much?' Again she dared to glance at him and, suddenly, the old passion, the remembered fire was still there in his eyes. 'We did our duty and produced a son and heir.' He grimaced. 'I suppose we should have provided a "spare" as well, but after Lawrence's birth, Celia flatly refused to go through the whole disgusting process, as she called it, again.'

Mary Ann rested her head against his shoulder. 'You'll have to take good care of him, then.'

'Mm,' Randolph murmured. 'Let's just hope there's not

another war.' His tone was bitter as he added, 'They have a nasty habit of devastating future generations.'

He put his arm around her and pulled her close. 'And what about you, my sweet Mary Ann, are you happy with Dan Ruddick?'

Carefully, Mary Ann said, 'He's a good man. He's kind and loving, but . . .'

He touched her chin with a gentle finger. 'But?' he prompted.

'But he's not you,' she said simply and raised her face for his kiss.

The school holidays presented problems for their trysts.

'You stay with your daddy,' Mary Ann said one wash day when she knew Randolph would be waiting, but Lizzie would not be coerced. 'I want to come, Mam. I like turning the mangle.'

'Let her go with you,' Dan said, unwittingly making matters worse. 'She doesn't want to be stuck on board ship all the holidays.'

'Besides,' Duggie called across the deck from where he was hauling on a sheet to bring in the sail, 'you might see young Tolly.' And he winked at his niece.

It was not Tolly whom Lizzie met that day, but Lawrence Marsh.

'There's a motor car coming,' Lizzie said, as she helped Mary Ann to fold the wet sheets. Dropping the end she was holding on to the dirty floor, she dashed to the door.

'Oh Lizzie, now look what you've done.' Exasperated already by the mere presence of the girl, Mary Ann snapped, but Lizzie was not listening.

'It's that man. The one we saw on horseback. He's got a boy with him.' The sound of the motor came nearer until it drew up outside the whitewashed building. The noise of the engine petered out as it was switched off and Mary Ann heard Randolph's voice.

'Good day to you, Miss Ruddick.'

Mary Ann held her breath. She hardly dared to move to the doorway. She was sure that if anyone saw them together, they would guess the truth. Then she let out her breath in a long sigh. She was being foolish. What could a couple of children know about the craving she had for this man? The mere sight of him made her knees tremble and her stomach churn. And when he touched her, the world seemed to explode in a firework of dazzling lights.

She swallowed the excitement that rose in her throat and moved to the door.

'Mr Marsh,' she managed to say, outwardly calm. 'Good morning.'

Her glance went to the boy, who was climbing out of the passenger seat.

'Mrs Ruddick, may I present my son, Lawrence. And this, I presume, is your daughter.' He was holding out his hand to Lizzie as he added, 'And what is your name, my dear?'

He was playing the part just as she was, Mary Ann thought. He knew very well what Lizzie's name was, just as she knew who Lawrence was. Mary Ann hid her secret smile as she watched Lizzie dip her knee and hold out her hand. The girl dimpled at the tall man and her eyes twinkled, but she swiftly lost interest in the adult and turned her attention to the boy.

'Hello. How old are you?'

Lawrence blinked at her directness, but after a moment's hesitation, he answered, 'Nine – at least nearly.'

Lizzie's smile widened. 'Me, too.'

The two adults watched in amusement as the youngsters eyed each other. 'You're tall for your age, aren't you?' Lizzie appraised. 'You're taller than me.'

The boy was thin, but his child's face promised to be handsome in adulthood with a straight nose and firm jaw.

'So what do you say to a ride in my motor car, little lady?' Randolph said. Turning towards Mary Ann so that the children should not see, he winked at her and added, deliberately offhand, 'And, of course, your mother may come too if she wishes.'

Five minutes later the car was speeding along country lanes, frightening squawking chickens and filling the quiet air with noise and smoke. The children bounced on the back seat, laughing, whilst Mary Ann clung on, terrified when Randolph hurled the car around corners throwing his passengers from side to side.

He brought the car to a halt at the edge of the wood and turned to the children.

'Run and play in the woods.' It was a command rather than an invitation.

Mary Ann felt Lizzie's eyes question her. 'Mam?'

'It's all right,' she reassured her. 'But only half an hour, mind.' Then she added primly like any good and dutiful wife should, 'We must get back then or your father will wonder where we've got to.'

The children clambered out of the car and ran shrieking and yelling into the wood and disappeared amongst the trees.

Still sitting in the car, Randolph reached for her. 'Oh Mary Ann, Mary Ann.'

An hour later, Mary Ann went to the edge of the woods and called, 'Lizzie, Lizzie. Where are you?'

She heard their laughter and then their footsteps

crunching through the undergrowth towards her. 'Come along. We're late,' she said briskly, pretending to be cross. 'We'll never catch the ship up at this rate.'

'Sorry, Mam. But Lawrence and me were building a den.'

As they walked to the car, Mary Ann held Lizzie back a pace or two behind Lawrence. 'Lizzie, we won't tell your father about this. About riding in a motor car. He might be worried. And you don't want to worry your daddy, do you?'

She felt Lizzie glance at her. 'No, Mam,' the girl said quietly.

'It would be best not to mention that we met Mr Marsh and his son. That way, you can't let it slip, can you?'

'No, Mam,' Lizzie agreed, but there was reluctance in her tone. She hated deceit of any kind and not being truthful with her father especially would cause her pain, Mary Ann knew. But she could not take the risk of the child letting out her secret.

As they climbed into the car, Lawrence was asking eagerly, 'Can we take Mrs Ruddick and Lizzie out again, Father?'

Coyly, Mary Ann glanced at Randolph. 'Well, I don't know about that. I expect Mr Marsh has better things to do than take us for rides in the country.'

She heard his low chuckle and then as he swung the starting handle and climbed back in beside her, beneath the noise of the engine he said, 'I can't think of anything I'd rather be doing.'

He took them back to the wash-house and even helped to load the heavy basket of washing into Mary Ann's cog boat. Already, Lizzie was sculling ahead down the river and Lawrence had remained in the car.

'When will I see you again?' he whispered.

'Next week,' she replied.

'A whole week,' he moaned. 'Oh, I can't bear it.'

'No. Neither can I.' For a moment as he handed the basket down to her, their eyes met each other's and held. There was such passion in his eyes that it seemed to burn into her. 'I know,' she breathed. 'I know. But there's nothing I can do.'

'There must be,' he whispered intensely. 'There has to be.'

'I must go,' she said, desperate to stay but knowing she had no choice.

'Mary Ann,' he said urgently, but already the boat was inching away from the bank.

'Thank you, Mr Marsh,' she called out for the benefit of Lawrence's young ears. 'Thank you for your kindness.'

As she sculled away, she knew he stood watching her, but she dared not look back.

If she had, she might well never have returned to the ship.

Forty

'Wherever have you been?' was Dan's greeting as they climbed aboard the *Maid Mary Ann*, weighed down with wet washing to be dried. 'I was worried. I thought something must have happened. I nearly had to anchor.'

'Oh, what a catastrophe that would have been,' Mary Ann snapped. 'Well, you can thank your daughter. She ran off playing and I couldn't find her.' She avoided looking at Lizzie, knowing that the girl would be gazing open-mouthed at her mother's lies. 'I shan't take her again.'

'But, Mam, I . . .' Lizzie began, but Mary Ann rounded on her. 'Not another word, miss, if you know what's good for you.'

She picked up the basket and walked along the deck away from them, praying very hard that her daughter would not give her away.

'Never mind, love,' Mary Ann heard Dan say behind her. 'You stay with me and Uncle Duggie.' He laughed, indulgent as ever. 'You can't run away far on board, can you?'

Their meetings went on through the summer and, despite her threat, Mary Ann was obliged to take Lizzie with her. Sometimes, Randolph brought Lawrence, at other times he came alone, but on those occasions there was no opportunity for a jaunt to the woods; there was no one to keep Lizzie occupied. On such days, Mary Ann could see her own frustration mirrored in Randolph's eyes but there was nothing they could do. One day, when Lizzie had been in mischief, Mary Ann used her naughtiness as an excuse to leave her with Dan, hoping to snatch a brief time alone with Randolph. But, not knowing, he brought Lawrence along.

They both heaved a sigh of relief when the school holidays were over and they watched in amusement as the two young people said goodbye to each other.

'I've got to go away tomorrow,' Lawrence told Lizzie haltingly. 'Back to boarding school.'

Lizzie pulled a face. 'Poor you. I go to your auntie's school. I stay with me grandma in the week when Mam and Daddy are away. It's nice there. Do you like school?'

Mary Ann saw the boy glance towards his father. With obvious diplomacy, Lawrence said, 'It's all right.' Then he turned back to Lizzie and in a low voice, added, 'But I'll miss you. We've had a great time this hols, haven't we?'

As the children continued to talk, promising to write to each other, Randolph murmured, 'Do you think this is the start of a romance? Is it going to be the romance of the century?'

'Oh no,' Mary Ann whispered, touching his hand discreetly. 'No, ours is the romance of the century.'

Randolph grasped her hand impulsively and said, 'Next week when we're alone, try to stay as long as you can. I want to take you for a drive.'

'I'll be here,' she promised. 'Same time, same place.'

But the following week, when she knew Randolph would be waiting for her in the shadow of the trees, she was aboard the ship in Grimsby docks waiting whilst a cargo of barley was loaded to be 'livered to a malt kiln in

Elsborough. She was angry and frustrated, but there was nothing she could do. She could not send a message and all she could do was hope and pray that he would be there the next week.

'I don't like to be made a fool of, Mary Ann,' Randolph said stiffly.

'Would you have liked me to have sent a telegram to The Hall?' Her tone was brittle, hiding her own fear that he would not come to meet her again. ' "Sorry, can't meet you on Monday. Love from your mistress." '

'Don't be ridiculous, Mary Ann,' he snapped.

'Ridiculous, am I? Randolph, I am at the mercy of the tides, the wind, Dan's cargoes and where they have to be loaded. It's a miracle that we have been able to meet as often as we have. It's only because he usually has a regular run on a Monday, and we pass here at about the same time each week, that I've managed it until now.'

'So what went wrong last week?'

Mary Ann shrugged. 'An urgent delivery that they were prepared to pay over the odds for.'

'And, of course, your thrifty husband couldn't miss such an opportunity, could he?'

'No,' Mary Ann said shortly, disliking the sarcasm in Randolph's tone that was directed at her husband. It was quite bad enough that she was deceiving Dan. In spite of all her faults – and she knew there were many – she couldn't bear to hear Dan ridiculed too. He didn't deserve that. In fact, Mary Ann realized in a fleeting and rare moment of honesty, he didn't deserve any of it. Dan Ruddick was a good man, too good for the likes of Mary Ann Clark.

'Come . . .' Randolph was holding out his hand to her,

all smiles now. 'Don't let's waste our precious time together in quarrelling. How long have you got?'

She couldn't resist him. As he had said, so long ago now and so prophetically, he only had to crook his little finger and she came running.

Pushing away uncomfortable thoughts, Mary Ann smiled impishly now. 'I told him I had a lot of extra washing to do this week, with having missed my turn at the wash-house last Monday.'

Randolph's returning smile was wolfish. 'Good, because I am going to take you on a long car ride.'

They took the country lanes and back roads where there was less likelihood of being seen by anyone who knew them. The car was bouncing down a long, rutted cart track towards a small, white cottage, on the far side of Raven's Wood, set against a backdrop of trees. They came to a halt outside the door and switched off the engine. Leaning back in his seat, he said, 'Here we are.'

Mary Ann looked at the cottage. It was painted white with a pretty garden and a climbing rose tree around the green-painted front door. Then she looked at Randolph. 'Here we are – where?'

'Home,' he said.

Her heart was racing and the blood was pounding in her ears. 'What . . . what do you mean?'

He leant towards her and took hold of her hand. Softly, he said, 'This could be yours, Mary Ann, if only you'll say the word.'

'You mean – it's yours?'

'Of course I do. It's part of the estate. It's really a gamekeeper's cottage, but I don't have need of as many gamekeepers as I used to have. So, it's been empty for a while. Oh, Mary Ann, Mary Ann . . .' He moved nearer and began to kiss her neck, urging her, tempting her between his kisses. 'Leave him, Mary Ann. Come to me. Be mine. You know how I need you, how I want you . . .'

For a while she gave in to his passion but afterwards, in the cold light of reason, she said, 'You know I can't.'

It was over Sunday lunch in Waterman's Yard that the trouble began.

'Have you seen Randolph Marsh's new car? It's a monstrosity of a thing.' Duggie, still interested in all things mechanical, laughed. 'But what I'd give for a ride in one.'

Mary Ann glanced worriedly at Lizzie, but she was concentrating on eating her favourite pudding – treacle sponge that Bessie always made for her – and didn't appear to be listening to the adult conversation going on around her.

'It'll have set him back a pretty penny. I think it's a Rolls Royce.'

'No, it isn't.' Lizzie took another mouthful before she said, 'It's a Bentley.'

Duggie laughed. 'How do you know that, our Lizzie?'

Lizzie scraped the spoon around her bowl to get the last drop of treacle. 'Lawrence told me.'

There was silence around the table as all eyes turned to look at her. Suddenly, Lizzie was motionless. Then her spoon clattered into her dish as she gazed, horrified, at her mother.

'Lizzie, go below.'

When they arrived back at the ship, Dan's voice was stern. Nothing more had been said around the dinner table, but there had been an awkward silence. Bessie had opened her mouth and Mary Ann had felt her heart begin to thump with fear. Nothing got past her mother-in-law, but then she saw Bert put out his hand to touch his wife's. Bessie had glanced at him, met his steady gaze, seen the slight shake of his head and had closed her mouth. But she had got up quickly from the table and began to clear away the pots, crashing them dangerously together so that Mary Ann was in no doubt that Bessie smelt trouble.

Even Duggie, usually blithely unaware of undercurrents, kept silent and, when the time came for them to return to the ship, he made an excuse that he was meeting some cronies in The Waterman's Arms.

Now Mary Ann was alone on deck with her husband.

'What's been going on?' Dan demanded. There was a tension in his voice, but she could tell that he was struggling to remain calm. 'How does my daughter – a child of ten – know the difference between a Rolls Royce and a Bentley? And how come she knows the boy?'

Mary Ann's laugh was brittle as she tried to bluff her way out. 'She's met him. Just once.'

'When? How?'

Mary Ann shrugged. 'That day she ran off and I couldn't find her. You remember? Well, that's where she was. They'd been driving past and stopped to speak to her. Mr Randolph and his son.' Embellishing her story, Mary Ann went on. 'They took her for a ride in their motor car.'

Dan was appalled. 'Took her . . .? She got in a car with strangers?' He paused and Mary Ann glanced away from him, her resolve wilting under his keen scrutiny. Now he was shaking his head. 'Oh no. I don't believe it. She wouldn't do that. Not my Lizzie. Not after all I've told her. She wouldn't get into a car with complete strangers.'

He paused and said slowly, 'Not unless she knew them.' There was a long pause before he asked, his voice now deceptively quiet, 'Did she know them, Mary Ann?'

'Of course not. How could she?'

'Mary Ann, I want the truth and I mean to have it. Either you tell it to me or I shall ask Lizzie. She will tell me the truth, I know she will, but I don't want to have to put a child in the awful position of having to tell me her mother's secrets.'

There was silence between them, the only sound the lapping of the water against the side of the ship, a fitful moon their only light in the darkness of the night.

'Mary Ann?'

Her resolve snapped. Her voice was a high-pitched shriek. 'All right. All right. You want the truth. All right. I've been meeting him. Randolph. He's my lover.' She paused and then, plunging the knife in even further, added, 'Again.'

He lunged at her and, grabbing her shoulders, shook her. He was shouting now. 'Why? Why, Mary Ann? Haven't I been good to you? Haven't I looked after you and cared for you?'

'I love him,' she screamed at him. 'I always have. And he loves me.'

'No. No. You can't believe that. He's just amusing himself with you. How can you allow yourself to be taken in by him? How can you be so stupid?'

Mary Ann pulled herself free of his grasp and ran to the side of the ship. 'Let me go. What do you know about it? What do you know about love?'

'How can you say that to me, Mary Ann? I gave up Susan for you.'

Appalled, they stared at each other through the darkness. He moved towards her. 'Mary Ann, I didn't mean it.

I love you. Really I do. Forget about him. We'll say no more about it, if you promise me not to see him again.'

'No, no,' her cry was anguished. 'I can't live without seeing him. I'm sorry, Dan. I don't mean to hurt you, but—'

'Listen to me. He'll leave you again, just like he did before, when he tires of you.'

Her voice rose hysterically. 'It's not like that. It wasn't his fault. He had to marry Celia. His family made him.'

'Don't be ridiculous. A man in his position can't be made to do anything he doesn't want to.'

A seed of doubt crept into her mind, rooted itself there and began to grow. But instead of gratitude, Mary Ann hated the person who had sown it.

She flew at Dan and pummelled his chest shrieking at him. 'I hate you. You don't want me to be happy. You want to keep me a prisoner on this blasted boat.'

Dan tried to catch hold of her, but she struggled free, crying hysterically. He raised his hand and slapped her face, not in fury, but to bring her to reason.

She fell back against the rail and at that moment the Aegir, moving majestically upriver, lifted the ship at its moorings.

Mary Ann, caught off balance, felt herself falling backwards over the side. Her arms flailed helplessly and her mouth opened in a terrified scream as she splashed into the black, swift flowing water.

She rose to the surface and heard, just once, the desperation in Dan's voice as he called her name.

'Mary Ann. *Maaary Aaan!*'

Then the dark waters closed over her head.

Part Three

Lizzie

Forty-One

1939

The rowing boat bumped gently against the side of the ship and Lizzie heard Tolly's voice calling, his face upturned as her father leant over the side. 'Mr Ruddick? Can Lizzie come fishing with me?'

'Where are you going, lad?'

Stifling her giggles, Lizzie watched as her uncle, Duggie, joined his brother to peer down at the boy, too. For a moment, Tolly seemed fazed by the two stern, weather-beaten faces staring down at him and his stammer became suddenly more pronounced. 'N-not far. Just – just to the bend in the river.'

'The Aegir's due soon and it'll be a big one,' Duggie warned.

'I know. That's why it's a good time. C-can Lizzie come, Mr Ruddick?'

The two men exchanged a glance. Lizzie, at fifteen, was a child of the river. Born and bred on the water, it had never held any fears for her. And now Dan, although still protective of his pretty daughter, was obliged to accept that, with her knowledge of the river and all its moods and her innate common sense, he should allow her a greater freedom.

'As long as you promise to be extra careful,' he said. 'Then, all right.'

Lizzie, already dressed for the expedition for she had known Tolly would come, climbed the last few steps of the ladder from the cabin and stepped on to the deck. The two men turned at the sound and Duggie laughed out loud. 'You little minx,' he said, holding out his arm and drawing her to him to hug her. 'You've arranged all this, haven't you? What if your dad had said, "No"?'

Lizzie, so like her mother in many ways, with dark unruly curls and dancing dark eyes, laughed, 'I'd have gone anyway,' she teased, although they all knew she would have done no such thing. Already, the girl seemed older than her years, far more mature than most girls of her age, and it seemed as if she had been blessed with the best traits of character from each of her parents. She had her mother's looks and her sunny nature and impish ways, but from Dan she got her honesty and, although this was probably a throwback to her grandmother, Bessie, she was forthright and afraid of no one.

'I've fried you a piece of steak each and there are potatoes, swede and carrots in the boiling pan.'

'Now, don't be late,' her father frowned. 'I want you home before dark.'

'Yes, Dad,' Lizzie called gaily as she swung herself over the side and down the rope ladder towards Tolly's boat. 'I'll bring you back a salmon.'

She sat in the bows of the small boat, whilst Tolly rowed strongly away from the ship and, reaching the middle of the river, rested a moment on the oars, allowing the boat to drift with the current. Lizzie gave a contented sigh, leaning back in the boat and allowing her hand to trail in the water. It was a balmy evening, a quiet time, when everyone seemed to be waiting for the swell of the Aegir surging up the river. The willow trees planted along the riverbank to strengthen it, the ducks swimming in convoy, the ships and the smaller boats, moored at the wharves or at the landings all seemed to be waiting for the great wave.

'I've got a job,' Tolly told her. Now that they were alone, all sign of his stammer had vanished.

Lizzie sat up and clapped her hands. 'That's wonderful. Is it with Mr Bryce, the basketmaker?'

On the Nottinghamshire side of the river, near the shipyard, were the workshops of Harry Bryce. Harry had served in the Great War and had been blinded, but he now ran a small cottage industry, weaving willow baskets with intricate skill. It was the root of the willow that strengthened the bank, the tree itself only serving as nature's ornament. So, with the permission of the authorities, Harry Bryce harvested the willow he needed from along the side of the Trent. Because of his blindness he was unable to do that work himself and so an army of schoolboys worked for him in their spare time, and to some, like Tolly, he had taught the rudiments of his trade.

To Lizzie's surprise, Tolly said, 'No. It's at the shipyard.' His face sobered. 'I wanted to work for Mr Bryce and he would have taken me on, if he could have afforded it. But,' he added hastily, 'I shall still be able to help him if he needs me.'

Lizzie smiled at him warmly. She knew he was very fond of old Mr Bryce, who had been very kind to him. The basketmaker's workshop had been a haven from the boy's unhappy home life.

As if reading her thoughts, Tolly said, 'He's like another dad to me.' He coloured a little and the stutter was temporarily back as he added, 'In fact, he's n-nicer to me than me real dad is.' Only to Lizzie did Tolly ever speak of his bullying, aggressive father, and she told no one, not even her own beloved daddy and uncle, although she was aware that they knew much of what went on inside the ferryman's white-washed cottage.

Tolly was smiling as he said, 'I shall row up the river to work every day and Mr Bryce has already said that if the weather's ever really bad, then I can stay with him for a night or two.'

'What will you be doing there? At the shipyard, I mean?'

'I'm to be an apprentice carpenter. Me dad's signed the papers already.'

'Is it what you want to do?'

Tolly shrugged. 'I don't know. I can't think of anything else.'

She leant towards him. 'Why don't you leave home? Why don't you get away from him?'

Tolly pressed his lips together and shook his head. 'I don't want to leave me mam. Now I'm older, maybe I can get between them a bit more.'

'Yes, and look what happens when you do. Like last week, you got the black eye.'

'I'd sooner that, than me mam get hit.'

'Oh Tolly,' Lizzie's eyes filled with tears. 'Why does he do it?'

The boy shrugged his thin shoulders and then smiled. 'Come on, it'll be here soon. Let's not think about him. Not tonight. Tonight, we're going fishing.'

He rowed a little further and then they sat waiting until they saw the wave coming towards them around the curve in the river.

'She's a big 'un. Hold on tight, Lizzie.'

As the Aegir rolled towards them, Tolly positioned the rowing boat bows into the wave. They clung on as the little boat crested the foaming wave and rode on top of it before meeting the smaller waves – the whelps, as the locals called them. The wave had stirred up the mud from the river bottom, so that fish were choked and swam about in panic.

The two youngsters waited patiently until the water began to settle and clear a little.

'There! Look!' Lizzie cried, 'I can see one. There's another – and another.'

'They're exhausted now,' Tolly said, reaching for his salmon net. He dipped the round hoop into the water and drew it along, scooping up the disorientated fish.

'Well, it's certainly fish for tomorrow night's supper,' Lizzie laughed, as fish after fish landed in the bottom of Tolly's boat.

'Just made it.'

Duggie was leaning down over the side of the ship to help her aboard. 'Your dad was starting to get twitchy because you weren't back and it's almost dark.'

'I'm sorry, but just look how many fish we caught.'

'My word, that is a fine catch. We'll be able to take some to your gran, Lizzie. She and your grandpa love a bit of fresh salmon. Here, Tolly, let me help you.'

'Where's Dad?' Lizzie asked, excitedly. 'I want him to see how many we've caught.'

'He's below in the cabin. He's in one of his moods.'

The delight fell from Lizzie's face. 'Is it my fault? Because I'm late.'

'Nah,' Duggie said, lifting the fish on to the deck. ''Course it isn't. Just go and make him a cuppa, lass, and put plenty of sugar in it.' He grinned. 'Sweeten the old grump up a bit.'

Lizzie sighed as she went towards the companion, feeling again the burden of guilt. For five years Lizzie had secretly carried the belief that she had been to blame for that fateful night when her mother had disappeared.

For weeks afterwards, she had cried, 'I'm sorry, I'm sorry, Daddy.' Her father had stroked her hair and though the sorrow never left his eyes, he had comforted her. 'It's not your fault, sweetheart. It's nothing to do with you.'

Five years later the haunted look was still there in his eyes. He never spoke about Mary Ann and no one had ever told Lizzie what had happened to her mother. Perhaps they didn't know, she thought, for all anyone would say was, 'She's gone away, love.'

Night after night, Lizzie would dream that she heard her mother's voice and would wake with the name on her lips, 'Mam?'

A girl at school – one who had never liked Lizzie, thinking her not the type who should attend a select private school – had said, 'They might hang your father. One day they'll find your mother's body floating in the river, all bloated and ugly, and then they'll hang your father for killing her. Just like they did your grandfather.'

Lizzie had run, crying, to Miss Marsh. Edwina had held her and comforted her, but even she had offered no explanation. Afterwards, the rest of her class had refused to include Lizzie in their games and, worse still, had ignored her completely, refusing to speak to her.

'She's a tell-tale-tit,' they mocked. 'Run and tell teacher, why don't you, Cry Baby?'

Lizzie had run home to the safe arms of her gran in Waterman's Yard. She had had nightmares for weeks, waking screaming in the night until Bessie had said one morning, 'You're not going to that school any more.'

So she had gone to the town's school, and there, Tolly had become her friend. Though the nightmares had lessened, Lizzie, deep within her, still believed herself to blame for the quarrel between her parents that night. And worse still, now, was implanted the terrifying thought that perhaps her mother had drowned in the river and that her father had been to blame. But Lizzie dared not ask, dared not put such a terrible thought into words. So she remained in ignorance. Outwardly, she was the sunny-natured, pretty girl she had always been, but deep in her heart she carried a leaden weight of sorrow. And what frightened her the most was that when she looked into her father's eyes, she saw that same fear mirrored there.

So Lizzie kept quiet and asked no questions lest she should bring more shame and sorrow upon her family.

She could not even talk to Tolly about it.

Forty-Two

From leaving school in 1938, Lizzie lived permanently aboard the *Maid Mary Ann*. She had always helped to look after her father and her uncle ever since her mother had gone, but, as she got older, she had taken on more and more of the domestic chores. Now, the only time she spent ashore was at the weekends when they all stayed with her grandparents in Waterman's Yard.

'There's going to be a war, you know.' If he said it once during the early part of 1939, Duggie said it a hundred times. But there were no clouds, war or otherwise, in the skies for Lizzie and Tolly that summer. Besides fishing for salmon and blobbing for eels, Lizzie would scull to meet him early in the morning before he went to work and together they would pick wild mushrooms, returning to the ship with a basketful. She made a rich, tasty pink sauce and served them hot to her father and uncle.

In early summer the two youngsters sought out the nests of plovers and moorhens, taking one or two eggs for their breakfasts.

'As long as you leave at least one egg in a moorhen's nest,' Tolly told her, 'she'll lay more. Just like a hen does.'

'I don't feel so bad about taking them, in that case,' said the tender-hearted Lizzie, who hated to think of the poor mothers robbed of their eggs.

On Sundays, after attending morning service in the

parish church with her family, Lizzie would often find Tolly waiting in Waterman's Yard.

'Are you c-coming blackberrying, Lizzie? I've f-found loads near Bourton.'

'As long as you don't go near Raven's Wood,' Dan would say and his frown would deepen. 'I don't want you going there.'

'All right, Dad,' Lizzie would agree cheerfully and off they would go for the afternoon, returning with their mouths and fingers stained with blackberry juice and refusing Sunday tea.

'Little scallywags, not eating that trifle I've spent hours making.' Bessie would pretend to be offended.

'Don't worry, Mam,' Duggie would say, winking at Lizzie. 'There's all the more for me.'

Then Bessie would gratefully accept the basketful of blackberries they had brought her. 'These'll make lovely jam and I'll have some apple and blackberry pasties ready for you next week to take back to the ship, Lizzie.'

'You enjoy yourselves,' Duggie said each time Lizzie went off with Tolly and, helping her climb down into Tolly's rowing boat, added, 'while you can.'

'Oh shut up, Duggie,' Dan said at last irritably. 'Anybody'd think you wanted a war the way you keep going on about it.'

Duggie only laughed and said, 'Well, it's the navy for me if it does happen.'

Lizzie stared at him. 'You wouldn't join up, Uncle Duggie, would you? Not really. What'd we do without you?'

Duggie put his hands across his heart. 'Ah, at least there'll be one pretty girl pining for me.'

Duggie had never married. Although he had come dangerously close once or twice he had always escaped 'the net', as he called it. He had never been without a girlfriend for very long, but as soon as rings and wedding bells were mentioned, he tactfully disentangled himself. It was to his credit that he had never left a girl pregnant, nor even particularly heartbroken. He was, at heart, a kind man and with his never failing good humour, he was genuinely liked by everyone as much as they loved him. The girls he jilted could never bring themselves to hate him and, in fact, he remained on good terms with most of them.

'I'll not be the only one,' Lizzie teased him. 'What about Janice?'

Duggie feigned ignorance. 'Janice? Who's Janice?'

Lizzie, joining in the fun, pretended to sigh. 'I see. Behind the times again, am I? Who's the latest then?'

'Well, there's this very nice girl who works in the jewellers' on the corner of Pottergate. Sheila, I think her name is. I was thinking of asking her out on Saturday night.'

'You want to be careful, Uncle Duggie. If she works in a jewellers', she might be able to buy things cheaper. She could have a ring on her finger before you know it.'

Duggie laughed loudly. 'She might well, Lizzie, my love, but it won't be me buying it for her.'

'Aren't you getting a bit old for all these young girls?' Dan said.

'I'm only thirty-four. They like an older, more mature man.'

'Older, yes,' Dan said. 'Mature – never!'

'You're just . . .' Duggie began, but then Lizzie saw him catch his lip. She guessed he had, in his teasing way, been going to say, 'You're just jealous,' but even Duggie stopped short of such a barb.

Dan walked away down the deck, a lonely figure, his

shoulders hunched. Lizzie stared after him and felt the familiar lump in her throat. Poor Dad, she thought, her love for him swelling in her breast. Whatever had happened that night, he was not to blame. She had to believe he was not to blame.

Now she murmured to Duggie, 'Will Dad have to go to war, Uncle Duggie?'

'Shouldn't think so, love. For a start he might be too old and even if he isn't, there are what they call "reserved occupations". He does a very useful job moving supplies about on the water. You never know, business for ships like ours might even pick up. Strange old world,' he mused more to himself than to the girl at his side. 'A catastrophe like a war can even be the making of people.'

'In business, you mean?' Lizzie asked.

'Aye, that and in a personal way too.' He grinned at her. 'Very character-building, is a war, young Lizzie.'

Soberly, Lizzie looked at him. The wind ruffled his dark hair, blowing it on to his forehead. For once his eyes had a serious, faraway look, as if already he was imagining himself sailing the high seas in a smart naval uniform.

Lizzie shuddered and reached out to touch his arm. 'If – if you do go, Uncle Duggie, you will be all right, won't you?'

The smile was back on his face as he patted her hand and looked down at her. ''Course I will, little Lizzie. It'll all be over by Christmas anyway. I'll be back before you've even missed me. You'll see.'

Everywhere the talk was of the war, but towards the end of August the annual regatta still took place. It was held, as always, on the stretch of river between Westlands and Eastlands, near where Ted Oliver ran his ferry.

'I've built a sea horse.' Proudly, Tolly showed Lizzie the barrel with the wooden horse's head he had made attached to one end. 'Are you entering the cog boat race, Lizzie?'

She nodded and her eyes twinkled with mischief. 'The blindfold race.'

'You're not!'

'I am.' She laughed. 'The worst thing that can happen is that I end up rowing down the middle of the river and have to be towed back by a motor boat.'

'No, no, you won't. I reckon you know this river as well as any of the men.'

'Are you going in for the greasy pole? My dad's having it on his ship this year.'

Every year one of the keel ships had a fifty-foot pole fixed in the bows pointing out over the water with a flag attached to the end of it. The pole was well greased, or soaped, and the person who walked along it and retrieved the flag won a prize and, later, it was also used for a pillow-fighting contest.

The day was bright and breezy and everybody seemed determined to enjoy themselves. Lizzie lined up in her cog boat with six other contestants. Tolly was not one of them as he had promised to try to shout instructions to her. Duggie would do the same from the opposite bank.

Solemnly, the brown paper bags were given out to each participant to put over their heads and the starter fired a pistol. Lizzie began to scull her boat away from the bank, but above the noise made by all the watchers, she could not distinguish Tolly's voice. For a moment she stopped sculling and let the boat drift, catching the feel of the current. Then, beneath the paper bag, Lizzie smiled and began to scull strongly in the direction she believed the opposite bank to be. It seemed to be taking her a long time and, for a moment, Lizzie thought she had miscalculated and that she was blithely sculling downstream to the amusement of all the onlookers. Then, quite clearly, she heard Duggie's voice.

'Come on, Lizzie. You're winning, lass. Just another two yards. Come on.'

A few more strokes and Lizzie felt the boat jolt against the bank and a huge cheer went up from the crowd. She removed the bag and turned to look back at her competitors. Three were tangled up with each other in the middle of the river, shouting and swearing, to the vast enjoyment of the watchers. One was rowing vigorously upstream against the current and another was sculling, supremely unaware, downstream. The last one hadn't even got away from the opposite bank and seemed to be going round in circles. Then, on the far bank she saw Tolly jumping up and down with excitement and waving his congratulations at her win.

Later, Duggie won the greasy pole competition and Tolly won the barrel race and everyone enjoyed the ale and sandwiches aboard a barge anchored in the middle of the river.

Although no one knew it at the time, it was to be the last time the regatta was held, for on Sunday 3 September war became a reality. The news was greeted by a lot of people with a sense of relief. At least the dreadful waiting was over.

'Well, now we know. Now we can get at 'em.' Duggie rubbed his hands gleefully as his father turned off the wireless and sat down in his chair. The whole family was squashed into Bessie's kitchen to hear the Prime Minister's broadcast.

'We'll just be left with young boys and old men to run the country,' Dan grumbled, 'whilst all the able-bodied men are away playing soldiers.'

There was silence until Bert's quiet voice said, 'It'll not be a game, son.'

Usually, it amused Lizzie to hear her daddy addressed as 'son' by his own father, but this morning, she was not smiling. Her face was serious, her eyes wide with anxiety as she listened intently to the conversation around her.

'Women did all sorts of things in the last lot,' Bessie murmured. 'Drove ambulances, worked in factories, even went to the Front as nurses. 'Spect they will again.' Lizzie felt her grandmother's gaze upon her. 'Even Lizzie here. She'll have to do her bit.'

'She's far too young,' Dan said quickly. 'Besides, I need her, 'specially if Duggie's going.' A strange bitterness crept into his tone as he added, 'At least she's capable of being a good "mate", even though she is a woman. She won't sit in the cabin all day doing her embroidery.'

Lizzie didn't understand his words or the look that passed between him and Bessie.

'Of course I'll stay with you, Dad,' she said, leaning against Dan's shoulder and smiling up at him.

Dan returned her smile and for a brief moment the haunted look went from his eyes. 'Aye, you'll never leave your old dad, will you, love?' he murmured softly.

'If it lasts as long as the last lot,' Bessie still insisted, 'she'll have to do as she's told in another three or four years' time and it won't be you doing the telling, our Dan. Not this time.'

When Duggie volunteered and was accepted into the Merchant Navy, Lizzie became her father's official mate aboard Mr Sudbury's ship, which he had skippered for the last sixteen years.

'You'll not always be able to take the lass with you, Dan,' his employer had warned. 'We shall more than likely get asked to go on some very odd missions, so just be prepared. By the way, I'm going to have the ship fitted out with a small diesel engine. You can still make use of the sails whenever possible, but it'll cut out wasted time waiting for a tow. Things are going to change, Dan,' Lizzie heard Mr Sudbury say to her father. 'And if we're to survive, we'll have to change with them.'

Dan bemoaned the fitting of a noisy, smelly engine to his beloved keel, but Lizzie loved its rhythmic phut-phut-phut. 'Wouldn't Uncle Duggie have liked it, Dad? I know just what he'd say. "Should have had one years ago."'

Dan's only reply was a baleful glance. 'I don't know why Mr Sudbury's bothered to have one fitted. Trade's dropped off that much, we look like being laid up for weeks. Everything's coming in by the ports on the west coast now. Besides, we're not allowed to move in the hours of darkness, so where's the point? The only cargo I've got this week is fifty tons of cement for building air-raid shelters.'

'It'll pick up again, Dad. It's bound to.'

A cold spell during the early months of 1940 kept the *Maid Mary Ann* moored at Elsborough and though Lizzie could find plenty to do ashore, Dan chafed at the enforced idleness. But when warmer weather came, with it returned some of the trade to the east coast ports.

Towards the end of May, Dan said, 'You can't come with me tomorrow, Lizzie.'

'Why not? Where are you going?'

Her father seemed tense and anxious and his answer was evasive. 'Oh, just into the Humber, but Mr Sudbury said you were not to go. He's sending one of his men down to go with me.'

The following morning, Lizzie helped her grandmother pack a basket of food for Dan.

'I think we'd better pack him a bit extra, love,' Bessie murmured. 'I reckon he's going to be gone a few days.'

'A few days?' Lizzie stared at her. 'Where's he going and why can't I go? And who's this man going in my place? Do you know more than he's told me?'

'Calm down, calm down,' Bessie smiled, but Lizzie noticed that the anxiety in her eyes was still there. 'All I know is that Mr Sudbury told ya dad it's something to do with the government or the War Office, or somebody.'

'What? Some sort of job for them, you mean?'

Bessie shrugged. 'I don't know and I don't even think your dad does. Mebbe this bloke who's joining him will know more. Now,' she added briskly, closing the lid and putting the peg through the fastening, 'can you carry this, love, 'cos I've packed enough to feed an army?'

'I know, I'll borrow Mr Eccleshall's pram wheels.' Lizzie darted out and across the yard to knock on Minnie's door. When their children had outgrown their old pram, Stan Eccleshall had removed the body and had fitted a sturdy wooden box on to the wheels. Through the years, it had seen good service for all his neighbours in Waterman's Yard.

At Miller's Wharf her father came down the gangway to help her lift the heavy basket aboard.

'I ought to be coming with you,' Lizzie grumbled. 'Who's going to look after you?'

'I wish you could come, Lizzie. I'll miss you, but he seems like a nice chap who's come. He's lost three fingers off his right hand so he didn't pass his medical for service, but it doesn't seem to stop him being able to handle a ship.'

'You . . . you will be careful, won't you, Dad?'

'Of course, now give us a hug and off you go back home to your gran.'

Lizzie watched him board and then cast off for him, waving to both him and the stranger on the deck of the *Maid Mary Ann*.

'Lizzie.' A familiar voice spoke behind her and she turned to smile at Tolly as he came to stand beside her. 'You not going on this trip, then?'

Lizzie shook her head. 'They won't let me.'

Tolly was gazing thoughtfully after the ship as it moved out into the middle of the river and began to sail downriver. Lizzie's gaze was still on her father's vessel, but Tolly glanced back upriver and then suddenly, he gripped her arm. 'Look. Just look!'

Lizzie turned to see several more of Mr Sudbury's ships coming down the river, following the *Maid Mary Ann*.

'Now just where,' Lizzie murmured, 'are they all going?'

'I don't know,' Tolly said, his gaze on the unusual sight. 'But it must be for something very important.'

Forty-Three

'You're like a cat on hot bricks, Lizzie,' Bessie grumbled. 'For heaven's sake find yourself something useful to do.'

'I'm just worried where Dad's gone, Gran. He's been gone three days.'

'Well, you're often away longer than that. How do you think I feel when I don't hear from you for days on end?' Bessie's needles continued to click as she sat beside the range, knitting a pair of socks.

'That's different. You know I'm with him then. You know I'll look after him.' She caught her grandmother's comical expression and laughed too. 'Oh, you know what I mean. We look after each other.'

Bessie chuckled softly, 'Aye, I know what you mean. You're a good girl, Lizzie.' There was a slight pause as she appeared to be thinking. 'I tell you what, love. You can go up to Miss Edwina's school for me. I'm running short of wool. She's become one of the mainstays of the local branch of the WVS and she's organizing all this war work that us housewives can do at home and still feel we're "doing our bit", as they say.'

Bessie, at sixty-five, now found it difficult to get about and rarely left the confines of the yard. She still struggled to the river now and then to watch the ships and she managed to get into the town once a week to do her shopping. But the effort exhausted her and her legs and feet pained her constantly.

Lizzie, despite her youth, realized that her grandmother still needed to busy herself to blot out the worry over Duggie. She jumped up, relieved to have something to do herself, something that might take her own mind off worrying about her father for a little while. She was missing, not only him, but the river too. She longed for the open air, the breeze in her face and the sounds and smells of the river. In Waterman's Yard, she felt stifled.

'Right,' she said. 'I'll go now.'

At the school, the door was opened by a tall, young man of a similar age to herself, who was vaguely familiar. Lizzie stared at him and he stared back. His fair hair was smoothed back and he was smartly dressed in a suit, white shirt and tie. But it was his bright, blue eyes that made her remember him.

'Hello, Lawrence,' she said at the same moment that his face broke into a grin, creasing the lines around his eyes, and he said, 'Lizzie!'

He pulled the door wider, inviting her in. 'I presume you've come to see Aunt Edwina?'

'Well, yes,' she conceded, but, greeting his smile with impish mischief, she added, 'But, of course, if I'd known you were going to be here . . .'

They laughed together.

'You've grown,' he said, as he led the way upstairs.

'So have you,' she countered and teased. 'However tall are you?'

'Six two in my stockinged feet.'

Tolly was tall, too, she thought, taller than she was, but Lawrence dwarfed even him.

He was opening the door into his aunt's study and ushering her in. 'You have a visitor, Aunt Edwina.'

Edwina rose from behind her desk and took off her spectacles. She came round the desk and held out her hands. 'Lizzie. My dear girl. How lovely to see you. I hear about you, of course, from Bessie. But it's ages since I saw you. Let me look at you.' Still holding her hands, she stood back and looked Lizzie up and down. For a moment there was a strange look in her eyes as if the sight of the pretty, dark-haired girl, with the sparkling brown eyes and cheeks that dimpled so easily with her ready smile, reminded her so poignantly of someone else.

Lizzie held her breath. She knew, without being told, that she reminded Edwina of her mother, Mary Ann. She remembered the closeness that had once existed between them, though the memories themselves were hazy now, mere fleeting childhood images that had left an impression rather than solid knowledge.

'I was just telling her that she's grown since I last saw her.'

Edwina looked startled as she glanced at her nephew and then back to Lizzie again. 'You – you know each other?'

Now it was the young ones who looked embarrassed. They glanced at each other and then swiftly away again. Lawrence cleared his throat. 'We met once or twice as children.' His voice dropped to a murmur. 'A long time ago now.'

Edwina let go of Lizzie's hands and turned away. 'Yes, yes, of course,' she said absently and then, gathering her wits, said briskly, 'Now, my dear. You've come to collect some wool for your gran, have you?'

She led the way across the room to a pile of boxes in one corner. Picking one up she handed it to Lizzie. 'There are two more. Bessie said that Mrs Eccleshall and Mrs Merryweather have offered to help too.'

'And Mrs Hamilton,' Lizzie said. 'She was the first to knock on Gran's door and offer.'

'Was she indeed?' For a moment, Edwina was lost in her own memories of the last war that gave her an empathy with the woman in Waterman's Yard. 'Well, every little helps,' she murmured.

'Lizzie can't carry all that lot on her own. Look, I'll walk home with her.'

'Oh Lawrence, I don't know . . .' Edwina began, but already he was picking up the other two boxes, resting his chin on the topmost one and smiling over the top of them at Lizzie, refusing to take no for an answer.

They walked the length of River Road laughing and talking just as if the intervening years since they had chased each other in the woods had never happened.

'Remember the den we built in the woods?' he asked. 'I wonder if it's still there?'

Lizzie laughed. 'We might need it, if we get invaded.'

'Oh, that'll not happen.' Lawrence was full of confidence. 'At least, not once we've got ourselves organized. I just wish I was a bit older and could do my bit too.'

'Here we are,' Lizzie said and led the way down the narrow alleyway between the houses and into Waterman's Yard, calling out as she pushed open the door of Bessie's home, 'I'm back, Gran.' She turned to Lawrence. 'I'll just put this down and come back for those two,' but Lawrence shook his head and followed her into the house.

'It's all right,' he said. 'I'll bring them in for you.'

Placing the boxes on the table in the kitchen, Lizzie watched as he went towards Bessie sitting in her chair by the range.

'Good day, Mrs Ruddick. I'm pleased to meet you.'

Bessie gaped up at him and then made as if to heave herself to her swollen feet.

'Please – don't get up. I don't wish to disturb you. I've only walked along with Lizzie to carry the boxes.' He smiled at her, his eyes crinkling. 'It looks as if they've set you a lot of work.'

Bessie, recovering her senses, said, 'Oh, I can still manage a bit of knitting, young man. It's just a pity I can't get about like I could.'

Without invitation, Lawrence sat down opposite her and leant forwards to talk to her, resting his elbows on his knees and linking his fingers. 'It must be very difficult for you.'

Lizzie watched in amazement as he sat there in her grandfather's chair, talking so easily and so naturally to her grandmother.

'Make this young feller a cup of tea, love,' Bessie said, her knitting needles never faltering.

As Lizzie busied herself, she listened to their conversation.

'It's sad that Holland and Belgium have surrendered, isn't it?' Lawrence began.

'Aye, and the papers are now saying that our lads are being driven back in France.'

'Right to the coast. They say the enemy has almost got them surrounded.'

At least, Lizzie thought, as she carried in the tea tray, there's no one belonging to us trapped on the French beaches and facing German guns and war planes. Uncle Duggie won't be there. For once, he was better off being out at sea.

'What a nice young man,' Bessie said, when Lawrence had taken his leave. 'Such nice manners and genuinely charming. Who is he, Lizzie?'

Lizzie gaped at her in surprise. 'Don't you know, Gran? He's Miss Edwina's nephew. Lawrence Marsh.'

Now Bessie did drop her knitting and struggled to her feet. She stood in front of Lizzie and, panting from the effort, wagged her finger in her face. 'And if I'd known that, girl, he wouldn't have been allowed across me doorstep. You're to have nowt more to do with him. Do you hear me, Mary Ann?'

Lizzie stared at her grandmother, but seeing how agitated the old lady had become, she said quietly, 'I hear you, Gran. I hear you.'

Bessie sank back into her chair with a sigh of relief, though whether from being able to rest her huge body once more or because her granddaughter had, as she believed, given her word, Lizzie couldn't tell.

She stared down at the grey head now bending over the box on her knee as she sorted through the wool.

Mary Ann, Lizzie was thinking. *She called me Mary Ann.*

Forty-Four

They were walking through the woods together. He had found her that morning at the wash-house just beyond Eastlands' Ferry, almost two weeks after he had met her again.

'I didn't know if you still came here.' Lawrence said, standing uncertainly in the doorway.

Lizzie straightened up from bending over the rinsing tub and pushed the damp hair from her face, shiny with sweat.

'Hello.' She smiled at him and then laughed. 'Yes. Modern inventions like washing machines haven't reached us aboard ship yet.'

He stepped into the steamy atmosphere. 'Have you time for a little walk? I thought we might take a trip down memory lane.'

'How have you got here? On horseback?'

'No. Bicycle.'

'A steed of sorts,' she teased, then added, 'I'll be finished in a couple of minutes when I've mangled these sheets.'

'Can I help?'

'You could turn the handle if you like.'

He stepped over the puddles on the brick floor and grasped the handle of the mangle. 'Tell me when.'

Lizzie fed in the folded wet sheets as he turned, the water flooding back into the rinsing tub.

'Thanks.' She laid the sheets on top of the other wet washing in the basket that Tolly had made for her in Mr Bryce's workshop and then she stepped outside into the sunshine. Although it was a warm day, Lizzie still shivered coming out from the steamy heat of the wash-house.

At once Lawrence removed his own jacket and slipped it around her shoulders.

'I heard about your father. I'm glad he got back safely.'

Lizzie beamed with pride. 'Yes, wasn't it a wonderful thing to do? All those little boats going across the Channel to rescue all those men off the Dunkirk beaches. And to think my father was there.' She shuddered again, but this time not from the cold. 'And there I was thinking he was perfectly safe somewhere on the Humber or on one of the rivers.'

Dan and his ship had taken part in the humiliating, and yet at the same time, glorious evacuation of Dunkirk. The British troops and their allies had taken their retreat badly, their pride wounded. Yet the way in which the country had rallied to bring thousands home had been a triumph of grit and determination. When the call had gone out for Operation Dynamo, Mr Sudbury, along with many boat owners, had responded with every seaworthy vessel he owned.

'However did he get down to Sheerness?' Lawrence asked. 'I didn't think keels went out to sea.'

'He was towed down there, I think.' She wrinkled her brow and added slowly, 'From what I can make out – though he won't say much about it – not many ships went from as far north as this, but Mr Sudbury and my dad were determined not to be left out.'

'Well, I can sympathize with that. I know how they feel,' Lawrence agreed. 'You must be very proud of your father.'

'Oh, I am.' Then she added jokingly, 'But I'm never going to trust him again when he says he's just going away for a couple of days without me.'

They walked on in silence for a while and when they came to the edge of the wood, she asked him, 'You know when we were younger and used to play here?'

'Mm,' Lawrence said. 'What about it?'

'Well . . .' She hesitated, knowing she might be treading on dangerous ground. Dangerous not only for him, but for her too. 'What were our parents doing?'

He glanced at her and for a moment he looked much older than his fifteen years, much older than she was, even though they were almost the same age. Whilst she did not think herself stupid or ignorant, she could see that he understood the ways of the world far better than she did.

He took hold of her hand and, instead of answering her question at once, he said, 'Let's sit down against this log, shall we? It'll be cooler still in the woods, but it's nice and warm here in the sun.'

As they sat down, side by side, still he did not let go of her hand. His touch was warm and dry and gentle.

'I expect they just sat and talked,' he began hesitantly, but now he was not meeting her eyes.

'Why?' Lizzie was every bit as direct as her grandmother. 'Why would a man like your father – a man in his position – want to spend his time with someone like my mother?'

Now Lawrence smiled. 'Same reason I came to find you today. Because I like you. Because I enjoy being with you and I want to get to know you better.'

'But – but they were both married.'

'That's never troubled my father,' Lawrence said wryly. 'My parents are barely civil to each other now. He's hardly ever at home and when he is, they quarrel. Oh, it's terribly civilized. No raised voices, no shouting. Just icy politeness, sitting at either end of the dinner table with me in between them. Sometimes, the only way they will communicate with each other is through me. You know, "Lawrence, will you ask your father to pass the salt," and "Tell your mother I shall be away on business for the coming week." That sort of thing.' He paused and then, his tone gentle and concerned now, asked, 'What about yours? Do they get on?'

Lizzie stared at him. 'Don't you know?'

'Know? Know what?'

'My mother . . .' She hesitated, choosing her words carefully. If her father had had something to do with her mother's sudden disappearance, Lizzie could unwittingly get him into serious trouble. So she repeated what the family had told her. 'She . . . she went away. Six years ago.' She found she was gripping Lawrence's hand tightly as she went on, haltingly, 'It was my fault. We were at my gran's. All the family was there and one of them, Uncle Duggie I think, was talking about your father's motor car. I didn't think what I was saying and I let it out that we'd had a ride in it. When we got back to the ship my father sent me below to the cabin. And on deck, they had a huge quarrel.' She shuddered as she brought back the dreadful memories of that night and Lawrence put his arm around her shoulders. 'I'd never heard them quarrel like that. Never.' Her voice broke as she finished, 'And then she . . . she went away.'

She had never been able to speak to anyone about that night, not even to Tolly, and yet now she found herself telling this comparative stranger all about it.

With gentle intuition, he said, 'You've kept all that locked inside you all this time, haven't you?'

She nodded.

'And you've no idea what happened to her?'

Pressing her lips together, Lizzie shook her head.

He pulled her to him in a swift, understanding hug. 'Poor you.'

It was nice sitting here in the sunshine with him; the only sound was of birds flying in and out of the trees. It was hot and she felt suddenly sleepy. Everything seemed so quiet and she couldn't remember having felt so at peace for a very long time. Even the war with its blackout and air-raid warnings seemed very far away at this moment.

'I must go,' she said, but with no real conviction.

'Must you?'

'Well . . .' Her eyelids felt heavy. It was so warm and comfortable sitting here in the quiet warmth of the day, resting her head against his shoulder. 'Just a few more minutes then . . .'

Something was tickling her cheek. Sleepily she brushed it away, but then was startled awake by a voice that said, close to her ear, 'Lizzie. I think you should wake up now. You've been asleep an hour.'

Lizzie sat up suddenly and then scrambled to her feet. 'An hour? Oh no! Dad will be miles upriver.'

Lawrence, getting up, said, 'Come on. I'll help you.'

She put out her hand, palm outwards as she said swiftly, 'No. I'll be fine.' Then realizing she had sounded abrupt, added, 'Thanks all the same. It's . . . it's been lovely to see you again. But I must go.'

Even before he had time to say another word, she had whipped his jacket from around her shoulders and flung it at him. Then before he could try to stop her, she was running across the field towards the wash-house. His voice drifted across the growing distance between them. 'I'll see you again, Lizzie.'

Lizzie didn't think she had ever paddled so furiously in her life. As she passed by the shipyard where Tolly now worked, she saw him waving to her from the bank. She sculled nearer and shouted to him. 'Can't stop. I'm late catching up with me dad. See you tomorrow. We'll be back then.'

Even from a distance, she could see the disappointment on his face, but he waved and smiled. 'See you then, Lizzie.'

When at last she caught up with the *Maid Mary Ann*, she was sweating both with the effort and with fear that her father would ask awkward questions.

Lizzie was a very honest girl and would only bend the truth a little if it was to save another's feelings. She would never lie to protect herself. Now, it was her father whom she wished to protect. Instinctively, after what her grandmother had said, she knew he would not be happy that she had spent time in the company of Lawrence Marsh. Deciding that it was best to stick to the truth as near as she could, even if it was not the whole truth, Lizzie said, 'I'm sorry, Dad. I fell asleep.'

'Asleep?'

'It was so warm in the sun when I'd finished the washing, I just sat down and next thing I knew I was waking up without any idea of how long I'd slept. I am sorry.'

Dan was smiling at her now and saying, teasingly, 'Am I supposed to believe that, you little minx? I expect you've been talking to Tolly, eh? Now just you be careful.' He tapped her lightly on her nose. 'Don't you go getting that lad the sack if he's seen talking to you when he should be working.'

Lizzie grinned up at her father. 'No, Dad, I won't.'

'You can hang the washing in the hold, Lizzie. There's room this trip.'

As Lizzie went forward and down into the hold to string lines from one side to the other, she breathed a sigh of relief. Then she opened two or three hatch boards fore and aft so that, as the ship moved forwards, the breeze would dry her lines of washing.

Her father had never minded Lizzie spending time with Tolly and, as long as she caused no trouble for Tolly at his place of work, it seemed Dan still had no objection. She wondered, though, just what his reaction would be if he knew with whom she really had been.

Forty-Five

Three times during the week that followed, Lawrence found her. Once, at the wash-house again and twice, as she sculled down the river, he appeared, on his bicycle, on the bank.

'Are you following me, sir?' she teased as her cog boat, the full-sized one now of course, bumped gently against the muddy bank.

Lawrence smiled. 'Yes.'

Lizzie laughed, delighting in his boldness that held no hint of apology or explanation.

He dismounted and slithered down the bank.

'You'll get muddy,' she warned, but took the hand he held out to her as they scrambled back up the steep slope.

'Now you look a real river urchin, just like me,' she told him.

'But not half as pretty,' he said gallantly. Then his teasing manner sobered as he added, 'Lizzie, I'm going away tomorrow. Back to school.'

'I thought you'd left. I mean, it's term time now, so why have you been at home?'

'The school got bombed and we were all sent home. But now they've fixed up some temporary accommodation, so we've got to go back. But I'll be home again at the end of July, for six weeks then. So,' he said, without any of the usual hesitance in a youth of his age, 'I'll see you then.'

A teasing retort sprang to her lips. She almost said, 'Not if I see you first,' but suddenly she realized that she wanted, more than anything, to see him again.

Lawrence reached out and touched her face, leaving a streak of mud on her cheek. 'You will take care of yourself, won't you? I mean, no going off in your father's ship to rescue soldiers.'

She pulled a wry face. 'I wasn't allowed to go last time.'

'But you would have gone, wouldn't you, if they had let you?'

Without hesitation, she nodded. 'Oh yes, I would.'

'I thought as much. See, I was right. So, I'm asking you, please take care. The bombing's going to get worse, you know.'

'It sounds as if it's you that ought to take care, in case they bomb your school again. Was anyone hurt?'

Lawrence shook his head. 'Not seriously. They'd had some very good shelters built in the grounds and we'd all crowded into them.'

There was a pause and they stood looking at each other until Lawrence said, 'I'm sorry, I'll have to go.'

'So will I,' Lizzie said, but neither of them made a move.

'I'll see you, then. Can I write to you?'

Lizzie thought quickly. 'Best not,' she said and pulled an apologetic face. 'We move about such a lot, you know.' There was only Waterman's Yard as a permanent address for her, and her grandmother was bound to ask questions. Swiftly, Lizzie added, 'Besides, it's only a few weeks until the end of July. You'll soon be home again.'

'Yes, of course,' Lawrence agreed, but the expression on his face seemed to mirror her own feeling that it still seemed an awfully long time. Aloud he said, 'I'll see you then.'

'Right. I ought to be going, too.'

Still, neither of them moved. Then he came towards her, put his arms about her and bent his head to kiss her firmly on the mouth. Surprised, Lizzie gasped. For a youth of only sixteen, he seemed amazingly experienced.

He released her, stepped back and picked up his bicycle. Throwing his leg over the cross bar, he paused a moment to look at her, then he gave a quick nod and began to pedal away. When he reached the far side of the meadow, just before disappearing amongst the trees, he braked, turned and waved once more to her.

Lizzie, standing motionless where he had left her, her fingers against her lips, now raised her hand in return.

At the end of July, Lawrence came home for the school holidays. He was waiting for her outside the wash-house as she sculled from the ship to the wooden landing on the riverbank. Fearfully, Lizzie glanced back to see if her father had seen him, but Dan had gone below to see to the engine.

'How are you? Oh, it's good to see you again, Lizzie. I've missed you. Is everyone all right? All your family?'

'Here . . .' Playfully, she thrust the heavy basket of washing at him. 'You can make yourself useful and carry this.' Then she marched ahead of him to the safety of the wash-house in case her father should reappear on deck.

'So?' he asked again. 'How have you been?'

'Fine, thanks.'

To Lizzie's surprise, Lawrence removed his jacket,

rolled up his shirtsleeves and said, 'Now, what can I do to help?'

Later, as they were walking through the cool shade of the wood, they heard the drone of aircraft overhead. Lawrence stood very still, listening intently. After a moment, he said, 'It's all right, they're ours.'

Lizzie's eyes widened. 'Can you tell just by listening to them?'

'Oh yes. The enemy planes sound very different. Those are British bombers, all right. That's what I'd like to be in when I join up. I want to go into the RAF and train to be a pilot.'

Softly, Lizzie said, 'Then it will be me telling you to take care of yourself, won't it?'

'I s-saw you. I saw you w-with him.'

Tolly's face was a mixture of hurt and anger and anxiety for her.

Lizzie glanced at him, noticing that his stammer was always more pronounced when he was upset or angry.

She almost said, 'Who?' but that would have been silly. She knew very well whom he meant.

'So?' she said, resentful at his intrusion. 'What's it got to do with you?'

The hurt on his face deepened. 'I'm s-sorry,' he mumbled and turned away. At once contrite, Lizzie grabbed his arm. 'No, it's me who should be sorry. I know you're only thinking of me. Sorry, Tolly.'

'He'll only hurt you, Lizzie. He . . . he's not for you.'

'But he's nice, Tolly. I'm sure you'd like him if only you met him.'

Tolly gave a rueful grin. 'I doubt it.'

'Why do you say that? You don't even know him.'

'I know enough about him. If he's anything like his father—'

'You shouldn't judge him by the name his father has got,' Lizzie cut in angrily.

Tolly looked at her strangely. He shook his head slightly. 'You really don't know, do you?'

'Know what?'

'About . . . about his father and your mother.'

'His . . .? My . . .?' she faltered, her eyes widening.

'Before she married your father, there were rumours that she . . . she was involved with Randolph Marsh. She . . . she worked at The Hall then.'

'How do you know all this?'

'M-my mother told me.'

'And how does *she* know?'

Embarrassed, Tolly looked away. 'She's very bitter about your father marrying your mother.'

Lizzie said nothing now, but the question was in her eyes.

'My mother was walking out with your father and he threw her over to marry Mary Ann.' Tolly moved nearer to her and tried to take her hands in his, but she snatched them away. 'I'm sorry. I shouldn't have told you. I thought you knew.'

'No,' Lizzie said slowly. 'It's evidently a big family secret.' Her mind was whirling and the terror which she tried to keep locked away – that her father had had something to do with her mother's disappearance – was pushing its unwelcome way to the forefront of her mind. Was that another terrible family secret?

Lizzie sat down on the bank and Tolly dropped beside her. She plucked absent-mindedly at the grass, her thoughts reeling. Clinging to a desperate hope, she said, 'If I ask you something, will you tell me the truth?'

''Course I will.'

'And will you also promise to tell no one that I've asked you such a thing?'

Tolly nodded.

The question that she had longed to ask for such a long time, but had never dared to voice before, came haltingly. 'Do . . . do you know what happened to my mother?'

His eyes full of compassion, Tolly shook his head. 'I don't think anybody really knows. There's always been a lot of talk, of course.'

'Has there?' None of it had ever reached her ears. Had the family protected her yet again, shielding her from the gossip? The only thing that had ever occurred – and she could never forget it – had been the cruel teasing at school. And then she had been quickly removed from its influence.

Tolly volunteered no more, so she prompted. 'What did they say?'

He shrugged. 'Oh, you know. That she'd run off with someone. That . . . that she'd drowned that night in the river.'

Lizzie shuddered. That was her biggest fear, for if it were true, then her father had been involved in some way, maybe innocently, but he had been there.

Tentatively, Tolly put his arm around her and when she did not throw him off, he held her close. 'Oh Lizzie, I'm sorry. But you do see now, don't you, how it would hurt your family to know that you were – well – meeting Lawrence Marsh?'

'We're only friends,' she murmured, but immediately in her mind's eye was his face – a face she knew already so intimately.

'You're going to go on seeing him, then?'

'It's not fair to judge him by his father,' she burst out angrily again and, before she could stop herself, she added, 'Can you be blamed for what your father does?'

Tolly looked as if she had physically slapped him in the face and immediately, she said again, 'Oh Tolly, I'm sorry.' She touched his face with her hand and he put his own over the top of it and held it, pressed to his cheek.

'You're right, of course,' he whispered. 'But I just don't want to see you get hurt. I couldn't bear it if . . .' He turned his head away from her and his voice was muffled as he added, 'If he ever hurt you. If he does, he'll have me to reckon with. And you can tell him that.' Then, with a sudden, coltish movement, Tolly kissed her. It was a clumsy, boyish bump against her cheek, rather than a kiss and, pulling back, his face flushed, he mumbled, 'Sorry.'

Before she could say a word, he scrambled to his feet and stumbled away.

Forty-Six

As the months went by, trade returned slowly to the River Trent and now the *Maid Mary Ann* was as busy as she ever had been. The Humberside ports were prime targets for enemy bombers, and stocks of food and other goods were moved to inland ports. The warehouses along the Trent, and particularly those at Elsborough, soon became storehouses for food and other essential items.

The engineering works in the town now produced the weapons of war.

'Do you know,' Lawrence told Lizzie excitedly, 'one of the firms in our town is building a gunner's turret that's going to be used on bombers?'

And, quite separately, Tolly said, 'We're working continuous shifts at the shipyard now, building barges and small coasters.'

In the town, the queues, caused by food rationing, grew longer.

'There's a British Restaurant opening in town,' Bessie told Lizzie, 'but they say the meat they use is whalemeat.' She pulled a face. 'Reckon I'll stick to fish and chips from our chippy. At least they haven't rationed that yet.'

It wasn't until 1941 that Elsborough got its own real taste of the Blitz, and bombs fell quite close to Waterman's Yard, but, thankfully, never in it. The Ruddick family had one narrow escape however. Aboard the *Maid Mary Ann*, Dan and Lizzie were approaching the town to moor at Miller's Wharf when a bomb fell into the river a hundred yards or so ahead of them. Dan stopped the engine as the swell of the ripples reached them.

'I'm going to drop anchor right here, Lizzie,' Dan said. 'I'm not going to risk going over that. We'll wait until morning.'

They waited through the night, but no explosion occurred. Only at daylight did they, very gingerly, dare to proceed to the wharf, holding their breath, as they sailed over the place where the bomb had fallen.

'I expect it's buried itself deep in the mud.'

'Will it explode?' Lizzie asked, leaning over the side to look into the murky water.

'Who knows?' was all Dan could say. 'It's a risk we'll all have to take.'

In May, enemy bombers dropped their bombs on a village on the Nottinghamshire side of the Trent. Speculation as to the reason for this was varied. Some believed that the enemy aircraft had seen the short stretch of light-coloured dual carriageway that ran through the village shining in the moonlight and had thought it to be the river. Accordingly, they had dropped their bombs on to farmland and isolated houses, believing that they were targeting the Elsborough factories. Others thought that the bombers had followed the railway line to the village and, when this disappeared abruptly, had calculated that they must be over an industrial area. Dropping incendiaries to illuminate the zone, they had accidentally ignited a dry gorse fox covert and, thinking they had hit something big, had then dropped their 'heavies'. But one ARP Warden on duty in Elsborough that brilliant, moonlit night insisted that he had seen an enemy pathfinder circling over the town and that an RAF night fighter had pursued it westwards over the River Trent. The enemy aircraft had then jettisoned its incendiary bombs, which resulted in the fires that led the larger force of enemy aircraft arriving later to bomb the burning area.

The village was relatively unscathed, although the railway line was hit, but one farmhouse about a mile outside was severely damaged. Watchers said later that the house seemed to jump up in the air when a landmine buried itself in the grass field a hundred yards or so away. A mother and her two children were the only occupants of the house, the father being away on night work.

'They'll not survive that,' the villagers said, but miraculously, the mother, hearing smaller bombs dropping earlier, had taken the children downstairs. As the huge landmine descended, whining through the night sky, she pushed the children under the kitchen table and crawled beneath it herself. The blast was terrifying, shattering every window in the house, breaking crockery and blowing doors off their hinges. Surrounded by broken glass and covered in soot that had been blasted down the chimney, the family stayed there for the remainder of the night.

'Poor things,' Bessie said, when she heard the story. 'They got it instead of us. Thank the good Lord they're not hurt.'

His shadow filling the doorway of the wash-house, Lawrence said for the umpteenth time that summer, 'Come for a walk?'

'I shouldn't really.' Lizzie's eyes twinkled at him. 'But I will.'

His face seemed to light up with pleasure. 'You little minx. You do like teasing folk, don't you?' He balanced himself on the balls of his feet. 'Come on, I'll race you to the woods.'

She dropped the wet sheet back into the rinsing tub, splashing her apron, but she scarcely noticed as she ran to the door and began to race after him across the meadow behind the wash-house and towards Raven's Wood.

Breathless and laughing, she fell into his arms. 'That's not fair. You had a head start.'

His arms were tightly around her and he was looking down into her eyes, his face serious now. 'Oh Lizzie, Lizzie, how I love you.'

And then he was kissing her as if he would never stop.

When, at last, they paused for breath, Lawrence whispered, 'Let's find our den, deep in the woods. Let's make it our own special place.'

Hand in hand, they went deeper amongst the trees until the sunlight was almost blotted out.

'Where is it? I can't remember.'

'No, I can't.' He stopped and looked about him, then leading her towards a clump of bushes, he added, 'But this will do . . .' Pulling aside the foliage, she saw that the centre of the undergrowth had been cleared. A blanket was spread on the ground and to one side stood a picnic hamper.

Through the dimness, she stared at him. 'Lawrence Marsh, you've planned this.'

He was smiling at her, sure and confident, but Lizzie's eyes narrowed thoughtfully as she said bluntly, 'I hope you're not thinking of trying anything.'

Lawrence laughed. 'Would I?' But his jocular sarcasm implied that he meant to do just that. She stepped into the clearing and he allowed the branches he was holding to fall back into place. Now they were cocooned, deep in the heart of the wood with only the birds for company.

'Champagne, madam?' Lawrence said, kneeling and throwing back the lid of the basket with a flourish.

Lizzie gasped. 'Wherever . . .?'

'Raided my father's cellar. I'm getting rather good at it.'

He pulled out a bottle, dusted it. It opened with a loud, echoing pop, startling birds who rose into the air calling alarm to each other. The liquid frothed out of the neck of the bottle as he tipped it into a narrow glass.

'I've never tasted champagne before,' Lizzie said, as she sat on the rug, took the glass and sipped the sparkling liquid.

'Well, life with me will be one long taste of champagne.' He filled his own glass and sat down beside her. Then, touching her glass with his own, Lawrence said, 'Here's to us, Lizzie.'

They ate cold chicken legs and hardboiled eggs with lettuce and tomatoes. There were even individual trifles in small glass bowls.

'Who packed all this up for you? Your mother?'

'Heavens, no. My mother wouldn't be seen dead in the kitchen. No, I smiled nicely at Cook and she packed it all up in a basket that I could carry on the back of my bicycle.'

Lizzie giggled and then hiccuped. 'Fancy having servants that you can just order to do whatever you want them to. Oh dear, I feel all funny. My head's sort of woozy.'

Lawrence took her glass and set it on the ground. 'There, lie back and close your eyes.' He lay down and put out his arm. 'Rest your head on my arm.'

'Mm,' she murmured, drowsily. 'This is nice. So cool out of the sun. I could stay here all day.'

'Then,' Lawrence was leaning over her now, 'why don't

356

we?' He bent his head and kissed her, gently at first but then with a growing ardour. 'Lizzie, oh Lizzie. I want you so much. Please, let me . . .' He was unfastening the buttons of her blouse and slipping his hand inside.

'No!' At once Lizzie was fully awake. She pushed his hand away and sat up. She looked round at him angrily, but Lawrence only lay there, his hands behind his head, smiling up at her. 'I'm not that sort of girl,' she said crossly. 'If that's what you're after, then you can find someone else.'

'I don't want anyone else, Lizzie,' he said lazily. 'I want you. I always have.'

'Well, not without a ring on my finger. And a wedding ring at that.'

She began to scramble to her feet, but he caught hold of her and pulled her down again so that she landed on top of him. 'I love you when you're angry, it makes me want you all the more. So, Lizzie Ruddick, will you marry me?'

'What? You're not serious.'

He put his arms around her, holding her to him. 'Lizzie, I love you. I want to marry you. Say you'll marry me. Please?'

Lizzie's heart somersaulted. 'Oh Lawrence. You know we can't. Your family would never allow it.'

His face darkened. 'My family aren't going to rule me. I can promise you that. I've no intention of having a marriage like my parents. I'm going to marry for love. It's you I love, Lizzie, and you love me, don't you? I know you do. Let me hear you say it. Please, darling Lizzie?'

Suddenly, overcome with tenderness, she stroked his hair and said, 'I do love you, Lawrence, but we're so young. We couldn't possibly marry until we're of age. They wouldn't let us.'

'We could run away.'

She laughed at the thought. 'Elope, you mean?'

Lawrence was serious. 'Yes, why not?'

But Lizzie was still teasing. 'To Gretna Green?'

He gripped her arms excitedly. 'I don't think we'd have to go as far as that. There are couples getting married all the time now in a hurry. Because of the war, I mean. Maybe we could find someone who wouldn't ask too many questions.'

'But we're only seventeen.'

His face sobered. 'I know and next year, I'll be called up. If I'm old enough to die for my country, then surely I'm old enough to get married.'

She laid her cheek against his chest and heard the beat of his heart, loud in her ear. 'Oh Lawrence, don't say such things. Don't even think them.'

He stroked her hair and whispered, 'I mean it, Lizzie. I have never been more serious about anything in the whole of my life. I love you and I want to marry you. And soon.'

A little later as they emerged from the shadow of the trees, brushing leaves and grass from their clothes, a man on a bicycle rode along the pathway that ran alongside the woods.

'Hello, Lizzie. All right?'

Startled, Lizzie looked up as the man passed close by them. He winked at her and then nodded knowingly towards Lawrence.

'Oh yes, thank you,' Lizzie said weakly to the retreating figure. As he rode away, the man was whistling, and the strains of 'Who were you with last night?' reached Lizzie.

When he was out of earshot, she sank to the ground as her legs gave way beneath her. She closed her eyes and groaned. 'Oh no.'

Lawrence dropped to his haunches beside her and stared at her in concern. 'What is it? Have you hurt yourself? Did you twist your ankle, or something?'

'No, no. But, that was Mr Horberry.'

'So?'

'His wife is only the biggest gossip in Elsborough and they happen to live in Waterman's Yard.'

Forty-Seven

'What's Gran doing on the wharf, Dad?'

Lizzie's sharp eyes had already spotted the lonely figure of Bessie standing on the edge of the wharf where the *Maid Mary Ann* was expected to dock. Throughout her childhood the sight of her grandmother waiting for them had not been unusual, but now, since her bad legs kept her almost a prisoner within Waterman's Yard, she hardly ever came to greet them.

As soon as the ship bumped gently against the planking, Lizzie scrambled ashore. 'Gran? Are you all right?'

'No, I'm not all right.' Bessie was seething with anger as she wagged her finger in her granddaughter's face. 'Not if what I've been hearing from Phyllis is right. And don't lie to me, girl, like your mother used to do.'

Lizzie returned the older woman's stare steadily. Quietly, she said, 'No, Gran, I won't lie to you, if you'll promise to believe me.'

'Ah, so you do know what it's about then?'

Lizzie nodded.

There was a pause before Bessie agreed, 'Very well, then. But you'd best come home. I aren't washing me dirty linen in public for the world and his wife to hear.'

Lizzie felt her grandmother's fingers, still surprisingly strong in their grip, grasp her arm. 'Come on.'

'Lizzie. Lizzie, where are you going? I could use a bit of help here.'

She glanced back over her shoulder towards her father, but before she could answer him, Bessie turned and shouted, 'She's coming with me, Dan. There's things we've got to talk about.'

'Can't it wait? We—'

'No, lad, it can't wait.'

'What's the matter? Is something wrong?' Now Dan was worried.

'I hope not, lad,' his mother said darkly. 'But that's what I aim to find out.'

Without waiting for any further protest, Bessie began to move away, grunting at the pain in her legs, but still keeping fast hold of her granddaughter. 'You just come with me, m'girl.'

Meekly, Lizzie went.

'Now then,' Bessie began as she sank into her armchair with obvious relief. 'Are you going to tell me what's been going on or shall I tell you what I've heard?'

'It's about Lawrence, isn't it?'

Bessie nodded.

Lizzie licked her lips. 'Well, it's true I've been meeting him and going for walks with him . . .'

'And?'

'And he's kissed me.'

'That all?'

Lizzie's eyes widened. 'Yes, Gran. I promise you. Except . . .'

'Go on.' The anger had not left Bessie's face.

'Except that the last time I saw him, he told me he loves me and . . . and that he wants to marry me.'

Bessie snorted. 'Did he, indeed? I hope you weren't daft enough to fall for that sort of talk.'

361

When Lizzie did not answer, Bessie sighed. 'Oh Lizzie, love. His sort don't marry the likes of us.' She wiped a tear from her eye as she murmured, 'Your poor mam could have told you that.'

'That's what I told him,' Lizzie said.

'You did?' Bessie's face brightened and some of the strain left her features. 'There, I knew you were a sensible girl. Oh, but you had me worried, 'specially when Phyllis said her Tom had seen you together coming out of Raven's Wood.' She frowned severely again as she asked, 'And were you, like he said, buttoning your blouse and him pulling up his trousers?'

Lizzie gasped. 'No, we weren't. Brushing the grass off our clothes, mebbe, but we'd only been kissing and cuddling. Nothing more, I swear.' Her eyes glittered with anger too now. 'I'm not that daft, Gran.'

'Aye well, there's no harm in that, as long as that's all it was.' Bessie smiled suddenly. 'I wasn't past a bit of kissing and cuddling in me day, neither. But don't you tell your grandpa that.' She wagged her finger again at Lizzie, but this time her mood was playful. 'And it never went any further than that. Your grandpa's the only man I've ever – you know – with, and I happen to be proud of the fact. And if you take my advice, m'girl, you'll not let any man have his way with you until you've got a wedding ring firmly on your finger. Oh they'll sweet talk you, ask you to prove that you love them and all that, but when it's over, they've no respect for you then.'

Lizzie was quiet. She knew her grandmother was right, but she still couldn't think that Lawrence would treat her so shabbily even if she did allow him to make love to her.

She felt Bessie's keen gaze on her. 'So, lass, are you going to promise me that you won't see Master Lawrence again?'

Lizzie returned her grandmother's gaze steadily. Quietly, she said, 'No, Gran, I can't promise you that. You see, I think I'm in love with him too. And if he asks me to marry him again, I'm going to say, "yes".'

The lines on Bessie's face seemed to sag. She shook her head and closed her eyes. 'Oh Lizzie, you'll break your poor dad's heart. You can't do it, lass. You just can't.'

'So what was all that about?' Dan wanted to know the moment Lizzie set foot back on board. 'Is everything all right? No one's ill, are they?'

'No,' Lizzie answered, trying to keep her voice light. 'Everyone's fine.'

'So what was all the secrecy and the hurry?' The smile that was not often evident these days lit his face briefly and drove away, for a moment, the sadness that rarely left his eyes. 'I bet Phyllis Horberry had a choice bit of gossip to impart, was that it?'

Lizzie stared at her father, her eyes widening, but then she realized that he was just joking. He couldn't possibly know how very near the truth he was. She took a deep breath. She'd never have a better opening and, knowing that she would have to tell him – wanted to tell him herself before someone else did – Lizzie said, 'As a matter of fact, it was about something Phyllis had found out . . .'

The dark, haunted look was back in his eyes and the smile was gone from his face. His frown deepened as she added, 'About me.'

'You? What on earth could Phyllis Horberry find to gossip about you?' Then his face cleared and he actually laughed as he said, 'Oh, you and Tolly, I suppose. Is that all?'

'No, Dad,' Lizzie said, trying to tell him as gently as

possible, but there was no easy way. 'Not me and Tolly. Me and Lawrence Marsh.'

There was a moment's silence, save for the sounds of the river all around them.

'Oh no. I don't believe it. No, oh no. My God! Not again.'

'Dad, please listen to me. Let me explain . . .'

'Where've you been meeting him, eh?' He took a step towards her and grasped her roughly by the shoulders.

'Dad, you're hurting me,' Lizzie squirmed in his hold.

'Tell me where?'

'In . . . in Raven's Wood.'

'You'll keep away from there. Do you hear me?' He shook her to emphasize his command. 'You're not to go anywhere near those woods.' Then, in what sounded almost like an afterthought, he added, 'And him. You'll keep away from him, an' all. From this moment, you will not leave your grandmother's house or this ship without someone – another member of the family – with you. Do you hear me? You are never, ever, to see him again.'

'Dad, please . . .'

'Not another word.'

He released her, turned and strode along the deck away from her as if he could not put a distance between them fast enough.

Lizzie watched him go, tears blurring her vision. She felt so alone. There was no one she could turn to. 'Oh, Uncle Duggie, I wish you were here,' she murmured. 'You'd understand, wouldn't you? You'd help me?'

And then she thought of Tolly. Tolly was her friend. He would understand. She must find Tolly.

*

When the cargo had been off-loaded, and she and her father had eaten their supper in the cabin amid a stony, uneasy silence, Lizzie lifted her chin and said, 'I'm going out in the cog boat. I'm going to find Tolly.'

Her father glowered and said gruffly, 'All right then. Just so long as you give me your word that it is Tolly you're going to meet.'

Lizzie's brown eyes regarded him steadily. 'Yes, Dad. It is.'

His voice was no more than a whisper, but there was a threat in his words. 'Don't you ever lie to me, Lizzie. Don't you *ever* lie to me.' And the unspoken words lay between them 'or else'.

Lizzie shuddered inwardly and the nightmare fears were back. Her mother had lied to him and then she had disappeared.

Lizzie sculled downriver until she came level with the shipyard where Tolly worked. She saw his small rowing boat moored beside the landing and manoeuvred hers alongside it. She did not have long to wait before she heard the hooter sound and saw the men begin to pack up for the day. Then she heard Tolly's boots clomping along the wooden boarding of the landing and saw him looking down at her.

'Lizzie!' Delight spread over his face and he jumped down into his boat and together they rowed away from the yard, a little way downstream. Then they rested, Tolly leaning on his oars.

'I haven't half missed you this summer. I expect you've been busy now you're full-time mate for your dad. And of course, I've been working long hours, but I have missed us going fishing and blackberrying and, oh just everything.' He brushed back the untidy flop of hair from his forehead and added, 'So where are we going tonight then? What about—?'

'Tolly,' she interrupted. 'Please, listen. We are friends, aren't we? I mean, you've always been my very best friend.'

The boy, several months younger than Lizzie, coloured. ''Course we are. Don't be daft.'

'So, if I tell you something, you will try to understand? You will be on my side?'

There was a sudden wariness in his eyes. 'I s-suppose so.'

'I've been meeting Lawrence Marsh. Tolly, we've fallen in love and we want to get married, but—'

'Married!' Tolly's harsh tone and the shock on his face were almost worse than either her grandmother's or even her father's. 'Marry him? You must be out of your mind.'

Shocked, she saw that there were tears in his eyes. 'Tolly, listen to me, please. I need your help. Will you find Lawrence for me? I must see him. I've got to talk to him.'

He pressed his lips together into a hard, tight line. 'No,' he said shortly. 'I won't.'

Lizzie gaped at him. 'You won't?'

'No, I won't. Lizzie, forget him. He's no good for you.'

'Don't you start. I've had enough from everyone else. I thought I could count on you. I thought you were my friend.'

'I am your friend. That's why I'm saying what I'm saying. And if everyone else is saying the same, doesn't that tell you something?'

Tears of rage started in her eyes. 'It tells me that not one of my family, nor even my best friend, wants me to be happy.'

'We do. That's all we want. You know that, Lizzie. But he won't make you happy. Not in a million years.'

Angrily, she picked up her oar and stood up in the cog boat. As she began to work the oar and the boat began to move away from his, she cried, 'I should have known better than to come to you. What would you know about being in love, Tolly Oliver? You're too young to understand.'

Then she turned her back on him and began to scull her way back up the river.

'Lizzie, Lizzie, wait . . .'

She heard him calling her, heard the anguish in his tone, but she did not look back, not once, for she knew he would be sitting there in his boat, watching her go, looking lost and forlorn.

She did not dare to look back and, for the first time in her life, Lizzie hardened her heart against Tolly.

Forty-Eight

The following week there was another occasion when Lizzie was not able to accompany her father aboard the *Maid Mary Ann*.

'You'll stay here with your grandmother and you will not leave the yard,' her father commanded. 'At least that's one thing I can be sure of. He won't come here looking for you.'

But Dan was wrong. The day after the *Maid Mary Ann* left for Hull, Lawrence knocked on the door of Bessie's house in Waterman's Yard. Lizzie, unsuspecting, opened the door. Startled to see him there, all she could utter was a surprised, 'Oh!'

Behind him, across the yard, she could see that already Minnie was standing in her doorway and Gladys was shaking a feather duster out of an upstairs window with such vigour that all the feathers threatened to come loose and flutter down into the yard. Their voices drifted across to her.

'Posh company yon lass is keeping now, ain't she, Min?'

'That's right, Glad. Bessie'll have to get her best tea set out to entertain young Mester Marsh.'

Recovering her senses, Lizzie pulled him inside. 'Come in, quick.'

She was thrilled to see him, bowled over to think that he had come to Waterman's Yard to see her, yet she asked sharply, 'Whatever have you come here for?'

'Well, that's a fine way to welcome your fiancé when he comes a-courting.' Lawrence was smiling at her, his eyes sparkling with teasing laughter. 'I'm relieved to see you're all right. I was worried when you didn't come to the wash-house yesterday.'

'You went there? You waited for me?'

'Of course I did. I saw your father's ship go by but you never came.'

'Lizzie,' Bessie's voice came from the kitchen. 'Who is it? Who's that you're talking to?'

'You'd better go,' Lizzie whispered. 'They've found out. I'm not allowed to see you.'

'Not allowed . . .?' Lawrence began. 'Oh well, in that case, I'll just come in and have a word with your grandmother.'

Before Lizzie could make a move to prevent him, Lawrence had stepped through the scullery and into the kitchen and was moving into the room, his hand outstretched in greeting. 'Mrs Ruddick, I trust I find you well.'

If the moment had not been so serious, Lizzie would have been convulsed with laughter at the look of astonishment on her grandmother's face.

'Well, he's got a nerve, I'll give him that.'

Bessie was lying back in her armchair as the door closed behind Lawrence and they heard his footsteps crossing the yard.

Lizzie sat down opposite her grandmother. She smoothed sweaty palms down her skirt. 'Don't you think he's nice, Gran?'

'He's very polite, but it's all fine talk, Lizzie love.'

Lizzie felt the stab of disappointment like a physical pain. 'Oh Gran, I thought you liked him. You've been sat here talking and laughing with him for more than half an hour.'

'He's nice enough, I grant you. Takes after his auntie, I expect.'

'There you are, then.'

'But that doesn't mean I want you to have anything to do with him, because I don't. I've told you before, Lizzie, it's not on. And what your dad'll say when he knows he's actually had the nerve to come here and me entertaining him in here an' all. He'll have me guts for garters. I must be getting soft in me old age. And what Miss Edwina will say if she gets to hear about it, I don't know. She'll be horrified.'

Lizzie's heart sank. Was no one, not even her dear friend, Tolly, on her side? But she shied away from thinking about Tolly. It was strange, but his disapproval hurt her more than anyone else's, more even than her father's.

'Of course I had to be civil to the lad. He was a guest in my house, but I left him in no doubt as to how we feel, now didn't I?'

Lizzie, the lump in her throat growing, merely nodded, for her grandmother's parting words to Lawrence had been, 'I'm sorry, lad, but her dad won't allow her to see you and there's an end to it.'

Miss Edwina called the following afternoon, but it was Bessie who was in for a surprise.

'So,' Edwina began, sitting down and withdrawing her gloves from her elegant fingers. 'You don't think my nephew's good enough for your granddaughter, Bessie?'

'Eh?' Bessie gaped at her visitor whilst Lizzie stood

quietly behind her grandmother's chair listening to the exchange, amazed herself at what she was hearing.

Calmly, Edwina went on. 'I understand that Lawrence wishes to marry Lizzie, but that you, and I presume Dan, too, object. Quite violently according to Lawrence. I believe you have forbidden Lizzie to see him. Isn't that a little extreme, Bessie?'

'Well, I never did.' Bessie was open-mouthed with astonishment. 'You of all people, Miss Edwina. Why, it was you who put a stop to all that business between Mary Ann and your brother and yet now you seem to be condoning what's going on between his son and her daughter.'

'It's completely different and you know it is, Bessie. Lawrence is very different from his father. Randolph was a rake and I knew he would only hurt Mary Ann.'

Lizzie watched as the two women exchanged a long look, before Edwina went on more briskly, 'But this is different. Very different. Lawrence is a good boy. He's not the sort to lead a girl on and besides . . .' She glanced up at Lizzie now and smiled. 'I don't think your granddaughter is the sort to allow herself to be "led on", do you?'

Bessie snorted. 'Huh, she's her mother's daughter too, don't forget.'

'Gran . . .?' Lizzie began, but Bessie only snapped, 'Be quiet, miss, and speak when you're spoken too.'

Lizzie bit her lip and retreated to sit in a chair by the window, although she could still hear every word that was being said.

'I'm sorry, Miss Edwina,' Bessie was saying stiffly, aware that the years of their friendship could be wiped out in a single moment. 'But Dan and the whole family are against this. There's no more to be said.'

'So, you're going to deny these young people a chance of happiness?'

'They wouldn't be happy, Miss Edwina. Are you going to tell me that your nephew would go and live on a boat with Lizzie?'

'Of course not. She would go to live at The Hall.'

Bessie's reply was grim. 'Exactly. And how do you think she would fit in there?' She leant forwards towards her visitor. 'Our sort are servants at The Hall, not mistresses of it.' With blunt sarcasm, she added, 'Unless it's the other sort of "mistress" he wants.'

Calmly, refusing to be goaded, Edwina said, 'I think that's the root of the matter. You don't really believe that he intends to marry her.' She stood up. 'Well, I'm very disappointed, Bessie. I had thought that in this uncertain world you would have allowed two young people a little happiness.' She stood looking down at the older woman as she added softly, 'Lawrence will be called up very soon now and who knows what will happen then.'

'And you'd have her left a widow? Mebbe with a child?'

Slowly, Edwina nodded, 'Yes, I would. If I had had the chance, I would have married Christopher and had his child. At least I would have had something, instead of a lifetime of loneliness.'

'That's as maybe,' Bessie's tone was still harsh. 'But you've money behind you. You would never have had to struggle to raise a child. It'd have been easy for you. What would she do, eh, left with a bairn?'

Edwina's face turned white and, shocked, she whispered, 'That's a cruel thing to say, Bessie. Cruel and heartless. I'd never have thought it of you.'

Unrepentant, Bessie said, 'I've never been one to shirk the truth, Miss Edwina, not even when it hurts.'

Edwina let out a shuddering sigh as she said flatly, 'I'm sorry, more sorry than you'll ever know, after all the years we've known each other and been friends. We have been friends, haven't we, Bessie?'

Lizzie could hear the sorrow in Edwina's voice, and her grandmother must be feeling it too, she thought as she watched and listened, for Bessie only nodded as if she did not trust herself to speak now.

Edwina went on. 'I'm sorry we have to part like this. Please think it over. Because you are wrong about Lawrence, truly you are.'

Lingering just a moment longer, Edwina stretched out a trembling hand to touch Bessie's shoulder, but the older woman remained seated in her chair, her head bowed, and did not utter a farewell or even look up as Edwina left the house. Only when she had been gone several minutes, and Lizzie got up from her chair and went to sit opposite her grandmother, did Bessie look at her, tears in her old eyes, and say bitterly, 'See what trouble you've caused? You've lost me one of the dearest friends I ever had.'

With a sob, Lizzie jumped up and ran from the house, through the yard and out into the street. For once, Bessie made no attempt to call her back.

Forty-Nine

Lizzie knocked at the back door of The Hall.

'Is Lawrence here?' she asked the young kitchen maid, who opened the door.

The girl gaped at her. 'The young master, you mean?'

'I suppose so, yes.'

'Wait a minute, miss. I'll ask Cook.'

The girl looked flustered, wondering why someone dressed as poorly as Lizzie and coming to the back entrance should be asking to speak to the young master and calling him 'Lawrence' in such a familiar way too. Understanding the girl's dilemma, Lizzie smiled to herself as she realized her own mistake. She should have walked boldly up to the main entrance, where the door would no doubt have been opened by a manservant.

'Come in, please, miss. Cook says she'll have a word with you.'

Lizzie stepped into the warm kitchen, where the smell of freshly baking bread was like a heady perfume.

'So,' the cook began without preamble. 'You're her daughter, are you? Setting your cap at the young master like your mother before you, eh?'

Lizzie drew herself up. 'Is that any of your business?'

'Oho, Miss Hoity Toity. Just like your mother, aren't you? You even look like her. Well, she came to a bad end, didn't she? And you will, an' all. You mark my words. And yes, anything that goes on in this house is my

374

business. When your mother worked here, she caused us all a lot of trouble. I got a right roasting from Miss Edwina for not having kept me eye on her. I'll never forget that. So you can turn yourself about and get out of my kitchen.'

Lizzie glanced about her. There were several doors leading out of the kitchen, presumably to pantries and cellars and store cupboards, but which one, she wondered, led to the upper part of the house?

'Do you hear me? If you know what's good for you, you'll be on your way and . . .'

At that moment one of the doors opened and a man, dressed like a butler, appeared. Lizzie sprang forward, dodged beneath his outstretched arm and was through the door before anyone could scarcely draw breath.

She entered a vast hall and stood a moment to stare around her in fascination. Then, behind her, she heard the sound of the man following her and she hurried on again, running the length of the room. She scampered along passages and up staircases, her heart thumping and yet she was enjoying the game of hide and seek. It was a wonderful old house, with nooks and crannies and plenty of hiding places. How the children of the house must have loved their games within its walls, she thought. What fun, what glorious fun life must be like to live in a place like this.

Her pace was slower now, for she had given the butler, or whoever he was, the slip and now she had time to peep into the rooms on either side and to marvel at the solid furniture and oil paintings hanging on the walls. In one room, she saw an embroidered wall hanging.

'Miss Edwina's been busy,' she murmured to herself, and then a door at the end of the passage opened.

'Lizzie.' She heard his voice and turned to see him coming towards her, his arms outstretched.

She ran to him and threw herself against him. 'Oh Lawrence, I had to come. Please don't be angry.'

'Angry? My darling, I'm delighted. I couldn't think how to get to see you, if you were being held prisoner by the dragon.'

'The . . .?' she began. 'Lawrence, please, don't call my gran that. She's wonderful, really. It's just that she doesn't think . . .'

'I know, I know. I'm sorry. I didn't mean to be rude towards her. But they won't listen to us, will they?'

The manservant was hurrying down the corridor towards them. 'Master Lawrence, I'm so sorry you've been troubled. I really don't know what Cook was thinking of to even let a gypsy woman into the house.' His voice was harsh as he spoke now directly to Lizzie. 'Come along, young woman . . .'

He was already stretching out his hand to take hold of her by the shoulder when Lawrence put up his hand. 'It's quite all right, Deakin. Miss Ruddick is a friend of mine.' Pointedly, he added, 'A very good friend. In fact, if I have my way, she could well be your future mistress at The Hall.'

For a moment, the man's face was a picture, and it was a credit to his professionalism that he managed with a supreme effort to mask his feelings, give a little bow and say, obsequiously, 'I am so sorry, sir. I had not realized. Pray forgive my intrusion.'

He turned away and marched, stiff backed, down the corridor whilst both Lawrence and Lizzie fought to stifle their laughter.

'Come in here. We won't be disturbed.'

He led her into the room at the end of the corridor. Intrigued, Lizzie glanced around. It was Lawrence's bed-room.

'Now my reputation will be in tatters,' she teased, but nevertheless she allowed him to lead her to the window seat. They sat together, holding hands.

'Oh Lizzie, let me look at you. It seems ages since I saw you.'

'I must look a mess.' She tried to smooth her tangled hair and scrubbed at her face. 'No wonder he thought I was a gypsy.'

'Darling, have you been crying?' Tenderly, he touched her face with his fingers and then drew her into his arms.

'They're all against us, Lawrence, everyone. At least, everyone except your Aunt Edwina.'

'Aunt Edwina?'

She drew back from him a little and looked up into his face. 'She came to see my grandmother. Came to plead our cause.'

Lawrence's eyes lit up. 'She did?'

Lizzie nodded. 'Yes, but she didn't get anywhere. They . . . they fell out. After all these years, they quarrelled and I feel so guilty about us being the cause of it.'

'They'll get over it,' Lawrence said, airily unconcerned. 'But don't let's waste precious time talking about them. Oh Lizzie, I've missed you so much.' He held her close again. 'I want to be with you for every minute of every day.'

He stood up and pulled her to her feet. Then he was kissing her, with an urgency that made her gasp. 'Darling . . .' he whispered and she felt his hands begin to caress her waist. His fingers moved up to unfasten the buttons of her blouse and with his other arm he was pulling her across the room towards the canopied old-fashioned four-poster bed.

'No, Lawrence, no.'

His eyes were ablaze with passion. 'Why, Lizzie? Why

not? I love you and we're going to be married. We're engaged now. Or as good as. I thought you loved me.'

'I do, you know I do, but . . .'

'Then prove it. Prove you love me as much as I love you. Oh, I want you so much. I've dreamed about this moment. Please, Lizzie . . .'

She pulled away from him, with tears of frustration. She wanted him too, just as much, but there were tears of bitter disappointment too. 'You're just like they said. That's all you want. You don't love me. Not really, or you wouldn't ask.'

Her words were like a douse of cold water to him. 'What do you mean? I don't understand.'

She was crying openly now. 'If I let you, you'd hate me afterwards.'

'I wouldn't. I swear I wouldn't.'

'Well, I'd hate myself and probably you too. I'm not going to give you or anyone else the chance to say that I'm just like my mother.'

'Lizzie, oh Lizzie.' She could see that his dismay was genuine as he reached out for her again, but this time only to take her gently in his arms to comfort her. 'I'd never even think such a thing.'

Her sobs, muffled against him now, began to subside as he stroked her hair and murmured, 'Then we'll be married, my darling. As soon as I can arrange something, we'll be married.'

She lifted her face to his. 'Oh Lawrence. Darling Lawrence, you really do love me.'

As he bent his head to kiss her once more, he whispered against her mouth, 'Never doubt it for a moment, my dearest love.'

Fifty

Lizzie was lucky that neither her grandmother nor her father, when he returned home, asked her if she had seen Lawrence. She didn't want to lie to them and, had they asked her outright, she would not have done so. She would have told them the truth. But, as they did not ask, she did not volunteer the information.

Her father, often morose and distant in the years since her mother had gone, was even more silent than usual. He very rarely smiled now and requests to her aboard ship became orders. It was as if she were merely an employed mate rather than his beloved daughter.

They made a trip to Newark where the ship was laid up for three days whilst necessary repairs and painting were carried out. Normally, her father would have suggested she stay at home, in Waterman's Yard, but this time he insisted she went with him, and she spent a miserable three days in a small hotel in the town with nothing to do, whilst her father was busy at the boatyard. Even when he was with her, they hardly spoke to each other.

When they set sail downriver once more, it was a relief.

'We're going straight through to the Humber,' her father said, 'before we go home.' Lizzie glanced at him, but said nothing. She could hardly ever remember a time when they had passed by Elsborough without calling.

Only when they were being towed in the days before they had an engine had they not stopped.

It was all a deliberate ploy, Lizzie fumed inwardly, to keep her away from Lawrence. He would be returning to boarding school soon. His father was adamant that he should sit his higher school certificate before joining the RAF.

'I'm not going back,' Lawrence had told her, but Lizzie believed that, when the time came, he would have no more choice in the matter than she had in obeying her father.

The trip to Hull was uneventful and on their return home, as they neared the Miller's Wharf, Lizzie could see her grandmother standing there.

'Oh, not again,' she breathed and sighed, bracing herself for more trouble. 'I suppose she's heard that I went to The Hall. Better get it over with, I suppose.'

No doubt, Lizzie thought to herself, Phyllis had heard the choice bit of gossip about this gypsy girl knocking at the back door of The Hall, demanding to see the young master. But as she jumped ashore and moved towards Bessie, Lizzie could see there was something dreadfully wrong. Something far worse had happened. Tears streamed down the old lady's face and she suddenly looked even older than her sixty-six years.

Lizzie stretched out her arms towards her. 'What is it? What's happened? Is . . . is it Grandpa?'

Unable to speak, Bessie shook her head. She clung to Lizzie and pressed her face into the girl's shoulder, sobs wracking her huge frame.

'Oh Gran, darling Gran. What is it?'

'Mam?' Dan was beside them now.

'It's . . . it's our Duggie. He's gone. He's lost at sea. His . . . his ship was torpedoed.' Her voice rose to a wail of untold grief and desolation. 'We've lost him, Dan. I've lost one of my boys. My baby.'

Dan put his arms around her and the three of them stood there clinging together, trying to find mutual comfort when nothing and no one could bring any kind of consolation. Lizzie was crying too now, 'Oh no. Not Uncle Duggie. Please say it's not true?'

Dan was the first to recover and said quietly, 'Come on, love. Be strong now for your gran's sake. Take her home and I'll come as soon as I can.' He looked down at his mother with such tenderness on his face that it twisted Lizzie's heart afresh. 'Come on, Mam. Lizzie will go home with you. Where's me dad? Does he know?'

Her body still heaving with tearing sobs, Bessie only nodded. 'He's sat at home by the fire. Won't move. Won't say a word. And Ernie. He's hardly said a word, either. And when he does, it's to say summat daft, like it ought to have been him and not our Duggie. He's just pacing up and down the yard, running his hands through his hair as if he'd like to pull it from his head.'

Dan said nothing, sparing a moment's thought for his taciturn brother, the one they always seemed to forget. Yet Ernie had been the first in their household to volunteer, only to be turned down by the medical board.

'You'll have to be strong, Mam. You always have been.'

Bessie shook her head. 'Not this time, lad. I'm done for. I'm too old to take any more. Mary Ann going fair broke me heart, but this . . .'

Her tears were unceasing as Lizzie helped her homewards. Bessie leant so heavily on her that the girl felt as if she were almost carrying her. But she was strong physically and now she had to be strong emotionally for all their sakes, for the woman who had always been the rock in their midst, the one to whom everyone, family and neighbours alike, had always turned in their troubles, was shattered and heartbroken.

When they entered Waterman's Yard, Ernie was nowhere to be seen, but Minnie rushed forwards. 'Oh Bessie, we've just heard. We're so sorry.' She dissolved into tears and covered her face with her apron.

'Thank you, Mrs Eccleshall,' Lizzie said. 'But I just want to get Gran home.'

'Of course, love. But if there's anything I can do, you've only to say. Oh, it's dreadful. It really is.' And she wailed afresh.

But what was there she could do? Lizzie thought sadly, as she helped Bessie, stumbling, across the yard. What was there any of them could do?

Amy Hamilton was standing by the door of Bessie's home, her arms folded across her thin chest. 'Well, Bessie Ruddick, now you know, don't you? Now you know how it feels.'

Feeling a shudder run through Bessie and hearing her groan, Lizzie braced herself as her grandmother leant even more heavily against her. Anger flooded through Lizzie and gave her a fresh spurt of strength. 'Excuse us, Mrs Hamilton, if you please,' she said with icy politeness. 'I want to get Gran into the house.'

Amy, with a strange look of surprise on her face, stared at Bessie, but she stood aside as Lizzie manoeuvred Bessie through the door and the scullery and into the kitchen.

'Sit down, Gran. I'll mash us a pot of tea.'

'I'll do it,' a voice said behind her, and Lizzie turned in surprise to see that Amy had followed them into the house.

'There's no need for you to trouble yourself, Mrs Hamilton . . .' she began, but the woman cut her short.

'There's every reason, lass. Every reason, but you wouldn't understand.'

Surprise robbed Lizzie momentarily of speech, and she sat down suddenly beside her grandmother, staring at Amy, who was busying herself about Bessie's kitchen and back scullery as if she were in her own house. Lizzie's glance went then to her grandfather sitting in his chair by the range. He looked in a worse state than her grandmother did, Lizzie thought, anguished. She felt helpless in the face of such grief. Her own sorrow was bad enough, but to see these two dear people so devastated broke Lizzie's young heart. It would have been bad enough for one of them to lose the other, their life's partner, but to lose one of their children went against nature. It wasn't the right order of things.

'His ship got torpedoed,' Bessie murmured again as if, only by repeating it, could she begin to believe what had happened to her beloved boy.

'It's a waste,' Amy said, placing a tray of teacups and saucers on the table and picking up the teapot. 'A tragic, senseless waste. That's what it is.' There was anger in her tone and even when she said, 'Here, Bessie girl, drink this,' it was said brusquely. She held out a cup of tea, but Bessie appeared not to have heard. Lizzie took it and gently patted her grandmother's arm.

'Mrs Hamilton's made you some nice tea, Gran. Come on, try and drink it.'

'Here you are, Bert.' Amy was standing over him, issuing an order she would not allow him to disobey. 'Drink this.'

Suddenly, Lizzie remembered and understood. This was the woman who had lost her husband and only son in the Great War. Lizzie felt her resentment towards Amy drain away. This woman, brusque though she seemed at this moment, was probably the only one of them around here who truly understood how Bessie must be feeling.

'Am I going to have to feed you, Bert Ruddick? Come on, rouse yasen.'

Tears running unashamedly down his face, Bert looked across at Bessie, who was lying back in the chair, her eyes red in a face pale with exhaustion. He closed his eyes and groaned.

Lizzie watched as Amy bent down towards him. 'Come on, Bert. You've got to be strong for Bessie.'

He shook his head. 'She . . .' he began haltingly as if even speaking was an effort. 'She's the strong one.'

Quietly, Amy said, 'Not this time, Bert. Poor Bessie's going to need you to be strong for her this time.'

Bert looked up at Amy and then slowly he reached out to take the cup of tea she held out to him. Though his hand shook and the cup rattled in the saucer, he picked it up and gulped the strong, hot liquid like a man thirsting in the desert.

Satisfied, Amy turned her attention to Bessie. 'Now then, let's be 'aving you an' all.' She smiled at Lizzie and her tone became gentle as she said, 'You go into the scullery, lass, and get a bit of dinner ready. I'll stay with them.'

At the sink in the scullery, as she peeled potatoes and washed vegetables, her own tears falling into the bowl of water, Lizzie could hear the low murmur of Amy's voice, although she could not hear what was being said. A little while later, Dan arrived and Amy came out into the scullery.

'I'm going now, lass, but I'll be back.'

Lizzie turned and opened her mouth to express her thanks, but Amy held up her hand. 'Don't say anything, lass, 'cos I might not like what you're be going to say.'

'I wasn't—' Lizzie began, but Amy interrupted.

'I lost me husband and son in the last lot and it was your gran who pulled me through. I'd have done for mesen for sure, if it hadn't been for her. I might sound a bit hard, a bit unfeeling, but I'm only giving her a taste of her own medicine.'

Lizzie gasped, astonished to think that the woman could be so vindictive after all these years. But once more, Lizzie had to admit that she was wrong as Amy explained. 'It's medicine that's hard to dish out and it's bitter to take, lass, but it works. It worked on me. I thought Bessie Ruddick was the hardest, most callous bitch around, but she knew what to do. Oh, she knew how to shake me out of me self-pity. I'm still alive today only because of her, Lizzie. And I'll never forget it. So, now I'm going to be here for her when she needs help.'

Lizzie's voice was unsteady as she said, 'Thanks. Thank you, Mrs Hamilton.'

If it hadn't been for Amy Hamilton, Lizzie thought later, the Ruddick family might well have lost Bessie and probably Bert too.

For days and weeks, Bessie hardly ate. The weight dropped from her and loose skin sagged beneath her jaw. Bert tried his best. He cajoled and pleaded with her, but to no avail. Even the taciturn Ernie was heard to plead, 'Come on, our Mam, try to eat something.'

Bessie retreated into a world of her own. Sitting beside the range, staring into the fire, she stirred only to answer the call of nature. She didn't even undress at night or go upstairs to bed, and soon her unwashed grey hair was lank and greasy, her clothes stained and crumpled.

It was Amy who finally broke through the wall of

misery. Once more she stood over Bessie. 'Are you going to sit there, Bessie Ruddick, till you rot? You're beginning to smell now.'

For the first time since they had received the dreadful news, Lizzie felt herself wanting to laugh. And yet she wanted to cry at the same time. Holding her breath, she watched as, slowly, Bessie raised her face to look at Amy. Suddenly, there was a spark of anger in her grandmother's eyes. 'What right have you to tell me what to do, Amy Hamilton, I'd like to know?'

'Oh you would, would you? Well, I'll tell you what right I've got.' She leant down so that her eyes were on a level with Bessie's. 'Same right as you had to save my miserable life all them years ago. Remember?'

The two women stared at each other, a lifetime of memories between them. 'And think about it, Bessie. You have got other family. There's poor Bert here, and your other lads, to say nothing of this poor lass who's bewildered and lost by it all. They're all hurting, Bessie. I had no one left, no one to live for, and yet you still wouldn't let me go, so I'm damned if I'm going to let you shrivel away and bring more grief to your family. You hear me, Bessie Ruddick. By heck, if you weren't so big and fat, I'd shake some sense into that stupid head of yours.'

Amy straightened up and turned to Lizzie and Bert, who were standing by listening, first shocked and then amused by Amy's antics.

'Lizzie, see if Mrs Eccleshall's at home. Tell her I need her help across here, but tell her to leave her tears at home. I don't want her coming in here weeping and wailing and making matters worse. And you, Bert, get the tin bath, bring it in here and fill it with water. It's time me and Min gave Mrs Smelly here a good bath. I'm just going to my house to fetch her some clean clothes.'

It had been the turning point and whilst the whole family still grieved, once Bessie started to recover, they all began to come to terms with their loss.

'I miss Uncle Duggie so much,' Lizzie told Tolly, who, their previous quarrel forgotten in the wake of such a tragedy, had been one of the first to arrive on the doorstep to offer his sympathy. 'He was always so happy and cheerful.' She smiled wistfully. 'I even miss him teasing me.'

They were sitting on the riverbank, watching the fish, but today neither of them had the heart to try to catch any.

'I expect there's a lot of people who miss him. Your uncle was what they call a lovable rogue. A bit of a lad with the women, but everybody liked him.'

'Yes. Yes, they did.' She sighed. 'I suppose that should be a comfort, but it isn't.'

'No.' Tolly reached out and took her hand. 'Nothing's a comfort really, because nothing can bring him back.'

'We're not the only ones to have lost someone, though, are we?'

'No,' Tolly agreed again. 'But that doesn't make it any easier either.'

She leant her forehead against his shoulder. 'Oh Tolly, thank goodness you're too young to be called up. Let's hope it's all over before you reach eighteen.'

He did not answer her and she could not tell him everything that was in her heart. Much as she loved Tolly – he was like the brother she had never had – she could not tell even him that with each passing day her fear grew that, before long, Lawrence would have to go to war.

Fifty-One

'Lizzie, I want to go to church this morning. Will you come with me?'

Bessie was standing in the kitchen, dressed in her best black hat and coat.

'Of course, Gran. I'll get my coat.'

'And find a hat,' her grandmother murmured. 'Doesn't do to go into church without a hat.'

The church was packed – every seat seemed to be taken.

'What's going on?' Lizzie whispered. 'I've never seen the church as full as this for a normal morning service.'

'It isn't a normal service,' Bessie said. 'It's a special service for all those families who've lost someone. That's why I wanted to come.' She nodded towards the congregation in front of them as they squeezed into a pew near the back of the church. 'Just look at all these poor folks who've lost loved ones. I'm not the only one and it's time I realized it.'

'Oh Gran,' was all Lizzie could say as tears threatened to choke her. She put her hand through her grandmother's arm and kept it there throughout the service. By the time it was over and the people were filing out, Lizzie wasn't sure whether coming had been such a good idea. Throughout the prayers and the hymn singing there had been the sound of people crying. Even Bessie, usually loath to let strangers witness her emotions, had dabbed at her eyes and blown her nose vigorously.

'Come on, Gran, time to go,' Lizzie urged, when Bessie made no move to leave.

'Hang on a minute, love,' Bessie said. 'There's something I want to see when everyone's gone.'

'What?' Lizzie asked, sitting down again.

'Amy reckons someone's embroidered a banner of some sort. It's on the wall near that little chapel at the side there. She says it's got Duggie's name on it.'

'Really?' Lizzie said, intrigued too, now.

When everyone except the verger, who was still busy, had left, Bessie and Lizzie walked to the front.

'There it is,' Lizzie said, pointing to the wall at one side. They moved closer and saw, embroidered in silks and gold thread upon satin, the emblems of the Merchant Navy and the words 'In loving memory of Douglas Ruddick, who gave his life in the service of his country, September 1941'.

'Who do you think has done it?' Lizzie asked.

'I suppose,' Bessie said slowly, her gaze never leaving the beautiful piece of work, 'there's only one person who could have done it.'

'Miss Edwina?' Lizzie suggested.

'I suppose so,' Bessie said, thoughtfully. Then, more briskly, she added, 'Come on, time we were going.'

But just before they turned away, Bessie reached out and touched the name of her son worked in gold thread.

In the spring of 1942, Lawrence volunteered for the RAF long before his call-up papers came.

'If you won't marry me, Lizzie, I might as well die the hero.'

Lizzie turned pale. 'How can you say such a thing to

me? You know how difficult it's been for me, losing Uncle Duggie and my gran and grandpa needing me.'

'I need you too, Lizzie.' There was a frown on Lawrence's handsome face. 'I'm beginning to think you don't really love me.'

They were in the shadows of the woods, deep amongst the trees where no passing cyclist could see them and, this time, they would be more careful when they left their secret place. Meeting at all had still been difficult, yet since the awful news about Duggie, Lizzie's grandmother had not once mentioned her involvement with Lawrence Marsh. The only time the matter had ever come to the surface again had been the time when Edwina had called at Waterman's Yard to see Bessie.

She had knelt on the rug in front of the grieving woman and taken hold of her hands. 'I'm not going to let a silly argument spoil our friendship, Bessie. I'm so very sorry about poor Duggie. You know, if there's anything I can do, anything at all . . .'

But Edwina had gone away without Bessie saying a word to her, for she had called at a time when the older woman was so lost in her grief she was speaking to no one. Since that day, Edwina had not called again and Bessie, either too proud or not even aware that Edwina had been, did not make the first move to restore their former friendship.

Slowly, the old couple had begun to come to terms with their loss, though their lives were altered forever. Lizzie was able to go back aboard the *Maid Mary Ann* to cook and care for her father, but there were still times when she was not allowed on a particular trip. It was only on these occasions, when she stayed in Waterman's Yard, that she had the opportunity to slip away to meet Lawrence.

'You know that's not true,' she said now, winding her arms around his neck.

'How do I know it's not true? You won't let me make love to you. You won't run away with me to get married. What am I supposed to think?'

'How could I leave my family after what happened?'

'Most families around here have lost someone. They don't all go to pieces. You have to get over it. Get on with your life. Our lives, Lizzie.' He took her gently by the shoulders and looked down into her eyes. 'I'm going away soon. I've joined up and I'm going to train to be a pilot, probably on bombers. I really want to be on Lancasters.' His eyes were afire with a passion in which she had no part.

Lizzie drew in a horrified breath at the thought of the danger he would be in.

'Before I go,' he was urging her, 'I want you so much. I want to make love to you so badly, it hurts. If you really love me, you wouldn't send me away not knowing, not having tasted such happiness.'

'Lawrence, I . . .' she began, but he cut her short, pulling her against him and resting his cheek against her hair.

'I know. I know what you're going to say, Lizzie, and I'm trying to understand. Truly, I am. So . . .' He paused and pulled back a little from her, looking down into her face once more, and now he was smiling gently. 'So, I've found us this vicar, miles from here, who will marry us.'

'Marry us? But he can't. We're not old enough to get married without parental consent.'

'He's a doddery old fool who hardly seems to know what day of the week it is, let alone still compos mentis enough to think to ask us our ages. All we need are some witnesses. I'm sure one of his church wardens would oblige and I thought we might ask Aunt Edwina.'

Lizzie eyes opened wide. 'Miss Edwina?' She shook her head. 'Oh no, that wouldn't be fair.'

'Why not? She and your grandmother aren't on speaking terms now. So she tells me. So what does it matter?'

'Aren't . . .? Oh no, you've got it wrong. Your aunt called just after my uncle was lost at sea, but it was at the time that Gran hardly knew what was happening. I don't think she was even aware that your aunt had called.'

Lawrence shrugged. 'Anyway, she might do it. Oh Lizzie, what do you say? Please – please, will you marry me?'

Swept along on the tide of his passionate pleading, and fearing that so very soon she might lose him, just like she had lost her dear uncle, Lizzie heard herself saying, 'Of course, I will.' And then he was kissing her so ardently that all thoughts of her father, her grandmother, even of Tolly, were driven from her mind.

Lawrence gave her no time for second thoughts or for doubt of any kind. He planned it all with such meticulous care that nothing could go wrong.

'We won't tell Aunt Edwina,' he decided later. 'She's such a one for truth and honesty that she might disapprove, not of what we're doing, but the way we're doing it. Now, are you sure there's nothing else you want? I've bought you a pretty dress . . .' He grimaced. 'Not a white one, darling, I'm afraid, but a very pretty one nonetheless. And flowers. I've ordered you a bouquet. And afterwards . . . oh darling, afterwards, I'm taking you away to a lovely little hotel in the country, where we can be completely alone. There'll be no bombs, no talk of war. Just the two of us, I promise.'

As she slipped home through the dusk of early evening, a shadow loomed from the entrance to the alleyway leading to Waterman's Yard.

'Tolly! What on earth are you doing skulking about in the dark? You frightened the life out of me.'

'Sorry,' he muttered.

There was silence between them before she said, 'Why are you here? Is something wrong?'

'You tell me.'

'What do you mean?'

'What do you think I mean?'

'Oh, do stop being so irritating,' she snapped.

She heard him take a deep breath. 'All right, if that's the way you want it. You've been seeing him again, haven't you?'

Her voice rising, Lizzie said, 'What's that got to do with you?'

'Ah, so I'm right.'

'I didn't say so.'

'You didn't deny it either and since you ask, it's got everything to do with me. Do you think I want to see you throw yourself away on someone like him? Someone who'll cast you aside like an old shoe when he's . . . he's had his way with you and then tired of you. He'll never marry you, Lizzie . . .'

'Well, that's just where you're wrong.' Angry beyond reason now, Lizzie's tongue began to run away with her. 'We're getting married this coming Saturday, so there.'

With that parting shaft, she strode away from him

down the alleyway. His voice echoed through the darkness, 'Oh Lizzie, no. Think what you're doing. Please.'

Tolly must have been waiting on the wharf the following morning when her father's ship docked. Or he might even, Lizzie thought bitterly, have rowed downriver to meet him.

'What's this all about?' her father thundered, when he stepped over the threshold of Bessie's house in Waterman's Yard, without a word of greeting to her after two days away. 'Is this true what Tolly tells me? That you've been seeing young Marsh again and that you're going to marry him?'

'Dad . . .' Lizzie began, but Dan was in no mood to listen.

'Well, just let me tell you, my girl, it'll be over my dead body if you do. Haven't I had more than enough trouble from that family? Hasn't his father caused me enough grief? To think that you could do this to me, Lizzie.' His anger seemed to die as he shook his head and said sadly, 'I thought you were different, but I see you're not. You're just like her. In looks, in everything. You're just like your mother.'

'Dad, don't say that.' Lizzie was crying now as she flung herself against him, trying to wrap her arms around his big frame, but, hurt beyond understanding, he flung her away from him as if he could not bear to touch her. 'Why won't you listen to me?' she cried. 'Why won't you try to understand?'

''Ere, 'ere, what's going on?' Bessie appeared in the doorway leading from the kitchen into the scullery where they were standing. 'What's all the shouting about?'

'She reckons she's going to marry young Marsh, that's

what's the matter,' Dan shouted. 'I thought you were going to keep an eye on her. Are you behind it? Has she wheedled her way around you, just like Mary Ann used to do?'

'Don't you take that tone with me, lad,' Bessie wagged her finger at him, some of her old spirit returning. 'Besides, she's isn't old enough. Without your consent,' Bessie added, calmly matter-of-fact, 'it wouldn't be legal.'

'I shouldn't think that'd bother *him* for a minute,' Dan sneered. 'It'll make divorcing her all the easier, won't it?'

'Doesn't anyone care about me?' Lizzie almost stamped her foot with anger. 'Don't you want me to be happy? He's joined up. He's going in the RAF in a few weeks. Going to be a bomber pilot. Don't you think he deserves a little happiness? Don't you think we have to snatch what happiness we can, while we can?'

She saw them glance at each other, but now they were silent, as if each were thinking the unspoken words. Had poor Duggie snatched what happiness he could in his life, cut short by an enemy torpedo?

Dan ran his hand distractedly through his hair. 'Oh Lizzie, it's because we love you so much and because there's so much you don't understand.'

'I'm sorry, Dad. The last thing I want to do is to hurt you, or Gran, but I'm going to marry Lawrence.'

His expression hardened again as he stared at her. Then through tight lips, he said, 'Then you'd better get on with it, but don't come running back to me when he casts you off like an old shoe.'

She shuddered at his words. They were the very same ones that Tolly had used.

Fifty-Two

Lizzie refused to let the rift between her and her family spoil her wedding day. The April sun shone brightly on the tiny church set high on a Yorkshire hillside as, dressed in her finery and carrying a bouquet, Lizzie walked up the narrow path, clinging to Lawrence's hand.

'However did you find it?' she asked.

He chuckled. 'It wasn't difficult. The church is on land belonging to my mother's family, to her brother now, actually. And he pays the vicar, who's as deaf as a post and can't see too well either. He hasn't even asked awkward questions about our ages or anything. So, there's no problem. Although making several trips up here to arrange it all did take rather a lot of my father's precious petrol coupons.' He looked down at her and any doubts she had were swept away. There was no denying the look of love and desire in his eyes.

They were wrong, she told herself, her heart singing with happiness. They were all so wrong. Lawrence loved her and they would be so happy together that her father and her grandmother would see it for themselves. And then they would forgive her. Lizzie was so confident in their love for her – she knew they were only concerned, like they said, for her happiness – that she knew they would all come around one day.

The old man in a dirty surplice shuffled forward to meet them. Twice during the service, he dropped the book and Lizzie had to bend down to retrieve it and place it back into his shaking hands. He stumbled through the words, squinting through grubby spectacles whilst the organist thumped out a hymn on the wheezing organ.

'I don't know who is the oldest,' Lawrence whispered. 'The vicar or that organ.'

'Ssh,' Lizzie hissed, but was soon in danger of being overcome with a fit of the giggles.

The service was over far sooner than she had expected and, once the register had been signed – the verger and the gravedigger having been commandeered as witnesses – they were outside in the sunshine.

'Could I prevail upon you to take a picture of us?' Lawrence stopped the organist as he hurried out of the church.

'Oh – er – yes, of course, but I am in rather a hurry.'

The man fumbled with Lawrence's camera. 'What do I press? Oh yes, I see.'

Quickly, he snapped three photographs and then said, 'That do? I really must be going.'

'Thank you,' Lawrence said, taking the camera, and then whispered to Lizzie, 'We'll take some more at the hotel. I'll take some nice ones of you. They've got a lovely garden there, with a little bridge over a stream . . .'

'I'm sorry, darling,' Lawrence said, as he rolled away from her after their first attempt at making love. 'I just wanted you so badly. It'll be better the next time . . .'

As he drifted into sleep, Lizzie lay, tensed and unsatisfied. If that was all there was to making love, she thought, all that heaving and pushing and grunting, then she didn't know what all the fuss was about. In the early hours, when Lawrence stirred and woke her, he whispered, 'It'll be better for you this time, darling, I promise.'

But still, despite his efforts to think of Lizzie's feelings, wanting her to experience the heights of passion along with him, he came to a shuddering climax long before her body had begun to respond to his caresses.

He tried to make light of it and pretended to leer as he murmured, 'It's going to take a lot of practice. An awful lot of practice . . .' Again, he slept.

By the fourth day of their honeymoon, Lawrence said, 'Things'll be better when we get home. We'll be among familiar surroundings then.'

Familiar to you, maybe, Lizzie thought, but she said nothing.

'And I expect you're still upset about your family,' Lawrence added. 'Once you've made up with them, you'll feel more relaxed.'

'Are you saying it's my fault?'

'Of course not, darling. You're just tense, that's all. It's only natural.' He took her in his arms and kissed her gently. 'I do love you so much, Lizzie. I just want every-thing to be so perfect.'

She kissed him in return and said, 'I'm sorry. Perhaps it is my fault. I . . . I mean it is the first time, for me. You're right, things will be better when we go home.'

He caught at her hands. 'Then let's go. Right now. Let's go home and begin our proper married life. With you as mistress of The Hall.'

Lizzie caught her breath. 'Don't be silly. Your mother is mistress of The Hall.'

Lawrence shrugged. 'In name only. Rather like their marriage. I think it's been "in name only" for years.'

'But she still lives there. And your father.'

'Supposedly. But he's hardly ever at home. God only

knows where he goes. I think he's got a fancy woman somewhere.'

Lizzie gasped. 'And ... and doesn't your mother mind?'

'No, she couldn't care less.' He grinned. 'Maybe she's got a fancy man somewhere too.'

'Well, I hope you don't think you can do that when you get tired of me,' Lizzie said, her eyes flashing.

'Oh darling.' He stroked her hair. 'I'll never get tired of you. For as long as I live.'

Their homecoming was unheralded and, consequently, devoid of welcome, although Lizzie doubted there would have been much of one anyway.

At dinner that first evening, when Lawrence had instructed her on how she was expected to dress, Lizzie was seated on one side of an enormous table, with Lawrence's father and mother at opposite ends, with far more than the length of the table between them.

The meal passed almost in silence, the rattle of cutlery and the chink of china the only sounds in the vast, cold dining room. If it hadn't been for the pressure of Lawrence's foot against her own beneath the table, Lizzie would have fled.

At the end of the meal, Lawrence cleared his throat and said, 'Father, Mother, there is something I have to tell you. *We* have to tell you.' He reached across the wide table to take her hand as he said, 'Lizzie and I were married last Saturday.'

Randolph stood up so suddenly that his heavy chair crashed to the floor and his red wine spilled over on to the table, the glass rolling towards the edge. Deakin hurried to catch it before it smashed on the floor. Then the manservant picked up the chair and set it behind his master before retiring to stand discreetly in the shadows of the corner of the room. He stood like a statue, ready to serve if needed, but more likely, Lizzie thought shrewdly, anxious to hear this latest piece of scandal with which he could regale the other servants.

'You did what?' Randolph, purple with rage, shouted.

Lizzie's fingers trembled but Lawrence's hand, she noticed, was warm and firm and steady. At a slight sound from the other end of the table, Lizzie turned to see that his mother was leaning back in her chair and holding her ribs. To Lizzie's amazement, the woman was laughing. 'Well done, Lawrence, my dear. You've finally shown you have got a spark of spirit in you after all. I was beginning to wonder.'

'Have you taken leave of your senses, boy? Married at your age. And about to go into the forces. What on earth were you thinking of?' There was a pause before Randolph added, 'Oh I get it. In the family way, is she?'

Quietly, Lawrence said, 'No, father, she isn't. Though I hope . . .' He smiled across the table at Lizzie. 'That she might be very soon.'

He released her hand then and stood up, turning to face his father. 'Wouldn't you like a grandson, father?'

'Of course I would,' the man thundered, and then flung out his arm towards Lizzie. 'But not with *her* as its mother.'

Randolph turned, pushed the chair that Deakin had so carefully placed behind him out of his way so that once more it toppled to the floor, and then he strode from the room. The only sound that followed him was his wife's laughter.

*

'He hates me. He doesn't think I'm good enough for you,' Lizzie said mournfully, when they were alone in their room later.

Lawrence sat beside her on the bed and put his arm about her shoulders. 'Well, your family hate me, don't they?'

'Perhaps they're all right. Perhaps we do come from such different worlds that it'll never work.'

'Lizzie, please don't say that. We'll make it work. We'll prove them all wrong. You do love me, don't you?'

'Of course I do.'

His lips were against hers. 'Then prove it, Mrs Marsh. Prove it.'

Fifty-Three

On 29 April 1942, a bright, moonlit night and only days after Lawrence and Lizzie had returned to The Hall after their marriage, Elsborough suffered one of its worst air raids of the war. A Dornier dropped bombs on the centre of the town, killing thirteen people and injuring many more. Gas pipes were fractured and fires broke out. Smashed water pipes gushed water into the streets and hampered the efforts of the rescue services.

Huddled in the deep cellars below The Hall with Lawrence, his mother and the servants – of Randolph, there was no sign – Lizzie could only listen to the distant thuds and worry about her family in Waterman's Yard. 'Dad's probably away,' she murmured to Lawrence, 'but what about Gran and Grandpa?'

'You've an uncle still living at home, haven't you?' Lawrence said, sounding unconcerned. 'He'll look after them.'

'No,' she said worriedly, feeling a fresh stab of guilt. 'Now I'm not there, he's gone with my dad aboard the *Maid Mary Ann* to take my place as mate.' She chewed her lip as anxiety gnawed at her. 'They'll be on their own.'

'Well, there's plenty of folk around who'll look after them.' Lawrence chuckled. 'That Horberry fellow, for a start. Time he did something useful instead of stirring it for others, eh?'

She was irritated by his seeming lack of concern for her

elderly grandparents, but she had to admit that what he said was true. There were plenty of people in Waterman's Yard who would look after Bert and Bessie Ruddick. They didn't really need her.

Strangely, the thought hurt her.

Her mother-in-law's voice, coming through the gloom, interrupted Lizzie's thoughts. 'What did you say your father's boat is called?'

'The *Maid Mary Ann*.'

'Shouldn't it be the *Maid Marian*?'

'It was,' Lizzie explained, pleased to have something to talk about; something to take her mind off the thud of bombs still falling somewhere above them. 'But because my mother's name was Mary Ann, the owner allowed my father to change the name slightly.'

'Mary Ann, you say?' Although Celia Marsh still spoke with her usual, seemingly disinterested, drawl, there was suddenly a different edge to her tone. 'Your mother's name was Mary Ann?'

'Yes.' Now Lizzie's answer was short. She had no wish to be drawn into searching questions about her mother.

'How strange,' Celia murmured. 'How very strange.' Then, with definite interest now, she asked, 'And where is your mother now, dear? Still aboard the boat named after her?'

'Er . . . no, she . . . I mean . . .' Lizzie floundered, knowing that in the shadows The Hall's servants were listening intently.

Lawrence came to her rescue smoothly. 'Lizzie lost her mother some years ago. She doesn't like to talk about it.'

'Lost, you say? You mean, she died?'

'Lizzie was very young. Her people just told her that her mother had "gone away".'

'Ah,' Celia said. 'I see.'

And to Lizzie, flushing uncomfortably in the darkness, it sounded very much as if Celia Marsh understood perfectly, perhaps even better than Lizzie herself had ever done.

With the dawn came Lizzie and Lawrence's first real quarrel.

'I'm must go to Waterman's Yard.'

'You're not going. It's too dangerous. I forbid it.'

'You . . . what?' Lizzie was scandalized. 'How dare you speak to me like that?'

'Of course I dare, you're my wife. And, if you remember, not many days ago you promised to obey me.'

'That has nothing to do with it . . .'

'It has everything to do with it. I won't allow you to go running back to the yards. They don't want you, they've said as much, and now that you're my wife, your home is here, at The Hall. And soon, with the help of my mother, you will have something of a position in the town.'

'A position? What sort of a position?' Lizzie was aghast, horrified at what his words implied. That she was to cut herself off from her family and, worse still, regard herself from now on as one of the gentry.

'A position in society. Mother knows everyone in the town who is worth knowing. She'll make sure you meet all the right people . . .'

'Lawrence, do you know what a prig you sound?' she flung at him, turned and walked out of the room, slamming the huge door behind her. Around her the old house seemed to creak in protest.

*

'Darling, I'm sorry.' That night, in bed, Lawrence took her in his arms. 'Please, don't let's quarrel. I have to go away next week. I'm to report to training camp.'

'Oh Lawrence.' Lizzie, contrite now, kissed him and put her arms around him. 'So soon? I thought you weren't going for another month. Darling, I'm sorry. I'm so sorry.'

'Well, my eighteenth birthday's next week, so I suppose the RAF think a few days doesn't make any difference.'

'You mean you won't be at home for your birthday?'

'No.'

'Oh Lawrence . . .' Full of remorse now for her behaviour, she gave herself to him, thinking nothing of her own needs now, only of his.

'You've made yar bed, lass, now you'll have to lie in it. It's no good coming back here because he's gone away to war and your ma and pa-in-law won't speak to you.'

Lizzie was in her grandmother's kitchen watching the older woman standing at the table kneading bread. Every so often Bessie winced and shifted her feet, trying to ease the pain.

'Let me do that, Gran. You sit down.'

'I'm not a cripple yet, thank you,' Bessie snapped and glowered at Lizzie. 'Hadn't you better be about your wifely duties? Aren't there luncheon parties and good works you should be attending to in your smart new clothes?' Bessie glanced resentfully at the new, well-cut costume Lizzie was wearing.

'Oh Gran, how long are you going to keep this up?' She sat down at the table and leant her elbows on it, though she was careful to avoid the scattering of flour.

'Who asked you to sit down, Mrs Marsh?'

Lizzie gaped at her and then stood up slowly. 'Well, if that's how it is. If I'm not welcome here . . .'

'That is how it is.' Bessie wagged her finger towards Lizzie, sending a further shower of flour over the table. 'You've hurt your dad more than I can find the words to tell you. It was bad enough what Mary Ann did to him, but you . . .' Words did, indeed, seem to fail her for the moment. 'You were the apple of his eye. He thought you could do no wrong. And you've done about the worst thing to him you could have done. Now he's all alone with his memories. And what bitter memories they are, an' all.' She shook her head. 'Poor Dan. My poor Dan. And don't you go running to him, either. He doesn't want to see you.'

Lizzie felt the tears spring to her eyes. 'I love Dad, he knows I do. I love all of you.'

'Well, you've a funny way of showing it, that's all I can say.'

Now anger spurted in Lizzie. 'And you've all a funny way of showing you care for me. You don't seem to want me to be happy.'

With that, she whirled around and ran out of the house and across the yard, almost bumping into Amy Hamilton coming down the alleyway loaded with heavy shopping bags.

'Oh morning, Mrs Marsh, ma'am. Doing a bit of slumming, are we?'

Lizzie gave a sob, dodged around her and hurried on, the sound of Amy's laughter echoing down the passage-way after her.

Fifty-Four

Lizzie felt as if she didn't belong anywhere now. At The Hall, Randolph Marsh ignored her completely and the servants were barely civil to her. To their minds, as well as to her own family's, she had betrayed her class. She was no longer one of them, but neither did she belong to the family she had married into. If only Lawrence had not gone away, Lizzie thought, things might well have been different.

Edwina might have become her friend, for she alone out of all of them had not been against the marriage. But Edwina rarely came to The Hall and Lizzie hesitated to visit her home.

Almost daily, Lizzie found herself going down to the river to stand on the wharves, watching the ships coming and going. Sometimes, she saw the *Maid Mary Ann* and her father or Ernie in the distance, but not once did they raise their hand in greeting or come to speak to her, even though she was sure they had seen her standing there. She longed to go aboard. Her need for sight of the cabin, so recently her home, for the feel of the ship beneath her feet and to breathe the damp smell of the river, to feel again its every mood, was like a hunger within her.

At nights, alone in her bed, Lizzie slept fitfully, dreaming that she was back on board in the middle of the River Humber on a calm, sunny day. Out there, away from everything, there was such peace and tranquillity, the only sounds the ship carving through the water, the wind billowing the sails and the seagulls calling overhead. She could hear her father's commands, 'Rise ya tack' and his long, drawn-out 'Let gooo', so clearly that she awoke with a start, her limbs already tensing to obey him. Then, with a sense of disappointment, she realized where she really was.

She was homesick for the river and its folk, but she was no longer welcome there.

At other times she wandered along the riverbank until she was opposite the shipyard. Once, she saw Tolly rowing homewards but, though she waved and shouted his name, he did not even glance towards her.

She felt so bereft, so cut off and alone.

Strangely, it was Lawrence's mother, Celia, who, in her cool, offhand manner, extended the hand of friendship. 'If you've nothing to do, my dear, there's plenty of voluntary work in the town you could help with. The WVS could certainly use another pair of hands.'

The 'good works' that her grandmother had spoken about so scathingly, Lizzie thought. She sighed inwardly, but summoned a smile. 'I'd be glad to help. Please tell me what I have to do.'

For the first time since Lizzie had known her, Celia became animated. 'You can join the local branch of the WVS. There are all sorts of jobs they do.' She ticked off a list on her fingers. 'Helping out at the rest centres and mobile canteens, providing hot drinks and food for Civil Defence workers. Then there's all the work we do for people who've been bombed out. Some of them have lost everything, all their possessions, clothes, absolutely everything. So we have a centre for the collection of clothes. You could help sort the bundles that come in there, perhaps.'

'I had been wondering whether to join up, too,' Lizzie murmured.

'Oh no,' her mother-in-law said swiftly. 'Lawrence wouldn't want you to do that. But he wouldn't mind you helping out in the town. I'm sure he wouldn't. Just so long as you're always here when he comes home on leave . . .'

Lizzie found the women volunteers were a mixed bunch: from the smart, town ladies, dressed in their fitted costumes with padded shoulders and pork-pie hats with long, curling feathers, to the housewives from the terraced street who came along to the centres in their aprons and their overalls. Yet there was camaraderie amongst them.

'We all muck in together,' Barbara, a young housewife from the backstreets of the town, told Lizzie, and she nodded towards one or two of the grander ladies, who were delving their well-manicured hands in amongst the grubby second-hand clothing without turning a hair of their neat heads. 'Who'd have thought it, a few years back to see the likes of them working alongside us, eh?' Then she laughed. ''Spect I shouldn't say such things to you, should I? You've just married Mrs Marsh's son, ain't you?'

Lizzie nodded.

'Bet you miss him, love, don't you? Ne'er mind, he'll soon be home on leave again. My old man's coming home next week.' She winked broadly at Lizzie and said, 'So I won't be here for a day or two. I'll be flat on me back giving comfort to the troops. Well, one of 'em, anyway.'

The raucous laughter echoed around them and Lizzie smiled.

'I'm off into town this dinner to get some frilly underwear,' Barbara went on. 'There's a man on the market selling knickers made out of parachute silk. That'll give my Harry a thrill. Why don't you come too, Lizzie? Give that new husband of yours a nice surprise when he comes home, eh?'

Lizzie thought about the fancy underwear that Lawrence had bought her for their honeymoon. Her lips tightened a little as she remembered his words. 'There's everything you need, my dear. I didn't think you'd be used to going into such shops.' It had been kind of him, she told herself, but she would have liked the chance to choose her new clothes for herself. With a spark of rebellion now, Lizzie nodded. 'All right, I will,' she told Barbara.

'Oho, madam from The Hall buying frilly knickers off the market. Whatever will Lady Celia say?' said a voice close by.

'You shut it, Vi. She's all right, is Mrs Marsh.' Barbara glanced at Lizzie and grinned. 'Both the Mrs Marshes are.' She linked her arm through Lizzie's. 'You stick with me, gal, I'll show you how to put a bit of spice into your marriage.'

'She don't need it,' said someone else. 'They've only been married a few months. They're still at the dewy-eyed stage.'

'Then she'll be ready to keep her old man from straying when the time comes, won't she?' Barbara countered, refusing to be shouted down. 'Come on, Lizzie, take no notice of them. We're going knicker shopping.'

'What on earth are you wearing?' Lawrence said, as they dressed for dinner on the first night of his leave.

Turning from the dressing table with a smile, Lizzie told him about her shopping expedition with Barbara. 'I was lucky to get them.'

410

'Lucky? I wouldn't call it that. Take them off this minute.'

Misunderstanding, Lizzie giggled. 'Oh Lawrence, not now, we haven't time.'

'I don't mean that,' he snapped. 'Get them off and put something decent on.' He strode across the room to the chest and dragged open one of the drawers. 'Where is all the nice underwear I bought you? That's real silk. Mind you,' he glanced at her over his shoulder as he added scathingly, 'I suppose I can't expect you to know the difference.'

Lizzie sprang to her feet. 'How dare you . . .?' she began, but he was walking calmly towards her holding out the undergarment of his choice. 'Here, put these on and mind you throw that rubbish where it belongs.'

For an instant Lizzie contemplated rebellion, but his eyes were suddenly so cold that she knew he was utterly serious. Remembering that he only had a few precious hours at home, she gave way and removed her knickers and put on the pair he had brought her.

'Is that better?' she asked tartly, and began to turn back to the dressing table.

He stepped close to her and put his arms about her, nuzzling his face against her hair. 'Much,' he murmured, and she could hear in his tone that at once his good humour had been restored. 'I shan't be able to eat for thinking about you dressed in those beneath your demure dress. And those stockings and suspenders. Oh,' he pretended to groan in ecstasy. 'Oh Lizzie . . .'

With a swift movement he picked her up in his arms and carried her to the bed.

'Lawrence, no. We mustn't. We'll be late for dinner.'

'It'll wait,' Lawrence murmured, his mouth searching

hers and his fingers pushing their way beneath her brassiere. 'This won't . . .'

Their coupling was soon over. Taken by surprise, Lizzie had no time to begin to enjoy it, even if she had not still been seething with anger at Lawrence's high-handed attitude with her over her underwear. But Lawrence did not seem to notice. He rolled off the bed, straightened his clothing and said, 'Hurry up and get ready. We'll be late.'

During the time Lawrence had been away, Lizzie had given a great deal of thought to what might be wrong between them in the marriage bed. She had listened to how the other girls had talked about their husbands and young men and she had been to the cinema twice where she had watched, fascinated, as the heroine seemed to give herself to the hero with complete abandon.

Later that night, lying beneath him once more, Lizzie closed her eyes and imagined she was Hedy Lamarr or Rita Hayworth. She caressed Lawrence and moaned and writhed, simulating pleasure.

'Oh darling, darling,' he murmured at last, panting against her neck in the aftermath of desire, 'that was glorious.' He raised his head and looked into her face. 'You felt it too, didn't you?'

She nodded, guilty at the lying, yet feeling it was justified for she had made Lawrence so happy.

He kissed her gently. 'You were wonderful – wonderful, my dearest love.'

They made love constantly throughout the week of his leave, seeming to spend most of the time in their bedroom.

'What must your mother think?' Lizzie said, feeling embarrassed.

'She'll understand, though . . .' he pulled a face, 'I

doubt their marriage has ever been as good as ours. Mind you,' he grinned cheekily at her, 'it did produce me, so perhaps they were happy at first.'

He laid his hand against Lizzie's stomach. 'Do you think you might be pregnant? I do so want a son.'

Lizzie glanced at him coyly, pushing away the guilty knowledge that, for her, their week of passion had been only an act. 'It won't be for the want of trying, will it?'

He was pushing her back against the pillows. 'One last time, Lizzie, please, just one last time before I have to go . . .'

Perhaps in time, she could not help thinking as his hands caressed her and his mouth found her breast, I will feel what he feels. Perhaps in time, it won't be just an act. She dug her fingers deep into his thick hair and held him close, arching her body to meet his, but as she moaned in pretended ecstasy, a tear squeezed its way from beneath her eyelids and ran down her temple.

Fifty-Five

Christmas 1942 was the most miserable Lizzie had ever spent. Lawrence could not get leave to come home. It was not the lack of traditional fare, for the Christmas dinner at The Hall was almost the same as in peacetime – roast turkey with chestnut stuffing and roast potatoes and Brussels sprouts, followed by Christmas pudding and brandy butter, made with real butter. There were trifles with real cream and real coffee to follow. How many other households would be able to afford, or even have access to, such luxuries? Certainly not her family in Waterman's Yard. Yet, with all the deprivations that the Ruddick family would be suffering, Lizzie longed to be there. She knew her grandmother would be fortunate indeed if she had managed to acquire a chicken for their dinner. More than likely the pudding would be a sugarless Christmas pudding from a wartime menu issued by the Ministry of Food, and the coffee would be made with acorns.

But Lizzie would have given anything to have been in Waterman's Yard amidst the laughter and the teasing, rather than sitting at the long table, handling the fine silver and eating off the expensive china plates between the silent Randolph and Celia Marsh.

It was a relief, after Christmas, to return to the WVS centre and to join in the lively chatter once more.

'Have you heard the latest?' At times, Barbara was almost as big a gossip as Phyllis Horberry, yet her tales were told with kindness. There had always seemed to be a hint of malice in Phyllis's tattle. 'You know the Olivers that live in the ferryman's cottage at Eastlands?'

Lizzie stiffened and found she was holding her breath. She listened, but said nothing.

'He used to be the ferryman, didn't he? Works in Phillips Engineering now, doesn't he?'

'Yeah, since the beginning of the war.'

'Who runs the ferry now then?'

Barbara shrugged. 'Not so much call for it nowadays with motor transport using the bridge, though I think a few of the locals still use it to get from Eastlands to Westlands across the river. I 'spect his wife operates it or his lad. They've got a lad with a funny name. Ollie or summat like that.' Lizzie bit back the reply that sprang to her lips as Barbara continued. 'Well, me and Ted Oliver were walking out together years ago, but I soon packed him up. He was a violent bugger, he was. He only ever hit me once, mind you, but that was quite enough for me.'

'He married Susan Price, didn't he? Old man Price's daughter?'

'Tale went,' someone else said, 'that someone jilted her. I forget who, but they say she married Ted Oliver on the rebound.'

'Aye,' Barbara said grimly, 'and I bet the poor woman has lived to rue the day, an' all.'

'What about him?' another, impatient for the juicy morsel of gossip, prompted.

'He's buggered off,' Barbara said bluntly.

Lizzie felt herself reddening, not at the language – she had heard far worse on the river – but her heart went out at once to Tolly.

'What do you mean?'

'What do you think I mean? He's run off with another woman.'

'He never has.'

'It's true. He's had a fancy piece for years, they say. In Westlands. She was married an' all, but her husband's been in the army since the beginning of the war and he's been killed. So Ted's moved in with her.'

'The bastard,' someone murmured. 'Didn't waste any time, did he? That's not nice, that.'

'It's the war,' said another. 'You've got to take your happiness where you can find it.'

'Mebbe, mebbe not,' Barbara said. 'But in this case you can't blame the war. This time, it's Ted Oliver.'

'I feel sorry for his wife. She's a nice little woman, by all accounts. The only good thing she's ever had in her life is her lad and now he's going in the RAF any day . . .'

The gossip flew around her head, being chewed over and digested, but Lizzie heard no more. Her mind froze. Tolly, her dear Tolly was going away. He'd be eighteen in a month or so's time, just after Christmas. And she hadn't realized. Wrapped up in her own life, she hadn't remembered that soon he, too, would be going to war.

Tears blurred her vision. Oh Tolly, Tolly, her heart cried. How could I have forgotten?

Lizzie's hand trembled as she knocked at the door of the small white cottage on the riverbank.

Susan opened the door. 'Why, Lizzie, how nice.' Her smile was warm and genuine and she looked happier than she had looked for years. 'How smart you look. Come in, come in.'

Lizzie stepped across the threshold and said, 'Has he gone?'

Susan's smile widened and her eyes twinkled. 'Who? Ted?'

Lizzie felt the colour creep into her face. 'Oh I'm sorry, I didn't mean . . .'

Susan reached out and touched her hand. 'I know you didn't, love. But I expect everyone knows – or they soon will. Yes, he's gone and to be honest, it's good riddance, Lizzie, 'cos he's made our lives hell at times. Mine and Tolly's.' Her smile faded and her mouth tightened. 'It was the biggest mistake I ever made. But my father was so for me marrying Ted and he wouldn't ever believe what was going on in this house. He sided with Ted against me, his own daughter. Can you believe it?'

Lizzie shook her head and fought to swallow the lump in her throat. 'It . . . it was Tolly I meant. I heard he'd been called up.'

Now Susan's face was sad as she nodded. Her voice dropped to a whisper. 'Not called up, exactly. He volunteered, but he doesn't go till January, until after his birthday. He's still here. Do you want to see him?'

'If . . . if he wants to see me.'

Susan smiled again. 'I'm sure he will.'

As she followed Susan through into the next room, Lizzie was not so sure, but the smile that lit Tolly's face when he looked up and saw her was reassuring. As he rose to greet her, he seemed to Lizzie to have grown even taller, and he had filled out so that the gangly youth had gone. Now his shoulders were broad and the floppy hair had been cut short and was smoothed back with hair cream.

'He's getting ready to be one of the Brylcream boys,'

Susan teased and her glance caressed her son fondly, although she could not quite hide the anxiety that lay deep in her eyes.

'Shall we go for a walk along the bank?' he said and minutes later, as they strolled beside the river, Lizzie murmured, 'It's just like old times.'

'Not quite,' Tolly said, in his gentle voice that was now deeper. He glanced her up and down. 'You're not quite dressed for salmon fishing, are you?'

She gave him a rueful smile and they walked on in silence for several minutes before she burst out, 'At least you're speaking to me. My family won't have anything to do with me. I haven't seen any of them for months.' She turned and looked up at him. 'Is my father all right? Have you seen him recently?'

Tolly nodded. 'He's fine as far as I know. Always gives us a wave as he passes by.' He grinned briefly. 'He doesn't chuck coal or veg or tins of fruit at me any more, but he always looks out for us.' His voice was even deeper as he added softly, 'Both of us. Mam and me. He always has done.'

Again there was a long silence before Lizzie said, 'You will take care of yourself, won't you?'

As if by silent, mutual consent, they stopped and turned to face each other. Tolly put his hands on her shoulders. 'Are you happy, Lizzie?'

She answered swiftly, too swiftly. 'Of course I am.'

Tolly said nothing, but he raised his eyebrows in an unspoken question. Then he let his hands fall heavily away from her and he thrust them deep into the pockets of his trousers. 'That's all right, then,' he muttered glumly.

Lizzie had the feeling that he would have been far happier if she had told him that she was lost and lonely and utterly miserable in her new life.

And it would not have been so far from the truth either, she acknowledged to herself, though the words remained unsaid as they walked on together.

Lizzie didn't see Tolly again before he went away, although she continued to visit his mother in the ferryman's cottage. She heard that he had completed his basic training and was learning to be a rear gunner on Lancasters.

'Isn't that dreadfully dangerous?' she asked Susan fearfully. Lawrence had told her that the rear gunner's turret was the most vulnerable part of the aircraft that he now piloted.

Susan had tried to smile bravely, but had failed miserably.

'I'm so proud of him, Lizzie, but I'm so dreadfully afraid for him. So terribly afraid . . .'

By the time Lawrence came home on his next leave, Susan had already heard that the aircraft in which Tolly had been flying had been shot down and that all the crew had been posted missing, presumed killed.

Lizzie sobbed against Lawrence's shoulder. 'He was my friend. My very best friend ever since we were at school.'

He held her but the soothing words she sought, needed, were not forthcoming. 'Aren't I your best friend now?' he asked, sounding hurt.

'That's different,' she murmured, her words muffled against him.

He led her towards the bed, tried in the only way he knew to take her mind off her sorrow. But lost in her grief for Tolly, Lizzie could not even make the effort to put on the act. She lay acquiescent beneath him, but not participating, whilst he took his pleasure, using her body.

At last he rolled away, frowning. 'You could at least pretend you're enjoying it,' he said bitterly, and she gasped wondering if he had guessed the truth.

Then, spiritedly, she flashed back, 'And you might show a little more concern when I'm so upset.'

They stared at each other, dismayed to find they were in the middle of another quarrel.

Fifty-Six

Although they had tried to make up, by the time Lawrence's brief forty-eight-hour leave was over, there was still a constraint between them.

'I'm sorry, Lawrence,' Lizzie said, genuinely contrite.

'It's all right,' he said, but she could see from the tightness around his mouth and the resentment in his eyes that it was anything but 'all right'. 'I don't know when I'll get leave again,' he went on. 'I'm being posted to Scampton to a newly formed squadron, six one seven. You mustn't tell a soul, Lizzie, it's all very hush-hush. We're to have special training, low flying over water at night. They won't tell us why, but it must be something big.'

'Oh Lawrence . . .' Now she clung to him, feeling a surge of concern. 'I do love you. I'm so sorry about . . . about everything. Try to get home again, soon. It'll be better, I promise.'

But it wasn't. When he came home again – for Scampton was only a few miles away and he could easily get home even for only a few hours – if anything, the situation was worse. Lizzie had been lonely and miserable with no one to turn to for comfort. She had visited Susan, but had found herself in the role of comforter. Now she had no one. Her father and grandparents were lost to her and Edwina was far too occupied with keeping her school running and all her pupils safe from the bombing, to say nothing of the war work in which she involved herself.

Even the work that Lizzie did for the war effort had become monotonous and now she was without the friendly camaraderie of the other girls. The one or two with whom she had formed a casual friendship, Barbara in particular, had moved on. Some had gone on to do other work, one or two of the younger ones had joined the forces and the new batch of women and girls seemed to view the wife of Lawrence Marsh from The Hall as an outsider. Lizzie was listless and mourning the loss of her friend. Then she was riddled with guilt because it should have been her husband and his safety that dominated her thoughts.

But all she could think was, *Oh Tolly, Tolly. I've lost you.*

When Lawrence arrived home again, looking wide-eyed with exhaustion, Lizzie tried hard to hide her feelings. She fussed around him, running a bath for him and using double the regulation amount of water. She laid out his suit herself on the bed and helped him tie his bow tie, although in fact, he was far more expert at tying than she was.

He smiled down at her, resting his hands lightly on her waist. 'I've missed you so much, Lizzie. How ... how have you been?'

She realized he was trying to show concern for her feelings and yet not wanting to open up the raw wound again.

'Fine,' she said brightly, but there was a brittle quality in her voice, a forced gaiety that she was afraid he could not help but notice. She patted his chest as she completed the tie and stood back. 'How about you, darling? You look awfully tired. Is it very dreadful?'

He nodded. 'We've been taken off all other operations, just to concentrate on this wretched special training.

We're getting such a lot of stick from the other chaps now. We just all wish something would happen.'

There were only the three of them at dinner: Lawrence, his mother and Lizzie. Celia made polite enquiries about his life in the RAF, but her interest was superficial and made out of the need for civilized, dinner-table conversation.

'Father away on business, is he?' Lawrence asked towards the end of the meal.

Celia leant back in her chair and fitted a cigarette into a long black holder. Deakin moved forward to light it for her and she inhaled deeply and blew smoke rings into the air, watching them float and then dissolve before she turned her limpid gaze on her son. 'My dear boy,' she drawled, 'your guess is as good as mine. I doubt the war is going to make your father change his ways.' She smiled, but the smile did not reach her eyes. 'Do you?'

Lawrence looked down at his plate and, beneath the table, Lizzie felt his foot find hers and press it. He needed her, she knew. He needed her to put her arms around him and hold him close and love him. He needed her to tell him that everything was going to be all right.

Lizzie rose from the table and smiled at her mother-in-law. 'That meal was delicious. I don't know how Cook manages it with all the rationing.'

Celia blew out the blue smoke again. 'It's what she's paid for.' She rose from the table, her movements languid, and moved towards the door. 'Good night, my dears,' she said offhandedly over her shoulder. 'If you're leaving early in the morning, Lawrence, please don't disturb me. I need my beauty sleep.'

Lizzie watched as Lawrence, who had risen to his feet the moment she had got up from the table, stared after his mother. 'Good night then, Mother,' he murmured. 'And

I'll say "goodbye" too . . .' but already the door had swung to behind her.

Lizzie held out her hand to him. 'Come on, darling. Shall we go up?'

He walked around the table and took her hand, clinging to it like a drowning person.

She tried, oh she tried so very hard, to respond to his desperate need of her. She willed herself to be swept along on the tidal wave of his passion, but there was a shadow between them, the shadow of a lost soul whom Lizzie could not forget.

At last, they lay in each other's arms in the huge bed against a mound of pillows. He buried his face against her neck and Lizzie could feel the wetness of his tears on her skin.

His voice was muffled as he said, 'It's over, isn't it?'

She held him tightly. She closed her eyes but her own tears squeezed their way from beneath her eyelids and ran down her face. She stroked his hair as sobs shook him. But she said nothing. There was nothing she could say.

She lay amidst sumptuous surroundings, her every whim pandered to by lackeys. She had no need to work for her living; she had no need to do anything. She had a wardrobe full of fine clothes, enough food set before her each day that would have fed the whole family in Waterman's Yard. And she was in the arms of a handsome young man who, she knew, loved her. And yet . . . All she wanted was to be back on the river, on her father's boat, standing at the prow, the wind in her hair, and watching for Tolly on the bank.

The truth came slowly, only moments before Lawrence lifted his head and, in the half-light, looked down into her eyes. 'Lizzie, my darling Lizzie,' he whispered. 'It's not me you love, is it? It's Tolly.'

She drew in breath. 'No, no . . .' she began to say, but very gently he laid his finger against her lips.

'Hush, my darling. Just let me love you one more time. For the good times, Lizzie. And we have had some good times, haven't we?'

'Yes, oh yes. Oh Lawrence . . .' Her tears flowed unchecked now and she clung to him. Now their loving was tender and giving, but they were crying, sobbing against each other, both knowing that the next time Lawrence came home, Lizzie would no longer be at The Hall.

Tomorrow morning, after Lawrence had gone, Lizzie was going home.

Fifty-Seven

Lizzie was waiting on Miller's Wharf when the *Maid Mary Ann* arrived. As soon as the gangplank was in place, Lizzie, her heart thumping in her chest, her mouth dry, ran up it and for the first time since before her marriage, she stepped on to the deck of her father's ship.

'Hello, Uncle Ernie.'

The quiet man nodded and said only one word, 'Lass.' It was both a greeting and a question. Lizzie looked about her and saw her father standing at the tiller. He was staring at her, but from here she could not read the expression in his eyes.

'Dad.' She made her way to him, tears stinging her eyes at the sight of him. He seemed to have aged since she had last seen him. His hair was liberally sprinkled with white, and lines of sorrow were etched deeply into his face. A few feet away from him, she hesitated, found she had to swallow a lump in her throat before she could begin to speak.

Then the words tumbled out, jumbled, scarcely making sense. 'Oh Dad. I'm sorry. Forgive me. I've come home. You were right. Please, will you forgive me? I was so dreadfully wrong. Please . . .'

For a long moment, in which Lizzie's hope plunged into despair, her father stared at her, his face expressionless. Then slowly, as if the action, so long unused, was rusty, he opened his arms wide to her.

With a sob of thankfulness, Lizzie ran into them to be enveloped in the safe embrace of his strong and loving arms.

Later, in the tiny cabin, they talked. 'Oh, it's so good to be back here,' she murmured, her glance roaming lovingly around the confined space, the polished cupboards, the tiny stove where she had cooked so many meals for her father and Uncle Duggie, the bed where she knew she had been born. 'I've missed it all so much.'

Already, Dan was able to tease her gently as they sat together on the bench seat, holding hands, almost like reunited lovers. 'All that grand living and you hankered for this?'

She nodded and pressed her lips together hard to try to stop the tears that welled in her eyes. But they spilled over and ran down her cheeks. Dan reached over and, with a callused hand that was surprisingly gentle, he brushed them away. 'Don't Lizzie, love. Don't cry. You're safe home, now. No more need for tears.'

'But I hurt you so. I hurt everyone. Gran and Grandpa. And ... and Tolly.' Now the sobs shook her and she buried her face against his chest. 'I can't ever tell him, Dad, how sorry I am. How wrong I was.'

'Ah.' She felt the breath sigh from her father's chest as he said softly, 'Ah, Tolly, is it?'

It was all he said and all he needed to say, for they both knew what lay behind that simple statement without another word being spoken.

He held her close whilst she cried out her sorrow and then, when she sat up slowly and dried her eyes, he asked gently, 'What about Lawrence?'

It was the first time he had spoken his name in gentleness.

'He's gone back to Scampton. He's . . . he's involved in some sort of special training. I don't know what. He . . . he couldn't tell me.'

'Of course he couldn't, love.'

'He . . . he knows I've come home. He knows it's over.'

Her father nodded. 'Poor lad.'

Lizzie's eyes widened as she stared at him. 'You . . . you feel sorry for him? For Lawrence? But . . . but I thought you hated him.'

Her father sighed heavily, releasing a lifetime of bitterness. 'No, I don't hate the lad. He can't help being his father's son.'

'What is it about his father that you . . .?' she began, but Dan patted her hand and said, 'Not now, Lizzie love. Maybe one day, I'll tell you it all. But not now. Now, I just want to enjoy you being back with me.' He put his arm about her again. 'For good, is it, Lizzie?' he asked softly.

She nodded and then, closing her eyes, she laid her head against his shoulder. The question could rest for now. There would always be another time to ask. She was home where she belonged.

'Now listen, Mam,' Dan began the moment he stepped over the threshold of Bessie's home, with Lizzie hovering uncertainly on the doorstep, nervous even to enter the house that had once been as much of a home to her as had the ship. 'Before you start, just let me have me say first, for once, will you? Me and Lizzie have sorted everything out between us.' He put his arm out and drew her in. 'She's sorry for what's happened. And she's home to stay and . . .' As Bessie opened her mouth, Dan held up his hand. 'That's all there is to be said.'

Bert had come to stand behind Bessie. He slipped his arms halfway around her ample waist – it was as far as they could reach – and peered around her shoulder. He was grinning happily. 'Bessie, my angel, isn't that just the most wonderful news? Come away in, Dan. You, too, love. Come and give your old grandpa a kiss.'

'Now just you wait a minute, Bert Ruddick . . .' Bessie twisted herself round in his embrace. 'I'm not having her—'

'Bessie, my angel, light of my life . . .' He reached up and kissed her full on the mouth. 'You have the loveliest mouth, but it don't half run away with itself – just now and again.' He lowered his voice, trying to hide what he was saying, but Lizzie's sharp ears caught the gist of his whispering. 'The lass is sorry . . . we don't know what's happened . . . taken a lot of courage to come back . . . just be thankful . . .'

There was a moment's silence before Bessie gave a shriek of laughter and clasped Bert to her, burying his face in the softness of her bosom. 'You're a good man, Bert Ruddick. The best. The very best.' Then she turned and held her arms wide to embrace Lizzie, the tears coursing down her plump cheeks.

It was on Bert's wireless that they all heard the news bulletin later that same week. The modulated tones of the announcer told them that a squadron of Lancaster bombers, flying at a very low level, had attacked the dams in the Rhur valley. Devastating flooding had been caused to the industrial region and the mission had been hailed as a great success, one that could possibly turn the tide of the war.

'Nine of our Lancasters are missing,' the announcer concluded in solemn tones.

Lizzie gasped and turned white, but she could not speak, not even when all her family turned to look at her.

Without waiting for the news that would surely follow in a few days' time, Lizzie knew, instinctively, that Lawrence would not be coming back.

It was Edwina who brought the official news to Waterman's Yard. She stood hesitantly on the doorstep, unsure of her welcome. The last time she had visited her old friend had been to offer comfort on the news of Duggie's death. Edwina had not come again to the Yard, but now, further tragic news had brought her unwillingly to Bessie's door once more.

But now Bessie drew her inside and hugged her. Any constraint between them fell away. 'We can guess why you've come, Miss Edwina,' Lizzie heard her say. 'Lizzie's in a right state, blaming herself.'

Lizzie looked up as they came into the kitchen. Edwina came straight to her, holding out her hands to take Lizzie's. 'You know, don't you, my dear?'

Lizzie, unable to speak, nodded.

'His plane went down over the target. It . . . it blew up. There was not the slightest chance of any survivors. I am so sorry.'

Shaking, Lizzie clung to Edwina's hands. 'I feel . . . so guilty. I should have carried on the pretence. I tried. I tried so hard, but he knew. He guessed. I . . . I feel as if I sent him to his death.'

'You mustn't think like that,' Edwina tried to reassure her. 'You probably gave him more happiness in these last few months than you will ever know.' Tenderly, she stroked a tendril of hair back from Lizzie's face and said, very quietly with a world of regret in her voice, 'It's more than I did for my man before he went away to war.'

'He wanted a child,' Lizzie sobbed. 'Lawrence so much wanted to ... to leave a son to carry on, if the worst happened. I haven't even been able to do that for him.' She raised her face to look into Edwina's. 'I would have done, if I could.'

'I know, I know.' Edwina put her arm around the girl and held her close. 'But it's over now,' she said, unwittingly echoing Lawrence's own poignant words. 'And now you must go on with your life, but before you do, can I ask just one more thing of you, Lizzie?'

'Of course. Anything.'

'Randolph is arranging a memorial service in the parish church. Will you attend as Lawrence's widow?'

Lizzie shook her head. 'His father won't want me there.'

'Oh, but he does,' Edwina said, surprising both Lizzie and the listening Bessie. 'It was Randolph who wanted me specifically to ask you to come.'

Fifty-Eight

There were fewer mourners at the memorial service than had been expected. Family members and local dignitaries, who attended out of duty only, made up the congregation. Once, the church might have been packed with the townsfolk paying their respects to a member of the unofficial squire's family, but Randolph was not liked and Lawrence hardly known. A few ladies from the committees upon which Celia served attended and only one person represented the river folk: Lizzie.

At the end of the service, Lizzie made her farewells to Edwina, who had sat with her throughout, but as she walked away down the long path to the gate, she heard a man's voice calling her name. 'Lizzie. Lizzie, a moment, if you please.'

With surprise, she turned to see Randolph Marsh following her. She stopped and turned to wait for him.

'My dear,' he said, taking her arm and urging her further down the path away from the small gathering outside the church door. 'You no doubt know that you will receive Lawrence's airforce pension, but . . .'

'I don't want his money,' her voice was shrill. 'That's not why I married him. I want nothing from you. Nothing.'

She could tell that he was fighting to hold on to his patience. 'Now, my dear, don't be so hasty. You are entitled to it and I certainly have no objection to make. What I wanted to ask you, my dear, was . . .'

Lizzie ground her teeth together, wishing he would stop calling her 'my dear', for there was not an ounce of affection in the endearment. But she said nothing as his next words shocked her. 'I don't suppose, by any miraculous chance, you could be pregnant?'

She stared up at him, her eyes wide with amazement. The audacity of the man, she thought. What an unfeeling, hard bastard Randolph Marsh was. Everything she had ever heard about him was true. Here he was at his own son's memorial service, and all he was concerned about was, was there any possibility of an heir for his family's fortune?

Lizzie's mouth was tight as she said shortly, 'No, I'm not.'

She pulled her arm free of his grasp and marched away from him, glad to be leaving the Marsh family for good.

'Oh Dad, Gran's waiting on the wharf again.' Lizzie turned towards her father standing at the wheel guiding the ship towards its mooring. 'Something must have happened. She only ever comes now when there's trouble.'

Lizzie had slipped back into her former life as if she had never been away. Her brief marriage to Lawrence Marsh was now never spoken of and the affection between herself and her father was, if that were possible, even stronger than before. As for Lizzie herself, she was as happy as it was possible for her to be, but deep inside she carried a heavy burden of regret. She felt such guilt that she had not been able to love Lawrence, as she should have done. She could not forgive herself for having hurt him. And worse still, when she realized at last where her true feelings lay, it was too late. Tolly was gone. She would never be able to make up her quarrel with him, not properly. Even though, that last time, they had parted on better terms, there was still so much that had been left unsaid. There was so much she wanted to tell him. And now she would never be able to. She would never be able to tell him how much she really loved him.

Lizzie and her father exchanged a troubled look as the vessel drew nearer to the wharf. Bert had been a little under the weather two days ago when they had left and the same thought was obviously in both their minds. Had something happened to him?

But as the ship drew nearer and Lizzie leant over the side, she could see that although her grandmother's face was anxious, she did not look devastated, as she no doubt would have done if something had happened to her beloved husband.

Lizzie was the first off the ship and running towards her. 'What is it, Gran? What's happened?'

Without the usual greeting, Bessie nodded her head beyond Lizzie towards Dan. 'It's yar dad I have to talk to, lass. Not you.'

'Just tell me, Gran, it's not Grandpa, is it?'

A brief smile chased away some of the anxiety on Bessie's face. 'No, lass. Your grandpa's fine. Better than he was.'

'Thank goodness,' Lizzie breathed. 'Then, what is it?'

Doggedly, Bessie said, 'You'll know soon enough, but your dad has a right to know first.'

Several minutes passed before Dan was able to step ashore. Lizzie could hardly contain her impatience and then, to her disappointment, as her father came towards them, Bessie waved her away. 'Just let me tell yar dad, there's a good lass.'

She opened her mouth to protest, but seeing the look

on her grandmother's face, she turned away and walked to the far end of the wharf. She watched them converse, although it was Bessie who was doing all the talking. Dan was just listening, staring down at his mother in disbelief.

'Whatever can it be?' Lizzie muttered to herself, standing first on one foot and then on the other.

She saw her father nod, say a few brief words and then her grandmother turned and, leaning heavily on the walking stick she now used, made her painful way from the wharf and towards her home.

Dan came towards Lizzie and stopped in front of her.

'What is it, Dad? What's happened?' She could guess nothing from his face, for his expression was a strange mixture of shock and disbelief.

His words came at last, halting and disjointed. 'She's come back. She's at your gran's house. She's very ill. She . . . she . . .'

Lizzie took hold of his hand. 'Who, Dad? Who's come back.'

For a long moment, unable to believe it himself, Dan stared at her. Then, his voice breaking with emotion, he said, 'Mary Ann. Your mother. She's come back.'

Lizzie felt as if her legs were going to give way beneath her, but whether from shock or relief that her mother was alive – and therefore the dark secret she had always dreaded had been entirely unfounded – she did not know.

'Where has she been all these years?'

Her father was looking down at her strangely now. 'You mean, you don't know, Lizzie?'

Lizzie shook her head and now, for the first time, she could whisper, 'I thought she might be dead. That night . . .' The question she had so desperately wanted to ask for so long, and yet had not dared, could now be voiced. 'I thought she'd drowned.'

'What?' His tone was scandalized. For a moment Dan closed his eyes and then groaned aloud. 'Oh, my dear girl, I never realized. Lizzie, I'm so sorry. I should have explained it to you. But at the time, you were so young and then, well, I couldn't bear to speak her name. I just wanted to blot it all out, to forget it. To forget her.'

But he hadn't been able to. Lizzie knew that. The haunted look in his eyes that had always been there told her so.

'It's all right,' she said now. It wasn't, but it was all she could say. She couldn't add to this poor man's burden any more. He was already suffering. He had suffered for years because of that night, and now . . . What now? Lizzie thought. Aloud, she said, 'So, where did she go?'

'She's been living in a little cottage just the other side of Raven's Wood.'

Lizzie gasped, understanding, at last, why there had been such anger when her father had learnt that that was where she had been meeting Lawrence. As if reading her thoughts, Dan smiled wryly. 'Yes, when you started meeting Lawrence there, I was always afraid you'd find out where she was.'

'But why – I mean, why was she living there?'

'Can't you guess?'

Mystified, Lizzie said, 'Not really. Unless she became tired of living on the ship and wanted a little house of her own.'

Dan sighed so heavily that she felt the waft of his breath on her face. 'If only that had been the case.' The hurt of years was in his tone as he added, 'No, your mother left me to go to her lover. She's been a kept

436

woman, his mistress, hidden away near the woods all these years. All I can presume is that he no longer wants her now. So, she's come back.'

'Her . . . her lover?' Lizzie began, and then it all fell swiftly into place. It was suddenly so blindingly obvious, that Lizzie was astounded at her own naïvety.

'Oh, my God,' she breathed and, not usually given to blasphemy, her father understood the depth of her shock. 'It was Randolph Marsh, wasn't it?'

Her father nodded and then added, his voice deep with emotion now, 'And that's not all. Your gran says she's expecting a child.'

Fifty-Nine

'You've told her?' was Bessie's greeting as Lizzie and her father stepped into the house.

Dan nodded. Then his voice was husky as he asked, 'Where is she?'

Bessie gestured with a slight movement of her head. 'Front room. I've had to rig up a bed in there for her. She's in a bad state.' There were tears in Bessie's eyes as she added, 'I couldn't send her away, Dan.'

The big man reached out and touched his mother's wrinkled hand. 'Of course you couldn't, Mam. I . . . I wouldn't have wanted you to.'

Woodenly, he moved towards the door leading into the front room. Big and strong as he was, Dan looked suddenly so vulnerable and afraid. Impulsively, Lizzie followed him, caught hold of his hand and smiled up at him. 'Do you want to go in on your own or shall I come in with you?'

He looked down at her and she felt his hold on her hand tighten. 'Come with me, Lizzie. Please,' he said hoarsely and, together, they went into the room.

Lizzie would not have recognized the woman lying in the bed. Apart from the bulge beneath the bedcovers that pronounced her pregnancy, she was thin to the point of emaciation. Her cheeks were hollowed, her eyes bulging from their sockets, and her hair hung, lank and unkempt, about her shoulders. Her face was an unhealthy pallor, devoid of any colour.

'Oh Dan!' Her voice was weak, little more than a whisper. Then her gaze came to rest on Lizzie. 'And Lizzie.'

With what appeared to be a great effort, she lifted her arm from the bed and reached out with trembling, skeletal fingers.

'There isn't long. Dan, please, will you forgive me? Please say you forgive me. I couldn't bear to go without making my peace with you.'

Dan moved suddenly, dragging Lizzie with him as he went towards the bed, his other hand outstretched to take Mary Ann's. 'My dear, don't say anything. You're home now and we're going to take care of you.'

He released Lizzie's hand and, sitting down on the edge of the bed, took hold of Mary Ann's with both his strong, warm hands. Lizzie, unable to speak, stood behind him, but her gaze never wavered from the woman in the bed.

'Oh, Dan,' Mary Ann breathed and closed her eyes. Tears pushed their way from beneath her eyelids and ran down her face. 'You're such a good man. I was such a fool. A stupid, naïve fool. So often, I've wanted to come back to you. You don't know how much I've missed you and . . . and Lizzie. And Duggie. I even missed Duggie and his teasing, too.' She opened her eyes now. 'I . . . I was so sorry about Duggie. Did you see the banner?'

Dan was puzzled. 'Banner? What banner?'

'The banner I embroidered in his memory. I gave it to the parish church. I thought they would put it up somewhere . . .'

'You? You did that, Mary Ann?'

Weakly, she nodded. 'It was the least I could do. It was

the only talent I ever had, wasn't it?' she said bitterly. 'Being able to embroider. I was useless at everything else. I even loved the wrong man.'

Lizzie watched as Dan said nothing now, but merely patted Mary Ann's hand.

'Dan, I was so wrong. So wicked . . .'

'Don't say that, my dear. A little foolish, maybe, but wicked, no.'

'I was. It was so wrong of me to leave a good and generous man like you. And I took you away from poor Susan too, didn't I? I did it deliberately, Dan. I couldn't bear to see you loving her, while no one seemed to love me. And then, to leave my child, my own flesh and blood. What sort of a mother does that? That was unforgivable.'

Her glance lifted now to rest on Lizzie and the slightest of smiles touched her mouth. 'She's pretty, Dan. Like I used to be, isn't she? And from what I've heard, she's been just as silly as her mother.'

Dan shook his head. 'No, no. She's come home. She's back with me now.'

'Since Lawrence was killed?'

'Well, no.' There was embarrassment in Dan's tone and he glanced apologetically at Lizzie before adding, 'She came home before that. She'd . . . she'd realized things weren't working out.'

Mary Ann gave a little nod and murmured, 'Maybe she's got a little more sense than me, then. I hope so.'

Lizzie was listening with a kind of bemused, shocked fascination. She had not seen her mother for nine years and yet Mary Ann knew all about her. She knew about her marriage, about her young husband's death – everything. But then, she would have heard it all from her lover. No wonder Randolph Marsh had been so incensed over Lawrence marrying Lizzie.

If it hadn't been such a tragic situation, Lizzie thought, it would be funny. But looking at the poor creature in the bed, there was nothing to find amusing.

'You've come home now, Mary Ann,' Dan was saying. 'And when you're better . . .'

Mary Ann was shaking her head. 'I'm not going to get better, Dan. This child is going to kill me.'

'Don't talk like that. I won't listen to such talk. You'll have the child and then, when you're stronger, we'll see what's to be done.'

Mary Ann was smiling at him sadly. In her huge, dark eyes Lizzie could see a depth of knowledge, a premonition, that what she said was the truth.

She had no will to survive any longer.

'I've come back, Dan,' Mary Ann whispered, 'for one reason only. To beg your forgiveness, so that I can rest in peace. Just say it, Dan. Please. Say I'm forgiven.'

His voice broke then and he lifted her hand and pressed it to his cheek. 'Oh Mary Ann. You're forgiven. You are forgiven.'

A week later, Mary Ann gave birth to a strong, healthy boy, who yelled constantly for the sustenance his sick mother could not give him. For the three days following the difficult and protracted birth, whilst the life drained out of Mary Ann, Lizzie sat beside her mother's bed, holding her hand.

Most of the time, Mary Ann was barely conscious, but Lizzie stayed there anyway. On the third night, at about three in the morning, Mary Ann awoke. Lizzie, dozing fitfully and uncomfortably in the chair, was instantly awake too.

'Is there anything you want, Mam?' she asked softly.

The room was illuminated softly by a tiny nightlight on the mantelpiece.

'No,' Mary Ann whispered. 'Just . . . hold my hand, Lizzie. And tell me you love your wicked, silly mother.'

'I do love you. We all do. Just get well and we'll be so happy together.'

'No, Lizzie. It's not going to happen, my darling.'

'Why not? You're not going back to *him*, are you?'

Mary Ann's smile was weak, but for a brief moment some of the suffering left her face. 'No, my love. I wouldn't go back to him. Not ever again. He's a cruel, harsh man. He uses people. But I couldn't see it. I was dazzled by his sophistication, his charm. I thought he loved me, but I doubt very much if the man is capable of love. And yet, I still couldn't seem to stop loving him.'

With an effort that was obviously painful, Mary Ann turned herself to face her daughter. For a moment her gaze lingered on Lizzie's face as if she were drinking in every feature of it to carry with her into eternity.

'Dan is a hundred times the man Randolph Marsh is. It's my tragedy that I didn't see it when I had his love. I did love your father, Lizzie, truly I did, but in a very different way. My feeling for Randolph was a kind of madness, a passion that wouldn't die. Dan's love was the true love. It was gentle and kind and good. Perhaps that sounds a little boring, but it's the only sort that lasts.'

She lay back against the pillows again, for a moment exhausted by the effort. 'You know,' Mary Ann said softly, 'I always thought you and Tolly might end up together.'

Suddenly, there was a lump in Lizzie's throat and she closed her eyes and pressed her lips together to prevent them uttering a sound.

'He always seemed so devoted to you, even as a little boy.'

Again there was a long silence before Mary Ann whispered, 'Find yourself a good man, Lizzie. A man like your father. A man who truly loves you for yourself . . .'

Her voice faded away and Lizzie could see that her mother had fallen asleep.

She sat back in her chair and closed her eyes, but the tears came anyway. Tears for her mother, who, despite Lizzie's own brave words, knew she was dying. Tears for Lawrence too, but most of all, the tears she wept were for Tolly.

Lizzie woke with a start as she heard a movement in the next room and knew that the house was stirring. The pale light of dawn was creeping in through the gap in the curtains. Lizzie stretched and then glanced towards her mother.

She was lying just as she had fallen asleep. She looked very peaceful and there was the ghost of a smile on her mouth. The lines of suffering had fallen away from her face and, though it was still thin, she looked more like the woman Lizzie remembered as her mother.

It was then she realized that the life had ebbed away from Mary Ann whilst Lizzie slept.

Sixty

'So, what are we going to do with this young man, then?'

Blunt as ever, Bessie was the one to voice the question that had been in everyone's mind, but the one that no one had dared to broach. They had buried poor Mary Ann in a corner of the town's cemetery the day before and now the most pressing question was, what was to happen to her baby son?

'I'd look after the bairn mesen,' Bessie added, tickling the wriggling infant fondly as he lay in his makeshift crib – the bottom drawer of the chest of drawers from Bessie's bedroom. 'But I'm really too old now.'

'I suppose I should go to The Hall,' Dan said, reluctantly.

'Oh no,' Bessie said fiercely. 'You aren't going there. No, I tell you what. Lizzie can go and ask Miss Edwina to come to see me.'

'Miss Edwina?' Lizzie and her father chorused together.

Bessie nodded firmly. 'Why not? She's the bairn's aunt.'

Lizzie glanced at her father, who shrugged. 'Aye, run along, lass. If your gran thinks it's the right thing to do.'

Lizzie walked the length of River Road deep in thought. What a muddle it all was, she thought. The child was her half-brother and would have been half-brother to Lawrence too. He was no blood relation to either Dan or to Bessie and yet they were concerning themselves over the infant's welfare.

Her mother had been right, Lizzie thought with a sad smile. Her father really was a good man. Despite the sorrow in her own heart, she felt a surge of happiness that she, at least, had been reconciled with her loving family. If only . . .

No, she told herself determinedly, I mustn't think of Tolly. Not today. Today I must think of that poor, nameless little boy. My half-brother. I mustn't think of Tolly now . . .

She was ushered into Edwina's private apartment at the top of the house.

'Lizzie, my dear.' Edwina came towards her, her hands outstretched. 'How are you? Yesterday must have been awful for you all.'

Lizzie nodded. 'We saw you in church. Why didn't you come back to the house?'

Edwina sighed. 'I was in two minds what to do.'

'It must have been difficult for you, too.'

Edwina pressed her lips together and nodded. She led Lizzie to the window seat and they sat down side by side.

'We used to sit here together, your mother and I. I used to teach her embroidery.'

Lizzie nodded. 'I know. There's a trunkful of it in Gran's house. Everything my mother ever made. Even the little baby dresses with the fancy smocking she made for me. Gran was showing me them only yesterday. She's kept it all.'

'Has she really?' Edwina was surprised, as she added, 'Fancy that.'

There was a moment's silence and then they both spoke at once.

'How is . . .?'

'Gran's sent me . . .'

They smiled and then Edwina said, 'You first.'

'Gran wonders if you could call to see her? She . . . they . . .' Lizzie bit her lip.

'Go on,' Edwina prompted gently.

'It's about the baby. They don't know what to do.'

'Baby?' Edwina's eyes widened. 'What baby?'

'You . . . you didn't know?'

Edwina continued to stare at Lizzie and, robbed of speech, merely shook her head.

Lizzie swallowed. This was proving to be even more difficult than she had imagined. 'When my mother came back to us, she was expecting. Almost on her time, in fact. The baby was born ten days ago and she died three days afterwards.'

Edwina let out a long sigh. 'I didn't know.' Bessie sent word about her death and when the funeral was, but she said nothing about a child.' Again they stared at each other as Edwina added softly, 'Of course, it's Randolph's child, isn't it?'

Lizzie nodded.

'So,' Edwina said, so quietly that Lizzie almost didn't hear her words, 'Randolph has an heir after all.' Then, shaking herself from her reverie, Edwina stood up and said briskly, 'I'll come at once. Just wait a moment while I get my hat and coat.'

They walked side by side back to Waterman's Yard without speaking, each lost in their own thoughts.

As she stood looking down upon the infant, a look of love and adoration drove away all the sadness that had for many years been in Edwina's face. Joy sparkled in her eyes as she bent and carefully lifted the baby boy into her arms.

'Oh,' she breathed, stroking his head with gentle fingers. 'He's just like Lawrence was as a baby and my mother always said that he was the image of Randolph as

446

a child.' She gave a light laugh and added, 'There's no denying whose this baby is.'

'Aye,' Bessie said bluntly as she and Lizzie watched. 'But will his father acknowledge him?'

'Not at once, no. I know my brother well.' Edwina's voice hardened. 'Too well. But I think in time, he will. His desperate need for an heir will override anything else. Eventually.'

'And in the meantime?' Bessie asked.

'In the meantime,' Edwina said firmly, 'if Dan will help me, I will adopt the child legally.'

'Dan? Why does it concern Dan?'

'Because, Bessie,' Edwina explained gently, 'Mary Ann was still legally Dan's wife, wasn't she? I think I'm right in saying that in the eyes of the law, this is Dan's child.'

Bessie sniffed, but said nothing. Edwina went on, 'But there's nothing to stop Dan allowing me to adopt him. I'll make sure everything is done legally and properly.'

'What shall you call him, Miss Edwina?' Lizzie asked quietly.

Again Edwina's loving eyes roamed over the baby's face, drinking in every tiny feature. 'Oh, there's only one name I could call him, Lizzie. Christopher.'

So it was all settled between them and the following day, Edwina came to collect her nephew, soon to be her adopted son.

'I'm surprised she's being allowed to adopt him,' Dan said, and added hastily, 'Not that I'm not delighted she is, but with her not being married . . .'

Bessie shrugged. 'We're in difficult times. There'll be a lot of poor little mites left orphaned because of the war. I expect the authorities have been able to allow this particular adoption because of the special circumstances. Besides,' Bessie added shrewdly, 'she knows all the right people, doesn't she? Moves in the right circles, so to speak.' She tapped the side of her nose. 'I 'spect it's a case of "not what you know, but who you know".'

'Now, now, Mam,' Dan teased.

'No, lad, don't get me wrong. I'm only too pleased she does. In this case, it's fully justified, however she's managed it.'

Dan put his arm around Lizzie's shoulder. 'Well, lass, are you ready? Time we were getting aboard.'

'I'm ready, Dad.' She bent and kissed her grandmother. 'Take it easy, Gran. Give my love to Grandpa. Tell him we'll see him on Wednesday.'

'Ta-ra, love. Take care.'

They were sailing past the ferryman's cottage when they saw Susan standing at the very edge of the riverbank, waving a piece of paper and shouting.

'I can't hear what she's saying,' Dan said. 'Can you?'

'No,' Lizzie said, shading her eyes against the sun. 'But she's looking very pleased about something.'

'I can't steer any nearer the bank, Lizzie. Take the cog boat and have a word with her.'

Minutes later, the cog boat was bumping against the bank, but before Lizzie had even the chance to climb out of it, Susan was reaching out towards her.

'Lizzie, he's safe. He's alive, Lizzie.'

Lizzie gaped up at her and the breath seemed knocked from her body as her heart began to thud painfully. 'Alive?'

'Yes. Tolly's alive. He's a prisoner of war. He's in a prison in Germany. But he'll be coming home, Lizzie. One day, when it's all over, he'll be coming home.' As Lizzie scrambled up the bank, Susan, tears coursing down her face, clasped her hands. 'Oh Lizzie, Tolly will be coming back to us.'

They hugged each other, there on the bank, dancing round with joy and singing together, 'He's coming home, he's coming home.'

Lizzie waved and shouted to her father, but still he could not hear the wonderful news. 'I'll go back in a minute,' she said to Susan. 'But tell me, is he all right? Was he hurt?'

'He broke a leg when they crash landed behind enemy lines, but he says he's received good treatment and his leg has mended well. They won't let him come home yet, of course, so we'll have to be patient until the war is over. Oh pray God, it isn't long.'

The war dragged on for another eighteen months, and for those who waited for loved ones with fear and longing, it seemed much longer. But then in May of 1945 came VE Day and soon afterwards, prisoners of war began to arrive back home.

'When will he be home?' Lizzie asked Susan constantly. Although she had written to him during his captivity and received a few letters in return, his words had been stilted and distant.

'It'll be because of the censor,' Susan tried to comfort her. 'They know every word is going to be read by the Germans. Mine are just the same.'

But his mother never showed Lizzie her letters from Tolly, so Lizzie could not be sure that the woman was not just being kind.

'He'll be home very soon now,' Susan was able to say

at last. 'But he's to go into hospital first to have a thorough check. He's fine. His leg's healed well, but he has been ill. Nothing serious, though.'

'Just prison camp conditions, I suppose,' Lizzie said, thinking of one or two men who had already come home after being imprisoned. Their skeletal figures had shocked Lizzie, but at least, she had told herself at the time, they are alive and home again, and she mourned for all those who would not be coming back. Uncle Duggie, Lawrence and so many more. Once, she had believed that Tolly, too, was lost to her forever. But now, her heart lifted as she thought that soon, very soon, she would see him again.

The weeks that passed before his arrival dragged interminably. Susan had received a letter from him and told Lizzie, 'He hopes to be home next week. When you come back from Hull, Lizzie, he'll be here.'

Now that day had arrived. They were returning home, sailing upriver towards Elsborough, closer and closer they came to the white cottage and Lizzie was standing at the bow of the ship, shading her eyes, squinting to catch sight of him.

And then there he was standing in the garden of his home, his mother hovering in the doorway of the cottage behind him. He was thin, Lizzie could see that even from this distance, but he looked resplendent in his RAF uniform, tall and with his hair blowing in the breeze. She waved but there was no answering wave from him. He just stood there, watching her.

Lizzie swallowed. He was still angry with her. He no longer loved her, if, indeed, he ever had done. Had her love for him coloured her imagination and made her believe that perhaps he had loved her too? Lizzie felt the tears prickle her eyelids and the lump in her throat grew, threatening to choke her.

Her father was at her side. 'Throw him this, love,' he said gently as he handed her a piece of coal from the cargo they were carrying.

'It's no use, Dad,' she said, her voice breaking. 'He . . . he's not forgiven me.'

'Go on, love. Just try it.' He pushed the piece of coal into her hands and hurried back to the tiller.

Lizzie balanced it in her hand and then threw it towards Tolly. It landed a little way beyond him, then rolled down the slope, coming to rest at his feet.

If he picks it up, she told herself, he loves me still. Or even if he smiles, or just – just waves. Anything, she found herself praying, just to show me that he forgives me. Please, oh please, Tolly. Don't you know how much I love you? Don't you know it was you all the time? Only I was too blind, too stupid to see it.

She found she was holding her breath as slowly the ship slid by the man standing on the bank. Tolly was perfectly still, his gaze upon her following the movement of the vessel as it carried her by him. Across the expanse of water, they stared at each other. The young man, solemn-faced, the girl, her dark eyes anxious, her lips parted.

Then slowly, oh so slowly, Tolly bent down. His fingers grasped the piece of coal and then, just as slowly, he straightened up. A smile spread across his mouth as he raised his hand to wave to her.

For a moment, tears blurred her vision as she raised her own trembling hand.

Behind him, Susan moved out of the cottage doorway and came to stand beside her son, linking her arm through his.

Susan waved too, although she was looking not at her, Lizzie noticed with surprise, but at Dan.

Lizzie turned to glance at her father, standing with his hand resting on the tiller of his ship. His gaze, however, was not, for once, on the river ahead, but on the woman standing on the riverbank.

The smile, which lit his eyes with a happiness for so long unknown, spread across his face and, as Lizzie watched, Dan raised his hand and waved to Susan.

extracts reading groups
competitions books new
discounts extracts extracts
competitions events
books
new reading groups
events books
extracts
new reading groups
interviews
events extracts
discounts
new books events
events new
discounts extracts discounts

extracts events reading groups
competitions books extracts new
books